Counterpoint

Counterpoint

Karen Turner

Published by Karen Turner

www.karenturner.com.au

First published 2022 by Karen Turner

© 2022 Karen Turner

The moral right of the author has been asserted.

A Cataloguing-in-Publication record is available from the National Library of Australia.

ISBN: 978-0-6450002-4-5 (pbk)
        978-0-6450002-3-8 (ebk–ePub)

Designed and typeset by Look Up Media

Cover image by shutterstock.com

*For all of you who
wanted more Patrick*

THE SUMMONS

1808

It was the persistent banging on the door that woke me. Every thump sent a crash through my brain. I groaned, attempted to move and found my right arm pinned beneath an inert weight.

"Christ!" I painfully cracked open an eye. The woman lay half over me; a naked, dead weight in the abandonment of sleep. Getting foxed always seemed like a good idea at the time but it never seemed so the following morning – how much had I drunk of that devil's piss they called wine in these parts?

I tested my arm again causing the woman to stir. "Wha's that bleedin' bangin'?" she moaned. Her breath was rancid.

"Patrick!" A familiar feminine voice came from the other side of the door. "I know you're in there. Get up this instant. We're late!"

"Shut yer gob yer bloody—"

"Quiet!" I growled and squinted at the woman beside me. The room was grey with the filtered light of early morning, but it was enough to make my eyeballs throb. Oh, Jesus ... I'd drunk more than I thought.

"Mornin' milord." She smiled at me; stained teeth. I groaned again and swallowed a wave of nausea.

"Patrick!" shouted the voice behind the door.

"Alright, Maeve!" I snarled and turned to my companion. "What the hell happened last night?"

"Don't yer remember, milord? Reckon we turned a right'un on, we did." She smirked in a way she evidently believed was attractive. I shuddered involuntarily.

"Come out now or I'm coming in!" Maeve threatened and recommenced her door-thumping.

"Bugger orf, yer–"

"*Fuck*!" I shouted, adding, "I'm up," and lurched off the bed and ... oh, I shouldn't have done that ... my stomach pitched, and my head spun. "Both of you shut up," I gasped, leaning against a grubby wall to steady myself.

"Last warning, brother!"

I snatched up what appeared to be my trousers and had just pulled them over my hips as the door was thrown open.

"Maeve, for Christ's sake!"

"Hurry up!" My sister's neat little foot started a staccato tapping beneath her green-velvet travelling gown.

"Oi! Who the bleedin' 'ell are you? Get outta me room!"

"We're late." Maeve spared not a glance for the naked woman advancing upon her.

That I'd been in the grip of drunken and lustful enthusiasm the night before was evident, as Maeve marched about the small room gathering shoes, stockings and coat from all corners while I eased into a limp shirt.

"Honestly, Patrick!" she remonstrated, as I dressed.

"Oi, I'm talkin' to you ... stuck-up li'l bitch!"

"Oh, *you're* addressing *me*?" Maeve haughtily raised her eyes to the woman who stood at least a foot taller. "Put on some clothes." Then looking me up and down, "Are you ready?"

Combing my fingers through my hair, I nodded.

"Yer not goin'... just like that, are yer, milord?"

"'Fraid so—"

Maeve snorted. "Of course he's going. What did you expect? Marriage, hmm? Presentation at court perhaps?"

"Nah see 'ere ... don' yer be talkin' to me like—"

"Oh, do be quiet!" Maeve dismissed the wench with a toss of her head. "Seriously, Pat, you never cease to surprise me. The innkeep's daughter? Got everything?"

I nodded again, my head foggy with pain.

"Come on, then," she said brightly, and strode to the door, my clothes over her arm.

"Oi, wha' 'bout money?" The naked woman was making a praiseworthy attempt at dignity. She stood in the middle of her sparsely furnished room, hands on hips, sagging blue-veined breasts resting on a fleshy, dimpled belly.

Maeve cocked an eyebrow in my direction. "Oh, she's delightful! No doubt she rifled through your purse while you slept." She turned to my erstwhile companion. "So it's payment you want?"

"Let's go," I said, in no mood for confrontation – my head was about to split open. But Maeve wasn't finished.

"Whoring is it? What do you think the master would say should he learn how you supplement your maid's wage?"

"Yer wouldn't ..."

"Perhaps not, but it's a tempting notion. Now, as for you ..." she wagged a finger in my direction. "You look a sight but we're too late to worry about it now. Let's get out of here."

∽

Maeve sat opposite me, her arm draped over a travelling crate containing her pet cat; fresh and well rested, and clearly undisturbed by the jerking movement of the carriage.

I, on the other hand, felt every jolt as we bumped along the country lanes of Yorkshire.

"You bring it on yourself, you know," she said. She hadn't moved her eyes from the patchwork of green fields rolling past.

I grunted humourlessly. "Ah, yes. Mea culpa. How kind of you to point that out." A cannon was sporadically firing in my skull.

"And did you see her teeth? Oh, Pat! You actually put your lips —"

"Yes, I did see her teeth and no, I didn't put my lips anywhere near her. You don't have to kiss the mantle when you stoke the fire."

She sighed, making a fog patch on the window. "I've heard that Broughton Hall's much smaller than Waterville, but pretty nonetheless."

"I should think it will be quite tedious."

"Come now," she scolded mildly. "I'm certain there'll be taverns nearby, wenches too, no doubt. You can whore until your soul turns black."

I grinned. I was not unfamiliar with Maeve's thoughts on my lifestyle. "You'll want to escape to the taverns too when you meet the woman Father's marrying. Just you wait!" I added with a laugh.

"It is going to be our new home, well, it will be for me. For you, only until you return to Oxford. You might consider being agreeable – even if neither of us wanted to come here. Anyway, I expect it will be rather nice. Yorkshire's quite beautiful, isn't it?"

"You find beauty in everything."

"Not everything," she said with a grimace. "I found no beauty in that trollop you woke up with this morning."

"Truth to tell neither did I, but I was bored – it was offered."

"You were foxed – didn't have to accept." She leaned forward. "You know, for the most part, it's only your rank they're interested in. You don't have to be so *available*."

"I know." I gazed out the window. Though my stomach had settled somewhat, my head was aching like the furies and there was horrid taste in my mouth.

Maeve's hounding was starting to irritate me. "Can we drop the subject?" I knew she wouldn't.

Perhaps the fact that we had no mother gave my sister license to hound me as she felt fit.

"You're a fine catch for a nice young lady," she continued. "If you don't die of the pox before you reach your majority."

I stared at her in feigned outrage. "What do you know about the pox?"

"Enough."

I groaned. The lecture she had planned promised to be more uncomfortable than her bursting into the room this morning.

"For example, I—"

"Drop it!"

She huffed and flopped against the padded velvet seat, but I knew she hadn't finished with me.

I counted 23 seconds.

"I just think," I rolled my eyes as she went on, "you could be more discerning, that's all ... a future earl should have a care for those beneath him."

Suddenly realising her faux pas, she flushed. "Oh ..." she visibly squirmed, and I laughed. "I ... I didn't mean ..."

"I care very much when there's someone beneath me." My amusement quickly wore off; even the slightest chuckle increased my headache. "You've said your piece. Now leave it."

"Father thinks you should be considering a wife. You can't marry these girls. Why don't you find a nice, suitable girl to court? Give up these ... these ..."

"Delicate flowers?" I finished for her. "I don't want to."

"All this drinking and carousing ... it's unseemly."

"It's perfectly seemly ... besides, I enjoy it."

"*Pfft*! You enjoy feeling like a carriage has run over you?"

"I enjoy fucking."

She lowered her eyes. "You shouldn't speak like that to me."

I blew out my breath in irritation. "Well, you shouldn't ask foolish questions," I snapped, grumpily. Ordinarily I love to make bold with language for the simple pleasure of witnessing its impact. But I should be more respectful of my sister; though she was feigning maidenly modesty, it was often tempting to push her to her boundaries.

"Look," I continued penitently. "We shouldn't be having this conversation in the first place so shut up. I'm going to sleep off my *unseemly carousing.*"

Grumpily, I turned my face into the padded corner of the coach and pretended to do just that.

But I couldn't sleep. The truth was I was unhappy.

Three weeks ago, I'd been contentedly tending my tenants and estates when the summons had arrived.

In my father's hand, it directed Maeve and me to journey north, to witness my father's marriage to a woman whom I mistrusted and disliked intensely. Afterwards I should return to Oxford to complete my studies – I was reading the law and I disliked that intensely too. Naturally, I would then find an appropriate young lady to wed and with whom I would breed.

Although I enjoyed a modicum of freedom, Father's instructions were non-negotiable and, having been raised on a tedious diet of aristocratic responsibility and protocol, I could do nought but comply.

It's true: I am a future earl, and the accompanying obligation lies heavily because I'm almost, but not yet, 17; too young, in my opinion, to consider marriage – even had I wanted to.

While it's understood that I should be weighing the financial and social merits of the string of eligible misses paraded beneath my nose by their social-climbing mamas, I do tend to ignore the eligible ones in favour of meaningless dalliances with a variety of ineligible ones.

I'm wealthy – or will be – beyond most people's wildest

imaginings, which guarantees my entry to the finest establishments and ensures I'm never lonely for company. That ladies find me incredibly attractive is clearly due to my heavy purse and ancient title. This fact irritates me, as do the hordes of sycophants I am at pains to ignore.

I hate pomposity and I loathe the innate snobbery that typifies people of my class. This type of arrogance tempts me to acts of such irreverence that complaints to my father generally result. Yet as I see it, if I can use my position for the betterment of others I can offer some contribution to the world – most of my kind are only interested in meaningless pursuits.

I sighed through my nose and shifted uncomfortably on the seat.

I know I should be more appreciative of my position, but I am not deliberately contrary. Soon enough the responsibilities of my birth will catch up with me and I will be forced to marry for the sole purpose of begetting the next Washburn heir. I can only hope that the young lady is at least intelligent – I can imagine few fates worse than being fettered to a fool.

I have large stakes in a variety of companies. I also have vast acres of land comprising villages and farms – it's no overstatement that lives depend on me.

Many landowners in my position are turning tenants off their estates because there's more money in growing crops and raising animals. Villages are emptied, homes flattened and the people flooding the overcrowded cities seek work that does not exist.

My tenants are safe from that.

Many will find this difficult to believe, but I genuinely care for these people and through my actions they will eventually come to understand this.

Attempts to communicate this fact to them have thus far been largely unsuccessful – I'm too young and untested in their eyes.

Having bedded several of their daughters probably didn't further my cause, but I *will* earn their trust.

Faithful to the times in which I live, I have a reputation for dissipation and debauchery that to great extent I have earned, even if many of my more outrageous exploits are wildly exaggerated.

I didn't lie when I told Maeve I enjoy fucking. Do I enjoy it because I'm good at it, or am I good at it *because* I enjoy it? Who cares ... in any case, this morning wasn't the first time she has extracted me from some wench's bed.

I yawned and stretched.

Won't be the last time, either.

∽

My head continued to ache through the brief snatches of unconsciousness, though it seemed only minutes had passed before Maeve, thumping the wood panelling beside my head, startled me into wakefulness.

"Dan!" she called. "Could we pause at the next inn, please?"

"Christ, Maeve," I groaned. "You'd have made an excellent timekeep on a slave galley."

She sneered across at me. "Head still sore?"

I returned her sneer.

"You need to wash and change your clothes ... you're not fit for company."

We arrived at an inn situated outside a village called Wharferidge. The coach had barely stopped before the innkeep, having evidently seen our arrival, dashed through the front door to make an embarrassing event of welcoming us to his establishment.

"You'd think they'd never seen a matched team before," Maeve whispered.

"May not have." I stepped onto the muddy road and addressed our host, requesting a private room and hot bath. Being a small wayside inn, it wasn't overburdened with conveniences so Maeve opted to wait in the coach.

Marsh, as the master introduced himself, knew only that I travelled in a crested coach-and-four, but practically fell over his feet as he bowed obsequiously and ushered me towards the door.

"Make haste, Your Lordship," Maeve called mischievously from the coach, "the earl awaits!"

Marsh's eyes popped like organ stops. "Yers friends o' the earl? I've 'eard Earl of Thorncliffe's in residence at Broughton 'all."

"Pay no heed to that lass, Marsh," I spoke confidentially as one man to another. "She's some random wench I found in a taproom ... wouldn't know an earl from a cooper but she's got one of those nice arses a man can hang on to. Now about that bath ..."

Inside the inn, it was dark, musty and populated by a handful of farmers and a pair of muddied sheepdogs, and if I'd hoped for Marsh's discretion I was doomed to disappointment. A great fuss was made ensuring his patrons were fully cognisant of my presence. I glared at my host as he ushered me into a suitable room.

A short time later, I returned to the coach – freshly bathed but no less seedy.

Maeve sat within, red-faced and indignant. "That man, Marsh, winked at me and made an indecent suggestion!"

"Did he? Strange behaviour, that."

"Strange indeed! What does he think I am?"

I shrugged dismissively and she narrowed her eyes at me.

∾

Broughton Hall lay about four miles from Leeds on the outskirts of a village called Wolstone. Its gates stood open and welcoming, and we turned in and rolled along a gravel drive cutting between neat lawns and terraced gardens.

The house itself, a double-storey pale butter-coloured stone structure, had large double doors that swung open as we approached, and my father appeared on the porch. He quickly descended the steps and waited at their foot as our coach drew to a halt.

His woman, Miriam Broughton, stood beside him, arrogant and swelling with his child.

"Look at that girl," Maeve whispered. "What a beauty!"

"Anne, I expect ... youngest of three. Supposed to make a career at court ... unlikely now Miriam's been banished."

Dan lowered the steps and threw open the door. Maeve and I emerged and were immediately gathered into Father's constricting embrace.

I love my father, something I often forget to mention as he regularly shows a marked lack of discernment – the woman he planned to marry evidenced that! However, in a world of corruption and excess, he stands apart as a kindly and selfless man.

When finally he released us, we were formally introduced to Miriam, Lady Broughton. She and I exchanged disdainful looks – this was not our first meeting – while Maeve bounced about in her typically enthusiastic way.

Realising belatedly that the two other Broughton children were standing beside their sister, we turned to the three: Simon, Alexandra and Anne.

Simon, about my age, was a baronet and probably one of the most handsome young men I'd ever seen – if I can say that without sounding odd. I glanced at Maeve, confirming she'd noted that fact too.

Anne, the youngest of the three and extraordinarily attractive, as Maeve had earlier pointed out, carried herself with the confidence of one fully aware of her beauty while not yet competent in its application. She peeked flirtatiously from beneath her lashes, and it was with a physical effort that I refrained from rolling my eyes.

I knew her type too well – she was her mother all over: selfish, vain and frivolous – unpleasant company and certain trouble!

Dismissing her, I turned to the middle child.

The human eye is unavoidably drawn to beauty. So, as I had addressed the attractions of the elder Broughton, Simon and the younger, Anne, I had initially overlooked the middle child.

Now, I met the sullen gaze of Alexandra Broughton. Brushing the hair from my forehead, I consciously shuttered my expression; I could control the external reactions of my body but not the internal ones.

This girl was not classically beautiful like her siblings, but she caused my throat to tighten in a most disconcerting way. Brown eyes surrounded by smudgy dark lashes glared at me with an expression of resentment that I knew and understood. Her nose, straight and small, was sprinkled with a delightful and unfashionable pattering of freckles, but it was her lips that intrigued me. Full and too sensuous for her age, they were at that moment set in the tight, grim line that resulted from a clenched jaw.

I suppressed a grin of solidarity for she was returning my scrutiny in a character assessment of an entirely unfamiliar nature: she didn't care for my title, wealth or position. She simply didn't care for me at all!

In fact, if I were any judge, I'd say she hated me on sight and wished me to the devil, all the while clutching the collar of an overexcited Border Collie.

Alexandra was as different from her sister as night from day.

Where Anne seemed self-assured and devious, Alexandra was entirely without artifice or deceit of any kind; her every thought was right there on her face for me to read.

And I was immediately drawn to her.

This young woman fascinated me in a way I'd not previously experienced and certainly didn't welcome. Mentally shaking myself, I ensured my expression of cool detachment remained intact.

Maeve, with her usual disregard for propriety, had embraced Miriam Broughton, oblivious of that woman's affronted grimace. Then in a moment of thoughtless reaction, responded to the calls of her cat and plunged into the coach to extract the travelling crate.

Alexandra, already struggling with the dog, was unable to restrain the animal and it leapt upon Maeve knocking the crate to the ground.

In a matter of seconds, all chaos had erupted.

The cat escaped, clawing the dog and raking Maeve's face before springing free and fleeing across the lawn into the forest.

There was much shouting and scuffling. The horses stamped and side-stepped in their traces. Dan and a stable-boy attempted to calm them while the dog leapt about barking and yelping hysterically. Miriam raised her voice above the racket to berate Alexandra before the entire group, humiliating the girl then directing the younger sister to fetch the stableman and have the dog dealt with.

Not one for public demonstrations of any type, I remained passive, although I didn't think I'd maintain passivity should the stableman indeed arrive to knock the dog on the head. It all seemed an overreaction to me.

Anne stared, horrified, at her mother while Alexandra pleaded the dog's case.

As Maeve cried into my father's coat, he assured her the cat would be found; they were ignorant of the drama unfolding – the drama that was quickly escalating out of control.

I hate conflict. I hate theatre and I hate hysterics. Moreover, I hate to see people humiliated and hurt – without reason, that is. I've been known to mete out my own brand of humiliation on occasion, but only with just cause.

Now, in the face of Alexandra's grief, I knew an intense desire to stand beside her in support – fuelled, probably, by my intense dislike for her mother. Nevertheless, such compassion was no pleasant sensation.

I groaned internally – there would be no happy resolution to this if someone did not step in.

Meantime, Anne, too young to do aught else, was about to carry out her mother's instructions.

Alexandra turned in desperation to her brother, begging that he speak up to save the dog's life, and it was then that it happened. In what I recognise now, but didn't consider at the time, was some kind of wordless, kinetic connection; Simon raised his eyes to meet mine. I thought, I need to end this.

I know I thought it, for no words passed my lips but Simon nodded, almost imperceptibly, and said to Alexandra, "Zan—"

She ignored him.

I turned to Miriam and said, calmly, "Give me the dog. I'll take it to the stableman."

Lady Broughton studied me speculatively, as I knew she would, then she nodded.

As I bent and scooped up the now petrified dog, Alexandra screamed and made to stop me.

Her distress disturbed me, but Simon caught and held her; I turned with the dog in my arms and strode away, leaving her struggling against her brother's grasp.

∾

Relieved to escape, I left the scene at the front of the house. Alexandra's cries faded behind me as I walked around the house to where I expected to find the stables. The dog remained a fur-wrapped lump of wood in my arms.

It was a short walk, through gardens that were neat and dignified, and upon arriving at the stables I found them clean and well maintained.

The stableman met me with a quizzical expression, but his face relaxed as I explained who I was and why I carried the dog.

"Keep it here until that woman finds herself more agreeable, would you?" I asked.

He nodded and didn't ask who *that woman* was. "'Ow long, d'yer reckon?"

"Don't know." I shrugged. "But just keep it out of sight, please."

∾

I had not wanted to come to Broughton Hall; coming here had disrupted my life and the lives of Broughton Hall's inhabitants from the moment Maeve and I alighted from the coach.

Though Simon seemed an intelligent chap – worth getting to know – I wondered if he'd make an entertaining companion. I was aware that Father was sending him to Oxford with me. Until now I'd rejected the idea, but the dog incident, during which he'd demonstrated a rare quick-wittedness, had elevated him in my opinion.

In the hours following our arrival, I retired to the room allocated to me and lay on the bed. Although I was exhausted from my activities the night before, I did not sleep; my thoughts were centred on my soon-to-be step-siblings.

Somehow I knew, each in his or her way, was going to change my life.

∾

At the appointed time, I obediently made my way to the family meals room and found Simon at the head of the table, with Miriam opposite.

The woman glared at me. *That's alright*, I thought, *I don't want me here either*. Though my head was beginning to ache again, I mustered my most charming smile, under the circumstances, and took my seat opposite Anne.

Alexandra was absent.

The urge to go to her, to comfort and protect her was confusing me. There was fierceness and passion in her that called to something within me – a recognition of like minds perhaps, for her thoughts, written clearly on her face, mirrored my own. I had spent most of my life shuttering my face, keeping my thoughts to myself. But Alex – as her sister called her – was no such master and her every expression was as transparent as glass.

Then, there was Anne. Christ, that child spent the entire meal pouting like a coquette and batting her lashes at me, demanding an unavoidable comparison with her sister.

I enjoyed my essentially selfish life and aside from my tenants, concerns for others, particularly a grumpy maid with a surly disposition, who at this very moment was no doubt wishing me to hell, left me particularly uncomfortable.

I ought to tell her that her dog was safe, but my tangled thoughts were too disconcerting. I needed to maintain my distance, regain my balance.

The girl – for what was she ... 14? – was skinny, suntanned and hostile – definitely the opposite of every woman I'd ever been attracted to. So why did I care? Why did I ... *oh, a pox on it*!

I needed to return to a place of familiarity. I needed to get foxed, perhaps lose myself between the plump thighs of some energetic bar wench with large breasts and a welcoming embrace – not some little fiend in a black mood!

There had to be a tavern somewhere in riding distance of this picturesque backwater.

Without finishing my meal, I placed my cutlery neatly on my plate and excused myself from the table.

I was going out.

A WELCOMING ESTABLISHMENT

Maeve had spent a good part of the morning in the surprisingly well-stocked Broughton Hall library. She'd flicked through several leather-bound tomes and trailed her fingers along the spines of a collection of novels – French and probably quite risqué.

She'd no need of such excitement. If it were racy she wanted, she need only ask her brother how he spent his evenings.

No, Maeve preferred history. She had selected an aged book filled with original sketches recording the journeys of discovery of some fellow by the name of Wilfred Heinz during his grand tour through Europe, a century and more ago.

Maeve sat in an armchair near the window overlooking the sweeping driveway. She had been enjoying the warmth of the fire and an hour of solitude when the door opened, and her brother peeked into the room.

"Where've you been?" She closed the book tenderly out of respect for its advanced years and rested it on her knee. "You didn't appear at breakfast."

Patrick closed the door behind him. "I slept late."

"Oh yes," she said, and nodded sagely. "I guessed you'd gone out last night. Make any new friends? A nice lady, perhaps?"

He smiled mysteriously and sitting on the arm of her chair, leaned over to read the cover of her book.

"Sketches?"

"Yes, and very good."

He nodded but she thought he seemed distracted.

"Out with it."

His emerald eyes caught her blue ones for a moment before he said, "What do you think of the Broughtons, then?"

"I take it you're referring to the three siblings? Simon is absolutely delectable – what a face! And by all accounts a thoroughly nice chap. I quite like Anne too—" She broke off at her brother's snort, then resumed, "Well, I do! Obviously, she's horribly vain but she's rather witty."

"She is horribly vain," Patrick agreed. "As for witty, I'd say cunning is more apt."

"The middle one," Maeve went on, "I don't know what to make of her. Very unfriendly ... clearly doesn't want us here."

"No, she doesn't want us here, but do you blame her? We wouldn't be here if we had a choice."

"You saved her dog, didn't you?"

He nodded and she went on, "Have you told her? She wasn't at breakfast either. I imagine she's quite distraught."

"I told her. She was not terribly receptive; threw a glass at me."

Maeve blew out her breath. "Ungrateful, and aggressive too."

Patrick shrugged. "I should've told her sooner, I suppose. I expect she passed an agonising night."

"I don't care. I was looking forward to meeting the three of them, and so far, she's been most unwelcoming."

"Give her a chance. I'm sure she'll warm to us."

Maeve made a doubtful noise and her brother flicked playfully at a silvery blond curl resting on her shoulder. "Of the two of us, I thought *I* was the difficult one."

"Generally, you are," Maeve responded, "but you're making excuses for that girl. There was no call for her to be so hostile. Oh, I know she couldn't control that dog, and Missy was found so all's well there, but ... even the narcissistic one's friendlier."

"The narcissistic one's friendlier because she thinks there's something in it for her. Alex is all right ... just young ... inexperienced. Everything she's ever known is being turned upside down."

Maeve narrowed her eyes and regarded her brother with interest. "Defensive of her, aren't you?"

He went to the window and looked out at the garden and drive below and she regarded him speculatively. "Nothing to say? Have I hit a raw nerve, brother?"

He ignored her question. "Simon asked if I'd accompany him into Wolstone tomorrow. It's market day ... a couple of his tenants are in dispute over wheat ... something about pricing or some such."

"Will you go?"

He turned and nodded. "Yes, I think so. I'm keen to see how trading works in these parts – Simon says the locals bring their stock in each month."

"Oh, that sounds *marvy*! I'm sure I can't think of anything nearly as exciting."

He laughed lightly. "Well, *I* will enjoy it."

❧

Neither horse seemed capable of more than a walk, but the day was mild and the countryside pretty. The lane leading to Wolstone was bordered on both sides by thick hedgerows that occasionally gave way to low, stone walls marking one property from the next.

Simon breathed deeply, enjoying the warmth of the sun on his back and the clean, earthy scents of late autumn. This was his land, his birthright, and young though he was, he already had the respect of his tenants and their families. Now, he had to work at keeping it.

He was glad of Patrick's company; already he'd found his future stepbrother entertaining, intelligent and humorous, and Simon was enjoying the possibility of having a male friend.

Not that there was anything wrong with his sister, but there were certain things he couldn't share with Zan; adventures and the experiences typical of wealthy young bucks on the brink of adulthood.

Patrick, he suspected, would make a perfect partner in his exploits. Already he sensed a similarity in their natures and interests. Additionally, Patrick had explained his similar position – with tenants and responsibilities – and had expressed interest in Simon's management of his own estate. All in all, Simon welcomed his companionship.

Although Simon was under no illusions – Pat's land holding could easily swallow at least ten of his own – he found the young lord markedly unpretentious and refreshingly irreverent for one of his class.

Simon had suggested the trip into Wolstone and received an enthusiastic response. Accurately guessing the reason, he had said, "There are a couple of very welcoming establishments in town. We may visit if you're of a mind to meet some of the locals."

The intense green gaze had held a spark of mischief as the young man responded, "I can think of nothing better than meeting some of the locals … in a welcoming establishment."

Patrick had grinned then, and Simon realised that he may well have a rival for the attentions of the Wolstone lasses. He was, nevertheless, keen to explore the unexpected friendship on offer.

Twisting in the saddle now, he looked over his shoulder at the fair-haired youth on the grade horse behind him.

Patrick rode the most inappropriately named animal in the Broughton stables. Nimble was clumsy, overweight and given to such episodes of costiveness as to be a thoroughly bad-tempered old hack. She was, however, very pleased to be going on an outing and Patrick, who was probably accustomed to more gently bred horses, treated her kindly, and was even now leaning forward to give her neck a good scratch.

"Mind she doesn't reach around and bite you," Simon warned.

Patrick straightened in the saddle, his hand dropping to rest casually on his thigh. "She won't bite, will you, old girl? Provided I respond as required," he added.

"Is that so?" Simon was amused. "And how might that be?"

"Every time she farts, I give her a scratch. She has an uncomfortable belly, poor lass."

"Well, the two of you best stay downwind from me ... you can enjoy one another all you like."

"In that case you'd better gee up your own shining example of horseflesh if we're not to overtake you at snail's pace."

Simon laughed. "Oliver enjoys the scenery, doesn't want to miss any – hello!" A small boy, sitting on a stone wall, now dropped lightly onto the lane in front of them. "What are you doing here?"

Any other horse might have shied at the sudden movement, but Oliver, always disinclined to unnecessary exertions, merely flicked an ear and took the opportunity to pull at the lush grass on the verge.

"Sir Simon?" the child asked.

Simon leaned towards the lad. "At your service, young man. What can I do for you?"

"Me pa's Ned Greenslope, Sir, and 'e's arksen can yer come to the 'orse 'n 'ounds t'meet 'im an' all. There's a' argument brewing."

Nimble pushed up to sample the grass for herself and Patrick said, "Horse and Hounds?"

"Aye, Sir."

"Very well," Simon said. "Run along home, then." The child grinned, pleased with having delivered his message.

"Aye, Sir Simon. 'Ave a good day, sirs," he added, with a touch to his cap and a quick nod in Patrick's direction, then clambering over the wall, disappeared whence he'd come.

"Are all local disputes settled in public houses?" Patrick enquired. "Sounds highly agreeable to me."

"Most are and it's agreeable to me too. Horse and Hounds is the largest of the public houses in Wolstone ... often functions as a local meeting place. Besides that, the innkeep's wife is proficient with an iron fire- poker, so arguments rarely get out of hand."

"And this would be one of your welcoming establishments? The bar wenches are also agreeable?"

Simon regarded his companion thoughtfully. Yes, Patrick was a seasoned campaigner. He'd wager a year's income that Pat's surliness the day of his arrival at Broughton Hall was the result of one hell of a raging hangover.

Simon, not one to drink to excess, nevertheless patronised Wolstone's inns with a frequency that suggested some form of entertainment was in the offing.

Now he waggled his eyebrows suggestively, "Bar wenches are both agreeable *and* welcoming, but mind that fire-poker."

Patrick laughed. "That's all right. I can run fast enough if I'm not too foxed."

The two steered their horses out of the grass and it wasn't long before the lane widened into a cobbled road that led to the township of Wolstone.

Market day was bustling and alive with sound and colour. Stalls were set up along the main road and within the town square selling everything from wool and ribbons to baked goods and live chickens, piglets and goats.

The locals greeted Simon with sincere good will, particularly the women and young maids; many were eyeing him with more than passing interest, before he noticed their eyes slide curiously in Patrick's direction.

Patrick acknowledged them with a nod here, a jaunty wink there and Simon laughed. "You're sure to be quite a success around here with that behaviour."

"Just being friendly. Perhaps your business will keep us longer than anticipated," Patrick drawled, smiling at one pretty young thing with a bold gaze.

Simon met Patrick's eyes with an approving grin. "That would be a pity – imagine being required to stay overnight," he lifted a shoulder in resignation "However, if duty calls ..."

"Exactly, and as landlord, your responsibilities include building rapport with your villagers. It would be negligent should you depart without ensuring everyone's concerns had been satisfactorily addressed."

"Negligent indeed. I make a point of satisfying all concerns whenever I've a call to visit Wolstone."

The two smiled in mutual understanding.

"Now," Simon dismounted and handed his reins to a waiting lad, "let's see about this dispute."

☙

The dispute, as it turned out, was twofold. Simon held court in a corner of the taproom at the Horse and Hounds, a mug of the thick local brew at his elbow, and sat patiently as the aggrieved farmer told how he had delivered 25 sacks of wheat to the miller, who after milling the raw grain into flour, returned only 19 sacks.

The miller, a large bovine man with meaty arms folded over his belly, rolled his eyes with exaggerated patience while Ned Greenslope poked a finger at him and called him a cheat.

"Six sacks missin' ... 'e thinks as ah can't count!"

Simon glanced to where Patrick sat quietly sipping ale. The argument seemed to interest the young man. With estates of his own, perhaps Patrick had had occasion to diffuse such situations himself. Turning his attention to his tenants, Simon explained to

Ned, who'd only recently inherited the farm from his father, that whole grain was bulkier than grain devoid of husk and ground into flour. It was, therefore, reasonable that 25 sacks of grain would yield 19 sacks of flour.

Mollified only slightly, Ned went on to claim that Miller Jacob had assured him of a buyer for 15 sacks of flour, which would cover the cost of milling. Ned was to receive any leftover money and the remainder of the flour for his own use.

"Now, 'e says 'e got no buyer for t'flour an' wants payment for t'millin'. What am ah t'do?"

Simon addressed the miller. "Who agreed to buy the flour?"

"Waters, Sir. Bakery in Leeds. Wanted fifteen sacks but they's gone an' got it from 'Arrogit."

"Hmm," Simon said and sipped his ale. "Then we need to find another buyer."

"But they's cheated me!" Miller Jacob insisted.

The miller's voice was incongruously whiny considering his bulky shape. Simon threw a subtle look toward Patrick who turned away, suppressing a smile.

Feeling eyes on him now, Simon glanced to the side and found the maid with the bold gaze from the marketplace earlier. Edith – that's right, that's her name. She was watching him steadily from across the room.

Dragging himself back to the matter at hand, he said, "They're entitled to buy flour from Harrogate or wherever." He swallowed a mouthful of ale. "Alright now, let's consider ..."

As he talked, Simon was distantly aware that Patrick seemed to lose interest in the dispute. He had risen and was weaving through the crowd of bystanders to where bold-eyed Edith leaned against a wall with her back arched and breasts thrust forward.

Simon was also losing interest in the dispute as each man presented his case. They argued back and forth with no resolution to be found and neither prepared to compromise.

Finally losing patience, Simon drained the last of his ale and clattered the mug on the table. "Alright!" he said, interrupting the two combatants, mid-sentence. "For now, Ned, see if you can find another buyer – your father must have had other buyers ... Miller Jacob, perhaps you have some bills of sale ... see if you've any names on them ... buyers Ned could speak to. In the meantime, you'll just have to give Ned time to pay you. It's in nobody's interest if you can't compromise."

The men looked at one another doubtfully but Simon continued regardless. "I'll go to Leeds myself and see what I can do. I have a number of friends and acquaintances with whom I can speak."

Miller Jacob's brow smoothed immediately. "P'raps, Sir," he suggested, "we could arrange a lasting agreement wi' 'em?"

Simon rose and clapped the man good-naturedly on the shoulder. "Perhaps, but first things first, alright? I need to talk to them, so you two put aside your disagreement. Give me a week to see what I can do. In the meantime, work together and you'll both benefit."

The two men nodded and stepped aside to let their landlord pass

∽

The taproom was becoming increasingly smoky and crowded as the market traders closed their stalls and gathered to discuss the day's events. Simon shouldered his way through the pack to where Patrick stood with Edith.

He paused a couple of yards away, smiling to himself. He'd spotted Edith making eyes at Patrick earlier and wasn't surprised that she'd wasted no time introducing herself. Edith was, for all intents, a good lass, if one didn't associate chastity with goodness. He drew a long breath and smiled to himself as he remembered his last visit to Wolstone only the week before.

At that moment Edith was leaning forward, ostensibly to examine something of great interest, and affording Patrick an unencumbered view down her bodice.

She was pretty up-close, slim with curling brown hair, full pouty lips and small round breasts – barely a handful, Simon remembered – though his tastes ran to more buxom lasses.

Simon came up beside Patrick and elbowed his future brother playfully in the ribs. "Hullo," he said, cheerfully, "you've met our lovely Edith here?"

"That I have," Patrick turned and the question, *yours*? passed silently between them. Simon gave an almost imperceptible shake of his head.

"Well," Simon said brightly. "Where's your sweet sister this afternoon, Edith?"

"Out t' back, Sir. Yer want me t' go fetch 'er then?"

Another wordless exchange with Patrick, and the maid was dispatched to find her sister while Simon ordered a private room, two bottles of wine and enough food for four.

∾

Simon yawned and trusted Oliver to step neatly around the potholes in the lane. Too weary to steer, he relaxed in the saddle and let his hands rest on his thighs.

He was aware that Patrick fared no better. His stepbrother had paid his respects to a bottle of brandy – and good quality it was too. Amazing that a place like Wolstone could offer such superior liquor, although being only four miles from Leeds they saw their fair share of travellers and kept a few bottles on hand.

When Simon spoke, his voice sounded rough to his own ears, "You seemed to enjoy Edith's company last night." He cleared his throat before continuing. "Like the skinny ones, do you?"

Patrick turned from watching the rolling fields beside him. His eyes were remarkably clear for a person who had spent the night drinking and smoking any number of cigars before laying Edith out on a rug before the fire in their rented room.

Patrick grinned. "Not generally, but I'm discovering that tastes change ..."

Simon nodded. "I tend to prefer the fleshy ones but Edith's eagerness makes up for it."

"Hmph! It's the eagerness you need to be wary of."

Simon threw him a questioning look and Patrick shrugged. "I'm just saying," Pat added. "They're all eager to fuck with a lord ..."

Simon detected a note of bitterness in Patrick's voice. He watched Pat's face, but it was unreadable, so he asked, "That sounds like you've been caught out?"

Patrick grunted noncommittally. "You need to, you know, be careful."

Now Simon was baffled. He frowned in confusion, but Patrick smiled good-naturedly and said, "Soak a sponge in vinegar or wine and ..." he gave a short, whistle that ended with an up note.

"And what ...?"

"What do you think?"

Simon shook his head causing his companion to laugh out loud. "Christ! Like playing with fire, do you?"

"I ... I usually ..." The colour rose in Simon's face and Patrick tried to restrain himself – and failed.

He took a moment to recover before continuing, "Soak a sponge, or cloth or something, in wine or vinegar – you can use lemon juice but it's not as readily available – and get the girl to *insert* it."

"Really?!"

"Or insert it yourself – just to be sure it's there. Very handy trick employed by ladies of the night and whores of Whitehall."

"Really." Simon repeated.

Patrick grinned. "More enjoyable than what you've been doing

– more effective too."

"We weren't drinking wine last night, and certainly not vinegar."

"Indeed not, but brandy serves just as well."

This time it was Simon's turn to laugh, and Oliver flicked his ears. "Expensive tastes you have."

"In some things ... in others I'm not discerning at all."

As the narrow path forced them to travel single file, the two fell silent and Simon pondered his new friendship.

Over the course of the last 12 hours, Patrick had revealed himself to be a young man of many facets. He swore expansively and drank excessively. Though intelligent and humorous, his conversation gave little of his deeper thoughts away. He had a demonstrated preference for expensive brandy, and though he enjoyed women, he didn't seem driven to pursue them.

On the contrary, they appeared drawn to him – as if he held some magnetic attraction for them.

Janet, his sisters' maid, had been extolling the young lord's virtues. Then, there was Anne. Simon was well aware that his youngest sister's eyes constantly followed their future brother.

Zan was different though. Simon frowned thoughtfully. Alexandra, normally so cheerful, was very unhappy with both Patrick's and Maeve's presence and was not averse to showing it. Simon guessed she was jealous; he and Zan had always been close, but now Patrick was here and ... well, he was enjoying the friendship of another male and Zan would just have to get accustomed to having Patrick around.

Simon smiled to himself as he recalled his future stepbrother, illuminated in flickering firelight, straddling a giggling Edith and raising her skirts. There were some activities Simon couldn't share with his sister, and he'd found in Patrick the brother he'd never had.

Much as he loved his sisters, it had been difficult, and in some respects lonely, growing to adulthood in a household of women. He didn't want to deliberately hurt Zan but adjusting to change was part of growing up.

He chuckled as he heard Patrick's horse deliver a rumbling fart and Pat's murmured, "Ah, enough now Nimble, you're making my eyes burn."

Simon was still smiling as they walked through the gates of Broughton Hall and nodded to himself. Zan would simply have to accept that her brother would be spending less time with her.

DISTRACTIONS

The world exploded in a million shards of light. I gasped and let my head drop against the back of the chair, eyes closed, and waiting for my breathing to return to normal.

My hair was sticking to the perspiration on my brow, and I was uncomfortable in my clothes.

Gradually, my heartbeat slowed, and my reality returned to the room ... and the unmistakeable sounds of fucking going on nearby.

With a final steadying breath, I opened my eyes.

I was sprawled in a lounge chair in the private room that Simon and I rented by monthly agreement at our latest haunt, The Red Fox.

Simon, across the room, was making a valiant account of himself judging by the rhythmic slapping and grunting coming from the chaise longue. Valiant, indeed, as this was his second whore of the evening – a dark-haired beauty with a full figure and experienced smile.

At this rate every apothecary in Leeds would be completely out of sponges. We'd bought a good supply of them on our trip to Leeds the previous week.

My own whore, Simon's first companion, knelt before me,

naked and smiling wetly.

She held my now flaccid cock in her hand. "Yer wanna go agin, milord?" Releasing me, she turned and presented her arse, round and ripe, and flushed like an apricot in the flickering firelight. "Yer like't like this ... like yer a stal'yin?"

I grinned. "While I'm flattered you think me capable so soon, I'm no stallion, nor am I ..." my voice trailed away, and I began adjusting my clothes. I was no longer interested.

I'd spent the greater part of the evening lounging in my chair by the fireplace, quietly seeing to a decanter of quality brandy; dulling my senses while my stepbrother indulged his.

It was only as Simon had finished with this lass and started on the second, that she had knelt before me. I had allowed her to open my trousers and convince me, in a most delightful fashion, that she was more entertaining than the brandy.

For the last ten minutes, I had been inclined to agree. Now, the brandy beckoned.

"Charming as you are," I said, "I must decline."

She turned onto her back and spread her legs – she was very flexible – assembling her face into an expression of such profound disappointment that I'm sure some of her customers would have been loath to deny her. As for me ... I laughed.

Not with unkindness, but I'd fucked enough whores in my time to know their ploys. To her credit she grinned and reached for her dress as I finished buttoning my trousers.

"Yer can't blame a wench fer tryin' t'earn a few shillin's more."

"Certainly not, and I applaud your enterprise," I said, tipping an imaginary hat. She paused – trying to fathom, without success – what I'd said. Well, she wasn't here for her cogitative skills. I smiled congenially. "Never mind. Finish dressing and come rinse your mouth."

I took up the decanter and refilled my glass. Simon had left his untouched brandy on the table. As she came up beside me,

I handed it to her, and she sniffed it indelicately.

"Smells 'spensive."

"It is, love, so sip it slowly and enjoy."

The grunts from across the room were reaching a crescendo and suddenly Simon shouted and collapsed over his woman. The two squirmed, laughing and jostling for position on the narrow couch. I turned away.

"What's your name?" I sipped my brandy and eyed the woman over the rim of my glass. She was young – not much older than the three girls at home: my sister Maeve and stepsisters Alex and Anne. She had a cloud of unruly hair, and was slim hipped and small breasted – like ... I shook off the thought but acknowledged ruefully that my tastes were definitely changing.

She swallowed hastily and licked her lips. "Michelle."

I raised my eyebrows. "Strange, you don't seem French to me."

"Maud," she admitted with a shrug.

"Ah," I gave a brief nod in salute. "Much nicer."

∾

"Better get up, man. It's nearly dawn."

I stirred, sleepily and squinted to where Simon stood at the window wearing only his underdrawers. He looked over his shoulder.

"C'mon. If we're not home for breakfast there'll be hell to pay. I was lying on the rug, spooning Maud, before the cooling hearth. My knees were pressed into the backs of hers, my arm draped over and around her. She was breathing deeply and noisily in her sleep and as I rolled onto my back she roused briefly, mumbled something, then returned to her dreams.

"It doesn't matter if I'm not at breakfast," I grumbled. The rug on the floor was grimy but I'd slept in worse places. I stretched and gave a jaw-cracking yawn.

"My mother will be furious," Simon said. "She bent my ear that morning Jackson came over to complain when he discovered you bare-arsed in his barn with the milkmaid." He pursed his lips and struck a pose reminiscent of my new stepmother. "*And that filthy farmer at the kitchen door ... mud and excrement still on his boots! The effrontery of him ... that son of yours, Gerard ... running wild, I tell you ... a barbarian! Now Simon, don't you* dare *get any ideas into your head!*"

I made a gagging noise – Simon was an excellent mimic. "Enough! It's too early and I've an empty stomach." I stretched. "God, this floor's rock hard."

"Then, get up." He moved about the room gathering his clothes and began dressing.

I grunted resignedly and sat up running my hands through my hair. I was tired but not hung-over; a quick glance at the brandy bottle: half-full. Just as well! If I'd woken hung-over after only half a bottle I should retire from society in disgrace.

Simon was almost dressed by the time I got to my feet. But for my shoes, I'd slept fully clothed – so had Maud. I nudged her gently with my toe. "Wake up, love."

"Hmm ...?" she murmured.

"Come on ... up." I nudged her again.

Her hair was a tangle of chestnut curls over her face. They spilled onto the rug when she rolled over and blinked up at me. "Wassamatter?"

"I have to leave."

"Oh ... s'mornin'?"

She extended a hand, and I hauled her upright. Her face was flushed with sleep making her appear younger than she was, bringing to mind, once again, a certain other young woman I'd been hoping to lock out of my mind.

She smoothed her dress while I pulled on my boots. "Where's t'other lass?" She asked.

"She left earlier," Simon responded. "You ready?" he asked me.

I nodded.

"Milord …" Maud followed us down the stairs into the darkened taproom. Several slumbering bodies lay on benches or under tables and the room smelt of smoke and greasy food.

"Hmm?" I was hoping to make a clean getaway.

"Milord …?" She repeated.

Shit, I thought. *Here it is …*

At the foot of the stairs, I sighed wearily and braced for the awkward scene that generally accompanied an early morning departure.

To my surprise she merely smiled. She was rather appealing with her hair sticking out at all angles.

"I'd a nice night, milord." She spoke shyly and I suppressed the urge to laugh at the incongruity of it – she was, after all, a whore who'd serviced Simon and, to a lesser degree myself, and been paid in good coin for it.

"Kind of you to say so," I made to turn away, but she placed a small, work-worn hand on my sleeve.

"Milord … I … if yers were t'come agin, I'd … be 'appy t' … t'see yers agin …" she blushed, "I mean … I like yer, milord."

I frowned, unused as I was to such amicable partings. "I like you too, Maud," I said. It was the truth. "If I find myself over this way, I'll be sure to come see you." *That*, I knew, wasn't *exactly* the truth. The truth was that I *did* like her, and I *would* see her again.

Her smile widened knowingly, but then she closed her eyes and leaned towards me, offering her mouth in farewell. I frowned and drew back.

Now, why would she do that? I hadn't kissed her all night, and I wasn't about to do so now – I never do. Lasses like Maud tend to have bad teeth and the kind of foul breath that accompanies the condition.

Where most things are concerned I'm not terribly discerning, but for some reason I am very fastidious about mouths.

I love kissing. I find the art of kissing an extraordinarily intimate expression. My first lover, Mary Whitmore, a young lady's maid at the Court of King George, had what I'd call a 'clean mouth' and I certainly enjoyed kissing her – very much.

Having drawn the conclusion that clean mouths were typical of well-bred young ladies, I was in for a very nasty surprise when I subsequently discovered that wasn't the case. Most people disregard their teeth, with the result that many of them avoid smiling from around the age of 30.

I hadn't noticed Maud's teeth, which was probably a good sign – I'd have noticed if her mouth were unpleasant.

In any case, I was wary because there was something else about Maud that morning as she stood before me in the dim light of the taproom. And, in spite of myself, I took her face between my palms and pressed my lips to her forehead.

My own actions surprised me. Abruptly releasing her, I turned and strode away. Simon was standing by the door with a smirk on his face.

"Don't say a word," I hissed as I stalked past.

He didn't have to – he was still chuckling to himself as we swung onto our horses and trotted out of the stables and into the predawn morning.

ॐ

Alex sat across the breakfast table from me. Simon, at the head, was leaning back in his chair regarding her speculatively.

"Are you certain?" He asked her.

She smiled smugly. "Of course," she turned to me. "Pythagoras has never been Simon's forte."

Since our discussion in the stables a few weeks ago, Alex had been making a genuine effort to be agreeable. She seemed more relaxed and had ceased making facetious remarks about my friendship with Simon, and no longer thumped around the house in a black mood.

An unbidden image of Simon fucking Maud's friend last evening flashed before me. Close as Alex and her brother clearly are, I couldn't imagine him sharing these adventures with his sheltered younger sister. I contained my urge to laugh with a snort that Alex interpreted as appreciation of her comment.

Her grin widened, showing perfect white teeth. "The square of the hypotenuse is equal to the squares of the other two sides added together."

"If you say so," her brother remarked. "I'm not on first name basis with the ancient Greek chap ... far be it from me to argue with you on this subject."

"You'd do well to acquaint yourself," she warned. "Master Baxter is planning a test of our understanding today."

"Christ!" I groaned. "That ancient Greek chap is no friend of mine either, Sime. Perhaps we can feign illness."

"Hmph! You wouldn't be feigning," Maeve said, coming into the room behind me. Anne followed and arranged herself prettily on a chair while Maeve draped her arms about my shoulders and leaned close to my ear. "What time did you two drag your sorry carcasses home last night – or was it this morning?"

Simon grinned and was about to reply but as Alex looked up from her plate, with more than mild curiosity in her face, I quickly leapt in, "Perhaps Alex can be persuaded to run through Pythagoras' theorem for us after breakfast."

"Count me out," Anne said, reaching for the teapot. "I couldn't care less. Alex, your grasp of the wretched thing is improper. Most unfeminine."

"Hmm," Maeve whispered in my ear. "A very timely and well-executed change of subject. One thinks one's brother has something to hide."

Kissing my cheek, she giggled and plopped into the seat beside me.

"One can't imagine what you mean," I replied blandly. She made a face and reached for a slice of toast.

Meanwhile Alex, flushed and indignant turned on her sister. "The fact that I enjoy Pythagoras isn't improper and doesn't make me unfeminine."

Anne made a derogatory sound. "Well, it doesn't make you a lady either. Don't expect the gallants to beat a path to your door any time soon. Mother says she'll be hard pressed to find anyone desperate enough to accept you in marriage."

Alex flushed and lowered her eyes.

I sucked my upper lip to stop myself speaking out. I felt the need to defend her, and I didn't like it! Damn her for ... just *damn* her!

Across the table, her bowed head revealed a riot of untidy curls instantly reminding me of Maud. I'd been content to sleep snuggled against Maud last night – knowledge that added to my displeasure because, despite Alex's tantrums and childish behaviour, in the three months since first laying eyes on my stepsister I'd been increasingly drawn to her.

I wanted to hold her and protect her, and last night I'd spooned a fucking whore because she reminded me of her! There: I'd said it and it was a ridiculous state of affairs!

"That's enough, Anne," Simon interjected sharply, bringing me back to the table.

"Well, it's true. That's what Mother said ... and any wonder ... look at her." Anne jerked her chin in her sister's direction. "Look at the way she's dressed, and that hair ... it's ..."

"I think Alex's hair is lovely ..." I spoke offhandedly and all heads swivelled in my direction.

There: I did it again, only this time I'd spoken out loud. *Blasted idiot*! I silently chided myself. I was growing soft and silly as an old maid.

I collected myself immediately and returned their stares with defiance.

"How—" Anne began, and I cut her off sharply.

"It's true." I asserted with a careless shrug. "Alex is unaffected ... unpretentious."

Maeve was watching me steadily, mouth twitching and a knowing smile in her eyes. Suddenly, she turned to Anne.

"Alex has a natural beauty. She may not feel at home at Whitehall, but there'll be suitors hammering on the door before long."

"Oh lovely, you too!" Anne sneered. "Are we having a praise Alexandra party?"

"Shut up!" Alex rose from the table and smoothed her skirt. "Oh, shut up, Anne, for once. If I don't spend an hour preening before my mirror each morning, it doesn't mean I ... I'm ... we're not all as vain as you."

She looked at each of us around the table, then turned on her heel and stalked from the room.

"Take that!" I threw at Anne who stuck her tongue out at me and reached for a slice of toast.

∾

Later that afternoon, I watched from the parlour window as the rain fell with dreary persistence. Standing where I was, the russet autumn colours of the garden appeared blurry through the water trickling down the glass.

At the swish of skirt behind me, I turned to find Maeve with Missy the cat in her arms. She closed the door behind her and approached with a coy smile on her face.

"What?" I demanded.

"I think you know," she responded. "Very defensive of Alex, aren't you?"

I shrugged with indifference. "You know me – I'll always stand up for someone if I think they need it."

"Alex doesn't need it. She can defend herself." She dropped Missy onto a settee and plopped beside her, her silk skirt puffed up around her.

"Besides," she went on, "the two of you seem to be rubbing along like old chums lately. What's going on?"

I returned to my study of the garden. "We had a little discussion ... we arrived at a truce ... there's nothing more to add. Have you reviewed your opinion of her?"

She considered her answer, "Y-yes. I think so." I glanced at her over my shoulder. She was absently stroking the cat as she thought. "She has a certain charm about her, I'll give her that, even if she's somewhat rustic."

"Hmm, rustic. That's unkind."

She waved her hand dismissively. "Though I may have led a sheltered life, I've more knowledge of the world than she, and *I'm* younger."

"Simon's protective of her."

"So are you. I think you both have a weakness for the female of the species."

"I'll grant you that. Simon's enthusiasm for ... er ... making new friends outweighs my own.

"That must take some doing." She smiled sweetly and I gave a little chuckle of appreciation. "Anyway," she continued, "with a face like *that* who can blame him? You must have difficulty competing."

"We don't compete. I'm content to take his leavings."

She laughed, evidently she didn't believe me. We fell silent for a few minutes, and I returned to my study of the garden.

The old tree they referred to as the Great Oak stood craggy and skeletal having shed its leaves for winter. It drew comparison with the lush green of the lawns, although unadorned, it had its own beauty. Contrary to my initial opinion of Broughton Hall, this was a very pleasant place. There was a presence here, something serene and inviting. And now that Alex and I had arrived at an understanding, of sorts, I was discovering a brotherly friendship with Simon and a ... tentative solidarity with his sister.

Yes, I was surprised to find myself content, for the first time since abandoning my posting at King George's court.

In any case, I knew I shouldn't become too comfortable. It wanted only a couple of weeks to Christmas and then I'd be expected to return to Oxford. I had missed a considerable amount of study last semester and the masters would expect me to make it up.

I smiled to myself and thought, expectation leads to disappointment. I had no intention of studying. I had given my father fair warning but if he insisted on throwing his money away by sending me to university that was his misfortune.

"You were horrid to Eleanor the other day," Maeve said, breaking into my thoughts. "Seriously, Patrick, even for you, pulling her wig off and hanging it from the chandelier? Seemed unnecessarily cruel to me."

I turned to her and leaned against the windowsill, arms folded on my chest. "Setting yourself up as my conscience?"

"Perhaps." She tried to look stern, but the corners of her lips curled upwards. "You don't seem to have one of your own. So what was it? Settling old scores or defending Alex – yet again?"

"Your life would be so much the pleasanter if you did not involve yourself in my concerns."

"But do I want pleasant? Perhaps I'd prefer interesting." She imitated weighing two items in her hands. "Pleasant or interesting? Hmm ... let me see."

I pushed away from the windowsill and bent over her, "Such a perfect little angel, aren't you?" Kissing my first two fingers, I leaned close to her face and pressed them to her lips, whispering, "be sure your halo doesn't slip and choke you."

A QUIET EVENING WITH FRIENDS

With good roads, Simon estimated that he and Patrick would arrive in Oxford within the week. Simon enjoyed riding, and although Oliver was notoriously lazy, he hoped that the changed terrain would entertain the horse sufficiently that Simon would not be required to repeatedly urge him forward.

Simon had always hoped to go to university – he'd been interested in medicine since he was a boy. When his father died, and he'd been forced to take up the duties required under his inheritance – although not official until he achieved his majority – he'd assumed the opportunity to further his studies would never arise.

He settled back in his saddle, comfortable and content, and very excited. His stepbrother was riding beside him. Simon often found it difficult to fathom Patrick's thoughts – the latter tended to keep much to himself. But over the months of their companionship, he'd found the other boy usually quite congenial and quick to laugh. That he was now silent and brooding led Simon to believe Patrick was grumpy about something – and he had a fair idea what.

He knew Patrick did not want to return to Oxford. Simon had

even been present during a rather heated argument Patrick had had with his father over the matter; however, Gerrard was adamant that his son must resume his education.

Patrick's reluctance to return to Oxford was borne out of a desire to purchase an officer's commission and join the war against Napoleon. His father, obviously hoping to distract his son, insisted the young man return to Oxford, complete his studies and defer all decisions pertaining to his future to a later date.

Evidently, the earl planned to keep his son out of harm's way long enough to see him married and producing a string of beneficiaries to the family fortune. With time, Gerrard hoped, his only heir would grow out of such noble aspirations and be content with a career at court, and wife and family tucked away in the country.

Simon gave a snort as he remembered Patrick's derogatory answer to that! Pat's response included words like parasite, hollow and meaningless; punctuated colourfully with less socially acceptable adjectives describing members of the idle aristocracy.

In reply, the earl stated that the family's title, wealth and position had been earned by their forefathers – none of whom had been idle – and should, therefore, be respected.

The argument had continued back and forth until the older man had, in a rare display of pique, put his patrician foot down and refused to discuss the matter further.

His son was going back to university and there was an end to it!

∽

As the days progressed and the boys made their way further south, Simon grew more excited. He was looking forward to exploring the old university town, and even more, he was looking forward to beginning his studies.

After the first couple of days on the road, the journey became tedious, although the further south they travelled, the better the condition of the roads. Though Simon hadn't travelled further from home than Leeds, Patrick was experienced in the ways of the road. Sticking mainly to ancient Roman routes ensured there were towns and villages along the way and no shortage of inns in which to stop, eat and sleep.

Their last night on the road was spent in a small village by the name of Blakeney and the unimaginatively named King's Arms Inn. As was their normal procedure, Patrick ensured the horses were suitably stabled for the night while Simon had their bags taken to their room.

Whichever of the two completed their task first, made his way to the taproom, ordered two jugs of ale and two meals, and awaited the arrival of the other.

On this occasion, Patrick entered the taproom first. He immediately made his way to a large fireplace and stood warming himself while stripping off his leather gloves.

∽

Deon Morehead was not well born but carried himself with more haughtiness than many who were. He associated with earls, barons and knights, and was quite comfortable in their company; indeed, his family was wealthier than most of them. But on account of his lack of title many doors were firmly closed to him.

Association with those whose ancient names could miraculously spring any establishment wide open, afforded Deon privileges to which he would not normally have access. While this fact had its advantages, it did nothing to soothe Deon's outraged dignity.

As Patrick entered the public room of the King's Arms, he immediately spotted Deon, sitting with yet another of his friends, Sir Anthony Dalton. The latter happened to glance up as Patrick stood on the hearth.

Elbowing his companion, Sir Anthony said, "Look who's just walked in. Might as well forget any plans you had to give that bar wench a good rogering."

Deon snorted and took a gulp of his wine. He was intending to get well and truly foxed tonight – his last opportunity before arriving at Oxford where he'd been barred from many of his favourite haunts.

"Ho, Washburn!" He called, and as the object of his salute nodded in response, he raised his glass and waggled his eyebrows. "Join us."

Deon's shout had attracted the attention of several of the locals. One in particular sat alone in a darkened corner. He'd noticed the pair of bucks when they first walked in and pegged them for a couple of students with well-lined pockets.

Now, as they shuffled along the bench to allow room for their friend, the man drew further into the shadows and lowered his hat. The recent arrival was mud-spattered and weary from his day's ride, but his demeanour and the cut and quality of his riding costume spoke louder than words – this young blade was a person of very high rank indeed.

Clearly some rich bastard's spawn sent off to school; usually these young men were reckless and vain – easy pickings for unscrupulous types – and as the group at the table was joined by a fourth member, the man knew this was going to be his lucky night.

For this latest arrival was as green and inexperienced as they came, but with a face that would reel in women like they were landed fish. With a surreptitious rub of his chin, the man gave the prearranged signal to a barmaid, rose and departed through a side door. The wench blinked twice in response and disappeared through an alternate door.

"Four of 'em," Wynne said, entering the private room at the back of the inn. Two men looked up from their mugs of ale as she spoke. "One's a lord or summat real fancy lookin'. Others look like they'd jingle well enough if yer shake 'em upside down."

A large, oafish man sniggered stupidly and wiped his nose on his sleeve. The other eyed Wynne narrowly. "One you can separate from the herd?" His voice was gruff and he was dressed shabbily, as was his companion.

"Aye, Ned," Wynne responded. "That real young one what come I last. Looks like 'e don't know what's goin' on."

"You'll take him?"

"Take 'im?" Wynne responded, archly. "With pleasure! Just don't youse be comin' in before I gets ter sit on 'is gorgeous friggin' face!"

The man with the running nose sniggered again and earned a sharp look from Ned. "You'll stick to the plan – no messing about."

Wynne rolled her eyes and raised her skirt to show the small knife tucked in her boot. "Good," Ned said. "Now, get back out there and give Peter the nod when you're ready. He'll wait ten minutes before coming to get us then he'll join you. Frankie and I'll take his friends if they come to find him."

Wynne nodded agreement and returned to the taproom, tugging the bodice of her gown lower. The barkeep glared at her from behind his taps and indicated a tray of ale jugs waiting for delivery.

She took the ale to a table of merchants, then on her way back to the bar detoured via the table of students.

"Evenin', lads," she purred, giving each in turn the benefit of her most inviting smile. The first was the arrogant, dark-haired one with the white skin; exotic looks perhaps but not to Wynne's taste. The second was a gangly youth with a newly sprouted beard and round-rimmed spectacles perched on the end of his nose.

The two new arrivals were more interesting: the first being an attractive blond with the most intriguing green eyes. This one was obviously high-born, but with a worldly shrewdness about him that caused Wynne to reconsider her plans – but only momentarily as her eyes slid to the youngest of the group.

This lad was the most devastatingly handsome creature Wynne had ever seen – and she'd seen a few. Be a pity if she was forced to use her knife on him. She hoped he wouldn't put up a struggle.

"Youse be wantin' another bottle o' wine?"

"Do you have brandy?" the blond asked.

Wynne smiled. "Certainly, milord."

"Good," he responded. While the other three sat around grinning like fools, this one was eyeing her carefully. "Bring a bottle and four glasses."

"Very good, milord." Wynne was rattled and made a decision. *Ned can go take a flyin' leap.* She thought to herself. *I'll tell 'im tomorra' – I want out o' this game.* She drew in her breath and smiled sweetly. "Can I be gettin' youse anythin' else?"

"Not at the moment," blondie stated flatly.

"Perhaps later, though," the beautiful one said, his eyes telling Wynne clearly what she wanted to hear.

Oh, pretty one, she thought. *You shouldn't have looked at me like that!*

～

"What the hell are you doing?" Patrick demanded.

Simon turned to his stepbrother in surprise. "What do you mean? Isn't it obvious?"

"It's obvious to me," Deon commented. "That wench is hungry for prick and she's chosen Broughton here." He clapped Simon good-naturedly on the back. "Get used to it man, none of us'll get a look-in with him around!"

Patrick sighed. "She's up to something. Don't go outside with her ..." he looked around the table, "any of you."

"Don't be ridiculous, Wa-Washburn," Anthony hiccupped. He was already well on his way to being pickled and incapable of bedding a wench himself. But he was not opposed to watching someone else have a go – in fact that was one of his favourite pastimes.

"I've seen her type before." Patrick went on. "She'll have a gang of cohorts waiting to jump whichever one of us is horny enough ... or foolish enough," he looked significantly at Simon, "to follow her."

"Well, I for one th-think you're jumping at shadows," Anthony said.

"Either that or you're jealous," Deon remarked. "Not used to having competition around."

Deon was spared Patrick's retort by Wynne's return. She carried a tray with a bottle of brandy and four glasses, which she placed on the table before her customers.

As she poured the liquor into the glasses, Deon snatched one up and drained it in a single gulp. Wynne arched her brows and refilled his glass then turned to Simon. "Decided if you want anythin' else?"

"Er ... no ... thank you." Simon knew better than to disregard Patrick's advice. His brother had a world of experience, and he could do worse than learn from him.

Deon drained his glass for a second time and wiped the back of his hand across his mouth. "He wans to show you his prick," he slurred, then burst into raucous laughter.

"Quite the gentleman, ain't 'e?" Wynne commented to Simon, who shrugged ruefully in reply.

"Quite," Patrick intervened. "That will be all for now. Thank you."

"You're a miserable pain in my arse, Washburn," Deon slurred, and reached for the bottle again.

☙

Wynne watched from the bar as the four youths grew gradually louder and drunker. Although the blond one had initially regarded her with suspicion and drank considerably less than his companions, as the evening wore on he was showing signs of boredom, and Wynne hoped he would take himself off to bed, thus leaving only three for her friends to take care of.

Two of them, however, were so foxed that she expected she could take them down on her own. The handsome young one was also quite pickled but remained reasonably alert – he seemed somehow to be under the protection of the blond one; she would have taken them for brothers but for the lack of common features.

When the pale one rose unsteadily and lurched across the floor towards the courtyard privy out the back, she sighed with resignation – she'd have preferred the handsome one – but she nevertheless gave a nod to the darkened corner where Ned had resumed his seat.

Wynne made her way around a couple of tables, collecting glasses and plates on her way. Weaving an indirect route toward the back door, she was careful not to attract attention, then when the time was right, she ducked through the door.

It was dusk, the evening quickly growing dark – timing was perfect. Wynne placed the tray and plates on the ground, and stood still, listening. There ... over to the right, the young man had just finished pissing and was fumbling clumsily with his flies. She stepped towards him.

"Here, let me 'elp you," she said and before he could react, she grasped his belt, pulled him towards her and pressed her mouth to his.

He tasted of brandy and smelled of horse and leather, and Wynne deepened her kiss as the young man pawed drunkenly at her bodice.

ॐ

Deon's head was reeling from the brandy and, taken by surprise as he was, his only awareness was of the bar wench's tongue exploring his mouth. As her hands delved into his riding breeches and grasped his limp cock he snorted and pulled his mouth away.

"It's going to need a bit more work, love," he said, and Wynne detected a light northern accent not present when he was sober.

"I can 'elp wi' that," she said and smiled invitingly. She took his hand and led him toward an old building to one side of the courtyard.

∾

"Think we should go look for him?" Simon asked. Patrick hadn't said anything but both boys were aware that Deon seemed to be taking longer than was necessary.

Patrick gave a grunt of annoyance. "That serving girl has disappeared too." He exhaled with irritation and took a sip from his glass. "She probably has her cronies watching us at this minute."

"Christ," Simon muttered, jerking his chin toward where Anthony was sprawled along the bench, snoring. "He won't be any help if there's trouble."

As though sensing his companions' eyes on him, Anthony stirred and delivered an explosive fart.

"We're better off without him," Patrick said, adding quietly, "I have an idea. Did you see that lane between this place and the stables?"

Simon nodded, and without another word, Patrick grasped the brandy bottle and rose from the bench, moving as one who was very intoxicated but trying not to show it.

Turning unsteadily, Patrick brandished the bottle at his brother and announced in a loud, slurring voice, "I know when's time fer bed! Stay 'ere an' drink alone fer all I care ... oh shorry, yer grace ..." he added, swaying into an elderly farmer.

As all eyes followed him, Patrick staggered toward a staircase, and made a painstaking job of climbing upstairs to the bedrooms above.

Once out of sight, he straightened and looked around. He was in a darkened corridor with doors at intervals along it and a window at the end. Moving swiftly and silently, he arrived at the end of the hall.

The window looked out over the kitchen; it was latched but opened easily, swinging outwards. Patrick's heart pounded with the thrill of adventure. *It's been a while since I've run along a rooftop*, he thought, grinning to himself. *At least this time I have my breeches on!*

With the brandy bottle clutched in one hand, he grasped the window frame with the other and climbed onto the ledge. He squatted there for a moment, then lightly dropped onto the tiled roof some four feet below.

∾

Simon was anxious. Painfully aware that this was his first venture away from home, he realised his nerve was about to be challenged. He had no experience with the kind of trouble Patrick seemed acquainted with, so arranged his face into what he hoped was an expression of bored, if slightly inebriated, nonchalance.

He estimated five minutes had passed before rising unsteadily. Muttering something that included the words, *throw up*, he stumbled his way toward the front door and out into the darkening street.

Pausing to ensure he wasn't being followed, he walked briskly around the side of the inn to the lane Patrick had mentioned.

As he entered the lane, he felt rather than saw, the two bulky shadows lurking about halfway down. One of them sniffed thickly, hawked and spat. The sound was followed by a hoarsely whispered, "Be quiet!"

Simon flattened himself against the cold stone of the inn and strained his ears for any sound of Patrick from above. He couldn't hear any sign of his brother but knew instinctively that he was close.

Glancing up, he saw the solid shape of him limned against the leaden evening sky.

No words were necessary. Simon edged along the stonework, aware that Patrick was keeping pace on the roof. Simon's hands were clammy and trembled slightly with nervous excitement. It hadn't occurred to him that the two men would be armed, but of course they would be, and now as one of the shapes moved, he heard the metallic hiss of a knife being withdrawn from its scabbard.

Simon drew in his breath and released it slowly to calm the thumping in his chest. He could feel the prickle of sweat on the back of his neck. Shooting a quick look above him, he could just make out the crouching shape on the roof. He counted under his breath, *one ... two ... three ...* and stepped into the middle of the lane.

"Waiting for someone?" He was gratified to see the two shapes start in surprise, but as they began to advance upon him, perspiration broke on his lip, and he mustered every ounce of bravado to hold his ground.

∾

"Waiting for someone?" As Simon's voice rang clearly through the night, the two men gave startled leaps and Patrick contained the urge to laugh. He thrived on escapades like these; the blood was pumping through his veins and his body was tense and ready to spring.

Balancing on the edge of the roof, brandy bottle in hand, he watched and waited, timing his moment.

The two ruffians below were moving cautiously toward Simon; one carried a long knife while the other appeared empty-handed.

He was a big brute, though gormless as they come, and no doubt relied on ham-fisted strength. So dopey not even his companion trusted him with a weapon!

Simon stood his ground. He was unarmed, but the thugs didn't know that and as he continued to stand confidently in the middle of the lane, the two cautiously measured their steps.

Patrick strained his ears and was sure he heard one whisper, "Ned, wot if 'e's got a pistol?"

Ned gave a non-committal grunt, then with a flourish of the knife said, "We were waiting for *you*." Without warning, he charged forward, but Simon was ready.

Years of tree climbing and outdoor pursuits paid off as Simon effortlessly dodged to the side and in one fluid lunge had leapt forward and kicked the big brainless bugger in the stones so hard, he squealed like a girl.

As his knife-wielding companion spun around, Patrick dropped from the roof to land directly in front of him. Grinning, the young lord swung the brandy bottle against the stone of the building, shattering its body and reducing it to a savage, jagged stump in his right hand.

"Come 'ere mother fucker," he whispered, menacingly.

Judging by the scuffling, thumping and grunting behind him, the idiot had made some kind of recovery. But Patrick was not about to be distracted. He and Ned circled each other like pugilists until Patrick suddenly feinted forward with a shouted, "*Ha!*"

The deceptive attack threw Ned off balance for the split second it took for Patrick to leap upon him and drive his shoulder into the brute's chest. The breath was thumped out of him in an *oof* that reeked of onions.

Recovering quickly, Ned flung the knife in a wide arc, but Patrick had anticipated the move. He dropped to a crouch, immediately springing upwards and ploughing his left fist into the man's midriff. Ned doubled over and Patrick grasped the hand still clutching the knife and slammed it viciously against the wall.

With a shout of pain, Ned dropped the knife, his eyes popping wildly as Pat pinned him to the wall with his shoulder and pressed the jagged edges of the broken bottle to his throat.

"Don't fuck with me," Patrick ground out, breathing hard with exertion. "Where'd the slut take my friend?"

Simon was not ordinarily one for violence. Nor was he prone to aggression. But when the huge brainless dolt turned on him, even after having his nuts kicked into his lungs, something inside him shifted.

The oaf clutched his balls but made a rather quick recovery under the circumstances, and Simon adopted a stance that he hoped mimicked a bare-knuckle fighter he'd once seen at the Wolstone market.

The fool was supposed to back down.

He didn't.

Instead, he swung such a punch that had it hit its target would have shattered Simon's jaw. As it was, it grazed with Simon's temple with enough force that his head snapped and he saw stars. His assailant hauled back for a second swing, but Simon had just enough wits left to duck and the fist flew harmlessly over his head.

With a roar of frustration, the large man bowed his head and charged like a raging bull.

As a surge of energy rushed through him Simon jumped aside, watching in disbelief as the halfwit crashed head first into the stone wall. There was a moment where a most comical look of surprise crossed the simpleton's face before he crumpled to the ground – out cold.

Breathing hard, Simon turned to where Patrick had Ned pinned to the wall on the point of a broken bottle. "Get the knife!" his brother snapped. "And see if he's got anything else on him." Simon jumped to obey, ears still ringing from the blow he'd taken. Ned was carrying no other weapons.

"Deon's in the wash house out back," Patrick told him; then, with a vicious jab of the bottle, turned to Ned. "Lead the way."

The trio stepped over the inert man on the ground and marched up the lane. It opened into a cobbled courtyard ringed by several outbuildings, indistinct in the half dark.

"Which one?" Patrick demanded. Simon watched a trickle of blood weep down Ned's neck – his collar was already soaked with it. He need not wonder how far Patrick was capable of taking this – he'd already seen the savage glint in his brother's eyes.

Ned pointed in the direction of a smaller building, more or less hidden by a curtain of ivy. "There."

In one movement, Patrick released him and threw him hard against a fence. Ned remained in place and his hand grabbed at his throat coming away dark and wet.

A less intelligent man might have taken the opportunity to attack, but Ned had also seen the wild look in Patrick's eye and wasn't taking any chances.

"Watch him," Patrick commanded, and Simon moved to stand before Ned with the knife aimed at the wound in his neck.

"Don't worry, I'll not move," Ned said to Simon, adding, "he's a madman!"

Simon might have been surprised by Ned's observation, but he wasn't going to relax his guard. He continued holding the knife on his prisoner as Patrick went to investigate the wash house.

ᴏᴠ

Moving carefully, the broken bottle held threateningly before him, Patrick approached the outbuilding.

He thought he could hear muffled sounds from within but

couldn't be sure. Edging closer, he crept along the wall. The door had long since rotted off its hinges, and now lay abandoned in the shadows leaving the entrance open and gaping like the black mouth of Hades.

Patrick waited, listening intently. There: a low moan and scuffling sound. Slowly, he moved up to the door and crouched low to examine the room discreetly from ground level.

The building was small and very dark with a packed-dirt floor and what looked like a stack of wooden crates along the near wall. Peering through the gloom, Pat could just make out what appeared to be a bundle of rubbish lying on the ground but was fairly certain it was his friend.

Taking a chance, he whispered "Deon!" The bundle on the floor jerked.

"Washburn? That you? They're gone!"

"Are you hurt?"

"No ... no, I'm ... perfectly alright."

Patrick rose to his feet and moved carefully into the room. "Where'd your lady friend go? What's all this?" He went over to look into the crates.

"How would I know? She had a companion waiting in here ... you lot ... making such a racket out there ... smashing bottles and such ... did what they had to and buggered off."

"Hmm," Patrick responded, absently. One of the crates contained bottles of wine. He held one and squinted at the label. "Can't see a thing."

"There's a lantern over by the door. Flint and char as well."

Patrick struck the flint to the char. After several attempts, he managed a small flame that he put to the lantern and a circle of yellow light leapt into the shed.

Only then did he clearly see his friend, and his eyes widened in surprise.

∾

Outside in the courtyard, Simon was startled to hear Patrick burst into laughter. He turned to where Ned was sitting on the ground, hugging his knees. "That your brother?" Ned asked. "Told you he's mad. I've had enough of this ... Just let me go check on Frankie back there."

A series of pained groans had been coming from the depths of the laneway – evidently Frankie was coming around.

"You know I can't do that." Simon replied, but as they heard the sound of shuffling steps coming toward them, he added, "I don't suppose you'll need to check on him now anyway – he's coming to us."

Frankie lumbered into the courtyard. A large, egg-shaped lump was clearly visible on his forehead, and he turned a stricken gaze on Ned.

"Can we go home now, coz? Mama's gonna kill us fer bein' out past supp' time. An' I don' wan' 'er takin' the strop to me again!"

"Who are you people?" Simon asked incredulously.

"Oh, I'm Frank Halbrecht an' 'e's me cousin N—"

"Shut up Frankie, you idiot!" Ned cried.

Simon watched the two for a moment and shook his head in amazement. "I may live to regret this," he said, coming to a sudden decision, "but just go, will you – both of you. Go! That way," he pointed toward the lane with the knife, "and don't come back."

Ned looked surprised while Frankie rubbed his swollen forehead. "Yer wanna come with? Mama's cookin's very good."

Ned grasped his cousin's arm. "No, he doesn't want to come with! Shut up and move." He gave Frankie a shove toward the lane and followed him without a backward glance.

Only then did Simon's heart stop pounding. He waited several minutes to make sure the pair had genuinely gone before going to the wash house.

Lantern light was jumping within the building, and as Simon

approached he could hear Patrick and Deon in companionable conversation, as though nothing untoward had just happened – perhaps for them it hadn't.

He drew close enough to peek around the door and was entirely unprepared for the sight that met his eyes.

Deon was completely naked and staked out like a starfish. Patrick was seated on the earthen floor beside him, calmly drinking wine directly from a dusty old bottle.

"What the hell …?" Simon strode into the room.

Both men looked up and grinned. "Care for a drink, brother?" Patrick brandished the bottle in his direction.

"You're just sitting there …? Drinking?" Simon demanded.

Patrick shrugged. "Waiting for you to get rid of the pair outside. We needed the knife to cut the ropes."

Dumbfounded, Simon turned to Deon. "But … what about you? Are you hurt?"

Deon tried to shrug but managed only a twitch because of his restraints. "Oh, I'm alright, except that the bitch stole every stitch I had on and didn't even suck my cock!"

TEA WITH MARY

Mary Whitmore.

It was a name certain to cause the blood to rush to my loins and make my trousers very uncomfortable.

Mary Whitmore had been my first lover, back when I was newly arrived at court. First, she had taken me under her wing; then she had taken me in her bed, under the stairs, behind the stables, in the orangery ... God! Where didn't we do it? And here she sat, all pink and blond and innocent as a babe, sipping tea from a delicate china cup in Adelene's Tea House on Cornmarket Street.

Her eagle-eyed chaperone was perched stiffly beside her, and Mary, or Lady Mary Ashwood, as she was now called, was carrying on a fluent and very detailed account of her wedding day, while her dainty foot firmly and relentlessly massaged my cock beneath the linen tablecloth.

A chance meeting on the street had led to Mary's invitation to join her for tea and explain that her new husband, having deposited her in his country home in Oxford, was currently in London in his capacity as assistant in the Prime Minister, The Right Honourable Perceval's office.

"So, my lord," she smiled, her teeth were like little pearls. *Christ, she had a kissable mouth!* "What news from you? I see you've returned to complete your studies ... how lovely!"

"Yes," it was all I could manage under the circumstances. My heart was pounding, and I was in danger of losing control. I hadn't come in my pants since I was fourteen, when Mary had spread her legs in a storeroom in Whitehall Palace. She'd demonstrated with her finger exactly what she wanted me to do, and in my inexperience, I ... did she just ask me something? I cleared my throat, "I'm ... sorry, what did you say?"

She laughed. It was like a tinkling bell, and as she touched her tongue suggestively to her lip, it took all my powers of concentration to prevent my eyes from rolling back in my head and my baser urges taking over.

Pulling myself together, I grasped my teacup and drank, while Mary cheerfully chattered on. Her chaperone saw only that her ladyship had met a friend on the street and invited him to a perfectly proper afternoon tea in a very public establishment.

Suddenly Mary's foot gave a little squeeze and I jumped, causing crockery and cutlery to clatter on the table.

Gathering myself, I discreetly withdrew one of my newly printed and addressed calling cards from my pocket and grasped her foot – oh God, her foot was naked! How'd she managed to strip off her stocking under the table? Struggling to compose myself, I shifted in a futile attempt to relieve some of the pressure building in my balls and wedged the card firmly between her two first toes.

Her conversation didn't miss a beat, but she withdrew her foot and smiled sweetly. She gave a subtle nod to the waiter who disappeared, reappearing shortly with her coat and hat, and those of her chaperone. Rather than rise, she acknowledged him with a very flirtatious smile of gratitude and allowed him to wait beside her.

The well-trained young man responded with a formal nod and turned to me. "Will you be leaving now, my lord? Shall I have your coat and hat brought over?"

"Yes please." I hoped he took his time about it – I was in danger of bursting my flies and in no mind to make a public exhibition of it.

Fortunately, Mary remained in her chair, and I was not obliged to stand. As a waiter arrived with my coat, I took it from him and rose with it held before me.

"Well, Brigitta," Mary spoke to the silent sentinel at her side. "Perhaps you could nip up High Street and make those purchases I need, then you can hire a cab to take you home."

Brigitta looked doubtful. "My lady, I really don't—"

"Now, how did I know you would argue with me?" Mary stood, and the waiter held her coat as she slipped into it. "Come along then. If you really think I'm in danger of being accosted on my way to my carriage you may walk me there."

She turned to me. I had quickly shrugged into my own coat and buttoned it up. Now I took her hand, and with a great show of courtliness, bowed over it.

"It was lovely to see you again, Lady Ashwood," I said, rising, correct in every way. "A very fortunate meeting. Perhaps you and Lord Ashwood will visit my home when next he is in Oxford."

"Perhaps we will, my lord." Turning to the stony-faced Brigitta, she said, "Let us go, Brigitta, you have errands to run and I must be getting home."

The waiter and I watched the two ladies stroll from the tea house – for pretty much the same reason: Mary was beautiful, witty and possessed of the most gravity-defying tits a man has ever seen.

Shit! Just as the pressure in my trousers was beginning to ease, I had the most delicious vision of Mary's rose-tipped breasts, bared and pert before my eyes. Nodding quickly to the waiter, I pushed such thoughts aside and strode out into the street.

Oxford, late March, was still prone to chill winds and today's gusty weather was an example. Fortunately, a cab was clopping by as I emerged from the tea house, and it stopped at my signal. I gave the address of the house my father kept for me as a residence while attending university and took a seat in the grubby interior of the public conveyance.

∾

The cab stopped at my gate, and in the time it took to climb out and pay the driver, Mary's coach had pulled up behind us.

I strode briskly up the walk and, without waiting for a footman, used my key to let myself in.

The entry was dim; the only furnishings were a hallstand with a bowl of cut flowers and a silver mail tray, and a hat rack. It was to this I turned while unbuttoning my coat, then casually tossed my hat onto a hook in a single movement – I enjoyed the challenge and was ludicrously pleased whenever I managed it first time. The hat snared on a hook just as the front door swung open.

Mary was immediately in my arms.

In a burning frenzy, our lips fused together and I crushed her against my chest. Oblivious to anything but our desperate need, we rebounded off the wall and crashed heavily against the hallstand.

"Oops!" Mary giggled, followed by a breathy, "*Ahh*," as my hands ruched up her skirts and cupped her naked buttocks.

"Is ... is ... anyone *oh* ... home?" Mary gasped, nibbling my neck, her hands tearing my shirt from my trousers.

"No ... *mmm* ... perhaps footman, housekeeper ... *mmm* brother ... won't be ... be disturbed ..."

Hands on her waist, I picked her up and dumped her on the hallstand, ignoring the bowl of flowers that bounced noisily onto the floor, followed closely by the clatter of the mail tray.

"Haven't ... much time ... oh *God, Patrick!*" She cried, frantically groping at my flies.

"Wait ..." I pushed her hands aside, unfastened my trousers and straight away her fingers delved within, applying firm, experienced strokes while I parted her thighs.

"Quickly ...!" she demanded, against my mouth.

I obliged.

Shoving up skirt and petticoat, I thrust into her, once, twice ... again ... and she gripped my arse and urged me onward, our mingled groans building rapidly to a crescendo.

I was vaguely aware of the hallstand thumping rhythmically against the wall as we clawed at one another, straining and pounding and aggressive.

Suddenly Mary's muscles contracted around me, and she shouted, "*Nng ... aah!*"

I followed her lead, smothering my own cries against her damp throat, my knees threatening to give way.

"Oh God ... oh God!" Mary gasped, arching her back while her hands clutched at my shoulders.

My breathing was returning to normal when a thought occurred to me. "Mary ... a sponge ... did you ...?"

She gave a breathless kind of snort. "Of course, silly ... couldn't you tell?"

I shook my head. "No ..."

"Don't worry. I ... prepared ... in the coach ... on the ride over."

I nodded, and eased myself away from her, and helped her to climb off the hallstand. She smoothed down her skirts and patted at her hair as I fastened my flies. "I must go," she said. She was still breathing hard. "If Brigitta should arrive home before me ..." Mary grimaced at the thought. "She reports to Gordon ... everything I do ... where I go, to whom I speak. He only hired her to monitor me."

"With just cause, I'd suggest," my tone was wry, and she

laughed, wrinkling her nose at me. I led her to the door and opened it, and as she made to step forward an odd expression crossed her face.

"What on earth ...?" she murmured. Reaching beneath her skirt, she withdrew a small gold-edged envelope. "Addressed to you, I believe, and stuck to my bottom!"

She placed a little kiss on my lips, dropped the note into my hand and skipped through the door and down the path.

∾

I slumped heavily against the wall and ran a hand threw my hair.

My God, she was a wildcat! I looked down at myself: my shirt was hanging loose and a button was missing, my coat was askew and my blue velvet trousers had a telling stain on them.

The bowl of flowers lay on the floor where it had landed surrounded by the combined wreckage of spilt water, scattered lavender and daffodils, and the silver mail tray.

Shrugging, I pushed away from the wall just as the parlour door opened and Simon emerged in company with a most offended-looking lady and gentleman.

"Ah," Simon said, as though surprised to see me, belied by the merry dancing of his eyes, "Lord Scarwood, may I present my—"

"You may not!" the very affronted Lord Scarwood declared, jowls wobbling indignantly. "Come, my dear," he grasped the elbow of the very flushed, and rather traumatised woman behind him who was clutching a fan to her throat.

I pressed myself against the wall as Lady Scarwood held her skirts close, for fear of contamination, and slid past me.

On the threshold, Lord Scarwood turned and pointed a finger in my direction. "You, Sir! You will hear about this!"

His wife snapped open her fan and employed it vigorously, glaring at me, nostrils flared in scandalised disgust.

"Your servant, Sir," I responded with the utmost courtesy and swept my most elegant bow. By the time I straightened, the pair had disappeared through the door and were marching down the walk to where their coach waited on the street.

I kicked the door shut. "Fuck off, then."

Simon could contain himself no longer. Clutching his stomach, he collapsed against the wall, and erupted into uncontrollable laughter.

When, finally, he regained his composure and stood before me wiping his streaming eyes.

I said, "Who the devil were they?"

"*They*," he responded, "were paying a call to *you*, to assess your suitability and whether you might be agreeable to the idea of paying court to their daughter. Apparently, Lord Scarwood had already addressed your father about the matter and your father suggested they visit you."

"I see – no doubt a practical joke on my father's part. Well, I'm not interested in courting their daughter – or anyone else for that matter. And in any case, they should have announced their intention to visit."

"They did," Simon smirked and nodded toward my hand.

I looked down at the envelope I was still holding, stained with body fluid, but clearly addressed to me despite the smudged ink after being stuck to Mary's firm arse.

"If you checked your mail more regularly ... anyway, I expect it won't be the last you hear about this. You should have seen the looks on their faces!"

I grinned. "I can only imagine."

"Lady Scarwood ... I was certain she was on the brink of a conniption. It was all I could do to keep a straight face and waffle on about my studies and how wonderful the university is, while the noises coming from out here sounded like you were slamming the hallstand through the wall with a battering ram."

"I was giving it my best."

We went into the parlour where a tea service sat; cups of tea left to grow cold, and a plate of biscuits lay untouched.

Suddenly hungry, I took up a biscuit and bit into it. "Hopefully, they'll get me expelled."

Simon toasted me with his teacup.

∾

Of course, my impromptu tryst with Mary was always going to come back and bite me. And so it did, two weeks later in the form of my much-aggrieved father.

Fresh from an unpleasant audience with the head of Oxford University, the earl rode his horse directly into the stables out at the back of his townhouse. He stomped unceremoniously through the kitchen, startling the cook on his way, then trudged up the stairs and into my room; where I, recovering from a night of debauchery involving champagne and Mary, was attempting to catch up on some much-needed sleep.

"Get out of that bloody bed!" my father bellowed.

Having heard the thumping of his boots on the stairs, I knew my day of reckoning had arrived. Groaning, I poked my head out from under the counterpane and squinted up at him.

I can honestly say I'd never seen my father so incensed.

His ordinarily ruddy complexion had adopted the hue of a thunderous cloud and perspiration glistened on his brow. He grasped the counterpane and stripped it from the bed, revealing me, fully clothed but for my boots.

Fragments of memory flashed before me: staggering clumsily into the room ... grey predawn light filtering through the window ... collapsing onto the bed ... kicking off my boots and rolling over ... dragging the counterpane over my shoulders ...

"Get up this minute," Father demanded, glaring down at me. "You're a bloody disgrace, you know that?"

"Mmph ..." I sat up and swung my legs over the side of the bed;

the movement caused my stomach to rebel. With a shove, I pushed my father aside and lurched across the room where I threw up in my chamber pot.

"You have fifteen minutes to clean yourself up and come downstairs. I'll have a full account of your behaviour."

With that, Father removed himself and slammed the door on his way out.

ॐ

I was still decidedly green when I presented myself in the parlour before my father. He was looking at the street outside and turned from the window when I entered the room. He seemed to have calmed himself.

"Where's Simon?" he asked.

I shrugged. "At lectures, I suppose. Never misses them. Very diligent and doing well too."

"So I believe."

"Yes, *he's* the credit to you," I added, and poured two cups of coffee from the pot left by a footman. "Unlike me ... See what happens when the student enjoys the study? Simon *wants* to be here."

He regarded me through narrow eyes. "They're not expelling you, if that's what you're hoping for."

I cursed under my breath. "Why? Because of my wealth and title?" I made a sound of contempt. "Anyone else would have been kicked out on his arse. But a scandal involving the earl's son – oh, that will be covered up, and Lord Scarwood's ruffled fur will be smoothed over."

I handed him a cup of coffee and he took a sip, eyes closing in appreciation of the flavour.

"Perhaps," he said. "So ... who was the ... er ... young lady? Someone of quality, they said. Drove away in a private coach."

"Doesn't matter who she was."

"Good lord, whores are one thing but if she was respectable ... you didn't take her maidenhead, did you?" He added, eyes widening with the implications.

I snorted at the irony. "On the contrary – she took mine!"

My father's mouth fell open and I suppressed a laugh. "Never mind," I said. "I'm toying with you. No, I didn't take her maidenhead, and no, I'm not saying who she was – it's irrelevant."

"She's married, then."

"Don't you go casting stones!" I was beginning to feel ill again and baiting him seemed to lose its appeal. I sighed heavily and dropped to a settee. "Very well. Are you going to lecture me? Mete out a punishment of some description? Get on with it, will you, I feel like shit warmed over."

"I'm your father! Show some respect!"

My head had begun spinning. I closed my eyes momentarily. "Yes, you're right, you do," I conceded. He did deserve my respect, but other than that, I needed to throw up again and wanted an end to the conversation.

Rising and moving with urgency, I left the room and staggered down the hall, through the kitchen and out into the courtyard. By the stone wall of the stables was a garden bed.

Bracing myself with one hand on the wall, I leaned over the pretty spring flowers and expelled the last of the champagne remaining in my stomach.

∾

As it turned out, there was nothing Father could do short of giving me a stern lecture that included words like obedience, family, responsibility, reputation, *blah, blah ad nauseam*.

It seemed that his biggest concern was that his wife – she who thrived on scandal but would not tolerate it within her own family – had been present when the messenger had arrived bearing a letter from the head of the university.

The letter described a visit one, Lord Scarwood, had made to the university head, an appropriately worded outline of my behaviour, and a request that my father attend a meeting to discuss said behaviour and suitable punishment.

The countess was furious and demanded my father address the situation immediately. Further, he was to ensure that her son, Simon, maintained his spotless reputation by avoiding association with me, and applying himself assiduously to his medical studies.

Little did she know that Simon's assiduous medical studies involved conducting nightly biology experiments in his room with a very willing subject.

While Simon was greatly amused by the entire event, I realised that my father was, in truth, quite upset, and I was sorry for it. He stayed two days with us, but before riding out he spoke to me in all earnestness.

He explained that while he couldn't control my behaviour, he trusted that in future I would be more discreet. He would not enquire further into the identity of my 'friend,' but hoped I would respect her marital status and break off any understanding between us.

He also insisted that I attend my classes.

I agreed, embraced him, and watched him mount Canto and trot through the courtyard gate to continue up the lane toward Yorkshire.

Simon stood at my side. He said, "You're going to keep seeing Mary." It wasn't a question.

Without looking at him, I said simply, "Yes."

∽

In the end, it was Mary who broke it off with me after we'd been seeing each other several times a week for about a month.

One afternoon, we were lying in my bed listening to the April rain pattering against the window. Mary was dozing after a vigorous and rather exhausting session, while I was propped on one elbow, lazily trailing my fingers over the contours of her body.

Brushing lightly over a nipple, I circled first one breast, then the other, before slowly drifting south. Dipping into her navel, circling around and down ...

She stretched languorously and sighed sleepily, murmuring, "Too tired ..." Taking the hint, I moved my hand further upward to settle lightly on her belly.

Her skin was silky and warm, her abdomen slightly rounded. I splayed my fingers over the shape of it and was gently massaging when she suddenly shoved my hand away.

"What?" I asked, alarmed.

"Don't do that!" She snapped, sitting up and clutching the counterpane to her chest.

"What's wrong?" I sat up beside her. "Mary?"

She slid out of bed and began dressing. I watched wordlessly until finally she sat on the edge of the bed to pull on her stockings. Only then did I speak.

"You'd better tell me."

She sighed deeply, then turned to face me with a look of resignation. "I'm pregnant."

I stopped breathing for a moment while a number of questions flashed through my mind. Then I took a deep breath and simply nodded, waiting for her to say more.

"You suspected I wasn't using the sponge," she said, adding, "there was no need."

Reaching out, she touched my hand where it rested on the counterpane. "It's not yours," she spoke softly, adding with a short, mirthless laugh. "If only it were."

"Whose is it?"

She smiled ruefully, "My husband's. Who would've thought the old man had it in him?"

"Are you sure?" I asked archly. " You haven't seen him in

months."

"I know. But you see, I became pregnant the first week we were married. I knew it for certain the day before I met you in the street. I'm nearly three months gone."

"You didn't say anything. Why didn't you tell me?"

"What difference would it have made? We have no future ... we've always known that. I suppose I could have told you, but I wanted to enjoy our time together without thinking of it. I do love you, Patrick."

Lifting a shoulder in a half-shrug she added simply, "I've always loved you."

I nodded and leaned in to receive her farewell kiss. She closed the door softly as she left.

⁊

That night I stayed in with a bottle of brandy. I acknowledged a certain pain in the region of my heart and allowed myself one night in which to indulge my misery.

The following night I went out, got well and truly foxed, found a willing bar wench and fucked her until we were both senseless. I awoke the next morning, sprawled in a pile of hay with an inquisitive pig snorting in my face.

Rising unsteadily and plucking stray straws from my clothes and hair, I staggered home.

The world had righted itself – I was back.

THE WAGER

Simon pulled the cork from a bottle of Bordeaux and poured a celebratory drink. Out in the hall, the front door of the Oxford town house he shared with his stepbrother Patrick, opened and closed, and Simon reached for a second glass.

He poured a generous measure and counted. Patrick would be removing hat and gloves and checking the mail tray before coming in.

By Simon's estimation, twenty seconds slid past before the door to the parlour swung open and Patrick strolled in. Pat's face gave nothing away, but Simon was innately aware of his stepbrother's unhappiness as he flopped into a chair and handed a letter to Simon in exchange for a glass of wine.

"Last day." Simon put the letter aside without looking at it. "Another university year over. You'd be happy with that, wouldn't you?"

Pat's face was flushed and damp, hair plastered to his temples where his hat had been. He raised his glass in salute, "I'll drink to that ..." and he threw back the wine in two gulps, then thrust the empty glass toward his stepbrother.

"You still going to Waterville?" Simon refilled the glass and sipped at his own.

Patrick took a more restrained mouthful of wine before responding. "I am. Are you coming?"

"I think so. Might be a change."

"If only to avoid your mother."

Simon grinned, the expression enhancing the beauty of his face. "I wouldn't say that specifically, but your father is far easier to deal with than my mother. Even when he was furious with you, he was still reasonable."

Patrick snorted, "I'll give him that I suppose."

"Well," Simon took a sip of wine, "you're not so unreasonable yourself. I expect he knows the effort you've been making. Old Feeble Peeble would've made damn sure the earl was receiving regular reports as to his son's behaviour."

Patrick smiled at the nickname the Oxford students had given the very uninspiring Professor Peeble. Old Feeble Peeble was responsible for making regular assessments of various students' progress and activities; Lord Patrick Washburn, the son of the Earl of Thorncliffe, headed his list.

These were students that had given the university cause for concern, and Peeble wasn't about to have the university's reputation suffer under his administration.

"He didn't believe I'd done my own study," Patrick commented, holding up his glass and peering through the ruby depths. "Accused me of paying someone to complete the assessments for me."

"You've drastically changed your study habits – and your attitude. Any wonder they're suspicious."

"True, but they wouldn't have been surprised had they known I'd kept seeing Mary – short lived as that episode has been. They always expect the worst from me."

"Hmm," Simon said, reflectively. He'd known that Patrick had felt more for his lover than he'd ever admit, and that he'd been hurt when she'd called off their arrangement. But then, Simon had been shocked by how completely his stepbrother had put the incident behind him, effectively cauterising the wound and moving on with a marked lack of emotion.

"In any event," Patrick was saying, "I've told Father I'll be going to Devon for summer to manage the harvest and any other issues, after which, I'll return to Oxford next year."

Simon looked impressed. "He'd have been happy to hear that."

"He was ... although when I told him I'd joined the rowing squad he was a bit sceptical."

His stepbrother laughed and drained his glass. "So, what now? You going to Lord Melville's birthday party?"

Patrick shook his head. "No," he placed his empty wine glass on a table and raised his arms above his head in a back-cracking stretch. "I'm planning a quiet night."

Simon regarded him archly. "Not unwell are you? No itching rashes? No oozing sores in unmentionable places? I am a physician in training, you know."

"I'm touched by your concern ... no, I'm very well thank you, Doctor Sarcasm ... just thought it would be nice to stay in. I owe Maeve a letter ... might spend the evening with pen in hand. What about you?" He waved in the direction of the letter he'd brought in for Simon. "Correspondence to deal with?"

"It's from Zan. She writes regularly, but I've trained her not to expect regular replies."

Patrick frowned. "Zan? Who's Zan?"

"Zan? Alex, my sister – *your* stepsister! I thought the two of you were rubbing along quite well ... how soon you forget."

Patrick felt a jolt in the region of his stomach. Indeed, how had he forgotten Alex? He shrugged sheepishly. "I suppose I don't think of her as Zan."

Simon watched his stepbrother speculatively. "How exactly do you think of her?"

"What does that mean?" Patrick was unaccustomed to feeling challenged and didn't enjoy it. Besides, he wasn't sure himself what he felt about Alex. Certainly she had fascinated him, attracted him even, during his time at Broughton Hall.

But since leaving ... If he was honest with himself, he would admit he had thought fleetingly of her from time to time. But he refused to be honest with himself – where his stepsister was concerned, at least. In most other things Patrick was brutally honest with himself, but just to be safe, he stubbornly blocked all thoughts of Alexandra Broughton.

"Well, by the time we left Yorkshire," Simon was on a mission, "the two of you seemed quite friendly, yet you haven't mentioned her once, or even asked about her since."

"So? What's your point?"

It was Simon's turn to feel challenged, but he wasn't as good at hiding it. He glanced uncomfortably at the empty glass he still held. "No reason ... just ... curious."

Having regained his composure, Patrick attacked. "She and I were amicable, but I'm not sure how that translates into an interest in the mundane daily activities of a countrified fourteen-year-old."

Simon gave a snort of laughter, "Give over. That approach might work with some people, but not me. I know you found my sister intriguing – it's alright to admit it."

Despite himself, Patrick smiled. One of the things he liked about Simon was the way his stepbrother saw right through him – to a degree. "Only when compared with your other sister – complete viper, that one."

"Oh yes! Our dear little Annie – viper indeed. Mother's going to want to marry her off before she creates a scandal." He eyed the man sitting opposite him. "Interested?"

Patrick made a rude sound. "She's pleasing to the eye, but I pity the man who wakes up to find her beside him every morning."

"You've woken up with worse."

"Of course," Patrick winked and rose from his chair. "But then I pay them and walk away."

∾

Exactly one week later, both boys were riding south toward Patrick's estate in Devon. Along the way, they stopped in Wiltshire to visit the standing stones and spent an uneventful night in an inn in Amesbury.

The lanes and byways of the country were the main thoroughfares from one village to the next, so from time to time they came across farmers herding stock or driving wagons laden with ale casks or vegetables bound for market.

The travelling was easy and the land rich, the air rang with early summer birdsong and the mingled scents of earth and ripening wheat.

Each evening they patronised a local inn for a meal and a room for the night before rising early the next morning to continue their journey.

By the following week, as they rode into Devon, it became apparent to Simon that the local population held Patrick in some regard. Feted like a person of some importance, the Young Lord, as he was widely referred to, responded to questions, accepted invitations to visit farms, and on more than one occasion, was forced to politely extricate himself from the clutches of numerous scheming matrons openly parading eligible daughters before him.

Laughing, Patrick deftly parried their approaches, swept off his hat in a chivalrous bow and kicked Equus forward in a clean escape.

"Regular occurrence?" Simon asked, amused, following on Oliver. They were leaving one of Patrick's villages, a small, prosperous wool farming community that went by the descriptive name of Glittering Brook. The afternoon sun was warm on their backs as they walked their horses down the lane.

"Afraid so. Most are more playful than serious," Patrick responded, equally amused.

"That red-head was ... interesting."

"It's marriage they're after, not a quick roll in the hay barn. Could you imagine my father's response should I announce my intended was a shepherdess from the village?"

Simon laughed, pulling his horse's head away from the grassy verge. "Not really, but I can imagine my mother's ... stick to the path, Oliver ... *that* would be worth seeing!"

Patrick grimaced. "I think I'd be pilloried."

"Would it worry you? To be forced into marriage?"

"I'd prefer it be my choice." He sighed, removing his hat and wiping his perspiring brow on his sleeve before replacing the hat. "But I will have to marry and get heirs some day – so will you. Provided she's intelligent, someone I can converse with, deal amicably with, I'm not that discerning."

He glanced at his stepbrother. "I don't plan to marry for love, if that's what you're wondering. I don't plan to *love* anyone, for that matter, but I plan to have a wife of appropriate pedigree for breeding, and a suitably qualified mistress for fucking. Two very different women; two very different roles."

"Good luck with that!" Simon said, with a short laugh.

Patrick shot a narrow look over his shoulder.

"I mean," Simon went on, "that you're no more impervious to Cupid's arrow than the rest of us – even if you *think* you are."

"Ha! I'll take a wager on that, brother."

Simon watched him for a moment, a knowing grin spreading across his face. "Very well, why not? I'll wager right here and now, that you will either marry for love or not at all."

Patrick smiled smugly. "What are you putting down?"

"What am I putting down?" Simon's eyes moved to the middle distance as he considered. "If I lose ... I'll ..." he paused thoughtfully.

"Can't think of anything suitably valuable?" Patrick teased. "Very well, what about this: if I lose, meaning I marry for love, I pledge unwavering monogamy – which just shows how unlikely I am to lose! I will be utterly and unquestioningly faithful to the one woman until death do us part. And if I don't marry, I'll take a vow of celibacy for an entire year."

"Good," Simon said, warming to the theme. "And if *I* lose, *I* will be celibate for a year."

Patrick burst into laughter.

"What's so funny about that?" His brother demanded, slightly affronted.

"*You*! Celibate? Who are you trying to fool? When it comes to getting your cock out, you're worse than me! The only difference is that you're more discreet about it. No one would ever suspect the rake you are! You couldn't abstain for a week let alone a year!"

"Exactly so, which illustrates my point. Do you think I would wager celibacy if I thought I would lose?"

"You *will* lose, brother dear," Patrick declared. "I hope you have a good relationship with your hand."

"Very funny. We need to put a time limit on it."

"Alright," Patrick stated. "Let's say by the age of thirty, if I haven't married for convenience—"

"No, too easy," Simon interrupted. "Let it be that *I* wager that by the time you are thirty, *you* will have married and will be utterly faithful to your wife. If you are unmarried – implying that you have fallen in love with someone unattainable – you will be celibate for an entire year."

"Done! And if I marry to fulfil the obligations of familial duty before I'm thirty you will be the loser and must remain celibate for a year."

"Agreed!" Simon stated and the two bridged the gap between their horses and shook on it.

∽

About an hour later, the sun was dropping toward the western horizon and Patrick shivered slightly in the late afternoon air. It was still only early summer, so the evenings tended to close in a little cooler.

He'd been considering his wager with Simon and now began chuckling to himself.

Simon was slumped comfortably in his saddle, relaxed to the point of drowsiness. Alerted by Patrick's soft laughter, he looked across at his stepbrother. "Hmm?"

Eyes glistening, Patrick turned to his companion. "Just thinking about our wager and how dangerous you're going to be the year before my thirtieth. By then you'll realise you're going to lose, and you'll be so fearful of celibacy you'll fuck everything that moves and wear your cock down to a bleeding stump."

"You think so?"

Patrick laughed again and nodded.

"Don't be so sure," Simon said, adding to himself, *I saw the way you looked at Mary Whitmore – you're not the stone-hearted brute you'd like us all to believe.*

∾

The brothers rode into Waterville the following day and were met by Patrick's team of household staff headed by Leonard the butler and Mrs Bath the very motherly housekeeper who greeted Patrick like a long-lost son.

More used to the overbearing Mrs Grainger, his own housekeeper, Simon was taken aback by the casual relationship the Young Lord maintained with the woman.

Immediately taking charge, Mrs Bath bustled them indoors while a gaggle of maids hovered about to take their hats, coats and riding gloves, and Leonard directed a pair of footmen to take care of their bags.

As Simon entered Waterville Place, he found himself in the

most incredible room he'd ever seen. This room was perfectly circular, lined with mirrored tiles and shards of coloured glass, and domed way overhead in a mosaic of vibrant glass panes that created a dazzling kaleidoscopic display.

Dumbstruck, he gazed about as the noonday sun bounced sparks of blue, red, green and yellow off the mirrors. So enchanted was he that he failed to notice the two maids waiting nearby, elbowing one another and sighing over the handsome young man.

"Mrs Bath ..." Patrick nodded significantly in the maids' direction.

"Back to work!" Mrs Bath clapped her hands and herded the two girls from the room then turned to her master. "Sir Simon is proving to be quite a distraction, my lord."

"Indeed," Patrick agreed, and clapping his stepbrother good naturedly on the shoulder added, "Come along, Eros."

"Huh ...?" Simon emerged from entrancement. "What?"

"Nothing, you big gormless twat," Pat said, and laughing, led Simon from the room.

∽

Waterville Place was enormous – the kind of grand mansion one could lose oneself in. Simon had been allocated a room in the guest wing, and Mrs Bath took it upon herself to escort him there herself.

Following the housekeeper's swaying rump along the gallery and corridors, Simon thought it might be wise to leave a trail of pebbles so he could find his way back.

Meanwhile, Patrick, relieved to be once again in his old room in the residential wing, closed the door on the outside world, and threw himself on his bed with a sigh of contentment.

He tugged the stock of his travelling suit loose from around his neck then consciously tensed and released each limb and muscle until he was completely and utterly relaxed.

It seemed only minutes had passed before a brisk knock

sounded at his door and Mrs Bath came in, hands folded respectfully before her.

"My lord?" She spoke softly and Patrick, opening a single eye to peep at her, promptly closed it again. By her stance alone he knew his tranquillity was about to end.

"Mrs Bath."

"My Lord, a word if you wouldn't mind."

She wasn't normally so formal when alone with him – that fact rang alarm bells too. He exhaled noisily through his nose and pushed to a sitting position.

"What is it?"

"Well, my—"

"Oh, for Christ's sake stop my lording and spit it out!"

Mrs Bath drew herself up. "It's about ... Sir Simon ..."

Patrick contained a smirk – he could guess what was coming next. "What about Sir Simon?"

"Well," the housekeeper paused, clearly uncomfortable. "I don't know how to say this ... delicately."

"Then just bloody say it."

"My l – I ... I have concerns about ... about the maids, my lord."

Patrick was enjoying himself so instead of rescuing the poor woman, he adopted a baffled expression and said, "*The maids*, Mrs Bath? I thought you said it was about Sir Simon?"

"The maids *and* Sir Simon."

"What about them?"

Damn him, she who'd known him all his life thought to herself. *He's going to make me say it.*

Taking a deep breath she said, "It's just that ... Bea and Hester, the two girls I've brought in from Astor, seem to have ... taken rather a fancy to Sir Simon and ... and I wondered, that is I ... I have *concerns* ... Young girls can be rather ... *forward*, you know, and ... tempting ..."

Her voice trailed off and she looked so thoroughly flustered that Patrick was forced to press his lips together to control their twitching.

At that moment, Mrs Bath, well acquainted with her Young Lord's penchant for mischief, studied him narrowly and Patrick, no longer able to control himself, burst out laughing.

After enjoying several moments' hilarity at his housekeeper's expense, he grew quiet and gasped, "Of course, I'm being very unkind to you, aren't I!"

She merely grunted in response.

"I take your point, Mrs Bath, I'm sure my stepbrother won't be diddling the maids – however tempting they may prove. But just to be sure, I'll have a word with him immediately."

"That's all I ask, *my lord*." Turning indignantly, she stalked from his room and could still hear him laughing when she reached the long gallery.

ᘇ

"I didn't notice," Simon admitted. "If they were making eyes or whatever ... I wasn't aware."

Patrick stood in the window in Simon's room staring down at the lawns to the rear of the house. "Look, you probably didn't, but I did and so did Mrs Bath. So all I'm saying is, if they engage in any ..." he shrugged and turned from the window to look at his stepbrother, "inappropriate or flirtatious behaviour, just ignore it, will you?"

"Of course ... but I would never give it a thought, anyway."

"I've ordered a light meal, come downstairs?"

Simon nodded and followed as Patrick left the room. "It goes on though, doesn't it?" he said to his brother's back. "I mean, the lord of the manor and the serving girl ... that kind of thing?"

Patrick whirled around and stared at him, genuinely shocked. "Jesus Christ! Are you serious?" He snorted in disbelief. "You are though, aren't you?"

Simon glared at him. "What did I say?"

"Of course it goes on! You know it goes on all the time! There's no happy ending for anyone. The girl ends up unemployed and in disgrace and the master ends up with a house full of disgruntled staff. If you haven't come across it among your friends, just wait! Jesus Christ," he repeated. Shaking his head in bewilderment, he continued down the corridor, with Simon behind him.

At the end of the corridor was a flight of stairs leading down to the long gallery, which ran the width of the house between the guest and resident wings. In its centre was the great staircase descending to the main living areas.

At the foot of the staircase, Simon paused and said, "Wait." The other man turned, a question on his face.

"Just wondering," Simon said, "have *you* ever ... you know, bedded one of yours?"

Patrick's face darkened and he leaned toward Simon. "No," he said firmly. "I haven't and never will – way too much trouble and you lose the respect of all of them and that leads to having to find new staff. So I haven't, and neither will you. Strictly off limits!" He went to walk on but paused and turned back with a wry grin on his face, "Besides, my father would fucking kill me!"

That evening, the brothers were enjoying an after-dinner brandy when Patrick suddenly and decisively drained his glass and placed it on the table.

Kicking Simon's outstretched boot he said, "Come on, let's go out. We'll go to Astor and I'll introduce you to some maids of my acquaintance who are definitely *not* off limits!"

BUCKSHOT

"**G**ood Lord!" The exclamation sounded like the shriek of an outraged thirteen-year-old girl but was in fact an outraged thirteen-year-old boy.

And it literally startled me out of the woman beneath me; the woman who turned out to be the outraged thirteen-year-old boy's mother. Bugger, she was older than I thought!

"For heaven's sake, Victor," Lady Ivana Orloff tucked the sheet around her shoulders as I slid to the side and rolled to face the intruder. "What have I told you about bursting into my rooms?"

"Unhand my mother, Sir!" Victor demanded, his face flushed and eyes bulging. Clicking his heels imperiously, he pointed at me. "Out of that bed! This instant!"

"Oh, I don't think that would be at all appropriate," I muttered. Victor's mother sniggered softly while a pimple on Victor's forehead seemed to grow before my eyes and looked set to explode.

Lady Ivana wriggled to a sitting position against the headboard and I shuffled up beside her, cocking a quizzical eyebrow at the boy.

"My God," Victor cried, his voice rising a semitone. "You're no older than me!"

Ivana frowned at me, "You're older than him, aren't you?"

"Of course. I'm at least four years older."

"You see, Victor? Lord Patrick is at least four years older than you."

Poor Victor hopped from foot to foot, clenching and unclenching his fists and emitting choking sounds.

"I'll have my satisfaction, Sir," he announced, mustering his dignity. "Name your second."

"Now Victor—"

"S-stay out of it, mother. I intend to defend your honour."

"Oh dear," Lady Ivana muttered. She was lightly trailing her fingernails up and down the length of my cock.

"Come now, Victor," I said calmly. I didn't want to humiliate the boy, but the situation was ludicrous. "Why don't you leave me to get dressed and we can talk about it, man to man, eh?"

"Don't man-to-man me you c-coward!" He stuttered in his fury. "I d-demand satisfaction, Sir! I'm calling you out!"

"Stop it, right now!" Ivana snapped and I squeaked like a thirteen-year-old girl myself as her nails dug into my prick.

She offered a conciliatory shrug, "Sorry, love. Shall I rub it better?"

"*Mother!*" Victor bellowed. "Out of that bed, both of you! Now!"

"Come on, son, be—"

"B-both of you! And you," he pointed at me, "Name your second you s-son of a b-bloody whore!"

I pushed Ivana's hand away. "Now, you've done it," I growled, and reached beside the bed for my trousers. "You don't disparage my mother. She's nothing like yours!"

"*What!*" Ivana thumped my shoulder as I swung my legs to the side of the bed. I shot a glare at her – *that fucking hurt* – rising with my back to the boy, I pulled on the trousers.

"Why, look at him ..." Victor sneered. "Not only is he a dog, he's also a cowardly one. What s-sort of woman b-breeds a man like that?"

"Oh, shut up Victor, for heaven's sake," his mother huffed, patting the bed trying to find her clothes.

"I'm t-telling you once more, you yellow-backed c-cur. Choose your weapon. I *will* defend m-my mother's honour."

I buttoned my trousers and turning, marched towards him. To his credit, he stood his ground; though I must have looked fearsome because the blood suddenly drained from his face.

I'm tall and being athletic, I'm quite well built. Naked from the waist up I know I was an imposing sight for this brave little chap, but I wasn't feeling charitably towards him at all.

Truth was, I was horny and frustrated – a bit embarrassed too – and this little shit's mother was in fact one of the greatest sluts of her time. I was not about to have my mother's name vilified for the sake of Ivana Orloff's honour.

"Now listen here you little arsehole," I grabbed the child by the throat and slammed him against the wall – not nearly as forcibly as I wanted to. "You listening?"

His head jerked in my hand and he gave a strangled, "*airck!*"

"Don't you *dare* ..." I shouted that last word in his face, "speak of my mother! Don't you *fucking dare* question her honour! While your mother's honour is *entirely* questionable, you don't have the right to even *think* of my mother! Now get the fuck out of this room before I forget you're just a spoilt little brat and kick the living shit out of you!"

I'd been aware of Ivana shouting and scrambling around behind me, frantically trying to throw some clothes on. Now as I released Victor and watched him slide limply down the wall, she ran over.

Sparing barely a glance for her son, she grasped my arm and spun me around. She had pulled on a silky wrap and as she slapped me across the face – hard – the shoulder slipped to reveal one luscious, dusky-tipped breast.

"Hmm," I murmured, my hand going to my cheek, eyes on her tit.

"Don't you touch my son, you bastard!" She tugged the wrap closed. "And keep your eyes to yourself!" Then she back-handed me across the other cheek for good measure.

"For God's sake!" I bellowed. "You two deserve one another." The second blow had more strength behind it than the first. My cheek went numb and blood started seeping into my mouth.

"Get out!" She stamped her foot and pointed to the door.

She had dropped to the floor and was making soothing noises in Victor's ear as I left the room.

Out on the street, I spat blood onto the road and hailed a passing cab. It was only as I gave my name and assured him of payment upon arrival that the driver decided I might be worth the risk of a forty-five-minute drive out to Waterville Place; I was, after all, still wearing only my trousers.

∾

The cab rolled up the drive and drew to a halt under the portico. The driver opened the door, lowered the stairs and I stepped out, barefoot and half-naked, and strode through the front door of my house.

"Mrs Bath!" My voice bounced sibilantly around the atrium as I passed through into the hall beyond. "Mrs Bath!"

My stalwart housekeeper had seen a lot in her time, but evidently not this. She appeared from one of the rooms and jerked in surprise at the sight of me standing there in all my glory.

"My lord?" I'd startled her into uncommon politeness. I grinned.

"Could you please pay the chap outside from the housekeeping tin and note down how much I need to reimburse you?"

"Certainly ... my lord." She shook herself as though throwing off a dream. "Of course."

I watched as she regained her composure and moved off to do as I asked.

ॐ

During the hour that followed, I was subjected to Mrs Bath's grudging ministrations. Not wishing to expose some innocent young housemaid to her half-naked Young Lord with purpling bruises on his face, she passed me a glass of some powerful solution with which to rinse my mouth and served up a thorough piece of her mind.

The mixture tasted horrid and stung like the blazes but the woman was not to be distracted from her course of action – which was to remind me of my position. I had servants, tenants and entire villages for which I was responsible. How on earth were they ever to place their faith in me when ... and on it went.

In the end I think she wore herself out, for her voice trailed off and she stood before me, hands on hips and glaring as though trying to set me afire with the double-barrelled force of her eyes.

"You're lucky I don't write immediately to your father, young man," she announced. "We do correspond, you know."

I shrugged. "Do you think you could arrange a bath, please?" I asked with exaggerated politeness.

She made puffing sounds with her lips and shook her head. "You're a horror, you really are. Your poor mother would turn in her grave—"

"Alright!" I snarled. Not again! My poor mother indeed! "Enough, Mrs Bath. I've endured your recriminations, your huffing and puffing, and that evil brew you made me gargle, but I'll not tolerate your bringing my mother into this. Arrange a bath for me, if you please, and kindly remove yourself so I can get some fu— bloody peace."

She made a snorting noise but left my room. I ran my hand

through my hair and stamped my foot like a petulant child.

Why the hell does everybody bring my mother into it? I wondered. It seemed the perfect way to stick the knife into me. I refuse to feel guilty over my behaviour.

∾

Simon arrived home shortly after Mrs Bath had ordered my bath and instructed my footman to leave me to relax – and with all due respect, wash some bleedin' foolishness out of myself – alone.

Encountering the housekeeper as he entered the house, Simon made a polite enquiry as to the cause of her obviously high colour.

Her response, a clipped, "Best discuss the matter with the Young Lord, Sir Simon," caused him to grin and make his way immediately upstairs.

∾

"What have you done now?" He asked without preamble as he strolled into my room. I was reclining in the brass tub, head resting on a towel, eyes closed. Oh, the relief of hot water!

"What makes you think I've *done* anything?" I couldn't be bothered opening my eyes.

"I just saw Mrs Bath and—"

I groaned. "Don't say any more."

"Then tell me. Sounds like it could be entertaining." He pulled up a chair and settled in.

I sat up in the bath, took a bar of sandalwood soap and as I lathered, told him the story of Ivana Orloff and the attempted defence of her dubious honour by a foolish, though gallant, thirteen-year-old.

By the time I'd finished, Simon was wiping his streaming eyes. "So," he said, waving his hand in the direction of my face, "Lady Ivana has a neat back-hand. Perhaps she's a tennis-player."

"Shut up and pass me that towel."

Rising from his chair, he tossed the towel at me. "Right, well I'm dining with Mrs Hudgeon and her two lovely daughters this evening, so I'll leave you now."

"Ah," I wrapped the towel around my waist and stepped from the bath. "The Misses Hudgeon. Beware their mother. She's a widow, you know."

Simon was heading toward the door but now he turned in surprise. "Christ, man! You haven't ...?"

I gave a jaunty wink. "Cannot tell a lie."

"Seriously? When?"

"Last summer. Just before Maeve and I were summoned to Broughton Hall."

"You *really* ought to keep it in your pants. It's a miracle you're not poxed – or dead!"

I threw off the towel and began dressing. "Agree, but you're the beneficiary of my experience." I grinned at him. "She was sizing me up as a potential son-in-law but decided against that idea."

Simon drew in his breath. "Is there any uncharted territory on your map?"

"I didn't touch the daughters."

Simon was laughing as he left my room, but once he'd gone, I did pause to think. It was true what he said: it *is* a miracle I'm not poxed, or dead.

It's probably only a matter of time, and I was not yet eighteen, for Christ's sake. I sighed heavily.

I was expected to attend a soirée this evening over in Astor – the perfect opportunity to practise behaving myself.

∾

The soirée was in full swing when I arrived. Some fifty people were milling about the drawing room of the Countess Barrington-Harford, or plain Daphne to her friends. For Daphne had been plain Daphne Walker when she met, snared and married Lord

George Cranshaw, Earl Barrington-Harford.

Those of us better acquainted with Daphne Walker, knew her as *Ambrosia* a successful *career woman.*

As the story goes, the aged and infirm but persistently randy earl had his attendants wheel him to a particular establishment on a particular evening. After booking a night in Ambrosia's company, the earl was charmed to say the least, for not many ladies could so inventively accommodate the earl's rather unusual needs.

Lord Barrington-Harford had been severely wounded during the 1776 war with America. Incapacitated in some areas, but not all, he made a thorough assessment of Ambrosia's skills and offered the talented young lass a permanent position on his staff.

Nobody could ever accuse Ambrosia of being neglectful of her career. A mere position on the earl's staff would never do!

She was coming toward me now, the enormous diamond on her wedding finger extended in greeting, but my eyes skimmed this minor detail going immediately to her bosom, which was not naked, but left little to the imagination.

For her gown, an exquisite sheath of translucent silver lace, shimmered as she moved giving the impression that it was wet, and she naked beneath.

The trouble for me was that I knew exactly what the countess looked like when she was wet, and naked.

I'd been ignoring the unsatisfied ache in my loins all afternoon. Now it bloomed into full-blown, urgent desire – *blast*!

"Lord Washburn," she purred, as I bowed over her hand. She did her homework; I'll give her that. Many people call me Lord Thorncliffe but that's my father's title. As the earl's son it's correct form to address me by our family name.

"It's been such a long time. So pleased you could ... *come*."

"Countess," I straightened, sweat was breaking on my lip and I resisted the urge to adjust my breeches. I allowed my focus to rest on her plump and painted lips, the corner of which twitched knowingly.

Slowly, my gaze rose to her dark eyes. She boldly returned my stare.

"Your poor face. Did you walk into ... a door?"

I smiled, feeling the tightness of my cheek beneath the bruising.

"But your eyes, my lord," she continued, "I declare are the most intriguing green ... no doubt you've heard that many times."

"Once or twice, perhaps," I drawled, "but never from such a delicious mouth."

That delicious mouth smiled languidly. She drew in a breath and leaned toward my ear to whisper, "Patrick ... I'm going to fuck you tonight."

My body's reaction was about to become embarrassing. I responded, candidly, "Can we do it now?"

The countess burst into loud and genuine laughter. Stepping back, she smiled about her as though sharing a joke. A number of people in close range tittered as though in on it.

"Sycophants," she murmured, smiling sweetly. Turning, she linked her arm through mine, leading me further into the room.

"Please, my lord," she said, releasing me before the buffet table. Gesturing widely, she said, "Enjoy the refreshments."

With that, she disappeared into the crowd.

Needing distraction, I selected a glass of wine and looked about for any familiar face – preferably of the masculine variety; no one with jutting tits, batting eyelashes or suggestive mouth!

There! I marched over and clapped Sir Daniel Forrester on the back – fellow Oxford student, erstwhile drinking partner and fanatical purveyor of horseflesh. "Good evening, Forrester!"

We bowed politely to one another, before launching immediately into a spirited discussion about his latest purchases and when I might be persuaded to part with Equus.

A short time later, two other chaps joined us, one of whom

produced a box of cigars and suggested we remove ourselves outside.

෨

The evening was winding to a close. Many of the guests had departed for dinner engagements elsewhere, while Dan and I lingered in rattan chairs on the veranda, blowing ribbons of fragrant cigar smoke into the balmy night air.

"Don't get up, gentlemen," Daphne's voice was husky from the effort of constant conversation and she looked rather fatigued. She dropped into one of the spare seats beside us and exhaled heavily.

We three sat some time in silence, aware that the last of the guests had now gone and we were alone.

Daphne stretched sinuously, then touched her hair. "You've no idea how painful it is having a headful of pins keeping one's hair in place."

One by one, she slowly withdrew each pin, dropping it onto the table before her with a soft tink, and shook out her hair in a black cascade over her shoulders. "Ah," she sighed in relief.

Dan was on his feet immediately, standing behind her and gently massaging her scalp. She groaned in pleasure, arched her back and leaned further into his hands, affording him a splendid view of her décolletage.

He looked across at me in confusion but despite my own gnawing frustrations, I nodded encouragement and observed his progress through heavy-lidded eyes.

Daphne drew a deep breath causing her breasts to heave upward and inch slightly above her bodice. Too much for Dan, whose hands left her hair and delved beneath the lace of her gown as his mouth came down on hers.

I was deciding whether to take my leave and afford them a modicum of privacy when Daphne's hand grasped mine, pulling me forward on my chair.

She broke away from Dan. Dropping to her knees before me, she unfastened the placket on the front of my dress breeches and wrapped those luscious lips around me.

I nearly exploded on the spot but managed to control myself as Dan knelt behind her. He lifted her skirt.

∾

It's fair to say that I was embarrassingly quick.

In some respects, I was also fortunate because while Dan was still occupied, I had put myself back together and was puffing gently on my cigar when the old earl wheeled himself into my periphery wielding some ancient hunting rifle.

I'd barely enough time to yell, "Get down!" before the shot rang out, spraying lead buckshot into the wall beside Dan's head and scattering plaster over the three of us.

"Unhand my wife, Sir!" the earl croaked, making a valiant attempt to reload, though his gnarled hands trembled violently.

Dan, clearly unsatisfied, quickly fastened his trousers and stepped back.

"Now Georgie," Daphne cooed. She was on her feet immediately, cool and collected. "What's the meaning of this? What are you doing with that funny old gun?"

"I know what he's up to – filthy young bastard!" George spluttered from his chair.

"Oh dear, where are your spectacles, my love?" Daphne soothed her husband. "I don't know what you think you saw, but Sir Daniel had dropped his cigar and was retrieving it before it marked the paving stones. I believe you owe him an apology, my dear."

The old earl looked doubtful but gazed up at his wife with pathetic hope in his rheumy old eyes.

"Come along, now. I've missed you tonight; such a pity you couldn't stay for the party. Let me help you into bed ... you know how you like it when I tuck you in."

She turned his chair around and with a last lascivious glance over her shoulder, wheeled her husband away.

"The devil take it!" Dan cursed, pushing at the bulge in the front of his trousers. "Now what?"

I smirked and dragged on my cigar, enjoying the flavour of exotic islands in its folds. "Find someone else or take care of it yourself," I suggested helpfully.

He glanced at me from beneath his lashes. "I don't suppose ..."

I shook my head. "Sorry, old chap."

"Some do, you know."

"Yes, I know. And some don't – and I fall into that party." I rose. "Think I'll go home." Nodding at his crotch, I added, "Good luck with that!"

ॐ

The wind had picked up a bit and out on the earl's porch I was forced to hold onto my hat while waiting for my coach to be brought around.

I felt no qualms of conscience over my moment with another man's wife. I supposed I should, but ... well I didn't. It wasn't the first time I'd been with a married woman, and it wouldn't be the last.

I knew one day I'd be married myself, and as I have wagered with Simon, I expected that it would be a convenient arrangement contrived to suit both myself and my wife.

Once she had produced an heir or two, she would be free to take her – discreet – pleasures where she chose.

I would be doing the same.

For now, however, my breeches were feeling marvellously comfortable for the first time all day.

ॐ

"Buckshot?" Simon was incredulous as, over breakfast the

following morning, I regaled him with my tale of the earl's untimely appearance.

"Hmm," I said, buttering a slice of toast. "The pellets took chunks of plaster out of the wall."

"I'm not surprised. But they could also have peppered you with lead and at close range it wouldn't have been pretty."

Shrugging, I said, "Well, my number's not up yet."

"Evidently not, but you won't know when it is until it is. You really should be more discreet."

"Funny," I muttered, sourly, "you don't look like my father."

Simon smiled and rose from the breakfast table, "Just keep it in your pants for once!" He took the last piece of toast with him as he strolled out the door.

"What about you?" I called after him.

He ducked his head back into the room, "In the last twenty-four hours, I've not been called out by a thirteen-year-old, beaten up by a woman, shot at by a cripple or propositioned by a drinking chum. What about me?"

He disappeared again and I toasted his back with my coffee cup, conceding ruefully that he may possibly have a point.

LAST DAYS OF SUMMER

"That should do it," I said, dropping to the ground, skipping the last two rungs of the ladder. I turned to Mrs Vickerage, removing my hat and mopping my sweating brow with my sleeve.

"Oh, milord, thank yer ever so much. I'd the bucket under it all through the night an' was that worried for winter coming."

I glanced at the clear blue sky – a far cry from last night's storm. "Well, the winter's a way off yet ... and I don't think it's going to rain like that again soon. Anyway, it's only a temporary repair ... should keep a few summer showers out."

"Hmm ..." She squinted into the horizon, just visible between the trees. "P'raps ... but doesn't stop me worryin' ... being alone an' all ..."

Mrs Vickerage was perhaps twenty-five years old ... no more – young to be a widow. She was pretty and curvaceous and standing before me in a posture calculated to attract my attention.

It worked – she had my attention – but I was wary. I'd been in a spot of trouble lately and, to quote my stepbrother, was attempting to *keep it in my pants*.

I cleared my throat and clamped my hat on my head. "Next time the carpenter comes to Waterville I'll send him over. He can check the rest of the roof for you."

"Thank yer, milord." She gnawed her plump lower lip and looked up at me from beneath chestnut lashes.

I was growing hotter, and not entirely due to the warmth of the morning. "Right ... well ..." I edged toward the tree where I'd left Equus cropping the grass. "Must go, I've—"

"Milord ..." she interrupted. She paused for only a split second, but I sensed her casting about for a reason to detain me. "This heat ... Can I offer yer a glass of ale?"

She strode purposefully into her cottage without waiting for a response.

"Ah ... Mrs Vickerage ..." I called. "I'm due over at Dan Dibble's ... he's a—"

"Can't hear you, milord," she shouted through the open window. "Best you come in ... get out o' that sun."

Her head disappeared and I resignedly blew out my breath.

∾

"Well, it's a conscientious landlord that cares for his tenants' wellbeing," Simon said, with a smirk. "Mrs Vickerage's needs obviously extend beyond the material. How lucky for her that you're the *obliging* type of landlord."

"Shut up!" I snapped and helped myself to a glass of fruit punch. I'd returned to the house to find Simon sitting on the porch poring over a medical book while sipping the cooling summer drink.

"This is delicious, by the way," he was holding a glass of the punch. "Your Monsieur Chartrain is a genius. You must have him send his recipes to Broughton Hall for Cook to try."

"I would never presume to have Monsieur Chartrain do *anything*. We have the perfect servant-master relationship: he does exactly as he pleases, and I pay his wages. I threaten him with dismissal, and he responds with obscene Gallic gestures."

Simon snorted and drained his glass. "So," he said, putting down his glass. "Did you end up getting over to that Dibble fellow's place? What was wrong?"

Stretching my legs out before me, I settled into my chair and peered at the gardens through the red-liquid window of my glass. "He has a very aggressive sow that found her way into his chicken coop ... decided to give birth in there. We both, and one of his neighbours, were trying to erect a fox-resistant coop for his hens – just until the sow can be enticed to vacate."

"Probably not until the piglets can be moved."

"Exactly, so it needs to be reasonably sturdy."

"How did it go?"

I sighed. I was tired and preferred to sit in silence; but Simon has tenants of his own, I reminded myself, and has a similar care for their welfare. His interest was genuine.

"Well ... er ... by the time I arrived, they'd already made some progress. He'll have to share his cottage with a couple of dozen birds tonight, but we'll get it finished tomorrow."

"In that case he should move in with Mrs Vickerage for the night – a win for everyone."

"Mrs Dibble might have something to say about that."

Simon nodded, "Ah. Then it's a good thing Mrs Vickerage has you to see t—"

"Right!" I jumped to my feet. "I'm off to bathe and dress for Sir Algernon's ball. Suggest you get yourself ready too." I doffed my hat in a mocking salute and left my stepbrother chuckling to himself.

∾

Being in the district over the summer months attracted all manner of invitations to dinners and balls. Most were tedious affairs during which Simon constantly defended himself from the hoard of local matrons assessing his social and financial worth as a potential husband for their daughters.

As for myself, the son of an earl, I held the title of Count in my own right – a title I never used – and I was independently wealthy. Combine these attributes with my position of local landlord and my worth had already been reckoned with insightful accuracy.

I had toyed, semi-seriously, with the idea of having my tailor create a coat with a target, such as one might use for archery, emblazoned on the back.

But Simon was a newcomer, titled and handsome; his appearance in Devon set them a new challenge and I'd been spared their attentions for the time being.

We arrived in our prerequisite white knee breeches, properly tied cravats and cutaway jackets. I hated the haughtiness of it, but the rules of masculine attire when attending a ball were immovable.

The moment we were announced at Sir Algernon Wainwright's door, every eye in the place turned toward us, and to my immense relief, focused immediately on Simon, skimming over me entirely.

Of course, I knew that Simon's looks would draw attention even if Prinny himself was standing beside him. And what a relief to be left to socialise with Algy and other pals from the district! I was released from the restraints of courtly banter, polite acknowledgement of inane feminine conversation and the defence of my continuing status as the county's most eligible bachelor.

I was still three months shy of my eighteenth birthday. The notion that I may be looking to marry so early in life was ridiculous. More troubling was the fact that these women would thrust their daughters beneath my nose regardless of the girls' ages.

A tray-carrying footman approached balancing a collection of glasses. Simon and I accepted a drink each while scanning the room for familiar faces.

Sir Anthony Dalton stood swaying in a corner. I hadn't seen

him since our escapade in Blakeney on our way to Oxford. Looking at him now, already foxed, I wondered if he'd been sober at all during the intervening six months.

He raised his glass in greeting and I nodded in response. "Shall we go over?" Simon asked.

"You can. Next time your mother complains about me drinking away my inheritance I suggest we introduce her to Tony."

"Hmm. I understand his father is buying him a commission ... futile attempt to dry him out."

I snorted. "Christ, help us all, if *he* ends up in the army!"

Across the room, Tony was gesturing, calling us over. I affected not to see him, but I felt Simon's uncertainty beside me. "Go ahead," I urged. "Give him half an hour, then pour him into his coach ... send him home before he can disgrace himself."

Simon drifted off in Anthony's direction, leaving me to occupy myself – but not for long! I'd hardly drawn breath before a large and bouffant matron was fast approaching like a ship under full sail.

She docked before me, bosom heaving and fan fluttering with affected girlishness, and I regarded her with an unguarded expression of surprise. She smiled in a manner she expected was beguiling.

I was about to enquire her purpose when a diminutive man, whom I vaguely remembered having met some years before at court, popped out – rather comically – from behind her, where he'd been hidden by her broad beam.

I swallowed a laugh, as Sir Somebody asked to present his wife and daughter. Summoning by most courtly manners, I bowed while searching my memory for his name.

Ah, that's it, I remembered as he introduced his wife, Lady Swinson, "Your servant, ma'am," I bowed over her hand, and turned to the daughter: Miss Abigail Swinson. I acknowledged her confident curtsy with a formal click of my heels.

Under normal circumstances, Swinson, a mere Baronet, probably should not approach me directly, but I've never stood on ceremony – most people are aware of that. I have a reputation for irreverence and licentiousness; they will dissect my character and take advantage of those attributes they can use to their benefit and disparage me for those they can't.

Consequently, I eyed him rather cautiously, wondering what he wanted of me. Lady Swinson's vigorous fanning of herself was irritating. It was quickly apparent that Sir Swinson's intention was for me to meet his daughter, but his silly wife was behaving with less decorum than the girl.

The Master of Ceremonies announced a minuet; for no reason other than to escape the fawning attentions of the parents, I invited the daughter to dance – pretending not to notice the two exchanging a satisfied look.

Stepping through the structured movements of the dance, I smiled absently as Miss Swinson indulged in the kind of absurd prattle I'd been hoping to avoid. The glance between her parents had amused me – but there was something troubling behind it too, because it was more than the usual hope that I would fall madly in love with their daughter and decide that I could not possibly live another moment without her as my wife.

And this girl, younger up close than she had first appeared, was attempting to engage me in conversation. I answered with a series of standard, "Oh, yeses," and "Oh, I sees," all the while aware that her mother was watching from the sidelines, with an expression befitting a hungry dog eyeing a sausage.

Warning hackles rose on my neck – she was too eager – and then to confirm my suspicions Miss Swinson seemed to stumble against me, appearing to swoon.

"Oh dear ... my lord!" she gasped, flapping a hand at her face. "I feel rather faint ... need some air ... Please, my lord ... help me outside ..."

Suddenly we were moving toward the doors leading to the gardens.

It's considered the height of bad manners to leave a dance before it finishes, so Miss Swinson was careful to draw as little attention as possible.

Discreetly, she drew me outside and closed the doors behind us. We found ourselves on a porch with a two-foot-high bordering hedge separating it from a lawn that disappeared into the night. The summer evening was unseasonably cool and Miss Swinson seemed to make a remarkable recovery.

Immediately, dragging me forward, she wrenched at my shirt causing it to hang untidily from my breeches. In the same motion, she loosened the ribbon on her bodice and tugged her gown into disarray. With hurried movements, she then slipped a ribbon from her hair, which tumbled over her shoulders.

I stood watching, caught between suspicion and amusement. Within seconds she'd transformed from a proper little miss into a dishevelled mess – she looked as though I'd just given her a good —"

"My lord ..." she breathed, "we don't have much time." Panting as in the throes of great passion and, reaching for my hand, she pulled me towards her. Coiling her arms about my neck, she attempted to draw my face down toward hers.

I resisted. Alarm bells were clanging in my head now. She must be ... fourteen? And I knew with certainty that I was being entrapped.

One thing she had said was right: we didn't have much time. The doors could be thrown open at any time and her parents, playing their part in the charade, would appear ... I would be discovered, caught in an act of rampant debauchery with their innocent, and *ruined* daughter.

The ton would not consider for a moment that I may have

been the one compromised – my reputation unfortunately precedes me wherever I go. I would be denounced, and my father involved and ... *oh, Christ!* Within a split second, the ramifications of discovery played out – to my great disadvantage – in my mind's eye.

Fired with anger, and an explosion of energy that always accompanies trouble, I quickly turned and leapt over the hedge. I heard Miss Swinson's startled shout behind me as I sprinted to the side of the house.

The gardens were black as pitch and most of the house was in darkness. The cream stone of the outbuildings had a pale glow beneath the silver of the moon, and for a moment I considered running toward them.

Just as quickly, I discarded that idea – Miss Swinson was no more the guilty party in this little escapade than I was. Her parents were entirely to blame; but with luck and speed, I could avoid trouble for us both.

Rounding the corner of the house and edging along the outer wall, I came across a door – it was unlocked and opened into a small room. Slipping inside, I silently pulled it to behind me and leaned against it, slowing my breathing and taking my bearings.

What the hell just happened? I wondered. This is the limit!

All was in darkness but for an oil lamp on a desk throwing a small golden arc of light. I seemed to be in Algy's study.

I took a moment to gather my thoughts, then straightened my clothes, tucked in my shirt and followed the strains of music coming from the ballroom. An adjoining door connected it to the study. This I now opened and casually strolled into the ballroom, taking up a glass of champagne from a passing footman on my way.

I was standing quietly and very composed beside Simon and Tony as the cry of alarm sounded from the porch outside.

Timing is everything. For an instant, conversations halted mid-sentence and the musicians skipped and slid on a discordant note from the violinist.

Lady Swinson had been so sure of what she'd encounter outside that she hadn't bothered to assess her daughter's situation. Rather, she had immediately set up such a racket that a crowd rushed outside – eager to witness a rape in progress.

Instead, they discovered a fully clothed child sitting on a chair, alone. Miss Swinson had had time to straighten her dress and was calmly combing her fingers through her hair, while her mother shouted to all within hearing range that her daughter's honour was compromised. "It was Lord Washburn," she bellowed in great distress. "He dragged my poor baby outside to have his wicked way … he's hiding in the garden. Find him!"

As a dozen sets of eyes swung to where I stood with Simon and Tony, they found me relaxed, holding my champagne in one hand, the other tucked casually into my pocket. I shrugged in a gesture that said, I'm just as bemused as you.

Sir Algernon's Master of Ceremonies pushed his way through the spectators and urged everyone to return to the ballroom and partake of the iced desserts. Algernon himself, no stranger to Lady Swinson's ways, suggested Sir Swinson gather his wife – who he suggested may be a little over-refreshed – and his daughter – who seemed a little tired – and take them home.

That was when I decided that Anthony's idea of drinking himself into oblivion was a good one. Draining my champagne, I took another from a hovering footman and ignored a wave of fatigue that washed over me.

Sir Algernon approached to offer his apologies, but I waved them aside. "Don't give it another thought, Algy," I said. "Lady Swinson is not the first mama to have tried that tack."

"That it should happen in my home is unacceptable," he grumbled, but I could see he didn't want to dwell on it any more than I, and when a footman drew his attention to a guest wishing to speak with him, Algy gratefully disappeared.

"Wh-what a drama!" Sir Anthony hiccupped. "Honestly Washburn, tr-trouble just seems to f-find you."

I grinned and clapped him on the shoulder.

I was still smiling as Simon nudged me. "See Lady Isla over there?" He nodded over the rim of his glass toward a pretty, soft-figured young lady who angled a sly glance in our direction.

"She has asked for an introduction. Feel like taking your chances with another young lady?"

"Yes please! I can't think of anything I'd rather do than meet yet another conniving vixen!"

Simon gave me a quick look. "You're being sarcastic."

"Oh, you're brilliant! See how easily you figured that out!"

My stepbrother laughed, good-naturedly. "I'm teasing you. But she did ask to be introduced. I'd hate to disappoint her."

"You're going to have to."

"I think she's lovely," he said, waggling his fingers at her. She lowered her lashes flirtatiously over her fan.

"What the fuck is wrong with you?" I snapped, finally losing my patience. That drew his attention back to me. I added in a modified tone, "Take my advice and steer clear. If you just want to bed someone, try her mother – much safer. *Her* father won't care if you fuck his daughter."

"Or buy a wh-whore," Anthony hiccupped.

Ignoring him, Simon stared at me for a moment before shaking his head. "By God, you're a cynic."

I shrugged. "Not by choice."

"And not without justification, I suppose," he conceded, as the Swinsons took their leave.

"These people ..." I shook my head in bewilderment. "They're wearing me out, Sime, honestly."

He nodded and smiled. "Well, you've had a run of it lately – but you're your own worst enemy too. Your reputation will destroy you in the end! Perhaps we need to stay away from these events."

"The ones frequented by young ladies with desperate, social-climbing mothers?"

"Or perhaps," he went on, attempting to tease me into a better mood, "we should only associate with the older ones ... Ivana Orloff? Perhaps Mrs Vickerage?"

"Safer on th-the Peninsula facing B-bonaparte," Anthony put in, helpfully.

Mollified, I raised my glass to him. "Agree." Turning back to Simon, I said, "Anyway, for your information, I didn't bed Mrs Vickerage. I went into her cottage, drank a glass of ale and repaired a rickety leg on her table. That's why I was late to Dibble's place."

I smiled pleasantly and clapped him on the back. "You have no faith in me, brother. Unlike you, I can keep it in my pants."

∾

The next morning, I stood outside Dan Dibble's cottage, my hands wrapped around a tin mug of tea while the Dibbles' cat curled around my legs. It was a fat black-and-white tom that seemed enamoured of my riding boots.

"'e's like that, milord," Mrs Sally Dibble told me. Sally had lived in the area all her life; she and her brother had grown up on my land and as children, the three of us had occasionally splashed around in the lake together.

It felt odd when she called me *milord*. As children we'd used first names. When did I become *milord* to her?

"Sorry ... what did you say?"

"Rats," Sally repeated. "Sound big – 'eard em scufflin' about under the house last night."

"Why don't you get this cat onto them?"

"That lazy freeloadin' bugger! Couldn't shift 'imself if 'e was on fire."

I gave a brief laugh and sipped my tea. It was hot and strong. I hoped Sally wasn't leaving herself short to make sure she brewed a good cup for me.

Many people did things like that – I wished they wouldn't. I can afford anything I want. These people cannot and yet they invite me into their homes and give me the best of the little they have – even if it means they go without themselves.

Charity is an insult, however, so I do what I can by donating produce and supplies of meat and staples that my estate has in surplus. I also sponsor gifts of food and goods at Christmas, May Day and mid-summer celebrations, harvest festivals ... and ensure, where possible, that Mrs Bath gives preference to the people in my villages when looking for staff. Other things, I do when I can.

Just then, Sally's youngest, a dark-eyed girl of about six, emerged from the cottage. Her face was alive with excitement and she rushed up to her mother.

"Mama, Lenny says I can ride up on the 'orse with 'im," she gasped.

"That's good. Mind the young lord, Alice. Where are yer manners?"

The child seemed to see me for the first time. "S'cuse me, milord," she said solemnly, dropping into a wobbly curtsy.

I bowed formally in reply. "Your servant, Miss Dibble," and the little girl giggled happily, then returned to her mother and hopped about impatiently.

"Mama, can I? Can I ride wi' Lenny?"

"Alright. But yer better go now else yer'll be late."

She watched fondly as Alice ran off to find her brother, then turned back to me. "They love that school, milord. Thank yer so much! Never thought they'd learn to read 'n' write."

I smiled, slightly embarrassed, and turned away, ostensibly to look for Sally's husband.

"Is Dan around, then?"

"Oh, 'e'll be in the shed."

I nodded. "Right ..." I drained my mug. "Time to get on with this chicken coop, then."

∽

It was late in the day when I rode Equus home to Waterville. I took her immediately around to the stables where Jimma ran over to assist.

"Later than expected, milord?" Jimma asked. He unbuckled Equus's saddle girth.

"Yes. The Dibbles kindly asked me to share their supper ... I'll do this, Jimma. You're probably in the middle of yours."

He grinned. "Thank yer, milord," and promptly disappeared.

I dragged Equus' saddle off and hung it over a railing, followed with her blanket. It was damp and warm and smelled strongly of horse. "A good honest smell, that one, eh?" I spoke aloud and moving around to her face, gave her a good hard scratch along her breastbone.

She whuffed and snorted in pleasure, "Ah yes, you like that, don't you?"

I set about rubbing her down, then began the rather therapeutic task of brushing her. I enjoyed being around horses; there was no deceit, no covert scheme – with animals you always got what you expected.

Unlike humans.

I didn't spend enough time with animals. Horses, dogs, cats, cows – even the Dibbles' grumpy sow – I liked them all for their candid and basic natures.

Unlike humans.

Well, most humans. Simon was easy and honest – not a deceitful bone in his body, to his detriment. Someone will take advantage of his good nature.

Someone like his sister – that Anne. I grunted and Equus blew into my hair. "Now there's trouble," I told Equus, "you mark my words." I pointed the brush at her and she tossed her head at it. "She'll give some poor fool a rough time of it one day."

Laughing humourlessly, I resumed my work, while my thoughts drifted to the other sister, Alex. What did Sime call her? Zan.

Suddenly I stopped. Alex.

A stubborn, grumpy, flighty and most disagreeable child; yet intelligent, passionate and, yes, honest ... and suddenly the urge to see her was overwhelming.

I put down the brush and sat on an upturned bucket. I hadn't thought of Alex in well over six months, yet now ... this minute ... my mind returned to an afternoon, a few days before Simon and I left Broughton Hall for Oxford.

He and I, with Alex accompanying us, ate a light luncheon at a local inn where the bar wench, Molly – if memory serves – was making her availability quite plain.

I was sitting on a bench opposite Simon, with Alex beside me, and for some reason, I had draped my arm across the back of the bench and let my hand rest on Alex's shoulder.

She had glanced at me in surprise but hadn't removed my arm ... and I'd enjoyed the comfortable, and completely relaxed, feel of her close to me. It seemed natural.

My own reaction to her confused me – it had since the first day I met her.

I've always been at ease in the company of women – I love women! But this was different. I was drawn to Alex in a way I did not understand; not as a sister, but not as a lover either. It was baffling, and for someone who prided himself on his self-assurance, it was most disagreeable!

The following day, Simon and I had returned to the inn. It had been my intention to bed the willing Molly, but upon arriving at the inn I had changed my mind.

A glass of brandy by the fire had kept me entertained while

Simon went upstairs with her.

The day following that, Simon and I had ridden away from Broughton Hall, and I had harnessed myself and turned my thoughts away from his sister, the most perplexing person I'd ever met.

Now, however, as I sat in the stables, restful in the sweet scents of chaff and the breaths of large slumbering animals, perhaps the stresses, debacles and trials of the past weeks were getting to me.

I was weary of deceit. I was weary of subterfuge and hidden agendas. Moreover, I was weary of all the pretence and artifice that came with my heritage.

I was ready to return to Oxford; to a masculine world of dark wood and books, to escape the insanity of grasping, avaricious, social-climbing, scheming women.

And summer was coming to an end.

RESURRECTIONISTS

"Can you hold the lantern higher?" Simon asked, and his fellow student, standing precariously on a chair, wobbled slightly, steadied himself with one hand on Simon's shoulder, and leaned forward.

A young man to Simon's left edged closer to the table while another opposite did the same.

The cadaver was thrown into gruesome relief beneath the wavering light. Bloated and mottled in shades of mauve and grey, the dead man lay on the stone table before them. Slit from sternum to pubis; skin, fat and muscle were folded back to reveal the inner workings of what had only days ago been a living, breathing human.

"Christ in heaven!" exclaimed a young man in a hoarse whisper. "What's that smell?"

"Bowel," Professor Danziger responded, his voice quiet and heavily accented. "You will always smell it, even when – Friedrich!" Turning to a lad lurking just behind him, he growled. "Go back and latch the door!"

"But *Vater* ... it's lonely up there." The boy shuddered, adding, "*und* dark."

The lecturer sighed and handed his bloodied scalpel to the student beside Simon. "Here – find *und* remove the gall bladder."

The young man blanched and opened his mouth to protest but the lecturer had already vanished into the dim recesses of the coal cellar he was using to conduct his clandestine lessons.

"Hop to, David," urged the student holding the lantern above them. "Haven't got all night, you know. Georgie Ainsworth owes me a jar over at the Smithy's Arms."

David, rapidly turning a nasty shade of green, thrust the blade in Simon's direction and staggered off into the corner. The sounds of violent retching followed.

Glancing to the student opposite, Simon shrugged and adjusted the sticky-handled scalpel in his palm, then leaned over the corpse.

"Swing the lamp over this way can you, John?" He squinted into the gaping cavity before him.

The lantern moved obediently and the dead man's innards glistened wet and slimy in the light. Simon quickly identified the liver. Reaching into the body, he lifted the liver aside to reveal the gall bladder beneath. A single, sure flick of the blade, and the small organ was extracted.

Simon was placing the gall bladder in a bowl beside its owner as the lecturer returned. "Very good, Sir Simon. Where is Mr Whitewood?"

"In the corner, throwing up, Sir," John responded, cheerfully. "Can I get down now, Sir?"

"*Ja, ja,* we must end this session for now, anyway. I have sent Friedrich home – bit young for this, I am afraid. We will have to find ourselves a new watchman."

"When can we get another cadaver, Sir?" the boy opposite Simon spoke for the first time. "A female perhaps?"

"We can try, Lord Draven."

John clapped his companion on the shoulder. "The only

chance you'll get to see a naked woman, eh Andrew?"

Even their teacher laughed then.

David Whitewood reappeared in the circle of light, wiping the back of his hand across his mouth, his complexion similar to the specimen laid out before them.

"Welcome back, Mr Whitewood," the lecturer commented. "I assume you ate something at dinner that did not appeal to you for that surely was not the reaction a future surgeon should have over a fresh corpse."

Andrew sniggered, "I think he had liver for dinner, Sir."

David groaned and seemed to sway slightly.

"Alright, that is enough." Professor Danziger was putting his instruments away in a leather bag. "It's very expensive to get these bodies, you know – *und* is a risky business. If you are all prepared to share the cost, I will see what I can do."

"Count me out," David murmured. "I won't need to know anything about this to treat rich brats with running noses."

"Very well ... You boys go now und I will tidy up here – *und* mind nobody sees you leaving."

"Yes, Sir. Thank you, Sir," they said individually, filing past and up the stairs that led to the cellar door and the unlit, secluded back lane behind Oxford's medical faculty.

Simon opened the front door of the house in Queen Street that he shared with his stepbrother. It was past midnight and he was sober, a considerable change from the condition in which he usually arrived home at such an hour.

He was also very tired. Closing and bolting the door behind him, he sighed in relief; he was looking forward to sleep. The house was dark and silent – Patrick was either out or in bed. Simon assumed the latter since Pat had been living the life of a monk lately. He had one foot on the stairs on the way to his room when suddenly he tensed, listening intently. He thought he heard a sound coming from the direction of the kitchen; yet the housekeeper, Mrs Baldoon, would have long since returned to her own home.

Cursing silently, Simon crept to the hallstand and reached for an umbrella – inadequate yet better than nothing – then began inching his way down the empty hall toward the sounds.

Heart pounding, he reached the kitchen door and paused, ear cocked. He held his breath and listened. All was silent within. He waited a moment more and just as he thought he'd been mistaken, there came a muffled clatter.

Raising the umbrella as one might a sword, Simon took a deep, steadying breath and counted one ... two ... and ...

On three, he threw open the kitchen door and leapt into the room, shouting, "Who the devil are you!?"

Instantly, the prowler sprang into an attacking pose; a single candle on a workbench backlit him as an unidentifiable silhouette wielding a large carving knife.

Simon took a step forward, breathing hard and brandishing his umbrella in what he hoped was a threatening gesture.

"God have mercy!" The trespasser cried with a squeak of terror. The knife clattered to the floor and the man dropped, cowering at Simon's feet. "Please don't run me through with that wicked blade!"

Then to Simon's astonishment, the intruder gripped his sides and all but collapsed on the floor in raucous laughter.

Simon's face registered his annoyance as he stood watching with one hand on his hip, not sharing the other's amusement.

Finally, Patrick controlled himself and straightened before his stepbrother, wiping the tears from his eyes.

"Finished your chortling?" Simon asked, acerbically.

"Depends," his brother responded, voice thick with mirth. "You going to sheathe that weapon?"

Simon made a noise of contempt. "I thought we had an intruder. You nearly scared me into next week!"

Patrick bent to retrieve the knife from the stone floor. "I found a game pie in the meat safe. You want some?"

Simon shook his head. Fatigue had made him irritable, but as Patrick sliced into the pie he had to admit it smelled good. His stomach made a sound of appreciation.

The other man turned, knife held aloft, "You're sure?"

"Oh, alright." Simon leaned the umbrella against the wall and came over to stand at his stepbrother's shoulder, watching as two slices of pie were cut.

Patrick took out a slice and bit into it, "This is good."

"Mmm," Simon agreed. "Mrs Baldoon forgiven you for throwing up on her marigolds?"

"I don't know. Has she forgiven you for taking her nephew out and getting him foxed?"

"I think so," Simon used the workbench as a seat while he ate. "But she doesn't know I took him to Madam's and introduced him to Luscious Lizette."

"Ah," Patrick swallowed, "best she doesn't find out about that." He took another bite and leaned against the workbench beside his stepbrother. "We may not get any more of these."

"Mphm. So, where'd you go this evening?"

"Smithy's Arms ... Deon Morehead's birthday."

Simon nodded and shoved the last chunk of pie in his mouth. "You're sober."

Patrick nodded. "Deon and Anthony had a head start on me and I couldn't be elbowed into catching up." He finished his pie and wiped his hands on a cloth on the bench. "Anyway, see this ...?" he tugged up his shirt and slapped his abdomen. "Getting fat ... need to cut down on the drink. I reckon that's what does it."

"You're not getting fat, but some exercise wouldn't kill you. What've you done lately?"

"Apart from riding Equus now and then ... nothing. Not even bedded anyone since we've been back in Oxford."

"Impressive."

"Isn't it!" Patrick agreed, cheerfully.

"They're looking for new members to join the rowing squad. Why don't you come down and try out?"

To Simon's surprise, the other man gave the idea some consideration before responding, "Where?"

"Friar's Wharf – not too far from here. I'm going down tomorrow morning – early – if you want to come."

"Alright." Patrick pushed away from the bench, "Wake me when you get up and ...What the hell's all over your shirt?"

The flickering candlelight had only just revealed Simon's state of dress. Patrick took the candle and held it close to Simon. "Is that blood? You've been in a fight?"

Hesitating for the briefest moment – Professor Danziger had sworn his students to the utmost secrecy but surely anything was safe with Patrick. Simon confessed, "I've been dissecting a cadaver – you can't breathe a word about it!"

"A *human* cadaver? Illegal, right?"

Simon nodded. "Highly illegal."

"Hmph! So what did you do? Murder someone?"

"Our professor got hold of a corpse they fished out of the river. Some lost soul no one has claimed."

Patrick grinned. "No grave robbing then? Didn't think that would be your style."

His stepbrother made a face of disgust. "Not me. There are fellows who do it for a living though. Tradesmen ... resurrectionists they call themselves. Distasteful occupation but there's no other way for us to understand the workings of human bodies."

"I see. Well, on that lovely thought, I wish you pleasant dreams and I shall see you in the morning."

❧

Patrick rose early the following day and joined Simon for a walk down to the docks where he tried out for the university rowing squad.

Being strong and athletic, it wasn't surprising that Patrick was accepted into the team. What was surprising, was Patrick's commitment to the sport.

Simon had to concede that his stepbrother had apparently undergone an unusual transformation. He was staying in most evenings, applying himself to his books and seemed to have reformed his wild ways. Additionally, and even more astonishing, was his evident disinterest in feminine company and preference for sobriety.

When Simon questioned him about his changed attitude, he merely shrugged, saying, "I don't know, Sime. I'm just tired of being in constant trouble and disappointing my father."

"And Lady Swinson's attempt to trap you ...?"

He nodded. "It wasn't the first time, and unless I start earning a modicum of respect, it won't be the last time either."

❧

"So, how long will this renaissance of yours last, do you think?" Simon's voice dripped sarcasm. They were walking past the ancient St Ebbes Church on their way back from a rowing session. Patrick had been in the squad several months and his ongoing sobriety continued to surprise his stepbrother.

Simon was also aware that Patrick was still avoiding feminine society – although there had been one or two girls at Madam's the richer for having met him.

Patrick now threw his stepbrother a wicked grin, "Oh, until I grow bored with it, I should imagine."

As they passed the churchyard a funeral was in progress. A

number of black-clad figures stood around an open grave. A young woman leaned heavily on an older man – evidently her father – the two clung together in shared grief.

Patrick suddenly grew serious. As he and Simon rounded the corner onto Pembroke Street he said, "Have you been attending any nocturnal classes lately?"

Simon looked narrowly at him. "Why do you ask?"

Patrick shrugged. "Don't know. Just the thought, I suppose, of that gentleman's wife being ..." his voice drifted off as they passed a pair of housemaids returning from the markets, laden baskets over their arms.

"You're wondering if we've employed the services of a resurrectionist?" Simon asked. His voice was sharper than intended, but the furtive gatherings Simon was attending on an almost weekly basis were highly covert; only the lecturer's most trusted students could know about them. All attendees risked incarceration if caught.

"You're not supposed to know about that remember, so—"

"Don't worry – I was just wondering ... I can't imagine what type of person could ransack a grave."

Simon shrugged. "I've often wondered that myself. Some of them go to incredible lengths too. I heard about ..." he broke off as an old woman walking a dog came toward them.

"You were saying ..." Patrick prompted. They'd arrived at their house and Simon waited while his stepbrother fished a key from his pocket and unlocked the front door.

Once inside, they turned immediately into the parlour and Simon continued.

"There was a fellow recently caught. He'd dug a network of tunnels beneath the cemetery. When there was a new burial, he would extend his tunnel to the top of the grave, break through the end of the coffin, tie a rope around the corpse's neck and drag the body back through the tunnel with him."

"Bloody hell!" Patrick exclaimed in horror. "That's disgusting. And you, or students like you, are the recipients of these poor people?"

Simon nodded. His own face showed his distaste but then he shrugged. "We need to learn. How else ... I mean we can't cut up living people, can we?"

"What happens to these resurrectionists if they're caught?"

"Well, that fellow was transported to New South Wales. They made an example of him. But – and this is where we must be discreet – it's common for the authorities to turn a blind eye to grave robbing because they understand the need for medical students to learn. They really only do something about it if the families find out and make a noise."

"Hell of a way to make a living, in any case," Patrick said. Then with a rapid change of subject he went on, "Is it Mrs Baldoon's day off? I can never remember which day she takes."

"No, it's tomorrow."

"Ah, good." He reached for a small bell on the sideboard. "I'm going to call for coffee if you're interested. Then I'd better bathe and get changed. I have a lecture to attend this afternoon."

Simon shook his head. "You're not unwell, are you? Whatever it is that's got into you these last few months ..." He grinned, "Well, let's just say your father would be a very happy man."

"Sime, I'm bored and that's the truth. I'm meeting with Tony next week – coffee please, Mrs Baldoon," he said, as his housekeeper responded to the bell. She made a small curtsy and returned to the kitchen.

"Sir Anthony Dalton?" Simon asked.

Patrick nodded. "You remember he recently bought an officer's commission? I want to talk with him about it."

"You're seriously considering this, aren't you?"

The other man didn't respond – he didn't have to. Simon had known for a long time that his stepbrother was restless and

and unhappy.

They sat in silence for several minutes while the parlour fire popped and snapped.

Mrs Baldoon returned with a tray laden with cups and a coffee pot. Her two employers were generally affable and informal but this morning she sensed an important conversation was taking place.

Laying her tray on the sideboard, Mrs Baldoon poured two cups of coffee and handed one to each of the young men, bobbed to them both and discreetly disappeared.

Simon and Patrick sipped their coffee in companionable silence, each lost in his own thoughts. Finally, Simon rose and placed his empty cup on Mrs Baldoon's tray. Turning, he said, "Let us finish this year ... I need to complete this year. Give me just a bit more time with my lecturers and ... and then I'll come with you."

Patrick had been staring distractedly into the fire. Now he raised his head and met his stepbrother's frank gaze.

"I'll go as a surgeon," Simon continued. "I understand how you feel, you know. You want to contribute – make a difference ... or try. I understand because I feel the same. But I'm not ready yet. I still have so much to learn ... a year would make that much difference. Just give me that."

Patrick allowed his surprise to show but still he didn't speak. More sensitive than he'd ever admit to being, he was touched by Simon's unexpected gesture. Finally, he rose and placed his coffee cup on the tray beside the other man's.

Then he turned. "You've never indicated you felt as I did." His stepbrother opened his mouth, but Patrick held up a hand. "Wait ... let me finish. I know how you pore over those newspapers and war reports, but you've never said anything. Why?"

"I don't know," Simon grinned and clapped his stepbrother on

119

the back, "but now I have."

Patrick exhaled gustily. "Very well. I'll stick it out for another year."

Simon moved toward the door, "Right then ... it's settled. Now, I've a lecture in an hour so I'd better get on with the day."

Patrick smiled. It wasn't that he needed his stepbrother to join military service with him, but the fact that he too was keen to purchase a commission, convinced Patrick that it was the right decision. Suddenly he felt a burden lift from his shoulders.

He'd always hated being a member of the idle aristocracy – he genuinely believed that most of his kind were social parasites, living off the hard work of tenants and staff – a career in the military was noble and honest. It was a way of giving back.

Patrick expected his father would be happy that his son had changed his lifestyle, but the earl will be most displeased to discover his only son and heir will be going to war.

Sighing, Patrick decided not to tell his father for the time being.

A PROPOSAL AND A DENIAL

"I'm a v-virgin," she hiccupped. Covering her mouth with a dainty hand, she giggled. "Whoopsie! I th-think I'm a wee bit tipsy!"

I glanced at Simon and suppressed a smile.

"C'mon, love," Simon said, gently leading her towards a discreet corner. He sat her on a bench, leaning against a wall, and we stood before her, shielding her from the prying eyes of the other guests at the Oxford Spring Ball.

"Now," he continued. "Who are you here with? You didn't come alone."

She hiccupped again and slipped slightly to the side.

"I came with ... Miss Ad-Adrienne Morehead. You prob-ah-probably know her brother Mr Meon Dorehead ..." she giggled again. "Whoopsie ... I *hic* mean—"

"That's alright," Simon said. "We know Mr Morehead." Turning to me, he indicated the footman standing by the door with a jerk of his chin.

I nodded my understanding, leaving him guarding the young lass who had just asked Simon to bed her – in very unambiguous terms.

As I approached the footman, he gave a respectful bow. "May I assist, my lord?"

"Yes. Please find Miss Adrienne Morehead and ask her to join Miss Havelock in the lower meeting room."

"Thank you, my lord."

The footman bowed and made to carry out my request when I stalled him, "Before you go ..."

He turned, "Yes, my lord?"

"Please exercise the utmost discretion. Ensure absolutely no one sees you."

"Certainly, my lord."

He bowed again and disappeared into the crowd.

࿇

We held Miss Havelock between us, cautiously leading her from the ballroom. Mindful of the young lady's reputation, we made every effort to avoid being seen as we slipped out into the hall.

The appointed room was in darkness but for a puddle of light spilling through the large windows from the gaslights along the outside walls.

Leaving Miss Havelock with Simon, I ducked back into the hallway, ostensibly to enjoy the portraits of past luminaries decorating the walls, while waiting for Adrienne Morehead to arrive.

Deon had told me about his sister, how she looked very much like him; but even so, as she came towards me, I was taken aback by the profound resemblance between them.

The Morehead siblings were almost identical – extraordinarily white skin, black eyes and glossy black hair. On Deon, the striking features might be considered effeminate; however, on his sister ...

Suddenly the corridor, the music, laughter and chatter fell away and the urge to propagate shot through me like a bolt of lightning. My vision narrowed to the pale, exquisite face that paused in front of me before she bowed her head and dropped a curtsy.

"My Lord Washburn?" Her voice was low and breathy, and I caught myself gaping like a horny fourteen year old.

Besides her being a friend's sister, this was a young lady of good character – certainly not some wench I could spirit off to a secluded corner. I gathered myself and bowed. "Miss Morehead."

With a cool smile, she waited for me to speak again while I mastered my baser urges and added, "Miss Havelock – she's in here and she's ... a little overwrought."

"I see. Well then, you'd better take me to her."

I held the door open, and Adrienne swept into the dimly lit room. Closing the door behind us, it took me a moment to become accustomed to the overpowering smell of vomit.

"Whew! What a stench!" Miss Morehead declared, hurrying to open a window. "She's been ill – you should have let in some air," she threw accusingly at Simon.

Miss Elizabeth Havelock was slumped in an armchair beside a cold fireplace. Simon was hovering around her, a vase at his feet – a vase that had evidently contained flowers, judging by the very expensive tulips strewn on the floor, but now served as a receptacle for Miss Havelock's considerable illness.

The night breeze billowed the lace curtains at the window as Miss Morehead turned, hands on hips, and addressed Simon. "What has been going on? Is she alright? Does she need a doctor?"

"No," Simon responded, "there's nothing wrong with her that a good night's rest and a hearty meal won't fix."

At that moment, Miss Havelock stirred, and Simon snatched up the vase and held it before her, but she brushed him aside.

"Adrienne you're here ... oh thank heavens!" Even in the weak light, her skin appeared pale and waxy.

Miss Morehead crouched at her friend's side. "Bessy, dear, are you alright? You're in a terrible state – look at your dress! How could you do this? You can't possibly return to the ball now." She rose to her feet, her exotic black eyes moving from me to Simon. "What on earth has she done?"

I stepped forward to stand beside Simon. "Miss Morehead." Her dark eyes returned to my face. She was lovely – and she knew it. She smiled and tilted her head to look at me through her lashes.

"Miss Havelock has been quite candid with my brother and me ... she explained her situation. As you so accurately observed she can take no further part in the ball. She must be taken home. Perhaps if you will accompany her ...?"

In that moment, Adrienne Morehead proved herself the perfect female replica of her selfish and narcissistic brother. Fluttering her dark lashes, she moved close enough to lay the palm of her manicured hand on my chest. "Why, my lord," her voice was low and intimate. "I'm not ready to leave yet. You haven't asked me to dance with you."

Christ! Her friend was ill and had spent the best part of the last hour in company with two men – a compromising situation at best – and here she was flirting with me!

Immediately, I changed my mind about finding her attractive. Very deliberately, I removed her hand from where her little fingers had begun plucking at my neckcloth, and let it drop. "Miss Morehead! Your friend is unwell and needs your assistance."

"Oh, come now!" She was entirely without sympathy. "So, she drank more champagne than she ought. Have the footman put her in a carriage – the driver can take her home. Why should *my* night be ruined because of this silly little child?"

"Miss Morehead," Simon interrupted gently. "Your friend told us her predicament – she's very distressed and you ought to have a care for her."

"Oh, she told you about Elderly Ellery, did she?"

Simon and I exchanged looks and he replied, "If that's the older gentleman she has been betrothed to, then yes."

She faced him and spoke very directly. "Did she ask you to bed her?"

"She ... suggested I might ... er ... assist with certain matters," Simon prevaricated.

I frowned. The girl had been terribly distraught when she'd made the proposition to Simon. A true friend would have been more sympathetic.

Adrienne turned to me. "And you felt sorry for her. How kind of you," she spoke sweetly, but her eyes narrowed cruelly, "that's probably not exactly what she said though, is it?"

I shrugged. "No, not exactly. She asked my brother to take her to his bed ... she didn't want to go as a virgin on her wedding night."

"Yes." Adrienne grinned at me. "Do you *know* Sir Oliver Ellery? You'd not be surprised if you saw him – dirty old fool, he is. She told me she would experience the touch of a young and pretty man of her choice at least once in her life before being presented like a slab of meat to a decrepit old man." She shrugged. "She's an idiot. He's marvellously wealthy and half-dead."

She swung around to face Simon again. Hands on hips, she looked him up and down, nodding to herself. "I trust you assisted her in her *predicament*. That is what you called her proposition? Hopefully you managed it before she made such a filthy mess of herself. Yes, I can see why she chose you – you're very pretty." She made a sound of contempt. "Ellery's only a baron, though – so are you, aren't you? My parents wouldn't be selling *me* so cheaply. Nothing less than an earl will do, and he will find *my* maidenhead intact!"

She gave me a long, meaningful look before dropping a curtsy. "Lord Washburn, Sir Simon, I bid you good evening."

"What about Miss Havelock?" Simon asked, as she strode to the door.

Adrienne Morehead didn't even stir a hair as she turned to face him, "You take care of her – if you haven't already." She added with a scornful toss of her head, "She's so foxed she probably won't even realise you've mounted her."

The anger rose in my chest. I marched toward my friend's sister. "Oh, you're a right nasty little—"

Simon stalled me with a hand on my sleeve and a low murmured, "Pat ..."

But it had been enough to give the selfish bitch reason to pause. "Well," she smiled spitefully, "if you're not up to rutting on the rug, I suggest you find her parents." She gave a breezy wave of her hand. "They're here somewhere."

Short of physically restraining her, we couldn't prevent Adrienne from leaving. At that moment, the hapless girl on the chair made a gagging noise and threw up again.

∾

"Have you ever known a more callous baggage?" Simon asked.

We were sitting beside the fire in the parlour in our Queen Street house. I poured two glasses of brandy and handed one to my brother.

"No, I don't think I have. She's Deon all over – not just to look at. He's as cold as she is when he has his mind set on something."

"Or some*one*," Simon agreed. "Remember that young lass he paid court to last year? Told her he wanted to marry her ... swept her off her feet, even spoke with her father. Did you know he bedded her? Then sent her a note to say he'd changed his mind. Changed his mind! Can you believe it?"

I snorted rudely. "The Moreheads are moneyed. Think it gives them the right to treat people any way they choose."

"People with money can be like that." Simon gently swirled the brandy in his glass and watched the fire flickering in the fireplace.

"Not *all* people with money."

He glanced across at me. "No." He agreed. "You're not like that. Your father's the richest man I've ever met and *he's* not like that."

I raised my glass in a silent toast. "At least Miss Havelock was safely escorted home – even without her so-called friend's help. How'd you get the mother away from the pack?"

Simon gave a crooked grin. "It's all in my smile. That, and the fact that I was about the only chap in the place willing to put his name on the old girl's dance-card. Once I got her on the floor, I simply told her about her daughter's sudden and unexplained illness.

"Fortunately," he went on, "Mr Havelock was on the winning side of a political argument and was happy for his wife and daughter to leave without him."

I nodded. "Don't you think it's sad, though? A young girl married off to some old fart. No wonder she propositioned you as she did – reckon I'd do the same in her position."

Simon exhaled a long, slow breath. "My mother would do it with my sisters if she thought the match suitably profitable. Anne's attractive enough to make a good match on her own, but Alex ..." he shrugged and sipped his brandy.

"What about Alex?" The thought of my wild and unladylike stepsister married to an elderly man made me feel rather uncomfortable.

"You know her! She's prickly and outspoken and certainly not the submissive young lady a young man might consider courting. Mother may have no choice."

I stared at him in surprise. "She's spirited, that's true, but surely ..." I found myself about to defend the child – and not for the first time. Simon was regarding me quizzically. I quickly changed tack, "You're head of the household, surely any such decisions are yours?"

He frowned. "Only once I attain my majority, you know that.

Why are you so concerned about Zan's marital prospects?"

I was wondering the same thing myself. I threw down the remains of my brandy, stalling, before answering as honestly as I could. I said, "I don't know. Perhaps Miss Havelock's situation has troubled me."

"Offer for the young lady yourself, then," he countered with an impish grin. "It's not as if they'd deny a future earl for the sake of an aging baron."

He'd trapped me nicely and I gave a brief inclination of my head in acknowledgement. "Not that troubled."

∾

It was a Saturday afternoon and the sun was shining. I'd been feeling stifled of late – Oxford, while pleasing, was nevertheless a thriving, busy city. I could neither stroll down the street nor ride Equus along the university walks without meeting someone I knew.

I longed for fresh rural air filled with birdsong and country maids with apple-red cheeks and no pretensions.

I was particularly weary of the 'chance' meetings I regularly had with fellow students whose pretty sisters just happened to be visiting. Naturally, these encounters always resulted in introductions, usually followed by an invitation to join the family for tea.

Since meeting Adrienne Morehead, Deon had been busting his balls to get me over to his townhouse. The girl, while beautiful, was a thoroughly unpleasant person – I'd no intention of calling on her.

Consequently, I stayed in my own townhouse waiting out Miss Morehead's visit to her brother. There were only a few days to go before she returned home.

That was a big thing for me – I was generally disinclined to remain indoors, especially when the sunshine beckoned. But today I lay on my bed, propped on pillows, Strad tucked beneath my chin, playing a mournful largo.

I vaguely heard the front door-knocker but continued with my music. Mrs Baldoon would answer it.

Suddenly I paused. Did Mrs Baldoon work Saturdays? I heard voices downstairs – oh good, seems she did work Saturdays.

Satisfied, I drew the bow across the strings and continued playing. By closing my eyes, I could picture the musical notes without needing the music before me. The fingers of my left hand moved automatically over the fingerboard while the bow swept across the strings.

My ear was good, enabling me to tune in perfect fifths without the aid of a tuning fork. I could tell now that my E string was flat but that was to be expected – I'd replaced it that morning, so it was stretching.

Pausing, I plucked the E string and it vibrated with a distinctive *scordatura* resonance.

"Mmm," I hummed the note, then inspired, turned the peg on the G string to create a sharp note. Plucked together, they created an eerie conflict – perfect for a Biber piece.

I began the opening chords of one of the Mystery Sonatas. The complexity of these sonatas was such that I'd never mastered a single one. Any wonder Biber wasn't popular with musicians.

The frustration was beginning to rise in me when there came a knock at my door and Mrs Baldoon called, "My lord?"

My housekeeper stepped into the room, pulling the door to behind her.

"My lord, Mr Morehead is in the parlour to see you. He has Miss Morehead with him."

I cursed under my breath. "Tell them I'm not home, could you?"

She made a gesture of helplessness, "They heard you playing the violin, my lord."

"Bugger." I went to get off the bed, then thought better of it. "Just go and tell them anyway. Deon will understand."

I settled back on the bed but she continued to stand there. "What? Go ... go!" I made a shoo-ing motion but she didn't move.

"Come on, now." She stood with hands on her hips, mouth set with determination. "Off that bed – I'll not lie to your guests." Then she turned and opened the door.

"Oh, for Christ's sake, Mrs Baldoon. What the hell do I pay you for?"

Already out in the hall, she stuck her head back into my room. "*You* don't pay me at all – your father does, and he wouldn't leave his guests waiting."

"Fuck it!" I grumbled.

"And your father doesn't use language like that!" Her voice drifted up the hall as she disappeared downstairs.

∾

I sat in the parlour; a teacup balanced on the arm of my chair. Across the room, Deon sat beside his sister, smiling innocently, while she repeated, for the third time, how grateful she was that Simon and I had taken care of her dearest friend last evening.

A complete volte-face from her previous attitude; I was having none of it, but she seemed oblivious.

"You should have seen them, Deon," she continued, "so assertive and self-assured. Pat – I mean, Lord Washburn, took the matter entirely in hand and—"

"I bet he did," Deon watched me through lidded eyes, a smirk playing about his mouth. "And did he offer to escort poor Miss Havelock home?"

"No, he did not," I snapped. I was feeling very unwelcoming at that moment. Despite being a bitch, Adrienne Morehead was an attractive woman, yet her blatant admiration was not sparking my interest. She was too self-absorbed for my tastes.

That she had decided I was to pay court to her was evident by the teasing looks she kept throwing in my direction. Clearly accustomed to getting her own way, she'd convinced Deon to bring her to my home. Wait until I got hold of him! I would wring his—

"... taking our leave now," Deon was saying, as he placed his teacup on a tray. I contained a sigh of relief.

We rose from our seats, while Adrienne, visibly unhappy about leaving so soon, reluctantly followed her brother's lead. I rang the bell for Mrs Baldoon.

"You will visit soon, won't you, my lord?" Adrienne was looking up at me, her fan flirtatiously resting on my sleeve.

"Of course you will, my lord," Deon interjected. "My sister is only here for another few days before she must return to the north. Shall we say tomorrow, at four?"

I was going to kill him, and the merry glistening in his black eyes told me that he was well aware of my intentions.

"Sir Simon and I shall be pleased to visit tomorrow," I responded placidly, as Mrs Baldoon came in. If I had to go to Deon's, Simon was going too. "Mrs Baldoon, please bring my guests' things."

My housekeeper bobbed and disappeared. Returning promptly, she handed Deon's coat to me – which I unceremoniously thrust at him – and held Adrienne's coat for the young lady to slip into.

All the while, Adrienne was smiling prettily at me. She could smile all she liked; after her abandonment of her friend last night, she would win no favour from me – Christ, though, she *was* beautiful!

"Why don't you go sit in the coach, my dear," Deon addressed his sister. "I would have a quick word with his lordship."

Adrienne simpered in my direction, and held her hand out for my kiss, which I delivered as perfunctorily and coldly as possible. "Tomorrow, it is, my lord. See you then!"

Deon and I watched her skip daintily down the path to the

waiting coach. I turned to my friend. "What the devil are you doing bringing Adrienne here?"

"What are you talking about?"

"You know what I'm talking about – I'm not going to court your sister!"

"She has a fancy for you."

I snorted derisively. "I don't give a shit! What makes you think I'd be even *remotely* interested in her?"

"She's beautiful and—"

"She's selfish, narcissistic and a fucking gold-digger!"

Mrs Baldoon accurately assessed the situation and hurried to shut the front door. I nodded my thanks, turned back to Deon and ...

He planted such a facer on me that the force of it threw me into the wall. Bouncing off, I responded with a quick left to his mouth and a right to his jaw, slamming him against the hallstand.

Mrs Baldoon yelped and leapt out of the way.

"*What the fuck!*" Deon bellowed, holding his jaw. He worked it from side to side, testing it before bunching his fists and retaliating.

I ducked.

He swung again. I ducked again.

So he kicked me in the balls so fucking hard, I hit the floor and lay curled in a heap on the rug.

"Tomorrow at four," he said, opening the door. "Don't be late!" And he was gone, slamming the door on his way out.

I groaned, my hands cupping the injured parties, and rolled over. Mrs Baldoon stood looking down at me, hands on hips and making tutting sounds. "Can I bring you a brandy, my lord?"

"Piss off!"

She snorted and turned away.

∽

Mr and Mrs Morehead shared a settee. Deon and Adrienne

another, while Simon and I perched on matching chairs.

Miss Bradbury was Mrs Morehead's unwed sister. Heavily rouged and vigorously fanning herself, she was sprawled on a chaise-longue, moaning about the terrible heat and how up north in Yorkshire, spring weather was much milder.

My brawl with Deon the day before was not our first, and was as quickly forgotten as previous ones. We sat opposite one another now, sipping tea and eating sandwiches while his parents asked Simon and me questions about our studies.

Through Mrs Morehead's remarks, I discovered that she was friendly with Simon's mother. Through her simpering and fawning over me, and repeated references to my title, I perceived her ambition. She and her sister spent a considerable amount of time extolling Adrienne's virtues as a gentle girl, intelligent and demure, very caring of others, and currently undergoing her mother's tutelage in the efficient management of a large household.

Meanwhile, Mr Morehead seemed unimpressed with his womenfolk. He spoke little and spent most of the afternoon quietly fingering the ends of his drooping moustache.

I finished my tea and placed my cup on a table beside me – a gesture I hoped would herald our departure. Unfortunately, it only seemed to prompt Miss Bradbury into saying, "Perhaps Lord Washburn would like to see our daffodils. Adrienne, would you accompany Lord Washburn in a turn about the garden?"

Simon quickly pulled a kerchief from his pocket and coughed delicately to smother a chuckle. I felt like thumping him but decided that strangling Miss Bradbury would be immeasurably more satisfying.

Redemption arrived in the form of Mr Morehead who cleared his throat. "I think not, good sister." His voice was deep and resonant – the kind that would make an impressive baritone. "I expect the young gentlemen will be keen to take their leave of us.

However, before they go, I would like a private word with you both, if I may."

Simon and I exchanged glances; standing politely as the ladies rose, we bowed formally and waited as Adrienne, her mother and aunt left the room. As Deon went to follow, his father said, "Stay, please. What I've to say involves you."

The door closed behind the women and Mr Morehead waved us to resume our seats.

"Now," he said. "Lord Washburn, I would ask you a number of questions regarding my daughter and I request that you respect me enough to be honest."

"Very well, but you must call me Patrick."

"Agreed." Rising, he went to a cabinet, took four glasses and poured four tots of some dark liquor. "Not too early in the day for a good whiskey, I trust?"

"No sir," Simon and I replied in unison and shared a smile as Mr Morehead handed out the glasses.

Dropping heavily onto his settee, he took a sip of whiskey, put his head back and released a gusty sigh.

We waited, sipping our drinks. It was good whiskey.

Finally, he sat upright. "I must commend you boys – including my son here," he nodded in Deon's direction, "on your incredible patience this afternoon. The machinations of my wife and her sister ... well, that's not what I wanted to talk about."

He leaned forward and stared intently at me. "Now, Patrick, let's not mince words. I have heard about you."

I wasn't going to delve into that – most people had heard about me and not in a good way. I gestured for him to continue.

"And you know that my daughter has taken a fancy to you."

"I am aware."

"So, I would ask you now, do you plan to call on her – as a gentleman?"

He had requested honesty. I breathed slowly in through my

nose. "No, Sir."

Another sip, then, "Do you plan to court her in the future?"

"No, Sir."

"I see." He nodded, thoughtfully. "In fact, I see more than you think because I am aware that my daughter has been throwing herself at you – ah, don't ... you're about to defend her, but don't. I know what she's like when she sees something she wants. And she wants you, my boy, make no mistake."

He drained his glass and got up to refill it; turning, with the decanter in hand, he raised his eyebrows questioningly.

Simon responded quickly, "No thank you, Sir."

The older man stoppered the bottle and returned to his seat. "Right then. What I ask is this. Given your disinterest in my daughter, I request that you not encourage her in any way, and that you behave at all times as a *true* gentleman – am I understood?"

"You're asking me not to take advantage of your daughter's fancy."

He inclined his head assertively.

"And," I went on, "you're asking me not to swive her."

Mr Morehead's eyes nearly popped out of his head. Deon spluttered into his glass and Simon seemed to hold his breath.

Suddenly, the older man exploded into loud guffaws.

When, finally, he regained control of himself he said, "I like you!" He saluted me with his glass. "Yes, I do, and it's a great pity you're not interested in my daughter. Well," he looked at the three of us in turn before continuing, "Deon, son. You did assure me that Patrick wasn't interested in Adrienne and now I have it from the horse's mouth. I trust you will now do everything you can to dissuade her from any foolish behaviour."

"I will, Sir." Deon sipped his drink and seemed suddenly to relax, while his father smiled benevolently across at me.

"Yes," he said, "I *have* heard a lot about you – not all of it to your advantage, mind, but for all you're young yet, I think you're a decent chap."

"Thank you, Sir."

"Do you think you'll take your seat in the House when you achieve the earldom?"

"I prefer not to think about losing my father," I replied. It was the truth.

"Hmm." Mr Morehead emptied his glass again. "Such a pity you're not inclined toward my daughter."

We grinned at one another – I liked him too.

THE ROAD TO YORKSHIRE

It was June 1810 and Oxford University students whose families owned country estates began drifting away from the city, returning to their rural homes for the summer. Corridors and halls became grey and lifeless, while the streets and markets, taverns, whorehouses and gaming hells were rapidly emptying.

It never occurred to Simon or Patrick that they might go their separate ways, each to his own estate in opposite directions. Simon had gone home with Patrick to Waterville the previous summer, and this year, without even discussing it, they both knew they would be riding to Yorkshire – to Simon's home, Broughton Hall.

Simon was looking forward to it, as expected – it was, after all, his seat. He had left a steward to manage his affairs, and Patrick's father, the earl, was there, but it wasn't the same as being there himself.

Patrick had understood that and would miss visiting his own estate but was just as happy to go to Yorkshire – Waterville was in good hands.

It was raining on the morning they rode out of Oxford. A steady, persistent rain that soaked through the thickest woollen coat and slid under the collar, to trickle uncomfortably down the neck and back.

Too cold and wet to consider doing anything else, they spent the night at an inn, sitting in a private suite, drying their clothes before a fire, eating a hearty meal and going to bed sober. The following morning, they departed early – only to repeat the previous day's sodden and miserable haul northwards.

By midday of the fourth day, the sky ahead was clearing, and the rain had reduced to a sullen drizzle that finally lifted in the early afternoon. As the sun appeared, clouds of steam rose off clothing and horses as they trudged along muddied lanes beside rain-logged fields.

A week into the journey, the pair had put the towns of Leicester and Loughborough behind them. By now the July sun was a white disc in an uninterrupted blue sky and the fields rolling beside them were green with swaying, stalks of new wheat.

They'd stripped off their coats and rolled up the sleeves of their shirts and were making faster progress as the roads dried.

Warmer weather meant they needed to rest the horses more frequently. During one such stop, they relaxed beside the road beneath a stand of trees, drinking small ale from stone bottles and eating grainy bread with hard, yellow cheese and slices of ham hacked straight from the bone.

They were on the outskirts of Ruddington, beside a small church and schoolhouse. The shouts and laughter of children playing close by made for pleasant background noise as they reclined in the grass.

ॐ

In no hurry, and grateful of the improved weather, Patrick contentedly drifted into a light doze. Unaware that Simon had wandered off, he was rudely awakened by Simon's voice, raised in anger – unusual in itself – but as he came to full wakefulness, Patrick realised that Simon's was only one voice among other enraged bellows and curses.

Leaping to his feet and grasping the knife they'd been using to cut the ham; Patrick followed the shouting around a thicket of brambles to find a pair of adolescent boys – one holding a knife – leaning over a bloodied and trembling lamb on the grass between them and a very outraged Simon standing before them.

"What's going on?" Pat asked calmly, although it was very evident what was going on and he was immediately incensed.

The two lads had obviously concluded that one man on his own was no threat to their game of torture. But at Patrick's appearance, at least one of them decided they were disadvantaged for he released his hold on the tiny creature that lay in the dry grass, panting and with eyes rolling in terror.

"Bugger orf, mister," the one still holding the petrified animal shouted.

Glancing at his stepbrother, Simon saw the shadow pass over his face – he knew the other man too well. "Pat ..." was all he said, but his tone was enough to cause the little shit crouching over the lamb to shoot a wary look at the newcomer.

The other boy, meanwhile, had begun to back away, arms up as though innocent of the crime still evident on his bloodied hands.

"I said bugger orf!" The first boy growled. He was becoming agitated, his eyes wild and darting. He held the knife threateningly over the lamb. "This ain't got nuthin' to do wi' you!"

"You're right," Patrick responded. "Carry on," he urged casually, nodding toward the bleating, terrified animal. "I don't mean to interrupt you." He took a couple of steps toward the boy.

"Wh-what are ya doin'?" the lad demanded uncertainly. He glanced from Patrick to his captive, back to Patrick again.

"Watching."

"Oh Christ!" Simon muttered from behind. He'd seen the knife his stepbrother held.

The boy was wavering. 'Wha' d'ya mean, ya *watchin'*? 'Ere, bugger orf, I said!"

"I told you," Patrick replied with a great show of patience. "*I'm watching.*"

The boy's friend began to whimper – he was obviously the smart one. "C'mon Lenny ... let's get outta here."

Lenny ignored his friend. He continued to hover over the lamb, who, having gathered itself somewhat, said, "*Ba-aa,*" and squirmed. The boy gave it a violent shove and threw a challenging look at the older man.

"Watchin' are ya. Some kind a weird toff are ya?"

Shrugging dismissively, Patrick took another step forward, then another. The boy held his ground, though his eyes widened ever so slightly. He clutched the knife menacingly above the animal that had begun bleating and struggling again.

"Well, watch this ..." he announced.

He raised the knife in a flashing arc, savouring the moment, eyes on Patrick.

"Wait ...!"

Lenny's smirk was triumphant. He brought the knife down, pressing its point against the animal's pulsing throat. The lamb kicked and bleated, its small legs flailing ineffectually.

"What?" His voice was smug. "Can't stomach it, my lord?"

"On the contrary." Patrick took another step forward; now he was almost close enough to touch the boy. "I would suggest you progress by inches," he explained. "Don't simply leap immediately in for the kill – take your time ... proceed slowly."

The boy's small eyes darted between Patrick and Simon, and he adjusted his grip on the knife.

"Why ...?"

"Prolongs the enjoyment."

The boy snorted. "Wha'da you care?"

Patrick leaned in, close and intimate, and whispered, "Because whatever you do to that animal, I'm going to do to you."

And then he grinned and drew his own knife from behind his back. Short, and greasy from the ham, it did not compare well with the boy's larger blade, but Patrick knew a malicious sense of satisfaction as the torturer squeaked like a terrified child and leapt away from the lamb.

Lenny lashed out with his knife, slashing inexpertly and shouting, "Ya think ya gonna do for me with that pigsticker, do ya?"

"No." Patrick was trying not to laugh. It was too easy, and he'd spent way too much time in drunken tavern brawls to be intimidated by a thirteen year old wielding a weapon so clumsily. He reached out and casually plucked it from the cretin's hand.

The boy squeaked again, and Patrick did laugh then and held up the child's knife. "No, I'm gonna do for you with this one!"

Before Lenny could react, he'd been thrown to the ground and leapt upon. Patrick straddled him in the thick summer grass and pinned the boy's arms beneath his knees. The boy's legs thrashed and kicked uselessly.

Patrick now held a knife in each hand. He brought the boy's knife up slowly, holding its dull point before his wide, staring eyes. "Remember what I said? Progress by inches, slowly ..."

"You're mad!"

"Thank you for noticing." His own knife was placed against the lad's youthful Adam's apple. "But I don't enjoy hurting the innocent. You, on the other hand, I shall enjoy hurting *you* very much."

He levelled his most charming grin on the boy, before sliding the blade down and around, coming to rest on the large vein visibly throbbing on the right side of the throat. The boy began to whimper, and tears seeped from the corners of his eyes.

Patrick leaned close and pressed his lips to the bastard's left ear and whispered, "You evil, fucking little prick. You like torture *now*, or only when you're perpetrating it?"

❧

Simon was holding Lenny's friend by the arm. He tightened his grip as the boy began to squirm. This was not the first time he'd seen that wintry glint of daring in his stepbrother's eye and knew it to be borne of a lust for adventure.

But today ... this was a thirteen-year-old boy. Alright, a thirteen-year-old boy bent on torturing a baby animal.

Many would argue that Patrick was giving the child a taste of his own medicine, and generally Simon would agree. But in this instance, as Simon watched the scene play out before him, he wondered at what point Patrick would cease tormenting the child or whether he might have to pull his stepbrother away.

❧

Meanwhile, Patrick was gradually increasing the pressure on Lenny's knife. He felt cold, emotionally detached and entirely in control as he pressed into the slight resistance before the pop of penetration.

It was no more than a slight piercing of the skin, and Patrick drew no satisfaction from the letting of the boy's blood, though the little arsehole deserved much more.

Leaning back slightly, Patrick took his own blade and slid the tip over Lenny's cheek to rest right between the eyes.

"Try not to squirm," he recommended, in a matter-of-fact tone. He didn't intend to seriously wound the boy; he aimed only to frighten him.

And it worked, for in that instant, the air was flooded with the hot, tangy smell of urine.

"Pissed yourself, have you? Not so brave after all. Not even that frightened little animal pissed itself!"

❧

The other boy screamed in terror. He twisted out of Simon's hands and took off at a sprint across the field toward the church while Simon came and stood over his stepbrother. Placing a hand on his shoulder, he said, "Pat ... come on. We need to go."

With a deep breath, his stepbrother sat back on his heels, took both knives and in a single angry movement, viciously stabbed them into the ground, either side of the lad's head.

The boy shrieked in terror and burst into tears. Patrick hauled himself to his feet and stood looking down at the child.

"Get up, you fucking coward, and go," he said, adding contemptuously, "you're unhurt and acting like a silly little maid."

But the boy remained lying in the grass in his own piss, sobbing pathetically.

"Look," Simon nodded toward the church. The other boy could be seen, arm raised finger extended, with the parish vicar looking their way. "We'd better go."

❧

Neither spoke as they rode away. Simon was disturbed by what he'd seen – it reminded him of the night in an inn in Blakeney when Patrick, armed with nothing but a broken bottle, had calmly and coldly taken on a violent thug set on robbing them.

He conceded that before Patrick had intervened to rescue the lamb his own thoughts had tracked a similar line; yet perhaps the burgeoning physician in him baulked at the idea of inflicting harm on another human.

In any case, he'd been unsuccessful in trying to *talk* the boy out of his pursuit. His attempts to reason with the child had seemed to only make him more determined.

Patrick's method had certainly proved more effective, although Patrick had toyed with the child, played with his fear, eventually drawing blood.

He glanced across at the other man, riding silently beside him, eyes fixed on the road ahead, expression unreadable.

Across his saddle, cradled in one arm like a sleeping, newborn baby, was the lamb. One ear had been partially severed and it bore several other bloody scars on its face and neck. Its small eyes drooped wearily; its little head nodded in rhythm with Equus' stride. Now and then it opened its eyes to gaze at its saviour before returning to sleep.

Yes, Simon allowed, at no time had Patrick lost control. He could see now that his stepbrother had acted, once again, with icy composure – the boy's life had never been in any danger. Patrick had set out to scare him, and in that, he had succeeded.

Simon had lived with Patrick now for over two full years. They had shared food, wine and the favours of women. They were as close as blood brothers – closer. And yet sometimes Simon saw something in his stepbrother that caused him to question whether he knew him at all.

This incident had been one such occasion. Simon recognised in Patrick the will to act as his own morals dictated, to protect the innocent, and defend the defenceless; he had behaved in a way that many would condemn.

And Simon had seen Patrick behave with extreme cruelty on other occasions.

He recalled Patrick's public humiliation of his mother's companion, Eleanor. That day, so long ago now, the five Washburn-Broughton siblings had been in the parlour at Broughton Hall when Eleanor had come in asking for his sister Anne for something or other.

At the time, Simon had been aware that Eleanor had made a derogatory remark about his other sister, Zan. Patrick had removed Eleanor's wig in an incredibly heartless manner, then had calmly returned to the game of chess they'd been playing, as though nothing untoward had happened.

Simon and his sisters had been stunned, having never witnessed such viciousness before, and Simon had wondered then what had prompted it.

Perhaps, Simon considered, Patrick may have been defending Zan. Surely not, but ... whatever other reason could there have been?

He shot a quick look at his stepbrother now and caught him glancing solicitously at the sleeping creature in his arms.

Simon puffed his cheeks in a gusty exhale, acknowledging ruefully that Patrick was going to make a strong and fair earl and landlord someday. He would certainly defend his people, adjudicate disputes and punish justly, and, when the day came that the two of them bought their commissions and joined the army, he knew that Patrick would be a fearless, soldier, an honourable officer and a ferocious enemy.

And yet here he was, nursing a frail little animal in his arms with all the tenderness of a new father. Simon smiled to himself – his stepbrother was a paradox!

Simon thought of their wager and knew he was going to win – Patrick would marry for love and no doubt about it. Of cruelty and violence, he was certainly capable, yet he had the heart and soul of a romantic.

He snorted, stifling a laugh as he remembered how his stepbrother had mourned the loss of his lover, Mary Whitmore over a year ago. How he'd denied falling for her – a married lady – and declared he would give his heart to no woman!

Now Simon laughed out loud.

The object of his mirth looked up at him, his green expression quizzical.

"What are you planning to do with your little friend there?" Simon asked, indicating the sleeping bundle in Patrick's arms.

His stepbrother shrugged. "Can't take her all the way to Broughton Hall ... not carried like this. When I grabbed her, I hadn't thought that far ahead ... just wanted to get her away from those bastards."

Simon nodded. "Well, we're nearly at Bingham. There might be somewhere we can leave her."

Patrick looked down at the lamb and smiled ruefully.

∾

In the end Patrick carried the lamb to Yorkshire.

The first night, when they stopped at Bingham, Patrick had washed the little creature's wounds and made a bed for her on a chair in their room at the Dun Horse hotel. From a market woman, the following morning, he bought a basket and strapped it to his saddle for the lamb to ride in.

The lamb was barely old enough to eat properly, so Patrick tracked down a shepherd who, for a small sum, allowed the lamb to suckle from one of his ewes and provided Patrick with a jar of sheep's milk for the lamb's ongoing journey.

For the next week, the travellers edged steadily northwards and eventually their road intersected with Ermine Street, the old Roman Road. Once on Ermine Street, the going was easier. The weather had cleared to produce crisp early mornings and warm, cloudless afternoons.

Meanwhile, the lamb was nursed and fussed over, gradually overcoming her fears. By day she travelled in the basket. At night Patrick fed her ewe's milk whenever possible, and chaff whenever not, and she slept in his room – he would not consider anything less.

By the time they rode into Huddersfield she was a happy, healthy, joyous lamb that followed him about like a dog.

Simon watched his stepbrother curiously one evening. They were staying in an inn on the outskirts of Kirkstall and expected to arrive at Broughton Hall on the morrow. Patrick was lounging in an overstuffed armchair sipping a tankard of beer, the lamb asleep across his lap.

"Have you named her?" Simon asked nodding toward the creature whose legs were twitching in a dream.

"No."

"Why not? I expect you're planning to keep her at Broughton Hall?"

"She's not a pet."

Simon made a snorting noise. "You're certain about that?"

"Yes." Patrick watched the lamb for a moment before adding, "I'm going to give her to Maud."

"Maud?"

He nodded. "Remember Maud? We spent some time with her at the Red Fox when we had a room there."

"Oh ... yes, I remember. Why Maud?"

"Because I vaguely recall her mother kept a small flock of sheep specifically for their milk. She makes a variety of soft cheese."

"So tonight is your last night together ... you'll miss her, won't you?"

Patrick smiled then. "Yes, I will miss her, but since I intend to renew my acquaintance with Maud, I expect I'll see her often enough to be glad I gave her away before she grew too big."

∽

The next morning, they rode out of Kirkstall, met the Harrogate Road and continued toward Wolstone. The lamb was sitting up in her basket looking about her as though she knew she was approaching her new home.

Close to evening, they rode into Wolstone, going immediately to the Red Fox where they were welcomed by the master with jugs of ale and a hot meal. Patrick's enquiries revealed that Maud lived in the last house on Bridge Street on the way to Wharferidge.

After their meal, while Patrick took his lamb and went to find Maud, Simon remained behind. It happened that one of Simon's tenants, wife and two children, were likewise staying in the inn and working to pay their way after their farmhouse had been destroyed in a fire.

Simon listened patiently to the farmer's concerns before agreeing to visit the remains of the farm the next morning. They would discuss plans for rebuilding and meanwhile, he agreed to employ the farmer during Broughton Hall's harvest to enable the man to earn an income.

When Patrick returned to the inn, he found Simon alone in the taproom, drinking brandy and sketching a design for a new cottage.

Simon looked up, assessed the expression on his stepbrother's face and decided not to ask about the lamb. Rather he showed him the plans and requested an opinion.

Patrick called for a glass of brandy and slid onto the bench across from his stepbrother. Turning the page around, he studied the design. "This looks good – fairly standard. How many children does he have? Can he afford this?"

"Two and another coming. I think he can afford it, provided he gets work."

"Hmm. You might want to consider something else. Maud told me that the old widow down near the grange died. That's Broughton land, isn't it?"

Simon nodded. "I haven't seen that place in years. Widow Browning kept to herself a lot … just her and her chickens. Did Maud tell you when she died?"

"End of winter. Maud's mother took the chickens. This place is probably close enough to your fellow's land. Why not move him and his family there?"

Simon mulled the idea over while draining the last of the brandy from his glass.

"Alright. I'll talk to him tomorrow. Sounds like a good solution, if the cottage is in decent repair."

"Apparently it is."

"And what about Maud? Happy to see you, was she?"

Now Patrick grinned. "Happy enough. I'll not be accompanying you to the widow's tomorrow, but I will meet you on the road later and we can ride to Broughton Hall together."

THE DEMANDS OF OTHERS

"Goin' so soon?" Maud watched me as I moved about the room collecting my clothes. She shuffled to a sitting position on the bed and let the sheet slip to her waist. "Will yer be visitin' tomorrow?"

She was slender and small-breasted, and very accommodating. In the beginning of our – *relationship* didn't quite fit – *arrangement*, perhaps, she was very agreeable and happily consented to the terms I proposed.

I would pay the rent on a room at the Red Fox and set up an account with the landlord, and she could live in the room and charge meals and expenses to the account. At her request, I agreed for a seamstress and milliner to visit so she could outfit herself in the latest fashions.

In return, she would be available to me, exclusively, in the evenings – she would continue to work in the taproom of the Black Horse during the day, if she chose.

It seemed the perfect arrangement for both of us – even though Simon expressed his doubts; but since he was diddling one of his housemaids he was hardly in a position to comment!

In any case, Maud and I had both understood the terms of our agreement, including the end date. In eight weeks, when I returned to Oxford, she would return to her former life. She could keep her new clothing and I would settle her account at the Red Fox.

The perfect arrangement – or so it seemed.

Within two weeks, Maud was asking to see more of me and suggested I move in with her at the Red Fox.

That went on for another week or so, until she asked me to accompany her home to meet her father. "You 'aven't met 'im yet, and I *know* 'e'd love to meet *you*, being a lord and all."

There it is! Impossible to escape.

I managed to extricate myself from that one, but a week later she asked me to buy her father a new plough horse. I couldn't be bothered with a quarrel, so I agreed that he could choose one and have the account sent to me at the Red Fox.

Finally, this evening, as we were lying in bed, she asked if I would take her to meet my family at Broughton Hall.

That was the limit! And definitely the end of our arrangement – Simon had been proven right. He'd warned that any woman I took as mistress should at least have a rank and sufficient means to support herself, otherwise she would sooner or later make demands of me. Being with a lord, he said, would only lead someone like Maud to more elaborate expectations.

I'd countered that a serving woman would have no such designs, would know her place and be content to profit from the arrangement as much as possible – this was not a courtship. I should have known better.

Simon, to my chagrin, had been the better judge. I pulled on my trousers and threw my shirt over my head, jamming my arms into the sleeves. I was sitting on the edge of the bed, stuffing my feet into my riding boots, when Maud crawled up behind me and coiled her arms possessively around my neck.

"Don't leave, Patrick. When yer go, I do miss yer."

I paused. Was she developing feelings for me? I hoped not – that would make things worse. I twisted around to face her, unwinding her arms as I did. "Maud—"

"Please, Patrick! I think yer know 'ow I'm feelin' for yer. Surely yer feelin' summat for me too?"

Oh Christ.

I took her hands and cradled them gently on my lap. "I am fond of you, love. That's why I wanted to spend time with you. But we both knew, *and agreed,* how it would be between us."

She snatched her hands away with a huff. "Fond o' me, are yer? Yer come in 'ere an' use me up like yer do an' you say yer fond o' me!"

"I'm not using you up – I'm paying good money to house and feed you. You're clothed in the latest fashions; your father has a new horse. I'd say you're doing very well out of—"

"Whore am I then?" Her voice rose sharply, and I glared at her, unrepentant.

Taking my silence for agreement – which it was – she pulled back and served a ringing slap across my ear.

"Right, that's it!" I rose immediately, collected the rest of my things and strode to the door.

"*No!*" she shrieked. Leaping from the bed, she flew, naked, across the floor. Clawing at my arm she cried, "Don't go, *please,* I'm sorry ... I didn't mean it ... oh Patrick, I'm sorry."

She dropped at my feet and huddled there, while I looked at the back of her bowed head. I hated that. "Maud, come on," I extended a hand and touched her bare shoulder. "Get up."

Raising her tear-stained face to me, I saw hope mingled with something else – cunning perhaps. Did she think her tears would soften my heart? Nevertheless, I knew the futility of continuing the arrangement.

Dropping my coat, hat and riding gloves on a chair, I went back to the bed and retrieved a blanket. As I wrapped it around her, she asked, "Will yer stay?"

"No." I gathered my things again. At the door, I turned toward her. "I will pay the rent on the room to the end of the month. You may continue to live here until then and I will settle your account when you leave."

With that, I opened the door and strode out into the corridor. Halfway down the stairs, I heard a loud, *"Fuckin' bastard!"* and something very much like a bottle smashing against a wall.

∽

The next evening, Simon and I both stayed at home. Simon's mother had houseguests from Italy – Isabella and her two, very charming, daughters.

Simon was smitten with the elder of the two, Catarina – an indisputable beauty. Her conceit was also indisputable, and she regarded all those around her as inferior. Perhaps for the first time in his experience, Simon's looks were not winning him any favours with a female member of the species. He was forced to satisfy his frustrated lust, by turns, on a lass named Jane Carter – a housemaid in his employ – and a village slut by the name of Molly Starling.

Grace was Catarina's younger sister, and in my opinion, a very nice girl. Her English was good, which was convenient since my Italian was poor; so we spent many hours together, talking, laughing and sharing anecdotes of our vastly different worlds. For the first time in my life, I learned that I could be friends with a woman without the thought of bedding her crossing my mind for an instant.

That was a revelation to me, and I discovered that I was thoroughly enjoying her company for the sheer pleasure of her conversation and friendship.

Another revelation to me was the discovery that my stepsister, Alex, in the year and a half that I'd been away, had blossomed into a lovely young woman. I'd always guessed that there was more to Alex than met the eye, but now that maturity had polished off the wilful brat in her, I realised she was witty, intelligent and mischievous. When I wasn't with Grace, I found myself drifting about the property looking for my stepsister.

It wasn't hard to find her. She spent a great deal of time in the nursery with our baby sister Meg, and the nurse Clara.

There was something about Alex that intrigued me – to be honest, there always had been something intriguing about her. But now, as I saw the young lady emerging from the chrysalis of a tearaway child, I was drawn to her.

That was my summer for discoveries and not all of them pleasant. One most unpleasant discovery was made late one evening.

Simon and I had attended a summer festival held by a group of his tenants. I stayed for some of the country dances, enjoying locally brewed ale and watching while Simon, as lord of the manor, blessed the forthcoming harvest in a rather pagan ceremony. At the earliest opportunity, I slipped out to the paddock, retrieved Equus and returned, alone, to Broughton Hall.

By the time I arrived, the stable-boys were abed, so rather than rouse them, I removed Equus' tack myself, fed her and put her to bed in her stall; then I went up to the house.

I let myself in through the front, and as I closed the great door behind me, the hall was plunged into almost complete darkness.

Almost, but for a sliver of light showing beneath the parlour door. *That's odd.*

Gently pushing open the door, I slipped into the room and closed it softly after me. The only light in the room was coming from a low-burning fire in the grate. Anne, my youngest stepsister, sat on the rug before it.

The sight of her kneeling there took my breath away, for there sat one of the most beautiful women I've ever seen.

Wearing only the sheerest of nightgowns, her naked young body was clearly displayed, backlit in gold by the fire behind her. Her head was bowed and a cascade of shimmering hair partially hid her delicate lips and nose, while pert breasts, flaring hips and curving bottom were outlined in a pink and rose glow. Immediately, my pulse quickened and the blood settled somewhere south of my navel.

I inhaled slowly, and moved further into the room.

She didn't seem surprised to see me as I came in, merely looked up to meet my eyes. She'd been crying.

The room was warm from the fire, and I stripped off my coat, flinging it over the back of a chair. Then I drew the chair up before her and reclined in it comfortably.

I'd like to say I was mesmerised by her loveliness, but it would be a poor defence. At almost nineteen, I was a man. She was yet a child of fifteen – and my stepsister. I also knew her for a scheming little wench – once again, as with most things involving women, I should have known better.

But I gazed at her for a long time before finally dragging my eyes away to watch the glowing red coals in the fireplace.

"Mother won't let me have a London season." Her voice was thick with tears and my heart stirred for her. All girls wished for a London season – although Alex and Maeve didn't seem to.

"She always promised that I could have a London season," Anne continued, "I thought ... I thought we could go with Isabella when she and the girls left. *They're* going to London to be presented to the king. But not me."

I glanced at her briefly, but my eyes were immediately drawn to the rosy tips of her breasts visible through the translucent fabric of her nightgown. I resumed my contemplation of the fire. "I don't suppose you *can* go now that your mother is no longer received at court."

She made a wet, snorting sound. "That's what *she* says. But what about me? What hope have I now? Stuck out here in the ... in the country?"

She gulped and began to cry again. "Patrick ... wh-what about *me*?" she wailed. "How am I su-supposed to make ... a good m-match when I ... can't have a ... a coming out ... in London?"

She sat before me on the rug, shoulders hunched, body shuddering with her sobs. "Anne, you don't have to rely on your mother to present you, you know. Any woman who has herself been presented, may present you. My father knows many such."

She brightened immediately, her beautiful face gazing at me hopefully. "Would you speak to him? Would you really?"

I shrugged. "I could. But there would be no guarantee, and you must still seek your mother's approval."

A little frown appeared on her brow and her weeping stopped rather abruptly. "Yes, of course." She thought for a moment and gradually I saw her expression undergo a transformation, for she was still too young to mask her thoughts.

I saw cunning and calculation, and as her eyes slowly lifted to my face, I sensed her mood had changed. She had an idea, and judging by the speculative way she regarded me, I wasn't going to like it.

Strangely, I was not surprised when she rose to a kneeling position before me, and moving forwards, nudged her way between my legs. Her small hands rested momentarily on my knees, tapered fingers weaving a delicate pattern; slowly, slowly insinuating their way up my thighs.

"There is another way," she breathed. Leaning over me, she pressed her stomach against my groin, her firm young bosom on my belly. "I wouldn't need a season to find a husband."

My body responded immediately: my breathing came hard, my heart began pounding. The smile of satisfaction on her kittenish mouth told me she'd felt the hardening within my trousers.

"*You* could marry me."

Before I knew what was happening, she'd taken one of my hands and thrust it beneath her nightgown. My fingers immediately detected crisp hair and hot, damp skin.

"Don't do that!" I snapped, pulling my hand away. Despite the reeling of my senses, I took her by the shoulders and pushed her back. "Stop this immediately!"

"Patrick." Her voice was almost a sigh. She arched her back, pushing her hips into my groin. I suppressed a groan.

"We could marry – *we* could! Mother would certainly allow it and ..." her hands moved to my belt and began unbuttoning my trousers, "and we would be good for one another. We're the same, you and I."

Suddenly, I grasped her hands – probably too firmly for she yelped, and her eyes widened in surprise. But just as quickly she smiled again – she knew I desired her.

But she was a child!

She was Simon's sister!

She was Alex's sister!

Alex!

Oh for God's sake! What if *Alex* walked in? What if *Alex* saw us like this! While I had absolutely no intention of bedding this girl, no one witnessing this scene would believe that.

Despite the fact that Simon would cut my balls off with one of his surgical instruments, and probably take my cock as well for good measure, it was as nothing compared with Alex finding out.

For reasons I could not even begin to contemplate, Alex's opinion of me was of utmost importance!

More than any*one*, I did not want Alex to find out what was going on here. More than any*thing*, the thought of Alex seeing me like this, with Anne groping at my erection, was like being doused with a bucket of icy water. I regained my wits, fired with anger and indignation.

Anne sensed my withdrawal but wasn't deterred. Even though

I had shackled her hands, she continued to move her hips wantonly, all to no avail. I had mastered my body's natural reaction and my arousal was withering. I was furious.

"Come on, Patrick. You know you want me – and if we were to marry ... just imagine! With my looks and your money, we would take London by storm! The world would lay at our feet."

"Stop it! We're not marrying, and we're not doing this, either." I tried to rise but the angle of the chair made it difficult with her full body weight now on top of me. "Anne, bloody get off me now or I'll throw you off!"

But she continued to press down on me, her lips finding the opening of my shirt. Her tongue darted out to touch my throat and my skin rippled involuntarily.

The only way to get her off was to forcibly dump her on the floor. I didn't want to hurt her but there was no other way.

I still had a firm grip on her hands. Now I jerked them down to the side and in the same motion, I twisted and pushed.

With a small cry and a loud thump, she hit the rug before the fire. I rose immediately and wiped my sleeve across the dampness she'd left on my neck.

"What are you doing?" she cried. She was genuinely shocked.

"You know what I'm doing."

"But ..." she jumped to her feet and stood before me, breasts jutting out, hands on hips. "Use your brains – this is perfect! It *would* be perfect if you—"

"It will *never* happen. Not in a million years. Don't you dare try something like—"

"... perfect, if you weren't such a ninny about it. I know you fuck everything in sight – why not fuck someone who would be perfect for you? We're perfect for each other!"

I was prepared to argue with her further, or walk away with my dignity intact, but I was truly stunned by her language – and not much ever stunned me!

"Well?" she went on. "Nothing to say? You know I'm right." She looked me up and down and snorted contemptuously. "You'll change your mind. You'll see reason. That's why I waited up for you. You're home earlier than I expected."

I stared incredulously at her. She'd planned this! She'd planned to seduce me and then run to her mother who would, doubtless, demand I marry her innocent young daughter, who, debaucher that I am, had been *ruined*.

Suddenly I exploded. My hands shot out and grasped her roughly by the shoulders, forcing her to step backwards.

"You ever lay a hand on me again ..." I snarled, "you ever presume to *touch* me without invitation ... I will destroy you, you scheming whore. The world will know what you are – no man worth the name will even look at you."

I still had a good hold on her and her face had paled in fright. Without pity, I pushed her into the chair I'd recently vacated, and she sprawled there gazing up at me with large, frightened eyes.

I leaned toward her, "Do you understand, *sister*?"

She nodded.

I snatched my coat from the back of the chair and stalked from the room, but not before I heard her mutter, "I won't forget this."

❧

The following morning, I awoke feeling drained. I felt hungover without having earned it. I felt bruised as though I'd been in a tavern brawl, and I felt jaded and world-weary.

And more than anything, I felt I wanted to see Alex; as though by her simple honesty she could expunge the guilt and anger roiling inside me.

Why I felt this way, why I had such guilt and anger, I couldn't tell. But I knew that Alex had not a single dishonest bone in her body; her every gesture and glance, her smile and laugh were entirely without artifice.

And I was tired of deceit.

The world I lived in was too sordid. I needed purity and candour and knew I'd find it in the rose garden.

So that was where I went.

And that was where I found her. The morning sun was touching her hair, sparking highlights of gold from the unruly mass of chestnut curls. Dressed as she was in a mint morning gown with stripes of darker green through the skirt, she looked fresh and clean.

Meg toddled at her side, and I could hear the little girl's chatter and Alex's commentary as they bent over an apricot bloom.

She wasn't aware of my approach and stood up suddenly, bumping into me, with a gasp of surprise.

"My apologies." I grinned at her.

She grinned back. "No ... I didn't realise you were there. I'm just surprised to see you about so early. It must want at least an hour until your usual rising time."

She was teasing me – it was a refreshing change from the devious, conniving, *demanding* women of my recent company. I felt instinctively that Alex was happy to see me, and not because I would *do* anything, *be* anything or *buy* anything for her. She was just happy to see me for my own sake.

"I returned early last night. Sime stayed out but I've had enough for a while."

"Growing too old for the wine, women and song, are we?"

I laughed and raked a hand through my hair. "I shall be nineteen soon and a man must know his limitations." I indicated our little sister with a jerk of my chin. "What are you doing?"

"Showing Meg the roses."

Crouching to Meg's level, I said, "And what do you think of the pretty flowers then, Meggy?"

"Dat! Dat!" the child responded, waving her arms. I glanced at

Alex, hoping for a translation.

Alex snorted humorously. "She's saying, *Pat, Pat.*"

"Oh, I see." I curled an arm around the little girl's waist and picked her up. She wrapped her arms about my neck, holding on tightly and giggling. "I have an idea. Let us see if there are any ripe apples to pick. Then, we shall ask cook to stew them with rhubarb and make us a treat."

Alex was smiling at the two of us. *Pretty*, I thought. *Not the great beauty that Anne will be, but very pretty in her own unconscious way.*

"Sounds good to me," she said. "What do you think, Meg?"

"Dat, Dat!" Meg responded and chortled happily to herself.

Alex's dog was lying on the lawn in the sphinx position, head raised to the morning breeze. I nudged her now with my toe, "On your feet, doggle!"

The three of us, with Jemima trotting at Alex's heels, made our way to the orchard, and I breathed deeply of the summer-scented air, feeling the constrictive bindings of demand and expectation loosen and fall away.

MATCHES AND FIRES

"They've found a husband for Zan." Simon's tone was flat and unemotional, and I sensed his resignation.

Something in my throat constricted and, not trusting myself to speak, I forced myself to breathe evenly.

Alex and I had only just parted company after a typical – for us – quarrel. She had dashed off to meet her mother's summons, while I had strolled along behind, coming across her brother lounging in the shade of the Great Oak.

Pulling up a chair, I had joined him, and waited now for him to continue.

He took a sip of lemonade and stared into the green, leafy canopy of the ancient boughs arching above us. Stretching his legs before him, he leaned back in his chair and exhaled noisily. "The son of some Scottish Laird – not the sort of fellow I would have chosen for her, but Mother says it's a good match – and it is, I must admit."

Why the news of his sister's betrothal would affect me as it did, I couldn't tell and didn't want to think about, but Simon took another mouthful of his drink and continued, "They're telling her now. She's not going to be happy, but I am not in a position to do anything about it. Even if I could, I doubt that I would."

I snorted and he glanced over at me, continuing, "Name's Hamish Glendenning. I've not met the chap, but I've heard enough about him. Mincing popinjay ... Mother says it's him or no one – Zan's way too stubborn, difficult ..." he shrugged and made a rueful face. "Well, you know what Zan's like."

"I know Glendenning – I know what he's like." I spoke for the first time since Simon shared the news. "I agree – he's not a good match for Alex; most incompatible."

"Mother's not looking for compatible. She's only interested in his title. As she sees it, Anne will be easy. With her beauty and ambition, Anne will effortlessly attract someone of rank, but Zan is too ... irreverent ... too difficult. She's just not cut out for society ballrooms and polite drawing-room conversations. Mother has always despaired of finding her a husband; so I expect, in that regard, the Glendenning match is perfect. He will be the Seventh Viscount Elginbury."

I spoke, not bothering to soften my tone. "If you don't prevent this, you'll be consigning your sister to a life of misery."

Simon stared at me in surprise. "Strong words," he said. "It's not that bad! She'll have a title, a home of her own ... this is Zan we're talking about, and you know I adore her, but I must be realistic. She won't do any better."

The annoyance rose within me. This was the brother Alex loved uncompromisingly, the one person she would follow to the ends of the earth, and he was showing her so little regard. "Don't you know anything about your own sister!?" I challenged.

"Of course I do," he retorted indignantly, "which is why I think Mother's right. Zan can be opinionated and antagonistic. Further, she's untitled with only a moderate dowry, although Mother's managed to contrive some kind of financial arrangement that will benefit the Elginburys. They've agreed to the terms; Zan will eventually be Lady Elginbury. It's unlikely another opportunity like this will arise."

"You shouldn't be thinking of it in terms of opportunity."

"What else is there?"

"Her happiness ...?"

"You can afford to say that – Maeve's dowry could purchase my entire estate, plus as the sister of an earl she'll have her pick of suitors. Zan hasn't that luxury."

"She'll be very unhappy with Glendenning."

"He's a viscount. It's a better match than we could have hoped for." I realised that my stepbrother was not being unkind. His assessment of Alex was the honest opinion of a brother who wanted a good marriage for his sister.

I sighed heavily. "So what if he's a viscount? He's not right for her."

Simon gave a grunt of laughter, "What would be right for her? A duke? You'll be an earl ... you think you're right for her?"

I was about to expose myself in a way that I rarely do, and I did not care. I responded simply and very seriously, "Yes."

Simon's eyes widened in surprise, but then he grinned. "Christ man, I nearly believed you!"

Grinning in return, I rose, doffed an imaginary hat and strode toward the house.

∽

Anne and Maeve were in the garden hitting a tennis ball back and forth between them. I sat in the window in my room, watching them play while my mind wandered elsewhere.

What had got into me?

It was one thing to admit quietly to myself that I found Alex's sincerity and rebelliousness very refreshing, even – if I was being completely honest with myself – attractive. It was also no secret that we rubbed along well together. Not for the first time, the urge to protect this belligerent girl washed over me.

But to tell Simon that I thought she ... that I thought *I* was right for her ... well, that was ...

What ...?

I frowned. What was that?

Stupid? I snorted derogatorily. Of course it was stupid!

But was it true? Definitely not! Alex needed stability and loyalty. I could offer neither of those attributes. And to be frank, I didn't *want* to be stable and loyal.

She also needed someone that would cosset and love her while taking a firm hand with her moods and prickles. She wouldn't find that in Glendenning. Nor would she find stability and loyalty in him.

In any case, the fact that I felt protective of her was simply the way any brother would feel. I felt protective of Maeve, and I might have felt similarly toward Anne too, had she not revealed her true, devious, calculating self.

Did my feelings run beyond those considered normal for a stepbrother? Now that was a thought I did not want to contemplate and was rescued from doing so by a knock at the door.

Her face was blotchy, and her nose was red and shiny. Alex stood before me, her eyes great wet pools, as she poured out her story and I affected an air of negligence.

I felt very sorry for her and did not trust my ability to conceal my thoughts so I turned away, ostensibly to continue watching Maeve and Anne.

"Haven't you anything to say?" she cried.

I knew she wanted me to agree with her and plead her case with my father, but I also knew the futility of such a move. For me, in that moment, the safest course of action was anger, so I turned back to her.

"What would you have me say?" I demanded. "I'm not

surprised – why are you surprised? Besides, isn't this what all girls hope for?"

She stared at me, and the hurt was plain on her face. "I ... I don't want to marry this ... stranger. I thought ... I hoped you might help me."

I hated conversations like this, and I didn't want to become involved in something I couldn't influence so I responded with an accusation.

"Why would you think that? If I recall correctly, not two hours ago you were wagging a finger at me."

She ignored me. "You could speak to your father ... I don't want to be married! Pat, I don't know what to do ..."

Her eyes were filling with tears and my heart twisted. Softening my tone, I said, "How can I speak for you? As if anything I said would change matters."

"Couldn't you try? Please ...?"

She had such hope in her face – she really thought I could help. She was definitely overrating my powers of persuasion. "Look," I wanted an end to the discussion, "you may be happy if you give this Lord Whatsit a chance."

"Hmph! I don't even know him."

I rose, taking her elbow, "Come on, it's supper time. We'd best go downstairs."

She jerked away from me. "Bastard!"

I stifled a laugh. "Oh dear." That was precisely why her mother despaired of finding a better match for her. "Such unladylike language."

Turning away, I hid my smile and left my room. She followed along the hall and down the stairs, thumping unhappily and it was all I could do not to chuckle aloud at the irony of it.

Aware that she was very close behind me, I deliberately stopped abruptly outside the dining room – I wanted her close when I turned and looked deeply into her face.

Tear-stained as she was, with eyes brimming and lips drawn tight to suppress her emotions, I found her most endearing – too appealing for her own good. The urge to kiss away her sadness was a physical pull in my chest, but that would never do.

Taking firm control of myself, I brushed a stray hair from her cheek. "You're so young yet," I said softly and as her emotions threatened to spill over, I added quickly, "Be brave – betrothals are broken every day. Who knows what the future holds?"

She seemed surprised and opened her mouth to reply, but my own emotions were too ragged. Before I could do or say anything that I might regret, I wiped a tear from her cheek and ordered, "Now, happy face!" and pushed her into the dining room.

ↄ

For the next week, I endeavoured to avoid being alone with Alex. Not because I did not enjoy her company, rather – the opposite was true. I enjoyed her company too much and did not understand my own thoughts and feelings.

Alex confounded me because I was drawn to her; appreciating her lack of pretence and sense of humour. The only other woman for whom I'd felt thus had been Mary, and we hadn't been able to keep our hands off each other.

Yet thoughts of touching Alex in any sexual or unbrotherly fashion never entered my mind. Consequently, I was often hesitant around her, puzzled by my own feelings – it was best to avoid being alone with her.

However, with Simon along, Alex and I were a safe trio, spending many long, indolent afternoons together, and the more time she and I spent with one another – even with Simon present – the closer I sensed we were growing. Yet to enjoy her company, to spend time with a woman without thoughts of bedding her, was foreign to me.

When I was not with Simon and Alex, I lazed away the

summer days with Grace, the Italian lass who was staying at Broughton Hall.

Unlike her mother and sister, Grace was gentle, genuine and possessed of a delicious sense of fun. I had not realised that it was possible to be pals with a woman in the same manner that I could be pals with a man.

My relationship with Grace was no simpler than my relationship with Alex. I was attracted to Grace, although, once again, it was not sexual.

These notions of platonic friendships with women were entirely new to me.

Grace and I were chums – had she been a man, I'd have understood myself much better. Perhaps it was a measure of maturity? I'd always considered myself rather mature for my age, but I could see now, that I'd been mistaken.

One afternoon, Grace and I were lying in the grass in the park enjoying a balmy summer breeze. She had confided that she was in love with a man she'd met in London.

My stepmother and Grace's mother were sitting beneath the Great Oak – they could not hear us, but they were whispering and watching us closely.

"They will be planning our wedding," Grace said, laughing.

"Then we must turn it to our advantage," I suggested.

She grinned wickedly and shuffled closer so that her head rested in my lap. She knew exactly what I meant. "His name is George," she went on, "and he is definitely not the man my mother would have for me. He is ... *come si dice* ... unsuiting for me."

I laughed lightly. "Unsuitable?"

"Unsuitable. He has no money, and he is not ... er ... he has no name."

"Untitled?"

"Ah, *si. Mia madre,* she say I must marry a man with an old family – *un conte* at the least."

"Nothing less than an earl? So I would just scrape in by the skin of my peerage, eh?"

She smiled. "*Si*, but *mia madre*, she would prefer *un marchese* or u*n duca*."

"Why stop at a duke? We have a perfectly obnoxious prince in London she could present you to."

"Oh, please do not encourage her!" She laughed and twisted around to look into my face and I stared down at her, an idea formulating in my mind.

"If we were to ... hmm." Our eyes met; the same thought was occurring to us. I continued. "If we led them to believe we were courting ..."

"Miriam would leave you in peace," she finished for me.

I nodded. "And you would be able to stay in England, supposedly to be with me, when your mother returns to Italy. You would need a chaperone."

"I have a friend in London I may stay with – she would be my chaperone."

"Perfect!"

She gave a little laugh, and reached up to touch my face in a sweet lover's gesture that would not be lost on our distant spectators. Grinning, I caught her hand and kissed her fingers.

"George is in Leeds, did you say?"

"He followed me here; he hope to seeing me, but we have had no opportunity."

"Send him a message. Tell him there is a room he can use at the Red Fox in Wolstone."

"Oh, he is in Leeds with a friend. He could not ... he has not the money for a room at this place."

"Never mind that. I have paid in advance for the summer. Most of the time it is not used. It is at his disposal."

She sat up abruptly and looked down at me. "You would do that?"

At my nod, she threw herself on top of me, arms around me. "Oh, you are so kind!"

Laughing, I held her back. "Listen to me. Send a message to him right away. Tell him you will meet him at midnight. I will take you."

"*Eee!*" she squealed and hugged me again.

This time I allowed her to hold me, returning her embrace, aware that her mother and my stepmother had grown silent and were openly staring as we lay enfolded in one another's arms.

∾

A little before ten that night, I crept along the hall toward Grace's room. I tapped lightly before slipping inside. She stood before her mirror in the light of a single candle, fastening the buttons on the bodice of her riding habit.

As I closed the door behind me, she wordlessly twirled, and I nodded my approval. "*Che bella!*" I said, and she glowed happily.

"*Spero di si!* Do you have ... did you bring the er ..."

From behind my back, I withdrew a new sponge. She blushed but approached, her eyes fixed on the object in my hand.

I felt no qualms about aiding her in this – if she were to give herself to George, the least I could do was help her prevent any unplanned results.

She held out her hand and I placed the sponge on her palm. "What do I do with it?"

Now it was my turn to blush – not a common occurrence – but there was no point giving it to her without instructions.

"Soak it in vinegar and ..." my face grew hotter, and she grinned cheekily. "Bloody hell, Grace. You know what to do with it!"

"*Si*, but you are very handsome when you are *imbarazzo!*"

I grunted. "Well, I *am* embarrassed, thank you very much. I have done my part; if you don't know what to do with it, I can't help you!"

She sniggered. "We go now?"

"*Andiamo!*"

Summer days in the north were longer than those I was used to in Devon. But by half past ten, the sun had dropped below the horizon and the sky was a magnificent indigo with a bright, crisp, sickle moon overhead.

We slowed our horses to a walk as we took a circuitous route through the quiet little village of Wharferidge. Although there was a more direct road into Wolstone, going through Wharferidge brought us closer to the Red Fox.

Kicking into a canter down the lane toward Wolstone, we clattered across Bridge Street bridge, up the lane past the Wolstone cattle market, and finally turned into the stable-yard behind the Red Fox.

I helped Grace to dismount, arranged for the horses to be watered, and escorted her through the back entrance, up the stairs, to the private suites above the taproom. Unlocking the door with my own key, I pushed it open and with an elegant gesture, ushered Grace into the room.

To say I was surprised by George is an understatement. He was reading, by the light of a lantern, a book I'd left during my last visit. He rose as Grace entered the room, and by the time I'd closed the door behind us, she was in his arms.

When at last he detached himself from Grace's lips, I saw that George was possessed of most unfortunate looks, but equally evident was his very gentle manner.

The fact that he clearly worshipped Grace, and that she returned his regard, was enough for me. When she introduced Lord Patrick Washburn to Mr George Poole, I was gratified that he respected my title, bowing congenially, without the obsequious fussing that usually accompanied it.

In short, I liked him.

Turning to Grace, I said, "It's ten minutes before midnight. I will come back at three o'clock. Be ready to ride back to Broughton Hall."

"I will," she said, embracing me. "*Ti ringrazio, mio caro.* Thank you so much. You are a very dear man, Patrick."

I refused to blush again, but turned away quickly just in case, leaving them alone together.

Out in the hall, I drifted down the stairs into the taproom, settling myself in a secluded corner where I could relax against a wall, unobserved and alone. When the bar maid approached, I ordered a large brandy. It arrived promptly, placed on the table before me with a plate of bread and cheese.

It was a little past two when I was awakened by a soft hand in my hair.

"Huh?"

"Milord? 'tis me, Molly Starling."

"Hello Molly. You looking for Sir Simon? He's not here tonight."

"I know 'e's not 'ere. I been watchin' yer sleep for an hour and more."

I stretched and looked around. The taproom was empty but for a snoring drunk sprawled along a bench. "I didn't mean to sleep. I must have been more tired than I thought. I'll be leaving soon."

She gave me a sly look. "Yer could come 'ome wi' me if yer wantin' to sleep."

I deliberately misunderstood her invitation. "Thank you, but I sleep better at home."

"Yer certain o' tha'?" With a fluidity of movement that suggested she'd done it before, she slid onto the table before me, hiked her skirt and spread her legs.

The sight before me was the stuff of every man's fantasy. I groaned as my body reacted without thought. Sweat broke on my lip and my riding breeches grew uncomfortably tight. Molly was one of Simon's regular doxies and close as my stepbrother and I were, I had no desire to plough his field.

"Alright, Molly, that's enough." I moved her leg aside and slid off my seat.

"Why milord?" she asked, reaching for my belt. "Sir Simon's beautiful an' all, but all't lassies talk about yer! They says yer not easy to get, but worth it when they do because yer—"

"Not interested."

"Oh no! That's no' what they says. They—"

"Enough, Molly. Why don't you go home, eh? I'm not in the mood tonight."

"Yer prick says otherwise." She made a grab for my swollen crotch, but I sidestepped.

"I'm saying no."

She pouted. "Can't blame me fer tryin'."

I laughed. "I would never do that – and one day I may even take up your offer but not tonight." I inclined my head politely, "Goodnight, Molly."

I reflected wryly that had it been anyone other than Molly I might have considered her invitation. Now, though, there was no way I could go upstairs and collect Grace in my current state.

The knowledge of what she was probably doing up there didn't lessen my condition. Relief would be welcome, I decided, but I was not inclined to change my mind and return to Molly.

The walk out of the back of the Red Fox to the stables was awkward and uncomfortable. The place itself was black as pitch and devoid of humans.

At this hour of the morning, the stable-boys were snoring contentedly in their loft. The horses shuffled and gently whuffed in their stalls. No one was about. Through the dark, I made out what looked like a bucket. Grasping it by the handle, I groped my way back out into the yard.

First, I took the precaution of removing my riding coat and shirt. Then, naked to the waist in the darkest hours before dawn, I plunged the bucket into the horse trough, filling it, and without another thought, dumped the entire contents over my head.

"*Nah*, Christ!" I growled through clenched teeth.

The water was not exactly fresh and was no doubt heavily laced with horse slobber, but it had the desired effect.

Shaking myself like a dog, I dropped the bucket back into the trough and reached for my clothes.

"Milord?" the voice came from behind me. One of the lads stood in the stable doorway, eyeing me curiously. "Yer alright, sir?"

"Yes, thank you. Could you please prepare my horse and my er ... sister's horse?"

"Cert'ly milord."

I was buttoning my shirt as I knocked on Grace's door. George opened it – he was also buttoning his shirt. He stood back to let me in, eyeing me curiously.

"Patrick!" Grace exclaimed. "What—"

"You're dripping on the floor, man." George raised an eyebrow but I merely grinned at him and turned to his companion.

"You ready, Grace?"

She was sitting on the bed lacing her boots. "*Si.*"

I busied myself putting on my coat while she and George said their goodbyes, then we were quickly down the stairs and back out to the stables.

We didn't speak until we were beyond the boundary of Wolstone and surrounded by open fields.

She twisted in the saddle to look at me. "Why are you wet?"

I smiled to myself. "I was putting out a fire. How was your evening with George?"

She grinned wickedly. "I also was putting out a fire."

SOBRIETY - YOU ARE NOT MY FRIEND

Simon had a hangover. A terrific source of amusement for me because I didn't have a hangover. I haven't had one for almost two months after discovering that I rather enjoyed sobriety, particularly while others settled well into their cups and were destined for the kind of suffering Simon was currently undergoing.

I glanced to where he sprawled in the grass, one arm flung over his eyes, a dandelion stem between his teeth. He'd woken up considerably the worse for wear today, and after picking disinterestedly at his dinner, he'd suggested that he, Alex and I go for an afternoon walk through the Broughton Hall forest.

I understood his motivation was to escape the cloying social environment of his mother and her friends back at the house. While the afternoon was warm, the forest offered a tranquil environment, even if it was not as cool as we'd have liked.

I smiled to myself – I was smug with temperance and robust good health!

Not only had I been sober for a while, but I hadn't bedded a woman since ending my arrangement with Maud. Time enough to debauch myself once Simon and I returned to Oxford. For now, I *wanted* to remain sober.

Propped on one elbow beneath a tree, I leaned back to watch a bird on a branch above me. She was holding her wings out to gain some relief from the heat, and beyond her, on a higher branch, was a nest. I wondered if there were hatchlings in there.

Feeling eyes on me, I turned and met my stepsister's lovely brown gaze. I smiled at her, slightly amused, slightly uneasy, about the flush that rose up her neck.

For there was a tension between Alex and me these days, of a quality that I had little practice with. The tone and nature of our banter held an underlying note of something that set alarm bells ringing in my brain.

And I knew why. I was attracted to her – not in a brotherly way – and my attraction was clearly reciprocated – not in a sisterly way.

Alex was ingenuous and being inexperienced in the teasing games women often play, her every thought was written in bold lettering across her face. Yet for my own sanity, it was imperative that she never should suspect that I regarded her differently than the way I regarded my sister, Maeve.

But I have caught myself watching Alex, enjoying the fluid vigour of her lithe, young form. Unlike the soft-bodied, pretentious drawing-room misses of my acquaintance, Alex was honest and irreverent. I love that she climbs trees, I love that she runs barefoot through the gardens and park, I love that she is hot-headed and passionate.

As we lingered in the warmth of the afternoon, she was sitting with her back against a tree, a book of sonnets on her lap. I was aware that I'd made her uncomfortable when I smiled – she had blushed and bowed her head.

Alex was attracted to me, she may even harbour a girlish fancy for me, and as the knowledge produced a ridiculous little flutter in my chest, I mentally shook myself. *You're behaving like an unkissed schoolboy!*

Yet it was true: I wanted to hear her laugh. I wanted to see her smile. I enjoyed lying in the grass with her, playing my Strad ... in Maeve's words, I was becoming silly as an old maid.

Perhaps the sooner I returned to Oxford, the better for all concerned. I was going to plunge myself into an orgy of fine brandy and energetic sex and put all thoughts of my stepsister behind me.

Yet she was pretty, and entirely unaware of the fact, for beside the dazzling beauty of her brother and sister, she could be considered plain. But in her own right, she was *very* pretty. Her hair was a messy cloud about her face as though she'd just been tumbled by a lover. Her arms were toned and strong, and unfashionably sun-browned. Her young bosom swelled above the neckline of her yellow summer gown and as we sat, a silent companionable trio, my mouth grew dry.

Suddenly, I wanted to touch her – I wanted to press my lips to the supple flesh of her throat and breathe deeply the clean, womanly scent of her, and it was my turn to grow hot in the face.

Shocked by my own reaction, I rolled onto my back, turning my face away. For the first time, I'd looked at my stepsister in a way that was not platonic – I wanted *her* ... and the wanting left me feeling uncomfortably aware of the inappropriateness of my thoughts.

In that moment, I knew I had to withdraw from her entirely – perhaps spend more time with Grace. And if Alex believed that my sham relationship with Grace was as genuine as I hoped her mother believed, all the better.

Alex may be hurt – but I couldn't help that. I hoped she grew out of her infatuation; it was dangerous for both of us.

As for me, abstinence could go to hell. I needed to get foxed and fuck someone.

ॐ

The tavern was dark and smoky. Simon was at a table across the room, in discussion with one of his tenants while two others shuffled about, waiting their turn. One of them turned to a woman beside him and her eyes slid in my direction. As the man spoke, she nodded and left his side.

Eyes levelled on me, she approached, and paused before my table with arms folded somewhat protectively beneath a shelf of a bosom. "Milord Washburn?"

I rose politely and inclined my head. Her face was rather plain but she was clean, her hair combed and covered with a neat little headscarf. Intelligent grey eyes sized me up shrewdly, even though she seemed anxious about something.

"I'm Maud's aunt." She smiled timidly at me. "Name mean owt t' yer? She's the daughter of me older sister."

"Oh yes, I know Maud. Am I in trouble, then?" I offered my most charming smile – to no effect.

Her eyes darted to the man across the room. "He sent me over 'ere to talk wi' yer."

I resumed my seat and slid across the bench, indicating the empty space beside me. She sat and rested her elbows on the table; I waited for her to speak.

The sense of her there caused my stomach to clench. I closed my eyes and could feel the soft warmth of her through my clothing. Breathing steadily, I tried to calm my heartbeat and distract myself by watching my stepbrother, but my traitorous body had other plans ... God, how long has it been since I was last with Maud ...?

"I've a proposition fer yer ..." the woman spoke, and I took another breath, exhaling slowly. "Not one I'm 'appy with, I might add. But, 'im over there ..." she nodded in the direction of the man across the room, "'E's asked me ter speak t'yer ... well, times are difficult, yer understand."

The back of my neck prickled like it sometimes does when I

was about to find myself in an unfavourable situation. I momentarily put aside my lecherous thoughts and took another sip of ale. My face was a blank mask when I turned to her.

The intensity of my green eyes often intimidates people. Using this to best advantage, I regarded her unblinkingly and waited.

The first to look away, but not diverted from her course, she clasped her hands in her lap and stared down at them. Without raising her eyes, she said, "It's like this, milord ... yer arrangement ... what yer had goin' on wi' Maud ... it helped me sister a great deal."

Now, she looked up at her husband, then quickly back down, continuing before she could lose confidence. "Me younger sister ... she's a virgin, yer see an' ... we, well we hoped ... we was thinkin'—"

I don't know what I'd been expecting her to say, but it wasn't that. Surprised, I pulled back to look at her as the outrageousness of her proposition slowly registered. I stared incredulously at her. "You're proposing to sell your sister's virginity? To me?"

My voice was calm, softly modulated and she raised her eyes to meet mine ... and shrank before the look on my face.

"I ... we ..." she rose and stood beside the bench, her face a picture of horror. "It's desperate, we are, milord ... an' me sister was sayin' what a relief havin' Maud out of the house fer a time an ..."

"Get out of my sight!" I growled, but to my abject irritation, she burst into tears.

"Oh Christ!" I blew out my breath and ran a hand through my hair, took up the tankard and gulped down the last of the ale. Snapping my fingers at a passing serving maid, I ordered, "Brandy – bring the bottle and two glasses!" Then I turned to the woman still standing beside the table, tears dribbling down her face. "Sit! For God's sake."

She obeyed, sniffing and dabbing at her eyes with the edge of her overskirt.

"What's your husband petitioning Sir Simon about?" I asked.

"He's not me 'usband. He's me *father* ... he's askin' Sir Simon fer work."

"Don't you have land? A harvest to bring in?"

"Aye, but I can do that. Me 'n' me boy."

"So you have a son? Where's *his* father?"

"Dead, milord. Came off 'is horse last winter – broke 'is neck."

The brandy arrived and I poured two glasses, handing her one. "Here. It'll do you good."

"Thank yer, milord," she took a larger than intended gulp and her eyes streamed again.

"I'm not going to bed your sister." I tasted the brandy. Not the finest I'd had but passable. "And I can't believe *he* – the girl's own father – would consider such a thing."

"Was 'is idea," she indicated her father with a nod of her head. "But me older sister says nice things o'yer. She says 'ow yer treated Maud right kindly."

"Too fucking kindly if you ask me." I muttered.

The woman gave a snort of laughter. "I'm glad yer refused, milord, an' me father won't be sayin' I didn't ask."

"Will he give you trouble over it?"

She shrugged and swallowed the last of her brandy. "Oh, 'e'll rant 'n' rave but 'e won't throw us out. We had t' move in with 'im when me Albert died."

I drained my glass and refilled both. An idea was formulating – an idea that I was not exactly proud of but one that might fulfil both our needs.

"What's your name?"

"Jilly."

"Well, Jilly. How much money do you need?"

I'd spoken just as she was about to swallow. She spluttered her brandy but the disbelief on her face swiftly changed to a coy smile.

She was quick, I'll give her that.

"Milord," she took another sip, weighing her answer, "that'll depend on what yer proposing t'invest against what yer expectin' t'get back."

My laughter caused a number of heads to turn in our direction but I ignored them. Rising, I bowed to her as though bidding farewell, and whispered, "Meet me in the lane outside in five minutes."

I threw down the last of the brandy in my glass and turned, "Don't leave that bottle behind," I said over my shoulder as I left.

∾

The lane was filthy. Broken crates, kitchen waste, horse shit and assorted, indiscernible forms of refuse lay about. Jilly and I shared the brandy, passing the bottle back and forth between us, discussing a fair price and agreeing on our terms.

She was direct in her negotiations, speaking plainly and setting expectations –a born businesswoman. "You've done this before." It was a statement, not unkindly meant, but she dropped her gaze.

"It's a hard life ... a woman alone in t'world tryin' t'feed her family. I reckon I've done alright. Just don't judge me, milord."

I raised her head with a finger beneath her chin. "I would never judge you. I know privilege I haven't earned. It's not for me to judge anyone."

She smiled and it made her face rather comely. "They do say yer a nice man."

I snorted at that and she went on, "They also say yer don't like no one knowin' yer a nice man."

That made me laugh out loud and she smiled again. "Shall we get down t' business, milord?"

She pushed me against the brick wall of the lane, pressing her substantial breasts into my chest, and proceeded to unlace my breeches. Her hand was rough and work-worn; the sensation, when she handled me, was extraordinarily arousing.

"Mmm, not so quick!" I removed her hand, then taking her by the shoulders, exchanged places with her, turning her to face the wall. I began unbuttoning the back of her gown, loosening it so that it hung open and I could reach in, and around, and grasp those pendulous breasts in my hands.

She made appreciative noises, as I pushed my groin against her bum. "Christ," I murmured into her neck, "my hands aren't big enough for your tits!"

She giggled and turned in my arms and raised her skirt.

She was not wearing bloomers. "*Oh Jesus,*" I groaned – my erection was beginning to hurt – I plunged into her.

It had definitely been way too long, but I held as long as I could, both of us breathing hard, writhing and thrashing against the wall ... until her muscles clenched and her cries reached a crescendo.

I paused; allowing her a moment, then quickly withdrew. She dropped to her knees and took me in her mouth – and almost immediately I gasped, shuddered and released.

ॐ

"Here," I handed her the brandy bottle and she took a swig, swished and spat.

Having rearranged my clothing and laced up my breeches, I leaned against the wall and pulled Jilly backwards into my arms. She rested against me and passed the brandy bottle back. I drank deeply and dropped my chin on top of her head.

"Milord?"

"Hmm?"

"It were kind o' yer t'ave a care fer my pleasure."

I gave a grunt. "Never let it be said I'm not fair in my business dealings."

"Milord?"

"Oh for God's sake, Jilly. Use my first name, hmm?"

"I suppose, milord. What is it?"

I sighed. "Never mind. So what did you want to say?"

She squirmed a little in my arms. "They's right, yer know."

"What about?"

"They say yer a nice man, but don't yer worry – I won't be tellin' no one."

∾

"I'm going to Wolstone," Simon told me. "I'm seeing the saddler about new tack for Oliver. Join me?"

We rode out together in the afternoon sunshine – I figured Simon's plans included more than just a visit to the saddler, and since I had no plans of my own, I decided to go along.

"What are you looking for at the saddler's?" I asked as we trotted our horses along the lane to Wolstone.

"I'm not really sure ... Catarina told me about the saddles they have in Italy – the cantle is shaped differently so the rider sits further forward."

"Which makes for ... greater balance? Comfort?"

"I don't know, and she couldn't tell me since she's not familiar with *our* saddles. I thought I might talk to the saddler about having one made so I could decide for myself."

I considered that for a few minutes, then Simon added, "Catarina sketched a picture. Might be more comfortable if I'm to be spending long hours riding."

Watching me, he waited for me to pick up on his clues. Finally, I gave in to him. "When we join up, you'll be going as a physician, won't you?"

He nodded. "I plan to, but military hospitals move around from location to location. If the Italian saddles are more comfortable, why not?"

"You won't be taking Oliver to Spain, I trust?" I regarded his horse through narrowed eyes. Oliver was a gentle, happy-natured horse, with a leaning toward plumpness and complacency.

Simon laughed and patted Oliver's neck. "No more than you would take Equus."

I grinned. He was right – there was no way I'd consider taking Equus to war.

The bridge into Wolstone was visible about a mile in the distance and the road was good. "Come on," I challenged, "race you to the bridge."

A quick kick to Equus's sides and she launched into a gallop. I gave her her head as we streaked down the lane; my hair, and her tail and mane flying, hooves pounding.

Two minutes later we arrived at the bridge, blowing and exhilarated. Behind us, Simon had managed to urge Oliver into a reluctant canter. By the time they joined us, Equus was cropping the grass on the bank of the river and I'd dismounted and was leaning against a tree.

❧

I'd hoped not to meet anyone we knew. I'd hoped in vain. No sooner had we left the saddler's than we met one of Simon's tenants, Mr Jacob. His *quick word if yer don' mind, Sir Simon*, turned into a lengthy discourse on the cost of repairs he'd had made to the grinding wheel in his mill.

Simon congratulated the man on having the work done in time for harvest, asked how his new Harrogate customers were going, and upon a favourable report, bade the man farewell.

As evening closed in, we dismounted outside The Cockerel and handed our reins to the waiting lad. Simon entered first, banging his head on the low lintel. He was an inch or so taller than I, but I was still forced to duck.

"Nice souvenir." I commented and he scowled in reply,

rubbing the reddening lump on his forehead.

Almost immediately we sat, I realised we'd chosen the wrong public house for there, leaning on the bar, was Jilly's father. He stood upright – bloody giant of a man, he was – and began weaving a drunken path towards us.

"Not grinning now, are you," Simon said with a smirk.

I groaned and looked up into the man's angry, unshaven face.

"You defiled my daughter!" He declared through gritted teeth.

I rolled my eyes. "I'd hardly say *defiled* – she has a son."

Simon gave a mirthless laugh. "Don't rile him."

"But it's true, she *does* have a child. Besides, who are you to throw stones? You tried to sell your other daughter, remember!"

"You toffs are all the same! You took advantage o' me daughter."

"It was a business transaction, and if I'm not mistaken, one that left her well satisfied – *fuckin' hell*!"

The man had balled his great meaty fists and planted a facer on me.

Simon laughed. "I warned you."

Rubbing my jaw, I climbed out of my seat and looked up at him, and by that I mean I tilted my head back to look up at him. Christ he was big! "Alright," I said, "I'll take that – I probably deserved—"

Whack!

I landed on my arse on the floor.

"Jesus! I *didn't* deserve that!" I gasped, slowly dragging myself up. I could taste blood and my vision was slightly blurred.

Simon was no longer laughing.

"Whatcha gonna do 'bout it?" the man demanded.

I was swaying on my feet. "There's probably not a lot I *can* do about it ... except—" I took a quick step back and struck twice with my left fist in rapid succession, and followed through with a right hook to his jaw.

When he raised his fist to retaliate, I ducked in beneath and elbowed him hard in the solar plexus.

He dropped to his knees, gasping.

"And *you* didn't deserve *that*," I said leaning over him, my hand resting on his shoulder to steady myself. With the exertion, I was on the verge of blacking out. "Sometimes it's better if you're the smaller fellow," I told Simon, before the man and I both crumpled to the floor.

∾

It was late when Simon knocked on Grace's bedroom door. There was no answer from within, so he opened the door and supported me into her room.

My head was spinning, and I felt rather ill, but he dumped me unceremoniously into a chair and approached the girl's bed. "Grace!" he whispered.

She rolled over, bleary eyed, half asleep. "*Simon, che cosè?*"

"Patrick needs your help ... please. Can you get up? He asked me to bring him to you."

Without hesitation, she slid from her bed and while Simon lit her lamp, she padded over to me.

Simon brought the lamp to my side and I squinted away from the light. "*Dio!*" Grace breathed. "Your face ... *cosa successo? Una donna, no?*"

"Yes," I admitted. "A woman – and a rather costly one too."

Turning to Simon, Grace said, "Do not worry, I will look after him."

"If you're certain."

I felt as though I was falling into a stupor, although I knew I hadn't drunk very much. As I relaxed in the chair, I grew drowsier, and I heard Simon, as if under water, suggest that I might have a concussion.

"*Si,* I know you are *il dottore.*" Grace said. "I will watch him tonight. He will be alright."

Satisfied, Simon left the room, closing the door silently behind him, and Grace knelt at my side.

"*Dio, mio caro.* When will you learn?" She pressed a kiss to my forehead, smoothing aside my hair. "Silly man!"

I tried to smile, but it hurt and I grimaced instead. But she'd leaned over me when she'd kissed me and I could tell she was naked beneath the sheer nightgown – and she smelled lovely, like soap and something exotic. It was making me giddy.

Curling my arm about her, I pulled her close and murmured into her neck, "You smell delicious."

"And you are *pazzo*." She giggled and pulled away, returning moments later with a bowl of water and a clean cloth from her washstand.

I was only dimly aware that she was bathing my face. At some point she removed my shoes and shirt, and there followed a hazy recollection of her wrangling me into bed.

∾

From what Grace told me, when I awoke the next morning, holding her in my arms with my nose pressed firmly between her breasts, I'd slept like a baby. I hoped she didn't mean that I'd tried to suckle from her – but by the teasing look on her face I assumed I hadn't.

From what Simon told me, the family was none the wiser, as they were accustomed to my irregular comings and goings. He kept watch on the hall to ensure nobody saw me sneak from Grace's room to my own, and there I remained until the following day – until I'd grown enough beard stubble to hide the bruising on my face.

COLLATERAL DAMAGE

"You want to bed her, don't you?"

Patrick spun around to face his sister, genuinely outraged. "What the hell does that mean? You have a filthy mind, Maeve. It's high time you—"

"Give over, brother." She tossed her head. "I know you better than anyone. You find her attractive ... I can tell."

"That doesn't mean I want to *bed* her. Give me some credit."

"Credit for what? *Not* bedding her?"

Maeve and her brother were strolling through Broughton Hall's gardens. He was returning to Oxford the next day and there had been talk about Maeve going to Italy with Isabella and her daughters.

The siblings were taking the opportunity to talk privately – neither knew when they'd see one another again.

Patrick sighed through his nose. "Look, she's very pretty – I'll grant you that I find Alex attractive. But she's a sixteen-year-old virgin who also happens to be my stepsister."

"So what you're really saying is that if she were some slattern from Wolstone, whose mother wasn't married to our father, you'd consider bedding her?"

Her brother's indignation was wearing off, although the accuracy of his interfering little sister's observation continued to rile him.

Attempting to lighten the tone of their rather inappropriate discussion, he said, "Ah, now you're losing your touch." He threw her a wolfish grin. "If she were some slattern from Wolstone, whose mother was not married to our father, I'd *already* have bedded her."

Maeve gave a snort of vindication.

"*And* the mother," he added, with a wink.

"Well, doesn't that prove my point – that you're without a shred of decency?"

Her brother merely smiled, and as they changed direction, he narrowed his eyes against the afternoon sun, and they continued their walk in companionable silence.

Patrick could make light of her accusations all he liked, but Maeve knew what she'd seen – and she'd seen it often enough in recent weeks to be uncomfortable about it. He could pretend that he was courting Grace Camelleri, but he couldn't fool his sister. She knew her brother too well, and she'd seen him demonstrate such tenderness toward Alex, as to attract his sister's consternation.

Maeve remembered watching him outside the dining room the other day. Arriving late for supper, she'd come across her brother and stepsister in the hall – Alex had evidently been crying, and Patrick was talking softly to her.

From where Maeve remained hidden, she could clearly see Patrick's face, and as one who knows him, she saw not only kindness, but genuine affection. And for the briefest of moments, Maeve was certain Patrick was about to kiss the girl.

But it would not have been a lustful kiss for there was tenderness in his expression and instead, he'd brushed a stray hair from Alex's face, and smoothed away her tears.

That Patrick had ordinarily reserved such intimate expressions for Maeve alone, and was now including Alex in his inner sphere, was not Maeve's concern, because Maeve was not a girl to harbour jealousies.

That Patrick was expressing himself so intimately to *anyone* troubled Maeve because she alone knew that her brother enjoyed women – far more than was appropriate – and any liaison with Alex would inevitably lead to the girl's grief and an ignominious drama within the family.

She did not worry that Patrick might be in love with their stepsister – she knew he was too shallow for that ... it was doubtful he would ever understand what true love was.

Hadn't he thought he was in love with that Mary girl he wrote about? And what about that ... *whatsername* he had dallied with in Ireland when they last visited their cousin, Aden?

No – Patrick was impervious to *real* love, although Maeve secretly hoped her brother would someday genuinely fall heavily in love, with a deserving woman, who would love him in return.

She smiled to herself. Knowing her brother, falling in love would not go easy for him – so it was just as well that he lived as he did.

Meanwhile, Maeve was aware that her brother's interest in drinking and carousing with Simon had waned; he seemed content to remain at home more often. And she felt the suppressed tension in him – he was strung as tightly as his violin.

She sensed a growing desperation within him to be on the road and back to Oxford before ... she knew not what, but she sincerely hoped that if he weakened for a moment and took any girl to bed, it would be the Italian lass, Grace.

Rake he may be, led by his manhood most certainly, but stupid? No, she wouldn't believe that!

∾

Simon sat on Oliver's back. He'd said his farewells to his sisters and stepsister, doled out hugs and kisses, and was now eager to be off and on the road to Oxford.

His mother and her friend stood, heads bent together, gossiping, as was their wont. Simon wondered why they bothered making an appearance at all.

A cool breeze suddenly gusted and he shivered slightly pulling up the collar of his riding coat. He was not generally the impatient type, but Patrick was taking his sweet-arsed time saying goodbye.

Simon looked over to where his stepbrother stood with Zan. Patrick had taken both her hands in his leathered ones and was speaking directly to her. By his expression and Zan's response, his words were serious and meant for her ears alone, and Simon gnawed at the inside of his cheek as he watched.

Zan was vulnerable and she was naive. She had also, Simon was aware, surrendered her original aversion toward their stepbrother. This fact had originally caused Simon some amusement – considering how fiercely she'd resented Patrick and his coming to live with them – but it was now giving him reason for concern, because as Simon watched, his stepbrother leaned in and said something, and she responded in kind.

There was closeness between them that went beyond what he might have considered normal for siblings – and Zan, sheltered as she was, was probably reading more into it than she should.

Patrick wasn't the sort of friend his naive sister ought to have, and Simon decided that upon arriving in Oxford, he would write to their mother to ensure Zan got to meet new people in the county.

She needed friends. Her one friend, Julia, was loyal and true, but Zan was a girl on the brink of womanhood. She needed to get out more!

In any event, Patrick seemed to be behaving respectably, as he should when dealing with a sister. He was grinning at her, kissing both her cheeks before pulling her into his arms in a brotherly embrace.

Releasing her abruptly, Patrick turned, jogged down the porch steps and headed towards his horse and Simon breathed again, satisfied that if Alex held a fancy for the young lord, it was neither reciprocated nor encouraged, and she was young enough to grow out of it.

Until that moment, Simon hadn't noticed Grace standing beside Equus; but now, as Patrick approached, the girl flushed hotly. Simon had only a heartbeat to realise something was amiss, as Patrick marched purposefully toward the girl, took her in his arms and kissed her.

"Hmph," Simon grunted, watching as Grace's head fell back into his stepbrother's cupped palm, their mouths fused together, and their arms wrapped around one another. "Didn't see that coming."

Patrick kissed Grace as deeply and ardently as a passionate lover would do.

While Simon's mother and Grace's mother had stopped their prattling, and Anne and Maeve had set up an indelicate whooping and cheering, Simon had a moment to consider that perhaps his stepbrother and their house guest were lovers.

Was that why Patrick had been less interested in the village girls of late? *He never said anything to me about it.*

So long did the two cling together that Simon began to feel rather voyeuristic in watching them. Shifting uncomfortably in his saddle, he turned away, eyes falling on his sister's face, and Simon's humour was rapidly replaced with trepidation.

For Zan had never been one to hide her feelings, and her feelings were plain for all to see; she was deeply, profoundly hurt.

If he's having a liaison with Grace, why the devil has he not told Zan? If he's been leading her on …

Simon didn't finish the thought, for the object of his irritation had finally broken his embrace and swung into his horse's saddle.

Doffing his hat, Patrick wheeled Equus' head around, and without a single thought for the young girl whose stricken face continued to stare after him, Patrick rode up beside Oliver and the two horses were under way.

∾

That evening, in the parlour, Maeve shared the settee with Grace. Both girls bent their heads over their needlework; Grace was working on a rather technical piece of embroidery while Maeve was repairing a torn sleeve on one of her dresses.

Leaning towards a lamp, Maeve squinted over her work. It was starting to get too dark to see what she was doing and she let her hands drop to her lap. The dress lay in a puddle of soft blue wool across her knees.

The room was silent but for the scratching of Anne's pen. She was seated at a small table – it looked like she was writing a letter. Alex and Catarina were reading, the countess and Isabella were sipping glasses of Muscat by the window, while the countess's companion, the silent, imposing Eleanor watched – her own glass of Muscat sitting on a table at her side.

The gathering was distinctly feminine, discussions were whispered, movements slow, gestures a study in elegance, and suddenly Maeve was thinking of her brother.

Patrick's thirst for adventure was a concern to Maeve. She knew that he found living in Oxford and attending the university mind-numbingly dull. And she knew that he was planning to enlist in the war – she just didn't know when.

That he was involved with the girl sharing her settee, was a surprise to Maeve. She'd have wagered a year's allowance that his relaxed intimacy with the girl was pretence or game.

Yet if he was serious about her ...

Maeve wondered how she could have judged her brother so inaccurately. She'd never have guessed he was involved with shy little Grace, and the fact that he hadn't told her drew Maeve's displeasure, for Maeve and her brother had shared confidences and adventures for as long as she could remember.

They were close; having no mother, and a frequently absent father, resulted in the two coming to rely on one another more than most siblings.

Maeve was aware of her brother's libertine lifestyle; she knew that he frequented inns and whorehouses. Over the years, she had learned to ignore his bumps, scrapes and occasional blackened eyes.

She forgave him because he was intelligent, generous and kind, witty and wicked, and she loved him unconditionally.

But this evening, she could happily throttle him because Maeve was angry. She'd been deceived and betrayed – her brother had told her nothing about this. And this, it seemed, was a romantic understanding with Grace.

What kind of understanding was it, anyway? Surely he was not planning to wed the girl?

Maeve's eyes slid sideways, noting that the girl seated beside her appeared tense and expectant. *Yes, sooner or later they're going to question you,* Maeve thought, with pity. *He dumped you in this jam and left you to answer for it.*

Feeling eyes on her, Grace turned to look at her companion.

Maeve smiled, and taking the opportunity to open the conversation, she leaned over and spoke, in her usual forthright manner, "I did not know you had an understanding with my brother."

Grace flushed and bowed her head, returning to her embroidery. Maeve watched the needle move in and out, punching through the fabric, aware of the passage of the other girl's thoughts by the expressions crossing her face.

Finally, the Italian girl looked up, a bold determination in her dark eyes. "I would like to tell you," she whispered conspiratorially, adding, "your brother said, that you would be the only one I could trust."

"I should like to think so," Maeve rejoined. "What has he been up to now?"

Grace leaned close to Maeve's ear and explained her arrangement with Patrick.

"I hoped that in pretending to have an understanding with him, I would be able to remain in England," she said, making no mention of her reason why.

"Your brother hoped," Grace went on, "that your stepmother would stop reminding him of his duty toward marriage and attempting to ..." she shot a quick glance across the room to where Anne sat, thoughtfully chewing her lip and gazing into space, "contract him to certain ladies."

So I was right ... it was a pretence, after all! Maeve thought. "Oh, this is simply marvy!" she said, with a devious smile. "Such fun! But he could have told me."

"I am telling you now," Grace said, with a wily smile of her own. "May I rely on your help? We must be convincing."

"Why, of course! I'd love nothing more!" And immediately, Maeve sat upright and released an excited squeal, and began chanting, "*Grace and Patrick, Grace and Patrick*! Do you think he will ask for your hand?"

As though choreographed, the other girl flushed with embarrassment and Maeve was satisfied that the countess and her guest believed the ploy.

Everyone in the room seemed to accept that Patrick was courting Grace; even Alex, who snapped her book shut and left the room in a pout.

☙

The two young men rode in silence, each lost in his own thoughts, for several miles. At length, Patrick turned to his stepbrother, "By your silence, I imagine you're waiting for me to tell you what is going on with Grace."

Simon drew in his breath and didn't reply immediately; he was still trying to understand his own thoughts, namely, why he felt such anger toward his stepbrother.

Finally he said, "There are two things I need to understand."

Patrick gestured for him to continue.

"Were you and Grace ... did you ...?" Simon's meaning was clear.

"After everything we've done and been through in the last few years, you still can't ask me a direct question."

Simon laughed lightly through his nose. "You know what I'm asking."

"You want to know if I took Grace to my bed?" Patrick paused and nodded to himself. "What would anger you more – that I was swiving one of your house guests, or simply that you didn't know about it?"

Simon glared at him but didn't respond. He knew his stepbrother very well and knew that Pat was provoking him. Patrick had not taken Grace for a lover – he would not be needling him now if he had.

Patrick grinned at him. "Of course she and I were not lovers. You already knew that. We have never been intimate, we never intend to be, and that kiss you witnessed was the first and only kiss we've ever exchanged."

Simon raised his eyebrows quizzically and his brother continued. "That little scene was for the benefit of Grace's mother and my stepmother. Purely so that Grace could stay in England after Isabella returns to Italy, and so that your mother will cease and desist her attempts to construct an arrangement between Anne and me."

"So," Simon summarised, "the entire show was contrived."

"Completely. Grace has a lover – a chap named George. Her mother won't approve but Grace and George are determined to be together. Grace needs a reason to stay in England – let them all think that I'm the reason. Works for both of us."

Simon eyed him suspiciously. "You spent a night in her bed, perhaps more than one."

"Only one, and I was totally abstemious."

"You did not touch her?"

"I did not touch her."

"Very disciplined of you," Simon conceded.

"Exactly. So why do you look as if you're about to skewer me?"

"Because of Zan. You didn't see her face as we left."

Patrick frowned, thoughtfully. He was silent, watching the road ahead for some moments. No, he hadn't seen her face – he'd deliberately avoided it, knowing the grief he'd see there and unwilling to witness it.

Hurting Alex was the last thing he ever wanted to do, but at the same time, Patrick needed to cauterise his own growing attraction for the girl before things got out of hand.

He'd almost kissed her recently when she'd been upset. He'd also caught himself admiring her healthy young body, in a not particularly brotherly fashion. He knew he must detach himself before his admiration became more than a young man's fancy for a pretty girl.

If, in the process of carrying out this farce with Grace, he had caused his stepsister to regard him unfavourably, it was all the better, for Alex was young, her fancy for him would, doubtless, be a passing thing.

Let her consider him a cad and put him from her mind.

He and Grace had decided to kiss before the gathering for maximum impact; it had achieved that result and Patrick was satisfied – some collateral damage could not be avoided. Alex would be alright – besides, she was betrothed now.

The two young men continued to ride in silence, their hips attuned to their horses' stride. They passed fields of yellowing wheat and barley, ready for harvest, without seeing them. Neither did they notice the cows and sheep in the paddocks, for the brothers were lost in thought.

Finally, drawing a long breath in through his nose Simon said, "Zan is growing up, Pat. She has little enough contact with the world outside of Broughton Hall – she sees you as a friend. You obviously did not tell her what you and Grace had concocted, so like everyone else, she must believe the two of you are courting. She will no doubt feel betrayed that you didn't confide in her."

Patrick frowned and settled his emerald gaze on his stepbrother. "Is that what you think?"

Simon looked genuinely perplexed. "Of course. Why else would she have been so upset? Anyway, even if she thinks she has some little fancy for you, she's betrothed. She needs to start growing up sometime."

"Indeed ..." Patrick murmured.

DARK PLACES

Patrick sighed and stretched his arms over his head. The details of the legal case Hennessy v Childrick that had been argued in the Court of Chancery during the spring of 1802, were beginning to blur before his eyes.

His neck ached from leaning over the text and his head was pounding with the effects of straining to read by the light of a flickering candle.

What the hell am I doing?

He pushed his chair back and rose, arching his back with a loud cracking sound as the vertebra adjusted. The clock in the downstairs hallway chimed the quarter hour – quarter of what? he wondered. He'd lost track of time while ploughing through the mundane details of the case the university lecturer had set for his students to read.

"Like wading through porridge," he murmured. He was upstairs in the spare bedroom that he and Simon had converted to use as a study. It was furnished with two desks, chairs and a cabinet for their books, a sideboard and a settee. Hours earlier, he'd banked the fire for the night, but had continued, stubbornly, with his reading; studies that he hated.

Now, he was cold, tired, his muscles stiff and sore, and he was irritable.

And more than anything, he was sick of studying the law. He'd promised Simon another year before they bought their commissions and joined the war on the Peninsula, and determined as he was to honour that promise, he was finding it increasingly difficult.

I could, he reasoned, *leave the university and remain at Devon until Simon was ready.* It was an appealing notion.

More often these days, he found his thoughts drifting toward quitting the university. He was wasting his time and his father was wasting his money. Patrick was aware that the only reason his father wanted him to study was to give him some focus – but the law? Seriously! It's not as if he would ever practice it so what was the point? Besides, he was more than happy to focus his attentions on the running of his estates down south.

The room had grown chilly as the bright orange glow of the coals in the grate had gradually dimmed, and finally lay dull, ashy and dead. With a shiver, he reached for the decanter of brandy on the sideboard, poured a tot and threw it back in one gulp, and stood facing the window. It looked out over the rear of his house, where there were a small courtyard and stables, but in the wee hours of the morning nothing was visible – neither stars nor moon; the night was completely lightless.

His reflection stared at him from the black mirror of the glass. In his shirtsleeves, he was tall and slim, though broad across the shoulders. His hair was untidy, resting on his collar and he was unshaven. The hand that clutched the bevelled crystal glass was strong with long, musical fingers and trimmed nails.

Patrick's eyes shifted upwards and he met his own gaze. The intense green was not obvious in the black and white image before him, but his eyes were clearly tired and vaguely troubled, and the source of that trouble lay on the table beside his study books.

He poured another measure of brandy – larger this time – and sat on the edge of his desk. Taking up the single page, he stared at the flowing, curvilinear strings of words.

Broughton Hall
Near Wolstone
Yorkshire
19 November 1810

My dearest brother,

By the lack of news, I assume you arrived in Oxford safely and have returned to your studies.

I trust you are aware that Isabella and her daughters have departed Broughton Hall with the intention of passing the winter in London – Isabella has engineered to have Catarina and Grace presented to His Majesty at Whitehall.

This is, I expect, no news to you, given your friendship with Grace. Ah yes, I did say friendship – you see, your friend confided the little ruse the two of you cooked up and I must say, my dear, that you threw yourself into your role with such enthusiasm that even I was persuaded.

Your parting gesture prompted much feminine speculation that evening, which has continued since.

Our stepmother is sufficiently irritated as to be convinced. Her house guest is sufficiently smug as to be swayed similarly, and as for our stepsisters ... Let me just say that one is baying for your blood while the other grieves.

Which brings me to the point of this mail.

What have you done? Do you even know? Do you care?

When you rode away from Broughton Hall that morning, you left a young woman with her heart in tatters. I had observed, on occasion, a closeness – an understanding perhaps? – between you but I had no idea that you had allowed it to progress as it had.

Our stepsister is naive and inexperienced, she is unhappily betrothed. In short – she is impressionable, and I believe that you have filled her heart with hope and fairy tales, with the result that she now entertains a fancy for you.

My brother, don't misunderstand me, I love you dearly, you know that, yet as I write this, I am most displeased with you and your actions, which can only be described as arrogant and insensitive.

Arrogant because you carried out a fiction to suit your own ends. Insensitive because you cannot possibly deny knowledge of the girl's feelings for you and yet you persisted regardless.

It is true that I originally found our stepsister difficult, but I have changed my attitude and would defend her in this. You lured her with a false pretence and took advantage of her inexperience. Further, you have wounded her most grievously.

Those dalliances that you regularly enjoy with ladies of a particular persuasion have led you to believe that all women are at your disposal, to treat, or mistreat as you choose.

You cannot persist!

I insist that you write to our stepsister and explain your actions and motives at once. She must harbour no false hopes. She is betrothed and must put such girlish fantasies from her head.

Further, you cultivated a companionship with her that has led her to regard you in a particular light and to expect certain confidences. Through your actions you have demonstrated a profound disregard for the sensibilities of others; this child now suffers an intense feeling of betrayal for you did not confide in her.

You must immediately apprise her of the true nature of your relationship both with Grace, and with the girl herself, so as to alleviate such daydreams your overtures have engendered.

With my love and regard, I remain your disappointed and disapproving sister,

Maeve

∾

Patrick still held the glass of brandy in one hand; Maeve's letter was in his other. He dropped it back onto his desk with an angry grunt and quaffed the brandy.

Maeve persistently took it upon herself to mother him, with an unfailing ability to home in on a sore point. Unfortunately, in this instance, Patrick knew that she was right.

He was acutely aware of Alex's budding feelings for him. It was one of the reasons, in the weeks leading to his departure from Broughton Hall, he'd tried to avoid her. The other reason was his reluctant acknowledgement of his reciprocal feelings.

There was more than a small sense of self-preservation in his attempt to keep his distance. She was such a young girl, betrothed – albeit to the bloody fop Hamish Glendenning – and as both Simon and Maeve were wont to point out, Alex was sheltered, inexperienced and naive. The very nature of girls like Alex was fickle.

But Patrick was feeling vulnerable, a sentiment with which he was both unfamiliar and unhappy. He had been very aware of his growing regard for Alex over the weeks of his stay at Broughton Hall and even as he attempted to avoid her, he could not.

Yet, he refused to expose himself to the changeable nature of a child with a fancy. By tomorrow she would have forgotten him, *but if I allowed myself, I would soon be in too deep*. This was uncharted territory for Patrick. Not even Mary Whitmore had evoked such feelings in him.

So, he'd tried, although largely unsuccessfully, to stay away from her.

At the time he'd kissed Grace, he'd only moments earlier been talking with Alex. The girl had been upset. Her eyes had gazed up at him with great sadness ... and other emotions. Whether she knew it or not, her feelings for him were revealed in all their fleeting, adolescent intensity.

Patrick's heart had leapt with a ridiculous joy that jolted him to the core, and admonishing himself for acting in the fashion typical of a foolish, untried schoolboy, he'd resisted the urge to farewell her in a less than brotherly manner.

He snorted irritably as he remembered chastely kissing her cheeks and pulling her into a brief, fraternal hug.

When, he'd turned to Grace, he'd been angry and frustrated.

As he took Grace in his arms, Patrick conceded that the passion of his kiss was genuine – except that in his imagination, it was Alex he held. Alex's lips that parted beneath his own. Alex's heart that pounded against his chest.

And for that very reason, he had prolonged the embrace, for far longer than was necessary to fulfil its purpose. Finally returning to awareness of his surroundings, Patrick realised that he'd intended to hurt Alex.

Let her feel betrayed, he told himself firmly. *Let her regard me as a cad. Let her believe the very worst of me ... and turn away before I am irretrievably lost.*

As she recovered from her childish infatuation, he would be released. Another reason for his eagerness to join the war: to remove himself from the temptation of her.

He could have kissed Grace with much less ardour and still achieved the desired result – to have his stepmother believe he and Grace were courting. But he had kissed the Italian girl with all the fervour of a passionate lover.

And Alex *had* been hurt, as he knew she would be.

It was selfish of him.

It was cruel.

It was necessary, to stop her gazing at him with those adoring brown eyes.

Suddenly resolute, Patrick returned to his desk, took up his pen and drew out a fresh sheet of vellum.

14 Queen Street
Oxford
Oxfordshire
27 November 1810

My dearest sister,

Mind your own bloody business.

Your loving brother

PW

❧

Patrick sat in the small room that served as their dining room.

The table was set for two, though he was alone, watching impassively as Mrs Baldoon poured him a cup of coffee then placed the pot on a cruet.

"Would you like eggs this morning, my lord? The new chickens have been laying already."

"Two please," said a cheerful voice behind them, "bacon, extra crispy and a large serve of buttered spinach."

"Good heavens, Sir Simon!" the housekeeper cried, in disgust. "You can't be sitting at the breakfast table like that! You look like you've been bathing in blood."

"Surgery, Mrs Baldoon, much the same thing." He winked and reached for the coffee pot. Though his hands were clean, traces of blood still showed beneath the fingernails and his previously white shirt was ruined.

"Don't you be touching that!" She snatched the pot from his grasp. "I'll pour it for you, and then you can take yourself upstairs to wash before I'll even consider your breakfast."

Simon shrugged good-naturedly, watched as she poured the coffee, then took the cup with him as he left the room.

∾

By the time he returned, Simon found his stepbrother peeling a boiled egg.

"Cutting up stiffs last night, were you?" Patrick asked, without looking up.

"No, for once. David Whitewood and I were leaving the Smithy's Arms just as some drunk staggered onto the road in front of a carriage. Poor chap went underneath the horses' hooves –" he broke off and inhaled appreciatively as the housekeeper returned with a heaped plate and placed it before him. "Ah, thank you Mrs Baldoon ... smells delicious."

"What happened then?" Patrick was spreading egg over a slice of toast with a knife.

The smile on Simon's face faded slightly. His stepbrother was making conversation but seemed distracted. "David's what happened," he replied. "The poor man had a broken collar bone – nothing too serious – but David, bloody fool, in trying to set it managed to sever the man's subclavian vein."

"How the devil did he do something like that?"

Simon shrugged and picked up a rasher of bacon with his fingers. "I like the fellow well enough but he's not a surgeon's bootlace. Put a scalpel in his hand and he's positively dangerous."

"Sounds like an idiot."

"He's not a bad stick. Just a ... well, you're right, he's an idiot. Anyway, as it turns out, the injured man was afflicted with what some American physicians are calling a haemorrhagic disposition."

"Oh, yes?" Patrick looked genuinely interested, for the first time. "What's that?"

Simon smiled to himself. His stepbrother's natural thirst for knowledge usually got the better of him – pity it didn't extend to his own university studies.

"Means he's a bleeder ... all we know is that it seems to be a hereditary condition ... can be fatal if the patient isn't taken care of properly. You must stop the bleeding – and sometimes it's very difficult."

"And your friend managed to slice through a vein while setting a broken bone. I don't think I'd trust him to sew on a button, let alone perform surgery."

Simon nodded, swallowing a mouth full of spinach. Mrs Baldoon had returned while they were talking. Now, she cleared her throat and Patrick turned to her.

"My lord, Sir Simon, if you're not needing me for the next hour, I'm going to the market. Is there anything you're wanting?"

Simon was pouring a fresh cup of coffee. He shook his head in reply but his brother said, "Yes, please Mrs Baldoon. I've left a a letter on the hall stand for posting, if you don't mind."

"I've already got it. Will there be anything else?"

"No. That will be all, thank you."

She made a small curtsy, and they heard the door bang on her way out.

Simon was regarding his stepbrother with speculation. He took a sip of his coffee then asked, "Is it the letter that has you so out of sorts this morning?"

Patrick looked up, frowning. "I'm not out of sorts."

"Yes, you are ... don't bother denying it. If you don't want to tell me I'll shut up, or ..." he cocked an eyebrow, "you can tell me."

"The letter was in reply to one I received from Maeve." Patrick snorted without humour. "A typical rant about my behaviour."

"What is she upset about this time?"

"Grace." It was partly true. "Seems she spoke to Grace and found out the truth about our deception. Maeve was unhappy that I hadn't confided in her."

Simon smirked, and Patrick glared at him. He wasn't finding anything humorous in his current situation. He said, "As you were. Pair of meddlesome buggers, you two."

"Hmm," Simon nodded, cutting his bacon. "What else? I know you too well. Maeve doesn't usually have this effect on you."

"Alright." Now Patrick pushed back his chair and crossed to where the fire leapt and popped in the grate. He shoved his hands deep into his pockets and stood staring into the flames for some moments before making his final decision. Drawing a deep breath, he felt a great burden slip from his shoulders.

"I'm quitting the university." He turned to look at his stepbrother. "I'll be writing to my father today."

Simon nodded. "I thought it would come to this ... sooner or later. What will you do?"

"I intend to honour our agreement. I won't enlist until you're ready ... I will return to Waterville."

"I won't hold you to it," Simon said, in honesty. "I know you want to go ... I know you're ready."

"I can wait. I'm going home."

"Very well. Let's say I quit my studies as planned – next winter. That alright?"

"Perfectly alright." Patrick smiled. "Now," he returned to the breakfast table, "another fortifying coffee, then I'd best be writing two more letters – one to the faculty head and another to my esteemed father."

∾

It was late and Patrick was seated on a couch in a dimly lit booth in the Bird of Paradise, an exclusive London club catering to the varied, and expensive, tastes of well-heeled gentlemen.

On a couch opposite, Deon Morehead sprawled, head lolling against the padded wall, legs stretched out, flies unbuttoned while a young lady in a yellow and orange feathered bird costume knelt before him.

A second bird, plumed in green and blue, stood beside him, one dainty foot rested on the couch at his hip, while his fingers moved in and out between her legs.

Patrick was watching the scene before him through ribbons of pungent smoke. He held a long opium pipe in one hand and was inhaling the vapours, savouring the giddy, numbing effects of the drug.

The green and blue bird was writhing on Deon's fingers, her hips undulating as though riding a horse. She was moaning and arching her back in a performance guaranteed to earn her a generous tip.

Patrick placed the pipe on the table beside his couch, then dropped his hand to cup his aching balls. His swollen cock strained against the front of his trousers – relief would be welcome.

He unbuttoned his flies and was about to take the matter in hand when slender brown fingers pushed his aside.

He glanced up to find a beautiful, dusky-skinned woman standing beside him. She had close-cropped, tightly curled hair and was feathered in fiery red, gold and bronze plumage.

Her long, sinuous limbs glistened in the light of the opium lamps, and as she moved in closer Patrick caught a whiff of some exotic fragrance.

"Allow me, my lord," she spoke in a smooth, chocolatey voice that left him incapable of speech. She knelt, her black eyes watching him all the while, and as she put her mouth to him, he slumped further into the couch while her full lips moved leisurely up and down his length.

Patrick heard Deon's shout of release through a drug-induced fog. His breathing was coming faster, and his head was swimming as the woman worked him with an expertise that rendered him on the verge of delirium.

Suddenly he felt hands on his shoulders. Deon's green and blue bird had moved across and was pinning him down. The sense of restraint, the lack of movement, intensified the pressure of the other bird's mouth and every flick of her tongue – but there was something more ... something his drugged mind couldn't grasp.

Sensing his thoughts, she drew back and released him, momentarily extending her tongue, and he caught a flash of a small gold nub.

When she put her mouth over him again, she allowed the stud to graze his skin ... it sent him crashing over the brink.

He came, almost immediately, with an explosive violence he'd never experienced before. It left him gasping, trembling and exhausted.

The green and blue bird released his shoulders and he slumped bonelessly to the side, to lie on the couch.

He was vaguely aware of small hands tucking him back inside

his trousers and doing up his buttons. It was some moments before he opened his eyes. At least it felt like moments but must have been longer for Deon was quietly sipping liquor from a short glass and the birds had flown.

Glancing around the room, Patrick realised that much of the smoke had cleared, and the girls, for the most part, seemed to have disappeared. One or two lingered in other booths, servicing their last customers of the evening.

"Welcome back to the land of the living," Deon drawled.
Patrick pushed himself to a sitting position. "How—" he broke off and coughed. "Christ! How long have I been asleep?"

"Oh, about half an hour – and you weren't asleep. You'd passed out. Probably from lack of blood to the brain – that exotic bird of yours sucked you dry, I'd reckon."

Patrick looked down at himself and grimaced. His shirt was hanging loose and was stained with wine and his white evening trousers were a grimy ruin.

Memory came rushing back through the tattered veil of drug fumes. He recalled drinking in a London public house with Deon ... running wild through the cobbled streets rousing slumbering Londoners with loud singing and shouting ... a carriage ride to the Bird of Paradise ... a dark-skinned woman with a golden stud through her tongue.

Just the thought of her was enough to make him hard again – almost. He realised suddenly that he was going to throw up if he didn't get some fresh air. Maybe he was going to throw up anyway.

He rose unsteadily, and nodding toward the table where the smoking paraphernalia sat, he told his companion, "Remind me never to touch that shit again."

∾

On emerging from the cloying warmth of the Bird of Paradise, the hit of icy winter air caused both young men to be violently ill.

Afterwards, they leaned heavily against a wall, bathed in cold sweat, bleary-eyed and debilitated.

Deon hawked and spat. "Come on. Let's try and find our way home, shall we?"

Home was a townhouse that Deon's father used when he was in London on business. No one was currently staying there except the housekeeper and a footman. The housekeeper opened the door to the two bedraggled men and tried not to recoil at the sight and smell of them.

She allowed them to sleep it off over the next twelve hours – whatever it was – she didn't know and didn't want to know.

Later in the day, when Deon knocked on his door, Patrick was awake, staring at the ceiling.

"Still alive, are you?" He was freshly bathed and shaved, and the other man was suddenly aware of how filthy he was. "I've got a bath coming for you."

"Thank you. I'm disgusting myself with my stench."
Patrick sat up and swung his legs over the side of the bed as his stomach gave a protracted growl.

"Oh, I have food coming too," Deon added. He went and sat on a chair by the window. "Now," he started, "about last night. I've never seen you like that before – you were ... you were crazed. Got it all out of your system, have you? You alright now?"

Patrick was surprised by the genuine concern on his friend's face, not to mention his acuity. He took a moment to self-assess. *Am I alright?* He wondered.

As he contemplated Deon's question, the housekeeper and footman arrived with steaming kettles to fill his bath. He watched them distractedly and thought about the last weeks.

He thought about Maeve's reprimand, his father's disappointment in him, the university head's obvious relief that he was leaving. He thought about Simon's concern for his welfare, and he thought about Alex – how he'd hurt her and how he was missing her.

He abhorred such sentiment in himself and had needed to exorcise it.

As the despondency had built within, he'd finally snapped, commandeered Deon and ridden to London.

He'd been unhappy for too long. He'd been frustrated for too long. And now that storm had subsided it was like a huge weight had been lifted off his shoulders.

The housekeeper and footman left the room and he looked up at Deon and smiled.

"I'm *perfectly* alright, and I thank you for asking. I will leave for
    Waterville today – it's where I should have gone months ago."

ALL'S WELL THAT ENDS WELL

"Can yer see anything? Any water or anything?"

I looked up the shaft to where a perfect disc of blue sky was interrupted by the wide face of Merry Carswell as she leaned over the side of the well. Her bulk eclipsed the sun shining directly overhead. "Not yet. But I'm only about half way. Tell him to let out more rope."

"Bull, let out more rope."

Bull, so called because of his close resemblance to a large, lumbering bovine, complied, and I was lowered, in sporadic jolts, further into the well. The rope tied around my waist had worked its way beneath my shirt and was rubbing against my skin, but not too much – it was only there as a precaution.

I was more or less lowering myself, hand over hand. I had my feet braced against the wall and was holding onto the rope, slowly edging backwards down the inside of the well as they let out more slack. Here and there, the rusted remains of a ladder still clung to the interior bricks but were definitely not stable enough to hold my weight.

"Yer alright, milord?"

"Keep going," I called up.

"More rope," Merry responded and I was dropped further down the shaft.

I looked beneath me and thought I detected movement. "Hold on! Stop for a moment."

"Stop!" Merry shouted. "Bull, stop!"

I hung momentarily, feet dangling over space before I rested them on a rung that appeared less corroded than some of the others.

Squinting through the dark, I could just make out the glistening motion of water some two yards beneath me. In the dimness of the well shaft, it looked black and oily, certainly not potable, and decidedly organic smelling.

"Merry ...?" I called, hearing my voice reverberate up the walls of the shaft. "Just a bit more – about a—"

Suddenly the rope gave a jerk and I hit the thick skin of the putrid water with a deadened splash.

"*Fucking hell!*" I spluttered to the surface. "*Fucking son of a fucking whore! What the hell're you doing up there!*" I roared, coughing and spitting.

"Sorry, milord," Merry's response filtered down. "Bull's hands slipped. You alright? Did you find water?"

"Yes!" I shouted. *Christ this stinks!* "Yes, there's water." Or liquid, at least and it was chest deep and so dense with muck that the rope was floating around me. God alone knew what was beneath my feet and as I went to move, a bloated and stinking lump drifted close by.

I peered at it. What the hell is – *oh fuck me!* "There are dead things down here," I yelled. "Merry! Pull me out!"

"Wait a minute, milord. Bull's hurt his hand."

I growled, taking a moment to look around. The sun above cast silvery dapples on the black surface of the water, and I was able to see how the well shaft opened into what seemed to be a naturally formed cavern. It was roughly four or five yards in diameter, and as I watched, the carcass slowly drifted past.

So there's a current in here, I thought. *But not a strong one, or else the water wouldn't be so foul.*

Taking a few tentative steps, I waded against the flow, through filth I didn't want to contemplate, breathing through my mouth to avoid as much of the stench as possible. I was trying to locate the underground channel through which the water ran.

Suddenly the rope gave a twitch. "Milord! You still there?"

"No, Merry," I called back. "I've gone home."

There was a momentary hesitation from above, then, "Milord?"

Christ! I grumbled to myself. "Yes! Yes, I'm still here! Give me a moment – I think I've found something."

By now I was in almost pitch darkness. My groping hands had found the wall of the cavern and I could feel, by the movement and the slightly cooler temperature against my shins, the small opening through which the underground stream was running.

I tried to reach down to it while keeping my head above the surface but it was impossible. *Shit and hellfire*! I was swearing a lot today, I observed, giving a humourless snort. Foul language wasn't helping my situation but I was impressing myself with my fluency.

All right, nothing for it! I took a deep breath, closed my eyes and ducked beneath the surface. My hands rippled over the contours of the cave wall, quickly locating the small opening through which the water flowed.

Probing further, I found what seemed to be a large rock blocking much of the opening. I pushed up and came to the surface, taking large gulps of air, readying myself for my next attempt.

Under I went, this time going directly to the stone. I gave it such a shove that I expelled my reserve of air, so once again I surfaced, took a breath and ducked back under.

My eyes were tightly closed against the sludge in the water – it was so dark in this section of the well that I wouldn't have been able to see anything anyway. Now, I ran my hands over the slimy surface of the boulder to where it rested, half-buried in the muddy bed.

It would need digging out and I didn't have anything to work with. But it seemed to me, this great lump of rock, and others like it, must have fallen from the roof of the cave and were blocking the flow.

Water always takes the path of least resistance. Given that this path was jammed, the fresh water must be coursing down some other channel. So, if the well was ever going to be usable again, these rocks had to be moved.

Fucking hell – I was going to have to come back down here. Neither Bull nor Merry could be expected to do it – which was why I'd volunteered to climb down in the first place.

These new tenants had agreed to move into an old shepherd's hut on the outskirts of my land, where it bordered the village of Astor. Our agreement was subject to me helping them build a new, larger home and assisting in getting them established. This well had been here for decades but had not been serviceable for some time. Hopefully, I would be able to get those boulders out, otherwise my agreement with Bull and Merry would be void.

Turning, I slowly waded back to where the light danced on the surface of the water in a vague reflection of the well's opening some five yards above. I looked up. Merry was still hanging over the edge.

"Merry!" I called.

"Milord! You're all right?" Her voice had a tinge of relief to it.

"Yes. Tell Bull to start hauling."

∾

They dragged me from the well, looking and smelling like some filthy creature coated in slow-dripping green mud.

I was ushered to the rear of the shepherd's hut, where they

both unceremoniously peeled my ruined clothes off and proceeded to douse me in clean water from the barrels they'd carted in.

I stood naked and shivering in the shadows of late afternoon while Merry subjected me to smirking scrutiny. "Cold, milord?" she sniggered.

Looking down at myself, I grinned. "Shows, doesn't it?"

"Only just," she rejoined, smartly.

"Merry!" Bull snapped. "Go inside and get milord some dry clothes."

Bull watched as she disappeared then pointed at my waist, "What's that mark? That from the rope?"

I nodded. The graze from the rope had been made worse once I was wet and they were dragging me back up the well shaft. Shrugging, I said, "If you've any wine or spirits I'll pour a bit on to clean it. But I'm going to have to go back down there so this won't be the end of it."

By the time Merry returned with a set of clean clothes, I'd explained the situation to her husband. He watched me dress, chuckling at how the trousers had to be pulled in, "Them pants looks like a sack with a drawstring."

The shirt was no better, hanging off my shoulders and needing to be rolled up at the sleeves. "Yours?" I suggested, observing the other man's massive bulk. He merely grinned – or that's what I assumed he did since all I saw was a set of notably white teeth behind the shrubbery of a thick ginger beard.

❧

I shared their meal that night – a hearty rabbit stew thickened with barley and peas, and flavoured with onions, parsley and carrots. It was simple and delicious.

I was seated opposite Merry and Bull's sixteen-year-old daughter, Lottie, who spent much of the meal pouting prettily at me from beneath her blond fringe and posing in a manner that showed off her budding breasts.

The family retired almost immediately after dinner. As their overlord I was offered the best bed in their small house – a straw-stuffed mattress on the floor – but I politely declined. Instead, I made a nest of hay for myself in a shed attached to the cottage, sharing the space with a plough horse, two cows, a sow, half-a-dozen chickens and Equus. I had, after all, slept in worse places.

Besides that, Bull's stern warning, "Touch me daughter, milord, and with all respect, I'll wring yer bleedin' neck," ensured I kept as much distance as possible between the flirtatious girl and myself. In any event, I was exhausted.

ॐ

In the end, it took almost four days of gruelling, filthy work to clear the rubble from the underground stream. A dirty and difficult job involving hauling rocks to other parts of the well and shovelling silt into buckets to be dragged up to the surface. It didn't seem to matter how much I cleared, there was always more to take its place; for years, sediment had banked up in the channel behind the massive rocks. This all had to be removed.

If I learned one thing, it was to ensure the rope didn't rub against my bare skin. Consequently, the burns on my abdomen began to heal reasonably well, despite being doused in God knew what putrid mess every day.

Over each evening meal, I endured Lottie's infatuated eye-batting and Bull's frowning growls, slinking off as early as possible to enjoy the simple companionship of barn animals. I slept like the dead every night, awakening in the morning to the smell of bacon frying, with muscles bunched tight and aching with fatigue.

When at long last, I had cleared as much of the rubble as I could, the water was flowing clear and clean – the well was usable once again.

I spent one last night in the barn, riding out towards Astor the next morning. Bull and Merry were profuse in their gratitude and Lottie slipped a sampler she'd been working on into my coat pocket with a wink indicating that I must not tell her parents.

Once out of sight I unfolded the sampler.

It was a red love heart, surrounded by little yellow daisies. I smiled at it and tucked it back in my pocket. Somehow, someway, this would be yet another source of trouble I would inevitably find myself in.

∾

I arrived in Astor just before midday, rode directly to Master Hodgkins, the local tailor, and asked him to make me, as quickly as he could, a set of underthings, trousers and a shirt. I couldn't keep wearing Bull's oversized garments beneath my riding coat.

Master Hodgkins took my measurements and assured me he would have my order ready within twenty-four hours. From there, I went to The Coachman's Rest, booked into a room and slept the entire day and night through.

The sun came streaming through my window the following morning. It splashed over my bed and puddled on the floor, quickly warming the room so that I awoke lying naked in a mild sweat, having kicked the blankets off.

I was meeting with a local businessman, Mr Bradford, a formerly successful importer of European wines. His import business had taken a downturn of late due to import embargoes imposed as a consequence of the war on the Peninsula.

Mr Bradford had approached me when I'd first returned to Devon to ask if we could meet. He had a proposition for me.

Before breaking my fast, I asked the landlord of The Coachman's Rest to send a message to Mr Bradford advising that I would meet with him that afternoon over brandy.

By the time I returned to my room, there were two items waiting for me. One was my new set of clothes from Master

Hodgkins, the other was a note from my father saying he had been looking everywhere for me, hoped I was here, and advised that he, his countess and stepdaughter had arrived at Waterville Place several days ago and looked forward to my presence at my earliest convenience.

Alex was in Devon! My heart gave a ridiculously childish leap of pleasure before I administered a mental slap to myself.

Stop it! Stop it right now!

Father's messenger was in the taproom awaiting my reply, which I quickly drafted and handed him on my way to meet with Mr Bradford.

∾

I'd expected Mr Bradford would be eager to offload his failing import business, either in full, or in part to a suitable investor. I was wrong.

Mr Bradford explained that he intended to retain his business against a time when trade with Europe had resumed. He believed – and I agreed with him – that sooner or later, he would be able to reconnect with his continental suppliers and pick up from where he left off. As he owned his ship outright, he could keep a skeleton crew to maintain it, and effectively have it on standby until the time was right to start trading again.

"No," he assured me, "what I'm really looking for, is someone to take my interests in a weaving factory off my hands. I can no longer afford the mortgage payments on it."

Well, that gave me food for thought. We discussed the matter at length, and I agreed that if he could put together all his paperwork and have his bookkeeper make available the banking records and inventories, I would give his proposition due consideration.

We parted amicably, agreeing to meet in a month's time when we could talk further and I could look over his accounts.

I arrived back at The Coachman's Rest just before eight of the clock. I ate a quick meal, and ordered the stables to prepare Equus.

I couldn't wait a moment more. And I couldn't deny myself a moment more. I was going home – immediately.

I was going home to see Alex.

THE AWAKENING

"Is he staying?" my stepsister asked, taking a sip of tea. From where I stood in the breakfast-room doorway, she couldn't see me, but I had time to observe her.

She had grown. She was a woman now, made beautiful by her lack of pretension and artifice, and eating bread and honey with her fingers, licking the sticky sweetness from their tips.

At the same time as she asked the question, my father raised his eyes and spotted me leaning against the door-frame. He nodded toward me, "Ask him yourself."

It was my cue to come forward, but I'd only taken a step when she bounced from her chair and threw herself into my arms, her own going around my neck. I laughed from sheer happiness, my heart swelling, pounding, my nostrils filled with the fresh verdant scent she always had about her from walking outdoors in the mornings.

Overcome by my own emotions, I quickly retreated into mockery. With my hands on her waist, I gave her a quick peck on each cheek and pushed her gently away, ostensibly to make a show of scrutinising her.

"Well, haven't you grown," I teased. "The extra year has

polished off the ruffian to expose the young lady."

Grinning delightedly, she seemed equally overwhelmed and dropped weakly into her seat, while I turned to greet my father.

After helping myself to breakfast, I quickly brought my father up to date with all that had been happening, including the offer from Mr Bradford to buy his weaving factory. My father seemed to think it might be a worthy investment, provided there was enough cotton and wool available.

"No point in having a weaving factory without fibre to weave," he observed, adding, "the government is buying up plenty of wool to make military uniforms. This is nothing new, so why your Mr Bradford isn't making enough to cover the mortgage on the place is a concern."

"And exactly why I need to examine his books and visit the factory in person. There must be a reason he can't make a profit during a time like this."

My father nodded. "Nothing like a war to keep factories pounding away."

While we'd been talking, I was aware of Alex's eyes on me. From time to time, I glanced over and smiled at her, if only to see the flash of neat white teeth as she responded.

The words Maeve wrote in a letter almost a year ago came flooding back, *you have filled her heart with hope and fairy tales ... she now entertains a fancy for you.*

Looking at my stepsister, I knew Maeve was right – she usually was, damn her!

... you left a young woman with her heart in tatters ... Maeve had written, and I daresay that was right too; for looking at Alex now, I knew her regard for me was nothing childish. But was it more than a mere infatuation? Probably not – girls of Alex's age seldom remained in love for long; shifting their direction as easily as the wind.

In any case, too artless for her own good, Alex's current

affection for me was clear on her face, and this was a very dangerous state of affairs, because as long as I believed her feelings resulted from a childish fancy, I could safely pretend the same of my own.

Seen now, in the cold light of maturity, I knew that Alex *believed* herself in love with me. Yet given the fleeting nature of a teenage girl's fancy, my head advised caution even as I smiled at her and revelled in her joyful reaction.

"So, the prodigal one has returned," my stepmother's acidic voice cut into my thoughts, and I contained a groan as I politely rose while she took her seat.

Without waiting for the maid, she poured herself a cup of tea and embarked upon a reasonably accurate observation of the estate and its prosperity beneath my care, before turning her invective into a commentary about the moral welfare of my serving women – I never touch my staff! – and the young ladies of the local villages – admittedly, I might have touched one or two of them!

My father's countess was beautiful and stylish – I could understand his attraction. She was also possessed of a sharp wit and equally sharp tongue. For these, I have a grudging admiration, or would have if she refrained from honing them on me! In any event, even she could not dampen my uplifted spirits this morning.

And, in order to keep it that way, I excused myself from the table. As I rose, my eyes met those of my stepsister. She was watching me from liquid chocolate eyes, her lovely face framed by a mess of undressed hair.

I had a sudden impulse to leap the table, take her face between my hands and press my lips to her mouth in a passionate, lover's kiss, and not *just* to shock my stepmother!

Instead, I opted for a more seemly approach – I winked at her, then left the room.

∾

If not for the fact that I was feeling so damned cheerful, I'd be steeped in misery. Misery because I now realised I was in love – a state of affairs that displeased me immensely because I'd always thought being in love made one vulnerable, which is a weakness – and moreover, the object of my affection was both unattainable and unfitting.

Further, I'd descended to the point where I was in danger of acting on impulses that were strictly off-limits!

As my father, his countess and Alex headed off on a day's journey to the seaside, I retreated to my office, supposedly poring over my account books, but instead, I was imagining what it might be like to kiss Alex, to feel her lips part beneath my own, feel her heartbeat against my palm as I cup her small breasts, and glory in her moans as I raise her skirt to slowly trail my fingertips along ...

Fucking hell! I ran my hands through my hair and got up to pace back and forth across the rug. These thoughts had to stop! They were entirely inappropriate, and further, they were futile.

I huffed and kicked at a book lying on the floor. It slid across the rug and bumped into the wall but I hardly noticed, so distracted was I.

If I continued with these adolescent fantasies, I was in danger of creating the kind of devastation my family would never recover from. I must, at all costs, never betray my feelings for her. I must never, ever give in to my urges.

She was betrothed to wed, and *moreover*, she was my stepsister, and even if they would pressure me to marry Anne, they would never accede to my marrying Alex while the Elginbury match still stood.

Jesus, that was a sobering thought!

Marry Alex? Where did that come from?

I had never wanted to marry anyone, although eventually I

would be required to perform my familial duty.

I gave a derisive snort as I remembered the wager I'd had with Simon nearly two years ago.

Pausing before the window, I looked out over my vast estate. I owned everything that stretched before me as far as the eye could see ... and beyond. I owned villages and trading ships, factories, warehouses and mines. I was richer than the Prince of Wales – but I was a captive of that wealth and all its associated responsibilities.

I sucked in my breath, returned to my seat and drew the account book towards me. There was work to be done and in the hours before my family returned from their visit to the shore, I would strap on my armour, and strengthen my resolve.

Alex is my sister and ever thus she will be. We will enjoy a pleasant summer together, *as siblings*. We will engage in games and activities, *as siblings*. I will escort her about my estate and we will entertain one another, *as siblings*.

And I will spend a small fortune on whores.

∼

I was in the garden with Briggs when I heard their carriages roll up the drive. My first thought was to hurry over and greet them. My second thought was to hide.

I did neither. I mustered my dignity and continued my discussion with my head gardener before removing myself to the far end of the property where an old tumble-down barn was used as a woodshed. It was ordinarily the job of a garden hand to chop the wood for the household, but today I'd assigned the task to myself.

Besides a supply of stumps and axes, the barn also housed several farming implements, and bales of hay harvested at the end of summer would be stored here to feed the horses over winter.

At this time of day there was no one about so I took up the axe and set to work. I enjoyed chopping wood. I enjoyed the bunching and stretching of muscles, the weighty balance of the axe that allowed it to do the work while I simply wielded it. I enjoyed the sweat of honest labour, and I particularly, in this instant, enjoyed the expenditure of energy that had been building inside me.

It was this energy that usually led me to the nearest brothel and the quick release provided by the skills of professional ladies. But today, I took the opportunity to forget myself for a good half hour of concentrated, physical effort, after which, I strolled back to the house, entering via the servants' stairs and was going directly to my room.

The hot bath water arrived within minutes of my ringing for it, and I was bathed and freshly clothed within twenty minutes. I had dressed hurriedly, smiling to myself when I realised that my shirt-tail was hanging loose but I'd never been concerned by things like that. My father had always argued that I wouldn't look as slovenly if I employed a valet, but right now I had way more pressing things on my mind.

I could put it off no longer, and I didn't want to. I left my room and took the brisk four-minute walk from the residential wing of my house to the guest wing.

∾

I heard Alex give a long sigh as I rapped on the door, and when she called something out – obviously taking me for a servant – I pushed open her door and waited on the threshold.

She was hunched over a bowl of water, skirt hitched to her knees, bathing her feet. When she looked up, her face initially showed surprise, followed quickly by delight. My heart gave a ludicrous leap and I casually strolled into her room.

In that moment I understood that what I had interpreted as love for Mary Whitmore had been unadulterated lust and nothing more, for as much as I saw Alex for what she now was – a desirable woman – I had not the slightest interest in fucking her.

I did, however, very much, want to make love to her. The fact that I realised there was a difference was an awakening for me.

Seated side-by-side on her bed, we sipped tea with an easy intimacy that felt gentle and natural. She told me about her trip to the seaside, and I poked fun at the sunburn on her face. A sense of peace washed over me; I was content.

When eventually we finished our tea, I put our cups aside, and led her by the hand on a guided tour through my vast house with an odd mixture of pride and sadness.

Pride because Waterville Place is, after all, a magnificent mansion. And sadness ... well sadness because as the future Earl of Thorncliffe, this estate would be my seat and it will require a countess.

I escorted my stepsister through room after room of exotic silks, works of art and treasures, unique and priceless artefacts from around the world, exulting in her delight and seeing many items I'd taken for granted, as fresh and special through her eyes.

We laughed and taunted one another and ran the length of the corridors, hand-clasped as children, and as we did, I deliberated the wisdom of showing her my own room. Then suddenly we were there and I was throwing open the door.

My bath had been removed but my clothes still littered the floor, and my bed was as yet unmade – I had, after all, instructed Mrs Bath to ensure the maids did not interfere with my belongings.

Alex stepped over the threshold, exhaling slowly and with great control. The buoyant mood between us had become something else entirely. She was staring at my bed and it was with the greatest effort of will that I did not throw her on it and kiss her breathless.

I knew she would not deny me – and that, perhaps, was my greatest reason for self-control. Turning, she caught me watching her; she too had sensed the shift in atmosphere and said with forced humour, "You ought to have your room cleaned."

Accustomed to hiding my emotions, I smiled nonchalantly, "I know. But I told Mrs Bath not to clean here. I've been reading and drawing up plans for the arboretum. When I'm finished, she may send someone in."

It seemed then that the spell had broken and I took her hand. "Come, there's one last place to show you – you'll love this."

∾

Late that night, I lay in bed, sleepless and tormented, recalling the day's events. Alex and I had spent several hours exploring my home. The last location I had taken her to was my grandfather's observatory, a magnificent dome of glass panels set into the roof.

The view from there was unsurpassed and even King George II had stood in awe when he'd visited back in the 1750s, only a couple of years before his death.

As Alex drifted around the room, gazing across the tiles of Waterville's roof towards the canopy of the distant forests, and the sea beyond, I watched her. Before I could stop myself, I said, "Have you heard from your Lord Whatsit?"

She rounded on me. "Why did you have to mention him?"

I shrugged, affecting a careless air, and she went on, "He visited shortly after you left last year. I haven't heard from him since."

"But the betrothal still stands?" I had to know.

"I've heard nothing to the contrary." She looked at me curiously. "And no line of suitors beating a path to my door."

"There ought to be," I said gently. Then realising I was on dangerous ground, I added, "you're rather appealing when you're not being a thorough bitch."

I was attempting to play with her, but she flushed and I realised that she was older now, and conscious of herself in a way she'd never had cause to be in the past. And unlike most women of my acquaintance, she was refreshingly lacking in arrogance.

She bowed her head. "Don't tease me," adding softly. "Who'd wed a country-rabbit with messy hair and narrow hips? I'm not built to be a brood mare, nor am I glamorous court material."

Of course, she was right. Our conversation continued for some time and eventually we made our way downstairs and went our separate ways to dress for dinner.

And now, here I was. This was set to be a very, *very* long summer indeed.

∾

Throughout the weeks of that blissful summer, Alex and I spent a great deal of time together. I took her riding with me through my villages and introduced her to the tenants we met along the way. I took her to markets and we visited nearby shops and tea-rooms. When the weather was inclement, we remained indoors making music and playing games, and I discovered a sense of frivolity in myself I'd not previously suspected I had. She was bringing out a different side of me and I was not inclined to resist it.

Alex had a sense of fun and adventure that was lacking in many of the young ladies of my acquaintance; she was a much more playful and entertaining woman than I'd suspected.

While others of her age were trained in rigid etiquette and unsmiling deference, Alex was irreverent and daring. She also had a strong will that I'd not given her credit for with a leaning toward stubbornness that could prove detrimental, like the morning she chose to take her usual walk about the gardens, despite my advice against it as the clouds gathered on the horizon.

Standing beneath an umbrella on the porch steps, I waved cheerfully as she returned, a sodden mess, running up the lawn. Her hair clung to her face in dripping tendrils and her cotton dress wrapped itself around her legs threatening to trip her at every step. I laughed smugly, until my, *I told you so*, attracted a most unladylike suggestion of where I could put my umbrella.

Later, over dinner, I caught her eye and she glared at me, which only made me laugh all the more.

∽

Christ, it was warm! Even for summer it was warm and the insects hovered low over the lake, while the lush plants in the gardens wilted sadly.

As I made my way to the summer house, the sweat trickled down the middle of my back along my spine. Standing outside on the deck, I watched as a heron rested in the shade of a tree. He and I both raised our heads at a dull thump from within the small cottage – it sounded like a book falling.

Curiously, I poked my head inside the door and found Alex there, asleep on the couch. Her face was flushed and slightly damp with the warmth of the day, and approaching softly, I enjoyed a rare moment of being able to observe her without attracting a smart remark.

While voyeuristic, perhaps, it was irresistible for she was refreshingly innocent and heartbreakingly lovely. I felt a quick and very unwelcome throb of pain in my chest – a completely foreign sentiment for one who'd always had any woman he'd ever desired – and suddenly, I was in uncharted territory.

I did not like the way I felt!

She gave a soft sigh and shifted slightly; the movement caused the bodice of her dress to gape. It provided me with an uninhibited view of the chemise beneath, clinging, and transparent with perspiration, to her breasts, creamy white and pink-tipped, and I was overcome with a sense of shame – another vaguely unfamiliar notion – and took a step to the side to avoid the view – a gentleman, in spite of myself!

I couldn't stand here gawping at her forever. Within three strides I was at her side, saying the most ridiculous thing that just popped into my head, "Is this where the prince awakens his true love with a kiss?"

She gave a start and blinked up at me. "How long have you been there?"

"Not long." I supposed it was true. I dropped beside her to pick up her book, turned it over to read the cover.

"Burchall – any good?"

Stretching, she responded, "Good enough, though I've read better."

She was flushed with heat and as I squatted beside her, a bead of sweat trickled down her hairline and before I could stop myself, I'd invited her to swim in the lake.

Naturally she resisted – what well-brought-up young lady wouldn't? But I could see she was tempted by the sight of the water glistening beyond the window and once we'd debated the question of what she would wear, I left her to get ready.

I was sitting on the deck, in only my underdrawers, dangling my feet in the water, when she emerged wearing only her shift. Her arms were self-consciously folded across her chest, but she was eyeing me with more than mere curiosity; I recognised admiration in them before she quickly looked away and dropped to sit beside me, hugging her knees.

We sat for some time, watching the heron going about his business, until finally, I slipped into the water. It was refreshingly cool and effectively purged my ardour and any inappropriate thoughts I might have otherwise entertained.

Maeve was right – Alex had a fancy for me – but how intense remained to be seen. Perhaps I was just a likely target for the affections of a bored young lady.

Nevertheless, I recognised that my own affections were more serious. My experience with Mary Whitmore had taught me that. I was in love with Alex and I was in danger of losing myself entirely in her.

God help me if I were to become some silly besotted fool! In any case, as we splashed and played in the lake, teasing one another, innocently pushing and shoving at one another, it was clear that I was already lost.

My heart swelled with happiness and I caught myself showing off like an idiot and teasing her as an infatuated schoolboy might. Lost in my musings, I was unprepared for her calculated attack as she used the buoyancy of the water to lift herself, throwing herself onto me and causing my feet to slip in the mud.

As I regained my footing and broke the surface, spluttering and laughing, I found her attempting to escape. She'd managed to get to the small decking on the edge of the lake and was trying to haul herself out.

For several heartbeats I watched as her shift clung to her back, the round shape of her arse, and wound itself around her legs. Despite the chill in the water, I was not unmoved. I closed my eyes in a long blink, only to open them again with a stern warning to myself.

Disobediently, I moved toward her and my hands on her waist, I dragged her back into the water.

Turning her to face me, I took her wrists, spread her arms wide and ... her face was open, caught in a breathless moment of laughter. There was water clinging in droplets to her eye lashes, her lips were parted ... inviting ...

We were both breathing hard as I stepped forward and felt the immediate warmth of her through the swirling water.

I could kiss her now.

I could lay her on the deck and make love to her.

And I wanted to. I wanted to love her with a fierce, painful yearning. It would be no lustful satiation. Had she the slightest worldly experience, she'd have seen it in my face, felt it pressing hard against her stomach.

But she didn't. Her actions were as primal, as instinctive as any female reacting to any male, regardless of the species. She closed her eyes and tilted her head towards me.

Our mouths were so close I could feel her breath on my face; I could feel her firm bosom against my chest. In that moment, time seemed to freeze as though the earth suddenly hung suspended among the stars, no longer spinning on her axis.

And I saw it all play out before me: I would kiss her and she would arch into me, urging me, inviting me and I would not resist, indeed with that first kiss it fell beyond my powers to resist.

Her lips were slick and wet, glistening in the sun and I would lean in to kiss them, nuzzle down her neck to the tops of her breasts where the skin would have puckered from the cold water. I saw myself lift her out of the lake and lay her on the decking. I watched myself strip the sodden fabric of her shift over her head, and peel off my under-drawers.

Then, I would lay beside her, caressing, tasting, exploring, until the last possible moment when I rolled onto her.

And then suddenly I knew I had gone too far. She was my stepsister, a virginal 17-year-old, betrothed to another man. She trusted me, and in her girlish inexperience she believed she loved me. That in itself was more than I could take.

I couldn't do it to her. I couldn't do it to my father. I couldn't do it myself.

By merely fantasising, I'd behaved foolishly. To act on that fantasy would be to risk everything. I must endeavour to never place myself in another such situation with her.

All this in but a fraction of a second, during which I came to understand what I was about to do and arrived at this most significant realisation. With so much riding on it, it was perhaps, one of the most sensible decisions I'd ever made: whatever I felt for this girl, it had to end now.

Abruptly releasing her, I stepped immediately aside, climbed out of the lake and thrust a hand at her. "Come on." My voice was gravelly, harsh with anger, desire and grief. "I'll help you out."

∾

In the end, I'd growled some unkind things at her, though what, I can't honestly remember. I do remember throwing a blanket at her to cover herself. I vaguely remember pulling on my shirt and trousers, and reluctantly helping her to button her dress.

She was humiliated and embarrassed, I knew, but it was a temporary state of affairs. She was hurt and angry with me, but that was temporary too. If I'd lain with her, taken her maidenhead ... the hurt, humiliation and anger would be a lot worse.

There were tears in her eyes when she ran away from me. She'd get over them, just as she'd get over me.

RESOLUTION

Kat Wheeler was blond and slender, radiating health and vitality. She spent the entire evening fluttering her eyelashes at me and squaring her shoulders to thrust forward her deliciously round breasts.

I could have told her not to bother; after the frustrating afternoon I'd spent swimming with Alex yesterday, I needed little persuasion. Nor was I in any mood to dissemble. I was horny as hell, and she was willing.

Unfortunately, the business with John Wheeler, Kat's father, was taking far too long for my liking. The man evidently considered it a great honour to have me in his home and intended to make the most of it. I'd come merely to discuss how much of the district's harvest wheat he was capable of grinding.

Every summer I spoke with several landowners in Devonshire and arranged work for my tenants – filling gaps in manpower that the Peninsular War had brought about. My tenants wanted the work, and I undertook the negotiations to secure it for them.

Talking with Wheeler was the final step in the process – all parties stood to benefit if the wheat, once harvested, could be milled into flour. I wasn't terribly fond of Wheeler – I suspected his dealings were not entirely honest and would have preferred to use another local chap – but my father liked him and had argued that John Wheeler was the only operator in the county that could mill large quantities of grain all at once.

I listened respectfully as the older man regaled me with stories of his youth, how he had fought at Yorktown in '81, all the while thinking about how I could assist one of the other millers in the area to expand his business.

That Wheeler wanted to feed me copious amounts of food, and open his finest imported wines for my sampling, was generous but unnecessary, and gave me a moment's contrition for planning to help his rival. Then he opened a box of cigars – brought with him all the way from the Americas after his discharge from the army, and I knew I was in for a long and tortuous evening.

Perhaps he suspected my interest in his daughter. He'd have to be blind if he couldn't see her enthusiasm for me! Yet as the night progressed, I realised that he was fully aware of his daughter's notions. He instructed his serving woman to prepare a bed for me – the room just happened to be right beside Kat's room.

I trusted he didn't expect me to become irretrievably besotted with the girl and demand her hand first thing the next morning? I could have told him that expectation generally led to disappointment. Nevertheless, I planned to pass the night between the girl's thighs – disallowing all thoughts of Alex to intrude.

In any event, my affections for Alex were doomed. Whatever fondness she held for me today would be fleeting at best, gone tomorrow. Alex fancied herself in love with me now because she loved my house and was enamoured of her summer in Devon. In her mind, I was merely part of the package.

Accordingly, I made not even a vague pretence of sleeping in the room allocated to me. After cigars and wine with John Wheeler, I went directly to his daughter's room where she was waiting, naked on her bed.

Before I'd even locked the door, she had risen and was walking towards me. I wasted no time closing the gap between us.

∾

The following day, I rode out to meet Mr Bradford. A few weeks ago I'd met with him for a second time, but after close scrutiny of his books, and a subsequent inspection of his weaving premises, I decided against purchasing his weaving business; the factory was too small, the equipment in poor repair, and the unfortunate Mr Bradford would be left holding a failing investment – but I couldn't afford to worry about that.

My own wealth, and indeed the financial well-being of my villagers, relied on my ability to make astute business decisions. To purchase Mr Bradford's weaving factory would not be an astute business decision.

The meeting with Bradford went better than I had expected. He had pre-empted my decision and already taken steps to dismantle his equipment and sell it as scrap to a boatyard.

Satisfied with the outcome, I spent the remaining part of the day with Mr Bradford in the Coachman's Rest discussing the war on the Peninsula. I was somehow not surprised when John Wheeler and his daughter joined us, and by the time it was very late and we had imbibed a considerable amount of wine, the innkeeper, whose name escapes me now, entreated us to pass the night in his rooms upstairs.

While Wheeler and the innkeeper remained downstairs, Kat and I acquainted ourselves with one of those rooms.

Did Wheeler hope I'd get a child on her and find myself trapped?

Regardless, the amount of wine I'd drunk seemed to bring on an uncommon fit of melancholy in me. Not usually given to sentimentality, I was unprepared for a sudden, overwhelming sense of guilt.

For there I was, sating my lust on a woman for whom I would never feel any romantic attachment, when I had an untimely vision of Alex lying beneath me. The intensity of my feelings shocked me. I realised, in that moment, that to make love to someone, to lay with them, to give and receive that most joyous pleasure, was sacred and special.

And bloody inconvenient!

Yet it was a turning point for me. I pulled back to look into Kat's face, hoping to find some spark of warmth beyond a momentary, gratifying release, but there was nothing.

I wanted Alex. I wanted to make love to *her* and the notion was wrong, and impossible on so many counts that I was engulfed by grief.

Guilt and anger quickly followed – both of which were directed squarely at my stepsister as, up to then, the sexual act had for me been an exciting diversion. With no shortage of willing partners, since the age of 14, I'd fucked my way from one end of the country to the other.

It was an unadorned, uncomplicated sport – until now. My breath caught in a sob with the realisation that I was as shallow and hedonistic as my stepmother accused me of being.

Maybe it was all the wine I'd drunk, but I wanted to be better than that. I wanted to be the kind of man that made love to the woman he adored and remained utterly faithful to her.

Such introspection was foreign to me and so mired in gloom was I that my desire began to wane. "*Oh God, don't stop!*" Kat panted urgently, and I snapped back to the present, realising that she deserved my full attention. Now, as my sense of remorse took hold, I lost momentum.

Feeling my withdrawal, she opened her eyes, grasped my arse firmly in both hands and bucked her hips, but it was too late. Finally, accepting the futility of her actions, she released me with a dissatisfied groan. I slid away and lay on my back staring at the smoke-blackened ceiling of the most respectable guest room the Coachman's Rest could offer.

"What's wrong?" she asked. Her hand moved beneath the bedclothes. The evidence was there. "You don't want me?"

"Kat, it's not that. You're very desirable. I ... the wine. I think I had too much tonight."

She snorted contemptuously and sat up; a moonbeam washed across her bare torso and in the light, her fair-skinned breasts looked large and soft, demanding comparison with Alex's firm young body, standing before me in her clinging, wet shift.

How I'd wanted her then. And with the acknowledgement came vulnerability and shame. Two qualities designed to do untellable damage to my lifestyle.

Thinking of Alex now, how the dripping garment had moulded to her lithe shape, I felt a stirring that owed nothing to Kat's hopeful fondling. But it served the purpose.

She straddled me and I managed to keep myself focused enough to fulfil her needs, even if I myself did not finish.

I did not care.

∾

I lay in the dark staring into space. Soon, Kat's steady breathing indicated she was asleep, so I rose, dressed and returned to the darkened taproom.

John Wheeler was alone, sitting at a table by the glowing coals in the fireplace, a glass of wine at his elbow, half-empty bottle beside it. As I entered, he wordlessly poured a second glass and shoved it across to me.

I threw it back and he poured another, and we sat in silence for a long time before he spoke. "She's not for the likes o' you, milord – I know that – but I also know that you treat your women well."

I grunted scornfully and he continued, "You have a

reputation, though. Men see you coming and lock up their daughters. If it wasn't for the fact that you're a bloody decent overlord, you'd be running low on tenants."

The expression on his face suddenly turned to horror and he passed a hand over his mouth as if to stopper any further comments. The rasp of his beard stubble was loud in the otherwise silent room. "Sorry, milord, I shouldn't have ... I spoke out o'turn."

I waved dismissively. "I am aware," I said. I knew my behaviour upset many of my tenants and resolved, in that moment, to mend my ways.

"Look," he went on. "Kat's one o' them lasses with certain ... she's forward, you know?"

Nodding, I sipped my wine and he went on, "If she's going to be," he made a gesture of helplessness, "like *that* ... well I'd rather it be with the likes o' you than one o' those slovenly lads out Wethersby way. Know what I mean?"

He emptied his glass and I refilled it. "Some o' your refinement might rub off on her, eh?" he added with a sardonic laugh.

"She's alright," I spoke at last. I was warming to the man's honesty. Perhaps I'd misjudged him all along. It's not uncommon for my father to be right about something when I've been mistaken.

"So," he took a sip of wine, "they've found some dreary society-chit to marry you off to yet?"

I smiled for the first time in what felt like weeks. "Not yet, but they're trying."

He laughed. "Don't let 'em force you, lad. I know in your position you've got to marry – probably sooner than later – but shackle yourself to a life of misery? You don't want that! I were lucky with Kat's mother. Loved her from the start ... and she loved me. Her family hated me though. She died bringing Kat into the world and didn't they blame that on me too! One thing I learned from it all was that you gotta be happy. Don't think about anyone else."

"Wise words."

"Got your eye on someone special then, have you?"

"What tells you that?"

"The fact that an oversexed young blade like yourself left my daughter's bed tells me a lot."

I laughed and raised my glass to him. "There is a lass," I said, wondering why I felt compelled to confide in this man. "She's unattainable."

"She love you in return?"

"Perhaps ... I think so. But her family would certainly not be approving."

"Spoken for elsewhere, is she?"

I thought of Hamish Glendenning, Alex's betrothed. "You could say that."

"He'd best be a prince, then. Why else would they quibble over their daughter marrying an earl? That's what you'll be – and bloody wealthy to boot, if you don't mind me saying so, milord."

I shrugged. "It's more complicated than that."

He made a deriding face. "She loves you, you love her – it's *never* more complicated than that."

∽

Once the bottle of wine had been drunk to the grainy dregs, Wheeler drifted upstairs to find a bed and I slipped to the floor and slept on the hearth before the banked coals.

I rose while it was still dark, went out to the stables to saddle Equus and left just as the sun was inching above the horizon.

It was a long ride, but the morning was calm, the sky opalescent and the birds in full voice. Equus was well-fed and well-rested and eager to be moving. I, on the other hand, felt like shit warmed up. I was dirty and hung-over and miserable.

Arriving on Waterville land meant a final twenty minutes' ride before I would come within sight of my house. When the first glimpses of it appeared between the trees, it took my breath away, as it always did.

My home was a palace. Its stone glowed pink and gold in the morning sun. Each end had a three-storey wing and they were connected by a gallery of some 100 yards in length. A great coloured-glass dome rose above it like a crown. The result was a wide, sprawling and very impressive mansion.

Approaching Waterville Place never failed to humble me and remind me of the fortune to which I was born – I have not earned this. Therefore, I must be worthy of being its custodian. I have been entrusted with its preservation for the generations that come after me.

I rode directly to the stables, coming around the house, passing manicured lawns and gardens and there, on the porch, she stood.

My heart leapt with pleasure at seeing her. Unconsciously pretty in the morning sun, with her hair undressed and tumbling over her shoulders, her skin was an unfashionable warm brown from hours spent outdoors. I waved, kicking Equus into a trot.

She stepped off the porch and crossed the gardens to the stables, meeting me there from the opposite side.

In that moment, I was prepared to throw caution to the wind. I intended to dismount and take her in my arms. I wanted to kiss her, embrace her, and hold her sweetness against my heart.

But my pleasure soon turned to dismay as her expression changed from happiness to concern ... then fury.

Self-inflicted illness, lack of sleep and long hours in the saddle compounded to cause me to be uncharacteristically clumsy. I practically fell out of the saddle and stood swaying before her like a disgraced husband while she rounded on me like a shrewish wife.

I'm not even sure what she said, suffice to say that I didn't enjoy receiving such a dressing-down! Nor did I enjoy being made to feel as guilty as I did – far more than any guilt or remorse I'd castigated myself for last night.

She need not berate me thus – I was quite capable of berating myself. I managed to stammer out a vague explanation, "Father's man ... Wheeler, had me at ... some tavern and ..."

"Forced you to drink and wench did he?"

Oh, for fuck's sake! She was relentless! That's when something inside me snapped.

I am known for my sharp tongue. There are times when I open my mouth and simply trust to the gods that whatever comes out will not result in a blackened eye or broken tooth.

I have a quicker wit than most, and a rather remarkable gift for using it to its most cutting, painful advantage. I used it now.

"And you're my keeper?" I demanded, scornfully. "Christ, Alex ... every time I turn around you're like shit clinging to a blanket. So what if I was delayed – it's none of your bloody business anyway!"

She stared at me. "That's so unfair," she said softly, and the hurt was plain on her face. She turned and strode away but I was not finished with her yet.

With all that I'd put myself through last night – and I somehow blamed her for it – she had the gall to question me now! She was labouring under an overblown infatuation, and she thought that gave her the right to question me as though we had some kind of ... I don't know – *understanding*? But we had *nothing*!

Nothing! And that's all we'd ever have!

I felt myself under attack and was angry with myself that I felt so vulnerable. I was also frustrated by the futility of my love for her. I was aggrieved and hurting, and more than anything, I hated that I felt this way.

Pain made me cruel. I opened my mouth without the slightest idea of what might come out, and I made no effort to censor it.

"Perhaps if you lived in the real world rather than a land of lovers and fantasies," I snarled, "you'd not be so involved in my life. Go find yourself some other unfortunate swain to level your adoration on."

I watched her pause mid-stride. My dagger had struck its mark right between her shoulder blades, but her hesitation was only momentary. I saw her straighten her spine and walk on. And my ridiculously foolish heart swelled with grudging pride: she was young and innocent but she was brave and strong too.

As for me, well I was a ... I sighed.

The worst word I had in my vocabulary was inadequate.

∽

I woke to my father's face peering into mine. My wine-fogged brain tried desperately to register what he was telling me. I grasped words like forest ... missed dinner ... still not home ... get up ... night ... dark ...

And suddenly it dawned on me – after our argument, when I'd been so cruel to her, Alex had marched off into the woods and had not returned.

"What time is it?" I murmured, climbing out of bed. I pulled a pair of trousers and a clean shirt from my wardrobe and my father watched as I dressed.

"It's almost ten. She missed dinner and now she's missed supper."

"Shit!" My stomach clenched with fear. What if she were hurt? She could be lost. Alex was familiar with forests, and not likely to scare easily. But given her enthusiastic appetite, not returning for meals would indicate that she might be either hurt or lost.

"Her mother's on the warpath, my boy, so you'd best find her. The stable-boys told her that you and Alex had been arguing and that she stormed away from you."

"Shit, shit!"

"So it's true?"

"I'll find her, don't worry."

It was divine intervention – I have no other explanation for how I'd managed to think so clearly. I'd gone directly to Alex's room where I grabbed the first item I found: a cashmere pelisse in a delicate lavender-grey colour.

I held it to my face and inhaled – her fresh, outdoorsy fragrance lingered on it – good. I sighed stupidly, then refocused ... "That'll do."

From there, I went straight to Briggs's cottage, where bouncing, blonde Tess met me with canine joy at the gate. I roused the old man from his armchair doze with a bang on the door.

Bleary-eyed, he responded to my request by fetching his pipe, packing it with stained, practised fingers, and closing the cottage door behind him. At the stables where Alex had last been seen, I gave Briggs the pelisse.

"Tess, 'ere girl, come 'ere," he thrust the garment into the dog's face and waved in an elaborate, *go-fetch* gesture.

The dog set off immediately, nose to the ground, with the old man and me following behind. Lanterns on the porch, evidenced my father, his countess and Janet, Alex's maid watching and waiting.

"We'll find her," I called. Mim responded and I was grateful I didn't catch her words.

We followed Tess's bobbing tail as she zigzagged through the tangled woods. I'm not sure how these things worked: did she detect the location by scent and take the shortest route over logs and under branches, or did she simply follow Alex's steps?

In any event, after the best part of an hour, the dog suddenly raised her head, eyes alert and excited, and with a crashing leap into a screen of shrubbery, she disappeared. A moment later, Alex's terrified screams echoed through the forest.

∽

In the kitchen, I sat with Sylvie and Briggs. Aside from hunger and fatigue, Alex had been remarkably unhurt. She was, however, still very angry with me but when she'd tried to stand and failed, I had scooped her into my arms and carried her back to the house.

She had turned her face into my neck and wept with relief, while I unchivalrously revelled in the necessity of carrying her in my arms.

They ushered her away as soon as we arrived back at the house and I sent Sylvie after them. "Tell her I would speak with her," I instructed my half-sister who nodded and disappeared upstairs.

Some time later, she returned. "She's tired, Master Pat, and angry," Sylvie said. "She refuses to see you." Her face was sympathetic. That, and Alex's rejection, were two very unfamiliar notions to me and as such, I was unprepared for the searing, uncontrollable rage that rose within me.

How dared she! After all the self-recrimination, remorse and anxiety I'd exposed myself to over the past few days, I was at the end of the line. Normally tolerant and even-tempered, my ensuing explosion caused much alarm among my household. The small gathering of servants backed away in horror as the air turned blue around my head with my most imaginative cursing. I denounced my stepsister for the most ungrateful and immature piece of baggage ever to darken my doorstep ... and on it went until finally I paused to draw breath.

Sylvie was the only one brave enough to approach. "Master Pat," she said soothingly. "Shall I fetch you some brandy?"

She wasn't worth it! She wasn't worth any of it and I would cauterise her from my heart. "*Fuck the brandy and fuck Alexandra Broughton!*" I roared.

Storming from the kitchen, I marched directly to the stables, leapt onto Equus' bare back and kicked her into a flying gallop across the lawns. Holding tight to her mane, I crouched low over her neck as she took a bed of summer roses in a single bound and we disappeared into the night.

∾

Equus and I passed the night in a shepherd's cottage on the far eastern border of my land. I'd taken her inside and when she reclined, as mares often do, in the hay, I'd laid against her for warmth, but I hadn't slept.

Steeped in abject misery, I knew I could not allow this situation to continue, but how could I not? I desperately needed to wrest back control of my emotions ... and my sanity!

But before I could do that, there was one last thing I had to do. I had to say goodbye. And it *would* be goodbye. Alex Broughton will, henceforth, be nothing more to me than a stepsister, and I will return to my licentious life in reckless pursuit of casual pleasure and careless, meaningless indulgence.

During the small empty hours of night, I realised that I'd arrived at my limit. Just before dawn, I roused Equus, and turned her toward home. I knew my stepsister was returning to Yorkshire this morning. I must bid her farewell – mend the fences, so to speak. It would be my catharsis. And then, it would be over. For good.

The sun had not yet peeked over the horizon when I rode up to the back porch. Monsieur Chartrain was ferreting about in his kitchen garden and wisely chose not to try my patience; perhaps it was the resolve on my face, but he obeyed my request to send Sylvie to me, without question. Minutes later, my little half-sister stood before me on the porch.

"She's out the front," she whispered. "They're preparing to leave."

"Bring her here. Don't tell her it's me," I added as an afterthought in case she was still angry.

But she wasn't. When Alex appeared on the porch, I drew in my breath expecting the worst, and I spoke quickly before she could shower me with abuse.

"I could not let you leave like this," I told her. The sky was gradually lightening over my shoulder; the morning promised a beautiful day ahead. "I can't tell you how rotten I feel for the things I said to you yesterday."

Before I'd finished my speech, she'd thrown herself against me. It was a luxury I couldn't allow myself. Taking her arms, I pushed her gently away. "Now listen well, Alex. I am sorry I hurt you, even though in your prideful way you marched into the woods and got yourself lost – it was my fault. I ask you to forgive me."

Then she was in my arms again and this time I responded, holding her close to my heart. It would be the last time. "Of course I forgive you," she cried.

I dared not close my eyes – I would lose myself if I did. Instead, I gazed at Sylvie over Alex's head, conveying a message that she read perfectly.

"Miss Alex! The countess is calling – you must go."

I dropped my arms, "I came home early ..." I spoke as I led her up the porch steps, my arm around her waist. Releasing her, I stepped back.

"Safe travels, Li'l Sis." It was goodbye – she was unaware, but for me, it was final.

She turned, giving a small whimper, and without warning, her mouth was on mine, her arms about my neck and I was incapable of containing myself further.

I responded. Every ounce of passion and love I had for her welled up within me. Her mouth opened beneath mine and I cupped her head in my hand, clinging to her in a lingering lover's embrace that must perforce sustain me for life.

I could have died in that moment; I did not believe I could love as I did. Time seemed suspended; my world narrowed to her scent, her heartbeat, the soft warmth of her in my arms and her mouth on mine.

In the end, Sylvie was the only one with any wits left. She tore Alex from me, dragging her up the porch stairs and beyond.

The last I saw of her was the billowing skirt of her travelling gown as she ran toward her coach.

Any grief I'd experienced in the loss of Mary Whitmore was as nothing compared with this. I sat in my office long after the crunch of carriage wheels died along the drive. Then I drew a page from a box of vellum, filled my pen with ink and drafted a letter to Simon.

I told him two things. Firstly, that I was going to buy my commission to the army immediately and understood if he were not ready. I would go alone, but go now I must.

Secondly, I reminded him of our wager – that I would marry for love or not at all.

You win, I wrote. *My future is with the army. I am resolved never to marry.*

NEW BEGINNINGS

Simon dismounted and led Oliver into the stables outside at the back of the Queen Street house in Oxford. The stable lad would have gone home hours ago so he set about removing Oliver's tack and brushing the horse down himself.

As he uncinched the girth-strap, he noted that it had been brought in a notch. "Hmph!" He ran his hands over the horse's ribs, noting the new definition. "Lost a few pounds have you, old boy?"

He took the curry-comb off the hook in the corner. "Not that it'll hurt you – you packed on a few the last time we were up north. You remember? We did discuss it."

Carrying on the one-sided conversation, Simon set to work. He didn't mind brushing Oliver down – the horse, too lazy to fidget and fuss, was quite happy to stand around and receive the attention. In fact, if Simon gave him a good hard scratch with the curry-comb on his protruding breastbone, Oliver virtually rolled his eyes in ecstasy.

Simon did that now, laughing lightly as the horse whuffed and snorted with pleasure.

An answering whicker in an adjacent stall caused Simon to

pause. "Don't go anywhere," he told the blissed-out horse as he peered over the half-door. "Oh, hello there. When did you get in?"

Equus's ears twitched at his voice but she flicked her tail in disdainful response. Unlike Oliver, Equus was a one-man girl, and Simon turned away to finish his work. "Ah, we both know what she's like, don't we boy."

∾

Half an hour later, Simon entered the house via the kitchen door. He was not surprised to find his stepbrother seated at the work-scarred table biting into a large slice of cherry tart. He was, however, quite surprised to find Patrick had made a pot of tea.

Pulling up a chair, he cut a slice of tart for himself and got down to the business of eating; the only sound in the room was the fire in the range slowly burning down for the night.

There were no words required, not at this stage anyway, for even though Simon was bursting to find out the meaning behind Patrick's recent letter, he knew better than to ask.

Patrick tended to keep himself to himself. If he intended to share his thoughts, he would, and no amount of pestering would unseal his lips.

Simon knew something had happened to bring about their current situation. The last line of Patrick's letter was still ringing in his head.

You win. My future is with the army. I am resolved never to marry.

It had been – he tried to think back – how long since he and Patrick made that wager? A couple of years at least. So what had happened? Had Patrick fallen in love with some whore or other? Someone unattainable?

Simon found it hard to believe – in all the years he'd known Patrick, Simon could count on one hand the number of women he'd bedded more than a few times each. In fact, in Simon's memory, there were only two, perhaps three? He was resolutely disinterested in forming attachments.

One attachment, albeit purely physical, was Maud, the barmaid he'd kept for a couple of months as his mistress in Wolstone. Simon was certain there'd been another briefly kept here in Oxford, but the name escaped him, some merchant's daughter – a chit of no consequence.

Of course, the one that had really stolen the young lord's heart had been Mary Whitmore – former court harlot, more recently the ostensibly respectable Lady Ashwood, who despite her newly wed status, had spent more time in Patrick's bed than that of her husband.

He watched as Patrick licked his finger and dabbed up the last tart crumbs, drained his cup of tea, then leaned back in a spine-cracking stretch.

"You been cutting up stiffs again?" Patrick finally spoke, eyeing Simon's hands somewhat distastefully.

"No. Not tonight." Simon swallowed the last of his tart. "I was over at George Gregson's place ... he'd invited a group of us over for a few rounds of whist."

"Hmm." Patrick was distracted and Simon thought he looked tired.

"Right then," Simon gathered the plates and took them to the side for Mrs Baldoon to wash up in the morning. "Do you want to talk now or later?"

Patrick made a face that said he didn't care either way but they both knew there was no other reason he showed up in Oxford.

"Well, have you laid plans or was that letter an impulsive gesture dredged up from the bottom of a brandy bottle?"

Patrick smirked at his stepbrother. "It was impulsive but not regrettable. I've made up my mind – it's for the best."

"Oh, I see," Simon said, resuming his seat and not really seeing at all. "Have you got some bourgeois lass into trouble and the father's demanding pistols at dawn – anything like that?"

"No. Nothing like that. You'll be pleased to know that, with this particular lady, I have been taking your advice and keeping it in my pants. But in any event, a future with her is impossible and I need to get away."

"You don't need a career in the military, you know. You'll have work aplenty and a more than adequate income in Waterville. Perhaps you only need to go over for a couple of years."

Simon realised he'd said the wrong thing as Patrick levelled that intense green gaze on him. "It's not about need. I *want* to go – I want to do something worthwhile with my life. You understand that! You don't need to be a surgeon but you want to make a contribution too."

Simon nodded. "I'm only playing devil's advocate."

"What about you?" Patrick asked. He tilted his chair back and eyed his stepbrother. "Still going to join me – I mean, not now, when you're ready?"

"I'm ready now."

Patrick's chair dropped back onto four legs. He'd assumed Simon was still enjoying his time at the university. "Seriously?" He asked.

Simon nodded. "Yes, seriously. I've made an effort to read ahead from the assigned textbooks and I've been thorough with my practical work. I'm ahead of the rest of my class and the lecturers are now starting to hold me back. It's not in their interest for me to advance myself. They rely on the income of my fees so they'll drag it out. Taking the initiative in one's own study programme is openly discouraged."

"What about that anatomy lecturer with the bodies?"

"Danziger? Well, he's the only one. I didn't know, but he'd been an army surgeon back in the seventies. Saw action at

Trafalgar."

"Decent chap?"

"I think so. After I received your letter I spoke with him – really honestly, you know? Told him that my brother was buying a commission and it was always planned we'd sign up together. I asked him to tell me truly, would I be better off staying at Oxford or going to the Peninsula. You know what he said?"

Patrick grinned. "I can guess, particularly if he's former military."

"He told me to go. He said I would learn more over there than they could ever teach me here. He said that a year in a military hospital and I would know more than the university lecturers put together."

"So, that's it?" Patrick asked.

"That's it," Simon confirmed.

The two brothers smiled at each other. Then Simon said, "Your father won't be happy."

Patrick's laugh was humourless and reckless, "Your mother's going to kill you! I'd rather face my father."

Simon yawned and got up. "I haven't quit yet, and I've a lecture at sparrow fart tomorrow so ... it's off to bed for me."

He pushed his chair in but instead of leaving immediately he stood staring down at the blond head hunched over the table, the world-weary way the shoulders slouched.

He must have felt Simon's speculative eyes on him for Patrick looked up.

"What?"

Simon smiled, but it was a rueful smile, certainly not one of pleasure. "Whoever she is, you've fallen hard, haven't you?"

"Fuck off!" Patrick growled.

But Simon wasn't deterred; Patrick's bark was worse than his bite. "I've never seen you so dejected. And you haven't even bedded her! She must be someone special."

Simon knew better than to expect a response, nevertheless, he couldn't resist, "Who is she?" he persisted.

Patrick raised his head and for a long moment he stared at his stepbrother. A sense of unease slipped along Simon's spine. But then Patrick sighed, long and deep. "You wouldn't believe me if I told you."

He got up, pushed his chair in and took the empty teapot to the sink and emptied the leaves.

"Mrs Baldoon won't be happy. She puts the tea leaves on the lemon tree," Simon told him.

"Thought you were going to bed."

Simon laughed, "I am! Just tell me ... do I know her?"

Patrick opened the tap and began rinsing out the teapot and Simon wasn't sure his stepbrother had heard him. He turned away and was about to leave the room when Patrick mumbled something.

Simon thought he was mistaken, but it sounded distinctly like, "Not as well as you think you do."

∾

Mrs Baldoon closed the door and glanced down at the message in her hand. It was very formally addressed to Lord Patrick Washburn – she turned it over – no return address.

"Hmph," she said. The handwriting on the front looked feminine, but unfamiliar – no surprises there. "Doesn't take them long to find out he's here."

His lordship was currently warming his feet before the parlour fire so she took the message immediately to him rather than leave it on the mail tray in the hall.

The Young Lord looked up from the documents he was reading by the afternoon light coming through the window. His feet were stretched toward the fire, and he pulled them in as his housekeeper approached with the mail tray in her hands.

"Message, my lord." She wrinkled her nose in disapproval at the sight of him barefoot, wearing only shirt and trousers. Familiar as she was with the master's casual manner, she was proud of working for a count – a future earl and one of the wealthiest young men of the day – she just wished he would comport himself accordingly.

Still, he was pleasant, polite and allowed her freedoms that others of lesser rank would not. Freedoms that included candid speech, a freedom she was prompted to exercise now.

"Couldn't you put some stockings and shoes on, my lord?"

He frowned. "Why? I'm in my own parlour."

"Well," she thought about it. Why couldn't he be one of those flashy lords she could brag to her friends about? "There is a level of decorum that you should adhere to, you know."

"Really?" he raised a foot and wriggled his toes at her. "Does the sight of my naked feet offend you, Mrs Baldoon? Or perhaps," he added with a lascivious grin, "you are one of *those* types, you know? Harbouring a secret fetish, hmm?"

He winked slyly, "Naughty girl!"

Mrs Baldoon flushed at his familiarity but pulled herself together. Clearing her throat, she gave the mail tray a small shake. "The message, my lord." *She* would be professional, even if he wouldn't.

"Thank you, Mrs Baldoon." He took it with a raised eyebrow; he evidently recognised the handwriting. "Did Sir Simon say when he was going to be back?"

"He said he was going to the opera tonight, but he expected to be home this afternoon to eat and change his clothes." She glanced at the clock on the mantel piece. "Within the hour, I should think."

Patrick nodded and glanced down at the note in his hand. "Who delivered this? A footman or a boy?"

"A boy, my lord, not in livery."

"Hmm."

"Will that be all, my lord?"

"Yes, thank you Mrs Baldoon."

⌒

The housekeeper closed the door after her and Patrick tossed the note onto the table. It was in a blank envelope, addressed in Lady Mary Ashwood's hand and delivered by a boy. If it had been delivered by a footman, and written on her stationery, it would be an open invitation to something.

This was evidently a private message from Mary. Probably an assignation. She'd provided her husband with an heir so he was no doubt allowing his wife more freedom nowadays.

Patrick had enjoyed his time in Mary's arms – and for a while he'd considered himself in love with her. He snorted self deprecatingly; he knew better now, and much as a sneaky dalliance with Mary would provide a delightful diversion while he finalised his departure plans, he was not in the slightest aroused by the idea.

His heart was bruised and he was nursing it. Some men might salve their wounds between the thighs of a willing slut, but not this man – not even for a well-born slut like Mary.

Patrick had not bedded a woman in over three months – the last being Kat Wheeler – and he had absolutely no desire to leap back into the saddle, as it were. He had other fish to fry, and one of those fish was a letter to his father.

The front door banged and Patrick raised his head – Simon was home already. He took the note from the table and flung it into the fire watching it brown, curl and ignite. By the time Simon came into the room, the note was mere ashes.

Simon entered the parlour looking a little worse for wear. Patrick took in his puffy eyes and streaming nose and raised his hand in the old horned-devil gesture common in the Middle Ages and said to ward off evil.

Despite his illness, Simon laughed – or would have if his nose wasn't so blocked.

"Suppose this means you're not going to the opera tonight?"

His stepbrother grunted in response; Patrick interpreted it as no.

"Is now a good time to discuss your plans for riding to Broughton Hall to speak to our parents?"

Simon shook his head, the movement causing him to sway on his feet. "Better sit down," he murmured thickly, then sneezed violently.

"Yes, you'd better sit down," Patrick agreed, indicating a chair in the farthest corner of the room away from him, "over there."

He watched his brother for a moment, noting the over-bright eyes and flushed cheeks. "You look feverish. You won't be embarking on a journey for at least a week, I'd say. What's your professional opinion?"

"I'm dying."

"Very astute diagnosis, doctor. How long do you have, and will you remember me in your will?"

"Shut up. I'm going to bed."

Patrick gave a snort of laughter and decided to go out.

∾

The morning dawned grey and miserable when Patrick knocked on his stepbrother's door. Simon was sitting up in bed studying a medical journal.

"No point in asking if you feel any better," Patrick said, with a grimace. "Anything I can get you? Hot toddy or something?"

Simon shook his head. "No," he rasped and pointing emphatically toward his throat, added, "losing my voice."

"Oh, all the better for me then." Patrick was cheerful. He'd gone out to the Smithy's Arms the night before but stayed sober – content to sit quietly in a corner nursing a brandy while Deon

Morehead shared the bench opposite with a very friendly serving maid.

After enduring an unpleasant half hour during which he was serenaded by the various grunts and wet sucking sounds as they kissed and fondled one another, he got up to leave, responding to Deon's, *Where're you going?* with, "Home. You two sound like a pair of cows trying to pull their feet out of the mud."

Consequently, he was alert and fresh as he sat on a chair beside Simon's bed.

"Mrs Baldoon said you wanted to talk to me," Patrick said. "We need to work out how we tell our parents."

"Yes," Simon's voice sounded painful.

"Don't talk if it hurts. We can talk later."

"It doesn't hurt ... I wanted to ask," Simon swallowed hard, and Patrick thought it may not hurt him to talk but it certainly hurt him to swallow. "I wanted to know if you were coming ..." swallow, "... to Broughton Hall with me?"

It was something Patrick hadn't considered. To his consternation, his first thought was that he'd get to see Alex again – one final time before leaving for the Peninsula – and his heart gave a brief leap of pleasure.

And she's the reason you decided to bring forward your enlistment, you idiot! He cursed himself but presented a carefully shuttered face to his stepbrother.

"No, I can't." His mind worked quickly trying to think up a plausible excuse. "I have to go back to Waterville to tie up a few last-minute details. I can meet you in London when you're ready."

Simon nodded. "I can tell your father, but ..." he swallowed and winced, "you really ought to tell him yourself."

"I'll write to him. I'll leave tomorrow and ride back to Devon. Once there I'll write to him."

"You only just got here."

"I know, but ..." he shrugged helplessly. "If we give you a week or so to get over this illness, my letter ought to arrive around the same time you do."

Simon nodded and swallowed, too ill to argue with Patrick's dubious reasoning. "Will you wait for me in London? At one of your father's houses?"

"Perhaps." Patrick frowned in thought. "But I think they all may be tenanted. It might be better for me to go to Grace's town house. I'll need to leave Equus where I know she'll be looked after."

"I could take her to Yorkshire with me." Simon knew, even as he spoke, that his offer would be declined. Patrick would want to ride Equus to London.

"So, we're decided then?" Patrick asked and Simon nodded and swallowed. "Don't speak any more. I'll come by and see you before I leave tomorrow.

Simon nodded again and the brothers' eyes met. There was no need of further words.

This was it – they were going to war, and though each was searching for his own future, their reasons couldn't be more different.

A FAREWELL

Patrick sat forward in his chair, while the young mother on the couch across the room fed her child. She had unbuttoned her bodice, to expose one large, milk-engorged breast, to which the infant attached itself with all the enthusiasm of a starving creature.

Grace looked up and met his steady green gaze and smiled. "One would think he'd had enough – I fed him only a short time ago – he is always hungry."

"Better that he be hungry than the opposite," Patrick commented.

"*Si*, I think this is so," the Italian girl agreed. Breastfeeding one's own child was not something to be encouraged among the gentry, much less doing so before a male friend, but Grace's friendship with Patrick was of an entirely different nature.

They were not lovers but there was a certain affection between them. They were not like brother and sister either, for Patrick had facilitated Grace's illicit love affair with her now husband – she couldn't imagine him doing something like that for his sisters ... and yet there was something between them.

She watched him watching her, his eyes fixed on her breast, but she knew there was nothing lascivious in his wistful observation.

"Patrick," she said gently. When he looked up, she asked carefully, "Who is she? This one you are running from."

Predictably, he adopted a shuttered expression and slumped back in his chair. "I am not running from anyone."

Grace shrugged. "You are going to Spain in a great hurry then."

"Simon and I are ready."

"*Si, si* ..." she nodded, unconvinced. "When will Simon arrive, do you think?"

"This afternoon, assuming he has not had any difficulties on the road from Yorkshire. It's a long ride on your own."

"And you did not go with him? I wonder at that." She studied him speculatively. "It is her, is it not? Your stepsister?"

Patrick got to his feet, "Grace! I wish you ... I'll be in my room." He strode to the door.

"There you go, running away again."

Swinging back to face her, he said, with an edge in his voice, "I am not running away. Simon and I planned to join up years ago. Now, the time is right."

"I know you, *mio caro*, better than the others. I know that your little stepsister is in love with you. I am ..." she narrowed her eyes at him, "I am quite certain you return her regard. *Beh* ...!" she added with a shrug. "Sit down, Patrick. I will not question you further. *Mantieni i tuoi segreti.*"

"I don't have any secrets," he grumbled, but resumed his seat.

They let the silence reign for several minutes and the only sounds in the room were the pops and crackles coming from the fire and the steady pulling of the suckling child.

At length Grace said, "You will marry one day, Patrick, and your wife will have a child of yours. You will allow her to feed the child or you will engage a wet-nurse?"

"I haven't thought about it." He watched as the Italian woman slipped a finger into her baby's mouth to detach him, then unashamedly released her other breast and shifted the infant to it.

"I imagine it will be my wife's decision."

"You like children, I know. I remember how you were with your youngest sister ... the baby ... what was her name?"

"Meg."

"Ah, *si*. Meg." She stroked the fine dark hair from the baby's brow as he fed. "You like children. You like animals. You are handsome, titled and wealthy. What a catch! It is no wonder that Alessandra—"

"Grace!" Patrick's voice adopted a warning tone but she merely smirked at him.

"You see, if she means nothing to you, you have no reason to be so ... *come si dice*?"

"Defensive?"

She grinned impishly at him. "You are defensive?"

"Grace, for Christ's sake, when are—" he broke off as the bell at the front door sounded. Grace's housekeeper responded and the two in the parlour could hear the older woman's voice followed by the lower tones of a man.

"That sounds like Simon," Patrick said, grateful of the change of subject. Grace had bettered him and he didn't like it. Not that he didn't mind a bit of verbal thrust and parry, but she'd made an uncomfortably accurate assessment of his position – and that's what he didn't like.

❧

Grace's housekeeper briskly knocked on the parlour door and put her head around it. Her eyes widened disapprovingly at the sight of her mistress feeding the young master before their male guest, and she certainly hadn't approved of the way Jean, the scullery maid had gone all fluttery when the young lord arrived the other evening.

The sooner he left the better, in her opinion, and as if this Lord Whoever weren't bad enough, Sir Somebody at the front door had a face on him likely to see an honest woman fall down in a dead faint. Lord knows what's going to happen when Jean sees *him*!

"Mrs Poole, Sir Simon here to see you and milord," she nodded vaguely in Patrick's direction.

"*Grazie*, Mrs Cockell," Grace said, buttoning her bodice. Please show him in and then tell Jeremy's nurse that I will bring him up to bed. I think he will sleep now."

The housekeeper backed out of the room, opening the door wider to usher in their guest.

∾

Simon immediately approached Grace, bowing formally before her, but she, never one to adhere to convention, rose and embraced him, kissing both his cheeks before stepping back to admire him.

"*Dio*, Simon, do you daily grow more handsome?" she asked, laughing. "I have a housekeeper, a scullery maid and, little Jeremy's nurse – women all. Please do not distract them from their duties!"

Patrick went over to greet his stepbrother with a masculine embrace and clap on the back, his good humour restored. "Good to see you, man," he said. "We were beginning to wonder where you'd got to."

"Oliver threw a shoe – had to walk him for a while and get him to a smithy. He's all right now though." Turning to Grace, "I understand you'll be housing Oliver and Equus in your stables? Is that still alright? I can arrange to have Oliver sent back to Yorkshire."

"It is perfectly all right, Simon, of course." Grace hiked little Jeremy higher in her arms and Simon noticed the baby for the first time.

"Ah, hello young sir," Simon said, sticking a finger out. Jeremy immediately clutched it in his fist and opened his mouth to show his new friend a milky set of gums.

"Time for his rest," Grace said, "I will take him upstairs and then have some refreshment prepared for you."

"Don't go to any trouble," Simon told her, but she was already heading to the door.

❧

After Grace left the room, Simon and Patrick sat, and Simon studied his stepbrother. "All set?" he asked.

Patrick nodded. "Paperwork's done and the commissions arrived last week. My steward and Mrs Bath are fully briefed so Waterville Place is taken care of. We're ready."

Simon continued to watch the other man, then finally he said, "Aren't you going to ask?"

"I would have ... eventually."

"Well, to save you the bother, no – it wasn't good. There were tears, recriminations and threats, and they were just from Cook. My mother was furious, your father unhappy and Zan was miserable. She instructed me – and you – to not do anything brave or stupid."

Patrick felt a warmth spread through him at the mention of his stepsister's name but controlled his expression. "I hope you explained that we did not *intend* to be killed."

"Pointless to tell her that." Simon rolled his shoulders and twisted to stretch his spine with a series of cracks, as the housekeeper came into the room with a tray of tea and cake.

"A room has been prepared for you, Sir Simon," she told him. "Would you like bath-water taken up?"

"Thank you, that would be just the ticket, Mrs ..."

"Cockell."

"Thank you, Mrs Cockell." Simon flashed her a dazzling smile.

Patrick grinned as he saw the woman unconsciously touch her

hair.

"Oh," she said, remembering. "Mrs Poole said she'll be down later and will see you at supper. Mr Poole will be home by then."

"Thank you again, Mrs Cockell."

As the housekeeper closed the door behind her, Simon watched as his stepbrother poured the tea and handed him a cup. He helped himself to a slice of cake and sat back to enjoy the food while continuing to study the other man.

Finally, Patrick looked up. "Something worrying you?"

Simon swallowed a mouthful of cake and put the plate down. "Well, yes there is, as a matter of fact. We didn't get to really talk, last time I saw you in Oxford. That letter you sent from Waterville ... what was that all about?"

Patrick had hoped to avoid the subject but realised now that Simon had only been biding his time. He grinned sheepishly. "I can see I'm going to have to rethink my opinion of you – you're much more patient than I gave you credit for."

"Thought you were going to get away with it, did you?"

Patrick shrugged. "What would you like to know?"

"You're forfeiting the wager? Doesn't have to be that drastic."

∿

The blond man took a deep breath and sipped his tea, thinking over his response. "You know, Sime," he began, then seemed to make up his mind about something. "I found myself in an unexpected situation." Patrick was feeling uncomfortable – he hated to talk about himself. But Simon sat quietly, waiting, and suddenly Patrick thought that to unburden himself, even if he were to keep the details vague, might be cathartic.

"I could have let myself be carried away by the moment," he began. "It would have been easy but she ..." he swallowed, how much to say without saying too much? His stepbrother was regarding him intensely. "She is young and unattainable. I felt ...

too much and under the circumstances, I decided ... I decided it would be better for all concerned if I removed myself."

∾

Simon nodded. When he'd first received Patrick's letter saying simply, *You win. My future is with the army. I am resolved never to marry*, a most unwelcome suspicion had insinuated its way into his mind.

Zan.

Simon knew that his sister and mother had been summering at Waterville, and his suspicions gained traction. Yet during his visit to his family estate, discussions with his sister had given him no reason to believe anything untoward had passed between his sister and stepbrother. He'd set his foolish notions aside.

That was until his mother had off-handedly commented about some falling out between Zan and Patrick that had resulted in Zan going missing for an entire day.

At the time, Simon had given it little thought, for on its own, it was of no particular consequence. Zan and Patrick had a long history of squabbling.

But taken in the context of the other details his mother had supplied – the inseparable nature of their friendship throughout that summer in Waterville – had given Simon pause.

Now Patrick admitted the woman in question was young and unattainable. A description which, Simon thought with growing trepidation, could as easily fit Zan.

∾

Patrick, watching Simon closely, realised immediately that he'd said too much. "In any event," he added, with practised off-handedness, "she is a peasant ... daughter of one of my tenants."

"Ah." Simon nodded, evidently eager to put his sister from his mind. That path led to certain trouble.

It was the first time Patrick could recall ever lying to Simon. He didn't enjoy it but he saw the muscles at the corners of Simon's eyes relax and knew it was for the best. No benefit – to anyone – would be served, if Simon ever discovered the truth.

At that moment, Mrs Cockell returned to announce that Sir Simon's bath-water was waiting in his room. "I will show you the way, Sir."

Simon rose and looked down at his stepbrother. "There is, however, the matter of a particular wager," he said, waggling his eyebrows.

The agreement, now that Patrick had conceded defeat, was that he remain celibate for a year. "I've already served four months," he said with a grin. "Does that count?"

"I suppose so," Simon allowed, magnanimously, and followed the housekeeper from the room.

Patrick sighed long and deep. Four months was nothing, he decided, nor was the remaining eight. For at this particular moment, he had absolutely no desire to bed anyone. It was unusual for him, and, he suspected, would be a fleeting condition. Yet that was how he felt, for now.

He and Simon had two days in which to kick their heels in London before reporting to their unit. He assumed Simon would use that time to acquaint himself with the seedier parts of town, and he, Patrick, would dutifully accompany him – as an observer.

༄

George Poole was not an attractive man, with his large head and bulbous nose, but his expression was kind and his pale-green eyes sparkled with humour. He didn't understand the nature of his wife's relationship with that handsome young blade, Lord Patrick, but the chap was a lot less stuck up than other toffs George had met.

Besides that, George would never forget how the fellow had

escorted Grace around town, facilitating a courtship between the fashionable Italian girl and the clumsy office worker, and covering for them during their occasional midnight rendezvous.

So Patrick Washburn was all right in George's books. When that evening he returned home from his clerical job in St Martin's Lane, George was not surprised to find a second gentleman in his wife's company – for he knew Simon was coming – but this fellow caused George to pause.

Despite his unfortunate looks, George had never known an ounce of ill-feeling toward any man – until he was introduced to Sir Simon Broughton.

Simon was witty, charming and confident. He was his wife's friend – indeed she treated him as one might a brother – quite the same way as she treated Lord Patrick. But George liked Patrick; from the moment he met Simon, George disliked him.

George disliked Simon intensely and irrationally, and it was a dislike borne of jealousy because Sir Simon Broughton was the most handsome man George had ever seen.

He resolved that he would speak with Mrs Cockell about ensuring her young scullery maid was kept strictly out of sight. Couldn't trust these rich handsome types, and Jean was just flighty enough to—

At that moment Mrs Cockell came into the parlour where George and his wife were sitting with the two gentlemen and George's heart sank as he witnessed the impossible – Mrs Cockell flirting!

Flirting with the handsome young buck and as the silly woman closed the door behind her, George made an audible and entirely involuntary growl of displeasure.

"Oh George!" Grace said, laughing. "Very few women are immune to Simon's face. You must accept it as the rest of us must."

Simon, to his credit, appeared somewhat abashed and, as

though attempting to divert attention, continued his conversation.

It appeared that he was stepbrother to Lord Patrick and the two had purchased commissions. "Yes," he was saying, "We are to report to the barracks in two days. Your wife has kindly allowed us to leave our horses here ... I trust that will not inconvenience you at all, sir?"

"Of course not," George quickly assured him, eager to cover his impolite behaviour. "As you've seen, our stables are large ... larger than we need. You're welcome to keep them here."

"You'll be paid, of course," Simon added, unnecessarily, since Patrick had already made those arrangements with Grace, but Simon was feeling uncomfortable, and he needed to say something.

"It is all arranged," Grace said. "And now we have had enough talk of the war. What plans do you two have for your stay in London?"

And from there, the talk flowed over George's head as he watched the easy repartee between his wife and these two young gentlemen. It was the first time in George's life, he'd been so aware of his ill-favoured face, and he didn't like it.

Not that it seemed to worry his wife, for even now she was smiling at him, and he recognised the glint in her eye – absent since the birth of their son – and George looked forward to an early night.

∾

Two days later, Grace stood on the porch of her London home, waving off the two young men as their hired coach pulled away. She had put on a brave face, for their sakes, but she was grieving nonetheless. She had a bad feeling about this and had asked Patrick, several times, to reconsider.

But he was determined to join the war, as was Simon. Grace understood Simon's point of view. He was minor nobility, and though going to war was not usually what the eldest son would do,

Simon had been studying to be a physician and saw this as an opportunity to do some good, to be more than just a landed gentleman.

If Grace could understand Simon's desire, she could not understand Patrick's. Patrick was a Count in his own right. He was to inherit the earldom after his father. A title as important as that should never be so easily disregarded, yet Patrick was going to war, where good men were dying in their thousands.

Patrick was the last of his name; he owed it to his ancestors to produce an heir and remain safe.

Her pleas fell on deaf ears. Patrick did not care for wealth or his title and as he hugged her to his chest and laughed at her fears, she knew he was resolute.

She also knew he was running away – a concept he'd firmly rejected – and despite her efforts, as recently as the previous evening, to talk to him, and encourage an honest discussion, he'd refused, stubbornly refuting her claims.

He continued to insist he was not in love with his stepsister. But Grace knew better. She knew what she'd seen between them; the comfortable rapport, the playful banter that disguised a deeper, dangerous intent.

If only he'd been open with her, Grace would have helped him, similarly to how he'd helped her with George, she would have supported him in any way he deemed beneficial.

Alexandra was betrothed, that much she knew, but such contracts were broken every day, she knew that too, and she would have ...

It didn't matter in any case. Patrick continued to deny her accusations and now ... she watched as the coach lumbered down the road and rounded a corner taking them out of sight. Clasping her hands over her heart she prayed, *Please God, keep him safe. Keep them both safe.*

UNEXPECTED MEETING AT BADAJOZ

In the Autumn of 1811, Napoleon Bonaparte ordered his French commanders in Spain to expand their control by continuing their offensive against Valencia. The effect of this was to reduce the number of French troops available to stand against the British.

Newly promoted, General Arthur Wellesley decided to use this attenuation to his advantage. Taking delivery of a powerful new siege engine, complete with fresh troops, he advanced across the border, to capture the fortresses of Cuidad Rodrigo and Badajoz.

I was ordered to march to Badajoz where I would join the thirty-second unit under his command. As part of this modern siege machine, I was outfitted in new white breeches, shiny black Hessian boots and a red woollen coat. My gorget hung about my neck, denoting my rank – by virtue of my commission and my title, I was an infantry captain.

Additionally, I was issued with a large-boned, and not terribly attractive horse and a greatcoat, which served as both day wear and as a blanket at night when we slept on the open ground.

Then, they gave me a Baker rifle with a detachable twenty-four-inch bayonet; I wore my own sword – a gift from my father for my sixteenth birthday, custom forged to my measurements – a nobleman's rite of passage as he progressed from childhood to manhood. I'd been trained in its use, as all young men of my rank were, and I was considered a reasonably competent swordsman. Yet I had never wielded it with any serious intent, particularly not in anger.

I expected that all that was about to change.

∾

Simon and I had left Dover on a dreary grey day. We'd sailed to Spain together, but as we'd disembarked at the port of Cadiz, we embraced and went our separate ways – he to join a medical team that deployed to Salamanca, while I met my unit, formed up and prepared to march to Badajoz.

Simon's team departed Cadiz first, and as I stood by to wave him off; it was a surprisingly emotional moment – over the course of the last few years, Simon and I had become legal brothers through our parents' marriage, yet we were closer than that. With four sisters between us – including baby Meg – we had quickly formed an alliance that could not have been stronger had we been born of the same blood.

I would trust Simon Broughton with my life, and I saw the reciprocal allegiance in his face as he marched out. I wondered *when* we would see each other again. I was not a superstitious man, but I refused to say *if* – even to myself.

∾

My company departed one bright, October morning, embarking on a long journey across unfamiliar terrain. I was given command of a small company of around 200 infantrymen, and we strode out in two columns. They were as excited as boys on an adventure, chatting, laughing and occasionally singing, and I smiled to myself as I rode at the head of a column.

I was dismayed to learn that due to my horse's lack of beauty, he'd been overlooked as an officer's mount and that he was only given to me because there were no others available. But I quickly discovered that he was an intelligent, gentle giant of a creature. I'd been told his name was Barnabus and introducing myself to him, I discreetly whispered in his scruffy ear that they'd saved the best of the herd for me.

Upon our enlistment, both Simon and I had received basic training, mainly in military protocol and so forth – it was considered that as landowners, and in my case, a member of the aristocracy, we were capable of leading and motivating men.

This may have been true up to a point, but I'd never been a leader and I doubted my ability to motivate anyone – beyond inveigling my friends to drink to excess.

Simon, in my opinion, would have made a far better leader than I. He was controlled and cool when under pressure, and compared with me, his decisions were more considered, his actions were less impulsive.

Given that, I supposed that my stepbrother was perfectly suited to a medical career. With no such vocation, I was merely a soldier – an inexperienced one at that!

Thus, I made a study of the behaviour of others more seasoned than I was. I noted how they rode at the heads of their columns, leading their men ever onwards, until nightfall when they handed over the direction of the evening ritual of making camp to their lieutenants.

There were animals to be fed, watered and made safe for the night. Weapons were to be cleaned, checked and secured, supplies stored and finally, the men themselves were to be fed and any medical issues taken care of.

These were injuries or illnesses that had arisen during the day's march – I was amazed at both the number and ridiculous nature of them.

They ranged in variety and included clumsy accidents like sprained ankles caused by tripping over exposed tree-roots, and burns sustained during cooking meals. One chap broke a finger when he dropped a heavy crate on it while another unfortunate fool somehow managed to perform an amputation of his own toe while chopping wood for a fire.

By far the worst two medical conditions we faced, with tedious regularity, were dysentery caused by drinking from contaminated wells or streams, and the pox. The former I instructed my lieutenant, a Welshman by the name of Hywel, to educate the men about, while the latter ... well, let's just say that neither Hywel nor I was a match for the gaggle of Spanish whores that followed us with the persistence of a swarm of blowflies. I was fighting a losing battle on that front.

I soon realised that the men would – for the most part – do what they would do. As for me ... I followed Simon's most astute advice and *kept it in my pants*.

Needless to say, I was still bound by our wager – I had seven months of abstention yet to serve. Even though Simon assured me that he would not hold me to such a condition, I'd have been inclined to join the priesthood before being tempted by the greasy-haired, gap-toothed camp followers whose spotty faces evidenced the ravages of the pox burning beneath their skirts.

Each evening, while the men caroused or sat around their campfires talking or singing, I was required to prepare a daily report for my commander, which I sealed and handed to a fast-riding messenger. I doubted that my reports were ever read, indeed I'd never even met my commanding officer, a Major Thorpe who was, I'd been advised, at Badajoz awaiting my arrival with my company of reinforcements.

My orders required me to get my men to Badajoz with all

urgency, so I drove them hard. We broke camp every morning before dawn, we marched all day with two brief pauses, and I only called a halt when the sun had disappeared over the western horizon. I set a brisk pace – we had nearly two hundred miles to cover, and the men were exhausted by the day's end.

But *my* day didn't end there. Besides my reporting responsibilities, I was required to read and respond to various letters and memoranda received throughout the day, and to maintain a personal log of the day's events. All this kept me busy well after most men had gone to their beds – or someone else's.

This forced separation from the men in my command, coupled with my relentlessly pushing them mile after mile, caused me to wonder how I could ever instil in them the necessary loyalty and motivation to face an enemy at close range. I certainly would expect more than that from a man who had the power to order me to my maker's doorstep.

With this in mind, one morning, as we broke camp, I decided to change the way I did things. Instead of riding at the head of my columns and leaving the ordering of the men to Hywel, I pulled Barnabus to the side of the column and as the men filed past, I randomly singled out a group and walked Barnabus alongside.

My belief that people love to talk about themselves was reinforced as I encouraged them to talk openly and casually. I was unsurprised to learn that they were, for the most part, single men, younger sons, with no prospects of work and, wishing to relieve their mothers of an additional mouth to feed, had joined the military.

It was important that I shared information about myself as well; rightly or wrongly, I decided that the best way to eliminate suspicion and garner loyalty was to be open and honest and to offer stories of my own. Therefore, when they talked about their families, I told them about my brother the army physician. If they mentioned their sweethearts or showed me the small pictures they often carried of lasses they fancied, I made suitably admiring comments while explaining that for myself, I'd rather face Napoleon.

That always got a laugh, then after inviting them to freely approach me if they had questions or concerns, I wheeled Barnabus aside before singling out my next group.

I followed this practice every day for several days, gradually working my way through the columns of men – ensuring that I remembered their names and the information I gleaned about them. Each morning as we broke camp, I made an effort – even if I could only spare ten minutes or so – to stroll about the campsite, mingling with them and addressing them by name as they gathered their equipment and made ready to begin the day's march.

Their inherent distrust of authority and the aristocracy caused them to be reticent at first, but it was only a matter of days before they began looking up as I wandered by, offering a casual tug of their caps or a polite greeting.

I was gratified to see that while maintaining a healthy respect for my status as their captain, they were learning to trust me, and from time to time, even greeted me with shouts of, *Mornin' capt'n* and *Nice day fer it capt'n*, as I passed by.

Some may accuse me of ingratiating myself with my subordinates, but I would deny the charge. It was my firm belief that if you were going to ask a man to put his life in your hands and obey your orders unquestioningly, then you'd bloody well better deserve it and respect him in turn.

Regardless of my motivation, it was evident that the men were increasingly relaxed in my company, and more importantly, during that ten-day march, I generated a rapport with them that grew into a certain loyalty.

I had no idea how invaluable that would prove, but I hoped I'd not have to test it.

❧

We rode into our camp on the outskirts of Badajoz late one afternoon. It was a city of grey canvas tents belonging to the senior officers, and cooking fires denoting the small personal territories of the enlisted men. It had been a gruellingly slow almost two-week march and although I'd set a cracking pace, a train of 200 men, equipment, pack mules and supply wagons, could travel only so fast.

Additionally, we were trailed by the assorted refugees and camp followers typical of a mobile army. The latter not only included whores, but also tradesmen such as farriers, carpenters and barbers whose services included dental procedures.

I rode at the head of one column, Hywel beside me at the head of the other, as we arrived. Our men were rapidly absorbed into the greater company of some 35,000 allied soldiers under the ultimate command of Viscount Wellesley

I was surprised to discover that ours wasn't the only company to arrive that day. In fact, our numbers were increasing as companies continued to arrive – sometimes two or three every day.

Upon my arrival, I was to present myself to my commanding officer, Major Thorpe. I took five minutes to remove my travel-stained clothes, dip my hands into a basin of water to rinse away road dust, and put on a clean shirt. I beat as much dust from my red coat as possible, and signalled to Hywel that I was leaving.

During my training period, I had learned that all British camps were laid out to the same plan. This meant that regardless of the camp, all the important tents were in roughly the same area and could be easily located.

For example, I knew without being told where I could find the medical tent, the officers' mess tent or the supply tent. It also meant that I knew where to find the tent belonging to my commanding officer.

Major Thorpe's aide, who introduced himself as Samuel Fitchen, met me at the entrance to the major's tent. He held the tent flap open and I ducked into the dingy space, my eyes slowly adjusting to the inadequate light of a single lamp on a large rectangular table in the centre.

Several men stood about the table. On it was spread a map showing Spain, Portugal and France, with coloured wooden pegs depicting what I guessed were the various armies.

The men surrounding the table seemed to be talking casually, and several had tankards in their hands. A number were leaning over the map, one in particular, whose face was turned away, was talking softly and indicating a point on the map. His hair was so black that the lamp cast blue shimmers through it, reminding me of someone I knew from Devon.

But I didn't have time to think about that now. Fitchen announced me and I cringed inwardly at the impeccably formal use of my rank and title.

"Captain Viscount Patrick Washburn, newly arrived, Sirs."

At which point, the officer with the blue-black hair, broke off his conversation and looked up. After only the slightest pause, I made my formal salute and was introduced to my direct commanding officer, Major Christopher Thorpe, and the other men of various ranks about the room.

I was offered a tankard of ale, which I gratefully accepted, and remained content to listen as the gathered officers discussed the current situation. It appeared that after the successful siege of Badajoz, Viscount Wellesley had decided that the thirty-second regiment should join a general advance upon Salamanca.

My first thought was for my men, who'd only just completed a long march, but as the discussion continued, I realised that the comfort of the men came second to a greater consideration.

Of urgent concern to the officers gathered in that tent, was lack of money. Lack of money resulted in the inability to purchase food and supplies, which led to parties raiding villages – definitely not the ideal way to garner support among the locals. Another result was that the men would not be paid, an inflammatory situation guaranteed to result in dissent and rebellion among the troops.

For my part, I sipped my ale and listened in dismay as the conversation continued. One young captain, I say young, although he was probably older than I was and certainly more experienced, suggested writing to the king.

This idea was quickly scotched amidst laughter and jeering, and the young captain removed himself, red-faced, to my side.

"Captain Washburn," he acknowledged with a nod.

"Captain ... apologies, I don't recall your name."

"No. I don't suppose you do. Too many of us, eh?" He shrugged carelessly. "Captain Emerson, at your service."

I nodded my acknowledgement, then, "When do you suppose we'll be pulling out?"

"Soon," Emerson responded. "Wellesley left last night, so he'll be keen for us all to join him. Major Thorpe's just going over the route on the map."

As we were talking, the gathering was breaking up. Major Thorpe swept the coloured pegs into a packet and rolled up the map. He handed it to an aide as he accepted the various goodnights from the departing men.

I placed my empty tankard on the table beside the others and prepared to take my leave when Thorpe spoke. "Captain Washburn? A word if you would. Please remain for a moment."

Nodding, I stood aside as the officers filed from the tent, casting curious glances in my direction as they passed.

∽

"Christie, you bastard!" I declared.

"Ha!" Thorpe responded, opening his arms to me and I walked up to him. We embraced, slapping one another's backs in genuine affection.

"What the devil are you doing here?" I asked, stepping back to admire the tall officer before me.

"I could ask the same of you, except that I knew you were coming."

"Ah, did you now."

Christie grinned and went across the tent to where a leather trunk sat in the corner. He moved with a loose-limbed grace that the gangly youth I'd spent many summers with in Devon, had never hinted at.

For Christie had been our closest neighbour and, until Simon, the truest male friend I'd ever had. His father was a Duke, Christie was a third son, and as such, convention decreed, it was either the church or the military.

He turned, a bottle in his hand, and waggled his eyebrows. "Napoleon's finest. Shall we drink to old friends?"

"We shall indeed." I made myself comfortable on the upturned crate he indicated. He pulled over a second one, and we placed the bottle on the table between us.

"No fancy crystal here, I'm afraid," he said, and I held out my ale tankard.

Christie had been a tall skinny lad with pale skin and the blackest of hair. Two years his junior, I had nevertheless dragged this quiet, thoughtful boy into all manner of scrapes and escapades – many of which resulted in his being chastised, for as the duke, his starchy old father determined, being the elder, Christie should have known better.

"To old friends," he said, and we drank together, both sighing in appreciation. "Told you it was good. Should call it the Little Emperor's best."

I laughed. It gladdened my heart to see Christie again. It had been ...

"How long has it been, Pat?" His dark blue eyes looked me over. I remember Maeve had gone all silly around him, declaring his eyes were in fact purple. Looking at him now, in the dimness of the tent, I was swayed to agree. "You look well," he added.

"It's been ... five years?" I said after a moment's thought.

He nodded. "At least. And you haven't changed."

"So is it coincidence that I report to you, or ..."

"What do you think? My father told me in one of his infrequent letters that you'd bought a captain's commission and shipped out. All it took was a word in the right ear and," he shrugged. "Here you are."

"I'm glad of it."

"So am I. If you're as daring now as you were when we were boys, you're the sort of man I want in my regiment." He sipped his brandy. "And from what I read in your reports, you are."

"Oh, you actually read those? I expected they'd be gathering dust in a pile somewhere."

"Not at all. Now, tell me. How's your lovely sister?"

My mouth fell open, suddenly disconcerted as Alex flickered through my mind. But then I mentally berated myself for a fool as firstly, Alex was not my sister, and secondly Christie would not know of her. I covered my momentary lapse by taking a large mouthful of brandy and swallowing it in several gulps.

Christie watched on, amusement pulling at the corners of his mouth.

Finally, I said. "Maeve's in Italy, no doubt driving the locals to distraction."

"Like she did us," he said, eyes dancing. "Quite a charmer, that sister of yours."

"I could say the same of your sisters." We both laughed for we knew that Christie's sisters were nothing of the sort.

"Well, Margaret, of course is married now and a bigger shrew there never was, while Susannah is not interested in marriage at all. My father is in despair but all she wants to do is read books and tend the herb garden."

I laughed. "And your father's ward. What was her name? Pretty little thing – used to follow us around all the time."

My friend shifted on his crate. "I trust she is well. I don't receive correspondence from home very often."

I wondered at Christie's sudden discomfiture and figured that in due course, as we renewed our friendship, we would share more intimate details with each other. But for now, I drained off my tankard and stood.

Christie stood as well, and we looked each other up and down. "So," I said nodding, pensively. "You not only outrank me at home, you outrank me here as well."

"Ah, that is not exactly correct," he said. "At home, I'm just the third son and people call me Sir Christopher. You will be an earl one day and will be called My Lord. Therefore," he added with a sly grin, "while you're here, I'll be making the most of my seniority."

I saluted formally. "Yes Sir! Goodnight, Sir!"

Turning in perfect military fashion, I marched to the tent flap, before looking over my shoulder. "Very fine brandy, Sir!"

Christie was laughing but he spoke soberly, "We pull out tomorrow, Patrick. Make sure your men are fit and ready to leave by dawn. We're marching to Salamanca."

I nodded and left the tent.

THE SEASONING

"Capt'n!" The shout seemed to come from a great distance away. "Oi Blake, I reckon that's Capt'n Washburn!" The voice sounded closer now and I stirred reluctantly, heavily, before deciding to return to sleep.

"Captain Washburn!" He, whoever *he* was, was persistent. But I was tired ... so thoroughly exhausted that I couldn't have risen if I'd wanted to.

I thought about pushing him away, ordering the man from my tent, but my limbs felt too heavy, and I was rapidly returning to a blissful, dreamless state.

Suddenly the lout had hold of my arm and was rudely shaking me. "Leave me alone," I mumbled, it was the most I could say, and it seemed to sap every last drop of strength from me.

"Hang about, Hopper. Did he just say somethin'?" A second voice.

"I reckon he did ... Come on, Capt'n, get up! We gotta get outta here." The first voice said again. It had a ring of urgency about it but unless my tent was afire, they could bugger off.

Perhaps my tent in fact *was* on fire; a thick mantle of smoke seemed to hang in the air and every time I drew breath it burned my throat and lungs.

But more than anything, I needed to sleep, and I allowed the voices to fade into the distance.

ॐ

The previous day

The morning after our arrival in Badajoz, my men formed up, and we filed out, one company along with two others, on a nine-day march to Salamanca.

By order of Viscount Wellesley, we were to join his thirty-second division, where we would be based for most of the winter in preparation for a fresh campaign early in 1812.

It was ironic that Simon would most likely be almost there by now, having marched directly to Salamanca from Cadiz. We hadn't expected to be reunited quite so soon, but if I was required to march my men another two hundred miles, so be it.

I returned comfortably to the routine of rising before dawn, strolling about the camp and greeting my men, mounting Barnabus and riding beneath the autumn sun for twelve hours, before making camp for the night.

Days on the march were not so difficult this time around – I suppose we all, man and beast alike, knew what we were in for. In any event, although we didn't commune during the day, Christie and I shared a glass of brandy each evening and did our paperwork together.

One such evening, we'd made camp just outside of Fuentes de Oñoro. The day had been warm, but as autumn progressed, the evenings were beginning to close in earlier and brought a cooling breeze with them.

Christie and I were in his tent. We'd completed our work and had poured the evening's brandy. Relaxed, he'd confided that he was estranged from his eldest brother. Thomas, I remembered from our childhood days, was a serious boy with a leaning toward religion. I was not surprised that he and the pragmatic Christie did not see eye to eye.

"He'd have joined the clergy if he'd had his way," Christie was saying. He was leaning back in his chair, examining the contents at the bottom of his brandy glass. "My father would never allow it, of course, Thomas being the eldest – the heir. Teddy would have been the obvious choice, second son and all, but ..." Christie smirked and gave a one-shoulder shrug. "You know Teddy."

"Still raising hell at court, is he?" I smiled, remembering the times Edward Thorpe and I had run amok through Whitehall Palace. And while my own attention was focused almost exclusively on Mary Whitmore, Teddy had arrangements with a variety of ladies' maids and the looks and charm that ensured he never passed a night alone.

If I had a reputation for licentious behaviour, I had nothing on Christie's brother. "Oh yes," I said archly, "I know Teddy."

Christie smiled indulgently. "Margaret says he'll die of the pox one of these days – that or mercury poisoning. He's part of Prinnie's inner sanctum."

"And you? I trust your father thought you joining the military a suitable occupation?"

He smiled ruefully. "Third son ... neither the heir, nor the spare. I thought it best to make myself scarce. I think Susannah was the only one who—" he broke off suddenly and cocked his head to the side.

"I heard it too," I said. "Sounded like a rifle shot."

It came again, closer, and undeniably the crack of a rifle. It was accompanied by shouts and several more shots.

We leapt to our feet. I was already wearing my sword; I had two pistols tucked into my belt but my rifle was back at my tent along with my coat and shako.

Suddenly the tent flap was thrown open and Fitchen, Christie's aide, stuck his head inside. "Major, the watch has fired on someone ... Frogs, they say, scouts, but there's more comin' over the rise. Looks like we got ourselves a bit o' evening's entertainment!"

Christie turned to me, all business now. "Always expect the unexpected. Call your men in, Captain, form up and await my command."

I saluted. "Yes, Sir!"

Outside the tent, all hell was breaking loose. Men were shouting at one another, running in every direction through the dark, while others were stamping out their fires, scrambling into their uniforms, several were pulling on their boots. One came running from the vicinity of the whores' camp, naked from the waist down, shirt-tail flapping, trousers and boots in his arms.

I was jogging towards my tent when Hywel grabbed my arm. How he'd found me amid the noise and confusion, I'll never know.

"Niall's saddling your horse, Sir," he shouted above the chaos and then he was off at a sprint.

Back in my tent, I hurriedly checked my pistols in the light of a lamp. I gathered a pouch of pistol balls and another of powder, tucked the pistols back into my belt and slung the pouches across my body. I slanted a quick glance toward my rifle but decided to leave it behind – I would be on horseback; a rifle would only get in my way. As an afterthought, I grasped a dagger I'd left on a table and slid it into my boot.

This is what they trained you for, I told myself, as I tamped the shako on my head. *This is what you're here for*. There was no time for any other thought as I emerged from my tent to find Niall holding Barnabus.

Niall was a young lad I had caught following me around early in our march from Cadiz to Badajoz. It seemed he was inordinately attached to Barnabus, and Barnabus seemed to like him in return, so I'd offered Niall a position looking after the horse, my equipment and my uniform along with various other personal tasks I required.

He told me he was 15, but if that were true, he was small for his age. In any event, I was happy with his service, and he definitely had a special way with Barnabus.

"I told yer, he don't like fightin', milord," Niall said, his face disapproving as I approached, buttoning my jacket. "S'why he were the only one left when yer arrived. No self-respectin' officer would have him."

His attachment to Barnabus stemmed, Niall had explained, from the horse's previous owner. It appeared the man had a vicious temper and a penchant for taking it out on horses. According to Niall, the massive horse had trust issues – whatever the hell that meant – was timid and had been beaten to the point where he was afraid of his own shadow.

Skittish though horses often were, I'd discovered early on that Barnabus was worse than any horse I'd ever known. He was afraid of almost everything from a low-flying starling to the sound of a stick snapping beneath his own hoof.

Over the month of our acquaintance, and with considerable patience, I'd earned a modicum of Barnabus's trust and he was gaining confidence, but I had no time or patience today. The great equine lump was showing me the whites of his eyes and dancing on the spot as I came up to him.

"He's a gentle soul, milord. Hates fightin' and suffers from this nervous thing where he gets so scared, he pisses himself."

"Oh Niall! Don't be ridiculous," I retorted as I swung into the saddle. "He's a warhorse whether he likes it or not. Wait here," I told the boy firmly, and gave him no time to respond. As I wheeled Barnabus around, I felt an unusual resistance in the horse's reaction and a strange tremor ran through him.

"Come on, boy," I said gently, rubbing his neck. "Time to grow a pair." I didn't have time for messing around. I kicked him sharply in the flanks and he jumped forward.

∾

Our combined regiments totalled around 800 men. Hywel and I waited at the front of our company, he on his chestnut mare, Dancy, and I on Barnabus. Flanked on either side by the other regiments we'd been marching to Salamanca with, we awaited the orders of our commanding officers.

Through the dark, I could just make out Christie. He was on his horse with a group of other officers, and what appeared to be a French soldier sent to parley. Rumours had flown thick in the air, all telling a different tale, but it was eventually confirmed that a small French scouting party had attracted the attention of our watch.

The overzealous, trigger-happy youth on duty, had shot the first man he'd spotted – no questions asked – right between the eyes. And before he had the chance to congratulate himself, he'd been shot dead in return by one of the man's compatriots.

As the scouting party fled back to their company, it now seemed that unless both the French commander and ours called the score even, we would shortly be engaged. For now, it was simply a waiting game.

Dawn was still an hour away. As I sat on Barnabus, I could feel the nervous energy coming off him. He stamped and snorted, his skin rippling with edgy tension. The leather of his saddle creaked as I leaned over his neck, rubbing and attempting to soothe him, but to no effect. He was breathing hard; his shoulders were grainy with his salty sweat.

One of the officers with Christie shouted some expletive and waved his arms angrily. Hywel and I exchanged anxious glances and Barnabus side-stepped in alarm.

The infantrymen at our backs were on edge and fidgety. The great adventure they'd been excitedly yammering about since the day we left Cadiz, was no longer such a great adventure.

I could hear one man muttering to himself – probably a prayer – while another seemed to have developed a persistent cough.

The waiting was the worst part; we waited for what felt like hours in the pearly-grey pre-dawn.

At length, Christie and the other officers broke apart, each cantering to his company. Christie came to me, and the two other captains reporting to him joined us – one of them was Captain Emerson, whom I'd met the night I'd arrived at Badajoz.

"We can't agree," Christie said simply. "Seems they were on the march, transporting goods – probably cannon. They believe we started it." He shrugged ruefully. "We did, I suppose. We'll be engaging at daybreak." Glancing off to the east, he added, "Soon. Emerson, go up over that flank – stay below the line of the ridge and prepare to move up behind them. If they have artillery – target that! Mason, go down that way – we are the larger force, skirt the boundary, and come up behind to block them in."

He turned to me with a wry expression. "Washburn, move your men up in line formation – present as narrow a target for their artillery as possible. We'll march right up the centre, meet them head on and engage with rifles and swords, distract them while Emerson and Mason get around the back." He glanced over my shoulder to where my men could be seen straining to hear. "Fix bayonets."

He pulled his horse around and moved off while I turned to Hywel. "Here we go." Then I addressed the men, "We're going to engage," I shouted. "Fix bayonets; let's give 'em a taste of pure British steel!"

The men roared their approval and the commotion started in earnest. I moved Barnabus aside and Hywel began shouting orders to form the men up. They erupted in a cacophony of shrieks and battle cries. At the same moment, Barnabus made an odd shriek of his own and a great gush of liquid splashed at his feet.

Leaning out of the saddle I looked down in dismay. "Christ, Barnabus, are you serious?"

A couple of the men noticed and called out, jeering and kicking up dust to cover the large, steaming puddle, for it was obvious that in the commotion, Barnabus had all but fallen to pieces. His withers and shoulders were shuddering; I could feel his sides rapidly expanding and contracting between my thighs with the force of his erratic breathing.

His bladder was finally empty but his angst wasn't over. As the frenzy and hysteria rose around him, Barnabus's distress grew. I could sense the weakness in his hindquarters, felt the shivering that was intensifying to the point where I feared his legs would give out from under him.

And suddenly Niall was there reaching for his halter. "I told yer so, milord! Didn't I tell yer so? Get off him before he collapses."

I threw the reins over Barnabus's head and did as Niall bid, making a promise to the horse that if I ever came face to face with his previous owner, I would kill the man with my bare hands. To reduce a great and noble creature to a quivering, useless wreck was unforgivable.

Niall took the reins. "Good luck, milord." And then he was gone.

"You want my horse, Sir?" Hywel leaned from his saddle. Dancy peered at me too, nostrils flaring, eyes alert – she looked ready to take on the entire French army.

I shook my head. "No," and I lined up with my men, the hubbub of their excitement flooding over me, lighting a fire within me. The sense of anticipation was such that I felt I was about to combust. My hands began to shake, my heart began to race, and I was imbued with a sense of lustful anticipation akin to taking a woman.

As the men around me worked themselves into a fever of madness, I had an untimely recollection of a book I'd read as a boy about Viking berserkers. These men drove themselves into paroxysms of insanity prior to rushing, crazed, vicious and virtually invincible, into battle.

I felt something of that now, surrounding me, buffeting me, infecting me with that bloodthirsty hunger. This was not bravery, this was not a group of young men embarking on adventure. This was raw ferocity, a furious, rabid dementia.

I could well see how men, deranged in the aftermath of battle, went on rampages of rape and butchery, oblivious to all but their most basic, savage urges.

And then the first of the sun's rays burst over the horizon. The signal came, the horns blew and I drew my sword.

∾

The first sign that we had been engaged was a heart-stopping explosion in the distance and some half-a-dozen cannon balls flying simultaneously through the air – they did indeed have artillery! It looked, from where I stood, like an oversized cricket game, with balls flying and bouncing all over the field.

But these balls were bowled with evil intent. To be struck by one was to be pulverised, to be in the vicinity of one coming to ground was to be buried alive in a shower of earth and rubble.

And we were off, running forward, towards the enemy in one great roaring swarm.

The boom and thunder of the cannon caused the ground to tremble while a barrage of rifle fire cracked and pinged past my ears and over my head as I ran.

Charging forward, my sword in my hand, my men either side and behind, I roared along with them. I was vaguely aware of the howls as men were struck and wounded, while others were felled without a sound.

My voice was lost among the hundreds charging across that field, the retorts of the rifles and the screaming of men.

We met the enemy as two great oceans crashing into one another in open water. We were without a shred of humanity as we hacked and slashed in an ecstasy of murder, and I hacked and slashed along with them.

In a moment of abstract clarity, I realised that if I did not attack, I would be attacked; if I did not kill, I would be killed – it was the most fundamental doctrine of any species.

And suddenly the moment was over as a huge French soldier loomed above me. I had a quick flash of drooping moustaches and flowing hair before I parried his sword attack and returned with an attack of my own that lacked any kind of technique whatsoever.

So much for all those lessons my father had paid for!

I was smaller, leaner and quicker. Although he was stronger, he was heavier and slower. Using that to advantage, I ducked and weaved, parried again and again as he swung and stabbed and thrust, forcing me backwards.

And then, I saw my moment. I gave him the lead and dropped to a crouch. He thought he had me – I saw the triumph rise in his face as he stepped in to make his kill. As he raised his arm, I leapt up beneath it, too quickly, too close for him to adjust. I hugged him to me with my sword arm wrapped around his back, and we were suddenly the only two people in the world.

The jarring of blade on bone sent shockwaves up my left arm. The man's eyes widened – he hadn't seen the dagger I'd retrieved from my boot. The victorious gleam in his eyes dulled. I continued to hold him as if we were engaged in some intimate and macabre dance.

But he was heavy. I gave him a backward shove and held the hilt of my dagger firmly, dragging it out as he fell – dead before he hit the ground.

As my knife came free, a jet of blood spurted from the entry point and showered me in a hot, sticky mess.

And I, in the middle of a raging battle, fell to my knees in the mud and bloody slush, and threw up.

∾

The horror of what I had just done passed quickly – it had to because within seconds the shouting, the flailing of limbs and crash of steel on steel was irresistible. I was on my feet, slashing and shrieking, caught up in the savagery, all over again. Knowing only that it was kill or be killed, I was one voice in a vortex of sound, and fighting for my life.

I faced one man after another, whirling and charging, while all around me was chaos, a maelstrom of fury and carnage. The sound, the sight, the smell, was one overwhelming assault – too multitudinous to be absorbed or recognised as individual elements, much easier to simply let it all wash over me like a great heaving, stinking tide.

An impenetrable black fog began to settle over the field; it was gunpowder and smoke from the fires used for the cannon. It was thick and acrid, burnt our noses and lungs, and blackened our faces and uniforms with smut. It was near impossible to discern friend from foe.

Yet, by now, the battle seemed to be waning, men lay dying or dead and the groans of wounded men and horses seemed to grow louder as the crack of pistol and rifle became sporadic. At least the cannon had fallen silent. Perhaps Emerson's men had circled around and taken their artillery down as Christie had strategised.

As blood and sweat mixed, my hands became slick and tacky. My eyes were stinging from sweat and smoke and suddenly I was standing alone, weaving dazedly on my feet, an island in a sea of dead or dying.

My sword arm dropped to my side.

At some point I had been wounded, but in the heat of the fighting I hadn't noticed. Now, though, I felt the burning slash across my breast and saw the blood stains around the ripped fabric of my coat.

The ringing in my ears reduced to where I could identify individual sounds. They were the cries of the dying, the groans of the wounded.

One sound seemed to stand apart. It was a sound that pulled at something within me; a perverse sense of compassion amid so much violence.

I turned towards it.

Dancy.

She was lying on her side, blood dribbling from her proud nose, foreleg at an impossible angle.

How was it that among so much death and violence, the life of a horse caused my heart to contract most painfully? I staggered towards her and hunkered beside her head. Resting a hand on her brow, I murmured, "Brave, sweet lass," and drew a pistol from my belt.

∾

Somewhat stunned by the events of the last hour or so, I watched detachedly as a French soldier wept over the body of a fallen comrade. Many Englishmen were doing the same – to what purpose? This entire event was the result of an impetuous youth and wounded pride.

Too small to be considered a battle, it would be called a skirmish. No ground was made, no side would claim victory, yet lives were lost – or changed forever.

Shaking my head, sadly, I turned away from the scene and came face to face with a blood smeared and very angry French man.

"*Enfoiré!*" he growled. "*Vous salaud goddams!*" Before I knew what was happening, he'd swung his rifle by its snout in a wide arc at my head.

I ducked, but not quickly enough to avoid being clipped on the temple with the rifle butt. I staggered and brandished my uselessly empty pistol.

He swung again.

☙

"Capt'n!" The young soldier shouted. "Oi, Blake, I reckon that's Capt'n Washburn!" Ensign Hopper looked up at his companion who was leaning over his shoulder. "Capt'n Washburn!" He repeated and grasped the captain's arm to give him a quick shake.

"Hang about, Hopper. Did he just say somethin'?" Ensign Blake asked, edging closer.

"I reckon he did ... Come on, Capt'n, get up! We gotta get outta here." Hopper sat back on his heels. "Don't look like he's hurt other than the bloody big lump on his head."

"Well, he's out cold now," Blake observed. "We'll have to carry him."

Hopper levelled a disdainful look on his skinny companion. "You mean *I'll* have to carry him?" He shrugged. "Hold this then." He handed Blake his rifle, crouched and threw the wounded officer unceremoniously over his shoulder.

☙

I woke up with the kind of headache that should accompany fragmented memories involving women and liquor. Unfortunately, that wasn't the case; in fact, I didn't seem to have memories of anything at all.

Opening my eyes was painful. There was a lamp on a nearby table and even its soft yellow glow seemed to cause my eyes to throb. But it was enough to catch a quick glimpse of my surroundings – it wasn't my room at Waterville, or even Oxford.

Groaning, I pressed my palms into my eyes and tried to sit up.

"Easy, there." The voice was close by and I heard movement as the man came up beside me. "You took a knock to the head. Bit of concussion, but you'll live."

"He's awake, is he?" A second voice, one I recognised.

Removing my hands, I squinted up at a handsome face framed by blue-black hair. "Christie. What ... what're you doing here? Did I ..." I frowned with the effort of remembering. "Did I fall off the barn roof again?"

Christie laughed lightly and shook his head.

"He's a bit confused, Major," the first voice spoke again. "A heavy knock to the skull can do that. He's just woken up and he's not thinking clearly. Should be easy enough to bring him back, talk him around, we need to make sure he's alright."

Christie smiled and I felt the edge of the bed dip. "Very well, Doctor. I'll sit with him."

The other man seemed to fade out and I was alone with Christie. "Patrick," he said with a grin. "You're in Spain ... the army, remember?"

I gave a protracted groan. Yes ... it was suddenly all there. Closing my eyes, I nodded and saw it all play out again behind my eyelids. These were not welcome memories, but there was no escaping them.

Finally, I said, "How many lost?"

"You're back so soon? Well, that was easy," he said, then sobering, added, "Twenty-two, for now. A score more still hanging in the balance."

I thought of my lieutenant. "Hywel?"

"He's alright. Came out of it without a scratch."

I sharply drew in my breath as another memory flashed before my eyes. "I shot his horse."

Christie nodded. "We know. The fighting was all but over by then. The sound of the shot attracted that French soldier. Luckily for you he'd run out of bullets – or you'd be dead by now."

I snorted. "He made good use of his rifle in any case," I muttered, remembering the wide arc of his arms, his double-handed grip on the muzzle and the butt coming at me.

"According to Ensign Hopper, you ducked the first swing, but he brained you properly with the second. Seems the Frenchie wanted to get a last notch on his belt before it was all over. You were unconscious before you hit the ground – he was determined to finish you off though and was preparing to cave your head in. Hopper shot him in the back, then he carried you here."

"Christ!" I let that sink in for a moment before speaking again. "So, I owe Hopper my life?"

Christie shook his head. "We're at war. We all look out for each other. You'd have done the same for him."

"Without hesitation."

"Now you understand. How was the fighting?"

I swallowed hard. "I killed men who were trying to kill me. Not something you can fully appreciate until you're in the thick of it."

"Bit different from a taproom brawl, eh? You take down the first and move on to the next – there's no time to think about it. It's life or death."

"The first was hard," I said, softly.

Christie arched his brows in question.

I snorted through my nose. "I threw up. Very unmanly."

"Most of us do. I don't think killing ever gets easier but you get over the throwing up part."

"I threw up after the second one too."

"And the third?"

I shook my head. "No, I was over it by then."

"Incidentally, you were cut – they stitched up your chest from here to here." He pointed at a spot just below my collarbone and another just above my nipple. "You'll have a pretty scar to show the ladies"

"Lovely – a souvenir."

Christie chuckled and got up from the bed. "Welcome to Spain, Captain. Sounds like you've been well seasoned."

CAMP AT SALAMANCA

Sixteen days.

That's how long we marched before we reached Salamanca, and in that time the wound on my chest was almost fully healed and the lump on the back of my head was long gone. As predicted by the regiment doctor, I'd survived my first taste of fighting.

The first time I saw Hywel after the skirmish, I eyed him cautiously, wondering what he'd have to say about my shooting of Dancy. I was sitting in a chair, the physician had just redressed the sabre slash across my breast, and Hywel was standing over me.

"She was a sweet girl," he said. He looked sad but smiled ruefully down at me. "Fortunes of war, I'm afraid."

"Well, I'm sorry for it, but not sorry for doing it," I told him sincerely, and he nodded. It was over.

When Barnabus and I were reunited, he seemed rather happy to see me; well, of course, he would be – who else would have been as foolishly charitable as I'd been in letting him leave the scene of the fighting? I rubbed his nose in greeting and he whuffed a warm composting smell in my face.

"Urgh! Enough, horse!" I pushed his great head aside and wondered again how anyone could have hurt this large, kind animal. Niall had been taking good care of him and he looked eager for a long march.

We'd remained at Fuentes de Oñoro for a couple of days before we broke camp and pulled out. It allowed us time to bury our dead and make arrangements for transporting the wounded.

Fortunately, I was able to ride. Most of the wounded had been infantry – foot soldiers; those unable to walk were transported on the carts that had originally carried supplies. The supplies were now carried by the men who weren't wounded.

Two of the wounded, regrettably, were unable to be transported. These we, perforce, left behind with a local nurse to watch over them. It was hoped that they'd be fit enough to rejoin us in Salamanca when they were able to travel.

So, we set out – sixteen days.

∾

We were quickly and thoroughly fed up with the ceaseless marching; the daily routine of setting up camp, breaking down camp, marching again ... a continuous tedium.

When at last we arrived at Salamanca late one afternoon in early March, it was with great relief. Many of the men had been separated from friends at Cadiz and were now raucously reunited.

For my part, I wondered where I would find Simon. I left Barnabus with Niall and made my way to where I expected to find the medical tent.

This camp was laid out as all other British camps were, and it was easy enough to locate where Simon ought to be, but on arrival, I paused in the opening of the large tent that served as a hospital and looked around.

Several people were milling about: nurses, doctors and two or three convalescents hobbling on crutches. Tables with stacked equipment lined the walls, along with cupboards and shelves. The centre of the room was filled with rows of the pallets that served as beds – mostly empty although several were occupied with men, sleeping or reading; one man seemed to be playing some solitary game with a deck of cards.

A pretty nurse eyed me curiously for a moment before approaching. She had gold-flecked, hazel eyes and a glorious cascade of blonde curls held off her face by a nurse's cap.

"May I be of assistance, Captain?" she asked in a rolling accent I didn't recognise, but which caused my blood to rush to my groin.

I smiled at her – I couldn't help it. She was the first woman I'd seen in months that I'd have considered cheating on my wager with Simon for. "Yes," I said, noting her slim figure, "I'm wondering if you might know the whereabouts of Captain Simon Broughton – a doctor. I expected to find him here."

Her eyes widened for a moment and she regarded me with something like recognition. "Would you be ... ah," she paused. "You must be Doctor Simon's brother?" Something in the way her eyes gleamed caused me to rethink my lecherous thoughts.

This lass wouldn't be the first to be smitten by my stepbrother's handsome face; if Simon hadn't already charted this territory, he wouldn't be far off it!

Still, I grinned, giving her the full benefit of my charm; I might as well, just in case. With a formal bow, I introduced myself, confirming that I was, indeed, Doctor Simon's brother.

She responded with a mysterious smile and turned away. "May I offer you a drink?" she said over her shoulder, "Simon tells me you drink coffee at your home."

"Really?" I followed her, admiring the sway of her hips beneath her nurse's uniform. "What else has *Simon* told you?" I wondered at her informality.

She faced me, a coffee pot in her hand and a coy smirk on her face, "That you and he are good friends – more than brothers are normally – and that is because you are not really brothers."

"It would appear then," I said archly, "that my *step*brother has been rather expansive in describing his family."

"Only his blond brother!" She grinned as she poured the coffee into a tin mug and handed it to me. "Simon is not here." She finally answered my question. "Not at the moment, that is. There was a report of illness spreading through a village outside of Salamanca. He and another doctor went there this morning. They should be back tomorrow sometime."

I sipped my coffee – it was horrible, but I was unlikely to find better. "Thank you. And since you know who I am, you have me at a disadvantage."

"I apologise." She gave a little curtsy, "I am Annika Lundgren ... your servant, my lord." She used the correct form of address in a way that seemed a little ironic and while I was deciding whether she was teasing me or not, she went to refill my coffee cup.

"No thank you," I said quickly, "I'm really not thirsty."

Annika snorted. "Not for this anyway – it is the worst coffee ever made." She laughed, a low breathy sound that was contagious even as it made me want to tumble her on the spot. I laughed with her, and she continued, "Nobody likes this coffee. They make it with chicory but they call it coffeeweed to make it seem more palatable."

"It doesn't work." I was watching her closely, the tip of her tongue darted out to moisten her lips. Her eyes rested on my mouth.

"No," she said, and she raised her eyes to mine.

We were standing awkwardly for a few moments, neither knowing what to say next, when suddenly there was a shout and the clatter of an enamel bowl bouncing on the canvas-covered floor. Across the tent, a patient was having a seizure and the doctor on duty seemed to be struggling to control him.

Annika practically threw the coffee pot at me and dashed in a flurry of skirts and blond curls to where the doctor had been joined by another nurse, yet between the three of them, they were still no match for the frenzied strength of a large man in the grip of a wild derangement.

Dropping the pot and cup onto a bench, I quickly followed. The man on the bed was screaming, thrashing about with arms and legs going everywhere. The doctor's nose had been smashed and was dripping blood down his apron.

Annika and the other nurse were trying to grasp the man's flailing limbs. Annika was struck across the mouth and knocked to the floor while the other nurse physically threw herself on top of the delirious man's legs.

"Hold his arms!" the doctor shouted to me through his flattened nose, and I snatched at the huge, heavy limbs, managing to catch first one, then the other. Standing close behind the man's bed I hauled his arms up over his head, effectively incapacitating them, both my hands clamped around his thick wrists and holding on with every ounce of strength I had.

Meanwhile, Annika had scrambled to her feet and rushed to a cabinet, fumbling with a key on a belt at her waist. "Hurry!" the doctor bellowed. He was sprawled across the man's chest pinning the massive man beneath his weight.

Annika finally got the cabinet open, rifled through it – bottles and packets falling unheeded to the floor – and with a yip of triumph, she virtually leapt across the gap to the bed, measuring a dose into a small glass. "Just pour it in his mouth!" the doctor demanded urgently. "He won't swallow half of it anyway."

The nurse obeyed, prising open clenched lips with one hand, she upended the glass with the other. As predicted, most of the fluid bubbled out of the man's mouth and soaked into his pillow – a brown, sickly sweet-smelling syrup that I recognised instantly.

Laudanum! The very thought of the opium it contained nearly

made me gag with the memories of a night spent in an opium den in London.

I swallowed hard and tried to focus on restraining the man on the bed while Annika poured another measure, this time with more success at feeding it to him.

It wasn't long before I felt the man's muscles relaxing and I was able to release my grip. Only then did I look up at the doctor. His nose was a mess, and purplish bruises were already blooming over his cheeks

"Christ!" I said. "Can I do anything to help you?"

The other man attempted a smile but grimaced with pain and shrugged instead. "No, thank you. I'll be fine." His voice was thick and he was clearly in pain but he gave a quick courtly bow and introduced himself, "Doctor Andrew Hurst."

"Captain Patrick Washburn."

"Simon's brother," Annika said. She held a basin of clear water and a clean cloth. "Sit down, Doctor."

"Washburn?" he said, taking a seat, as instructed. "Yes, I remember, Simon mentioned you ... Oxford – you had that house on Queen Street."

"Hurst?" I repeated, uncertainly. I didn't recognise the name.

"Lord Draven," Annika supplied helpfully.

"Ah, yes, I remember now. You were one of those chaps that ..." I paused. Simon's clandestine anatomy classes were highly illegal, and from what I recalled, this man had been a party to them. "One of those chaps that Simon studied with in the evenings," I finished discreetly.

"That's right – sss!" He sucked in his breath as Annika bathed the blood from his nose. "Simon and I used to study – in the basement of old Danziger's building."

I nodded. "Yes, he had told me ... er ... some things."

"I'm going to have to set it for you," Annika said, and I winced and looked away. The patient in the bed was now sleeping peacefully, and the other nurse was tidying up the mess he'd made in his crazed state.

"Look," I said, quickly turning back to Hurst, "it was a pleasure to meet you – *both* of you," I added significantly for Annika's interest. I offered a polite nod to the doctor, a more meaningful smile to the nurse, and took my leave before Annika went to work on Andrew's nose.

∽

I went back to the hospital tent the next morning, ostensibly to see if Simon had returned – knowing full well that if he had, he would have come to find me. So, the real reason I went was to see Annika again.

A couple of other nurses were there, and a young girl was sweeping the floor, but there was no sign of Annika. Doctor Hurst was seated at a table, writing in a notebook. He looked up as I approached.

"Good morning, Captain," he said, closing his notebook and filing it on a shelf. His nose was swollen and the colour of a beetroot; the bruising had formed purple half-moons beneath his eyes. "Looking for your brother? Simon hasn't come in yet."

"I expected he hadn't. No, I have come to see your nurse, Annika. Is she here?" I asked looking around.

He shook his head. "It's her week to check on the camps."

I assumed he meant the camp followers and when I asked, he said, "Yes. A couple of pregnancies – to be expected," he added with a wry shrug, "several cases of the pox and a ten year old with a bullet wound."

"Ten year old?" I repeated, aghast.

He nodded wearily, "Wrong place at the wrong time – it's war. It could have been worse. Children are conceived, born and killed on these battlefields. Life is cheap. Some of the mites have never had a permanent roof over their heads." He sighed. "Anyway," I followed him as he wandered down the rows of occupied beds, checking a patient here, another there, "the nurses take turns making a weekly visit. This week is Annika's turn."

He stopped suddenly and regarded me speculatively. "Be careful of that one – I would only say this because you're Simon's brother. I wouldn't ordinarily discuss my nurses with anyone but ... just be careful."

"What do you—" I began but he'd already turned away and was striding along the row.

"I must apologise, Captain," he said over his shoulder. "I am rather busy. I'll be sure to let Simon know you were looking for him."

∞

Later that day, I was summoned to Christie's tent. He was sitting at his writing desk, putting his signature to a document. Fitchen stood beside him and as I waited, Christie folded the paper and slipped it into a satchel.

"See if you can get it to the mail coach before it leaves – if not, bring it back and I'll keep it until the next one. Ah, Captain," he said, rising and coming toward me as Fitchen left the tent. "I have an errand for you."

He took another leather satchel from the desk and handed it to me. "I need you to take this to Coronel Felipe Vargas of the Spanish army. They're camped on the other side of Salamanca, on the outskirts of Villares de la Reina. It's about five miles from here."

I took the satchel. "Will there be a reply? Should I wait?"

"No. It's only information for him. Wellesley wanted us to pass instructions to the local divisions – make sure they're kept informed."

"When do you want me to go?"

"Right away. He must receive it today."

I nodded. It would be good to take Barnabus out on the road, let him relax into a comfortable stride for a couple of hours.

We saluted formally and Christie added, "See you this evening. I purchased a bottle of *Cuarenta Y* from an elderly local gent."

"I haven't heard of it. This evening then." I left the tent and went in search of Niall, easily finding him in the yard where the horses and mules were enclosed.

"Saddle Barnabus," I instructed, "and have him ready for me in twenty minutes." I then went to my tent to change into my riding boots, coat and shako.

I was already wearing my sword – officers were required to wear their swords at all times – so I needed only to load my pistols and tuck them into my belt.

There was a sound of clopping outside my tent and Niall stuck his head through the flap. "He's ready Capt'n."

"Very well. Please advise Hywel that I'm taking a message to Villares de la Reina. I will be back before sunset."

Niall nodded, holding Barnabus's head as I mounted. He whispered against the horse's cheek – no doubt some parting words of endearment – and stepped back as I gave Barnabus a nudge in the flanks. He moved forwards in an easy walk through the compound, past the rows of tents and supply wagons, then onto the dusty road.

∾

It was early afternoon when I left the campsite, riding along a dirt road that had been so baked and packed over the years of traffic that it was hard as stone. There'd been a light rain that morning that lay in puddles, the earth being too hard for the water to penetrate, and now it steamed beneath the bold blue sky.

Low yellow grasses sprouted by the side of the road and olive trees growing in the fields created a sea of grey. The flora was parched, easily fortified by the smallest amount of rain in this arid, rocky landscape. Spain was so vastly different from my home of rolling green fields and cool, lavender-coloured mornings that I knew a momentary pang of homesickness – only momentary. I might as well have been on the moon – I was not going home any time soon and despite the harshness of this place, it had a unique beauty of its own. I was content to be here and happy to do my duty.

We moved through the tent village on the outskirts of our campsite, passing by the various trades – all with their families in tow – that trailed in the wake of an army: farriers, carpenters, entertainers, snake-oil salesmen, prostitutes. I wondered if Annika was there at this moment, dealing with the assorted illnesses and injuries that arose.

Barnabus seemed pleased to be going on a journey. He snorted and stepped lightly – cheerfully obedient when feeling safe and secure – along the road. I leaned forward in the saddle to give his neck a rub and felt my heart lift in a way it hadn't done for many months.

So we, Barnabus and I, were content to put our worries aside and enjoy the outing and the scenery on our way to Villares de la Reina. From what I knew already, it was a typical Spanish agricultural village, such as I'd seen frequently over the weeks since arriving in this country.

The village had a small population of mainly farmers and tradespeople, housed in neat stone cottages that had probably seen generations of the same family come into, and pass out from, the world.

Allowing Barnabus to set the pace, we moved along at an easy trot, and I let my mind drift. I wondered why I'd gone to see Annika this morning, wondered at what I wasn't telling myself. When did I start avoiding the truth? I'd always been brutally honest with myself – until Alex – there, I said her name! First time in weeks.

Acknowledging my feelings for my stepsister had caused me to accept certain facts about myself that I'd been stubbornly ignoring.

Fact one, I'm an idiot.

Fact two, I have used my wager with Simon as a convenient excuse to avoid women.

Fact three, I have been avoiding women because I am behaving like the petulant child who, when denied a particular toy, refuses to play with *any* toy.

Fact four, I am an even bigger idiot than I initially thought.

Fact five, Annika is the first woman I have met in many months that I have been physically attracted to.

Which led me directly into another fact: Andrew Hurst, a friend of Simon's and therefore someone whose opinion should be respected, warned me about Annika. He didn't say why, though, and there was no time to think about it for Barnabus gave a sudden snort, as though to snap me from my reverie. We had arrived in Villares de la Reina.

∾

It was easy to locate the campsite of the Spanish army. Not so easy to locate the *coronel*. A few enquiries, in the limited Spanish I'd managed to pick up over the last couple of months, led me on something of a journey of discovery through the entire camp.

When I, at last, located the *coronel*, he was in the middle of an afternoon meal – why the fellow felt he *needed* an afternoon meal was beyond me. He was a mountain of a man, wide as he was tall, with a fleshy gut that hung well below his belt. His round swarthy face sported a drooping moustache, of which he was evidently proud, judging by how frequently he fondled it.

Coronel Felipe Vargas was ebullient in his greeting. He explained in heavily accented English that was nonetheless better than my Spanish, that he considered the British practice of taking tea in the afternoon very civilised and invited me to join his repast.

Thanking him, I regretfully declined, handed him the satchel from Christie, and took my leave as politely as possible.

A boy had taken Barnabus to a trough to drink. The great beast was now waiting for me, hitched to a post, watered and relaxing with his eyes drooping. He greeted me with a snort that left a spray of horse snot on my jacket. I grasped a handful of his tail and duly wiped it off.

He flicked his tail at me indignantly as I mounted, "Well, you started it," I told him, wheeling him toward Salamanca, and we set off on the return trip.

There is nothing quite as uncomfortable as sitting in a saddle with the urge to relieve oneself. I was aware that the sight of an accomplished horseman, attuned to the rocking motion of a horse, was considered by some ladies as rather sensual – I'd used it to my advantage on numerous occasions – but I laughed now to think how awkward I must, at that moment, appear as I painfully adjusted my seat with each step Barnabus took.

A narrow ribbon of trees to my left indicated a water source, so I dismounted and walked Barnabus into what was a small glade. A cool stream bubbled through it, and I left Barnabus to drink while I made my way through the tangle of grass and wildflowers to a suitable-looking tree some five yards away.

Unfastening the placket on the front of my trousers, I set to business. I had just finished and was tucking myself away when I heard a startled intake of air behind me.

Whirling about, I was surprised to find a young Spanish girl, dressed in a ragged skirt and blouse. Her face was grimy and bore the traces of tears, her hair was long and hung about her face in matted hanks.

She stared at me fearfully, her gaze dropping to my open trousers and suddenly her eyes widened and she raised filthy little paws as though to ward off an attack – as if she could defend herself against a grown man!

Such bravery, coupled with the fact that she felt she had to defend herself, caused my heart to twist.

She was a child, for God's sake, perhaps twelve, thirteen at best. *What has been done to you to make you so fearful?* I wondered.

Thinking to reassure her, I held out my own hands, but my trousers were still open and seemed to make her more afraid. She took a step backward, then another.

"I won't hurt you …" I said in English, my mind running down the list of the few Spanish words I knew, but there was nothing for this situation.

She took another step in the direction of the river. I could see Barnabus standing there with his front hooves in the water, neck bowed, slurping, savouring.

"Let me just …" I slowly reached down and began fastening my trousers, eyeing her carefully through my lashes. She was terrified, watching intensely, her small skinny body poised for flight. She wouldn't get far over the stony terrain – she was not wearing shoes and there was blood on her feet.

Finishing my task, I straightened and showed her the palms of my hands. "See, all safe."

Over at the water's edge, Barnabus gave a grunt of pleasure and the child noticed him for the first time, saw the saddle bags. "*Alimento?*"

Her voice was barely above a whisper, her throat sounded dry.

"*Alimento?*" I repeated, I'd heard that word before, but …

"*Alimento, por favor …*" she made an eating gesture.

"Food!" I said, eagerly. "You're hungry!" Foolishly pleased that I'd understood, I nodded and made a sudden movement toward Barnabus. Stupid mistake.

The child, standing between me and the horse, misinterpreted my intent. She shrieked, a bright sound that pierced the quiet of the trees and turned to run. Barnabus, knowing only that some unexpected and horrible sound had rent the air, gave a shriek of his own, turned and bolted through the trees.

"Shit!" I bellowed and lunged for the girl, catching her by the tail of her blouse. The sound of ripping fabric seemed overloud in the quiet of the glade, but I'd caught her, and she wriggled and squirmed in my hands.

The horse, on the other hand, was gone in a matter of seconds, ears flat, eyes wild, the last I saw of him was that bloody tail disappearing through the trees. "For fuck's sake!" I cursed after him. "Fucking horse!"

I looked down to the child cowering in my arms. Her eyes were wide and her small limbs were frozen – petrified. It was only in seeing her this close that the bruising on her face was evident.

I released her and we regarded each other intently.

She needed medical attention. She needed food. I wondered if she were lost ... orphaned perhaps. Either way, she couldn't stay out here alone. Evening would be coming in a couple of hours, cold and dark – dangerous.

"*Vieni*," I said, resorting to Italian and hoping it was close enough for her to understand. I held out my hand. "*Vieni con me, ti aiuterò.*"

She was breathing hard and staring at me like I was the devil himself. I crouched beside her. "*Alimento.*" I used her Spanish word.

Apparently the Italian *aiutare*, to help, was close enough to the Spanish *ayudar*, that she understood. After several minutes of gentling, she gradually relaxed and straightened to her full, meagre height.

"*Alimento*," I said again, "*andiamo. Ti darò alimento, se venissi con me.*"

I saw a glimmer of understanding, and if she didn't trust me, she was hungry enough to follow me all the same. I assumed Barnabus hadn't gone far and fortunately I was right. We emerged from the trees and only had to walk a hundred yards or so before we found him grazing, happy as could be, on the side of the road.

"We'll talk about this later," I assured him through gritted teeth as I checked the saddle hadn't slipped in his mad dash.

My bag didn't contain much, but there was a shrivelled apple I'd forgotten and a piece of hard bread wrapped in linen. I handed everything to the child who quickly devoured the apple then discarded the cloth and began gnawing at the bread.

Swinging into the saddle, I looked down at her, wondering what to do now. I couldn't leave her, not a little girl, out here like this. With a resolute sigh, I held out my hand. "*Venga!*"

She looked up at me, looked about her, and seemed to be weighing up her options. Evidently, she came to the same conclusion I did for she passed the remains of the bread to her left hand and held out her right.

Leaning from the saddle, I pulled her up behind me, catching as I did so, a quick flash of naked thigh beneath her skirt.

It was a lean, child's thigh – smeared with dried blood. The sight of it alarmed me; although the blood could have a perfectly natural explanation, I suspected otherwise.

"*Sono* Patrick," I told her. She put her thin arms about my waist. I could feel her chin bumping against my back as she chewed the bread.

"Maja," she whispered.

∽

Barnabus had not absolved himself of his crimes, but he did go some of the distance because his gentle manner and rolling stride rocked the child to sleep against my back. I cursed the gods of war that caused both a horse and a small girl to be so traumatised.

At length we rode into camp, and I directed Barnabus to the hospital tent. Simon was there and much as we were both pleased to be reunited, I didn't have time for personal matters. Simon was eyeing the sleeping child as I carried her in and laid her on a pallet.

"I found her down by the river outside of Villares de la Reina," I told him. "She was starving and she's been … I think someone has hurt her badly."

Simon was examining the bruises on her face and skinny, brown arms. "Hmm," he said. "Looks like it."

"Not just that," I added, "I think she's been raped."

Now he looked up at me and cursed under his breath. "Do you know how common this is?" Gently he lifted her skirt. He said, "Hmm," again and I knew I'd been right.

"Now what?"

He lowered her skirt and laid a light hand on her forehead. Her eyes flickered open and for a moment she looked alarmed.

"Shh," Simon soothed, "*este es un hospital. Estás seguro.*"

She looked from Simon's handsome face, to my relatively more familiar one, and seemed to relax. It was only then that I noticed Annika by another patient's bed. Simon waved her over, issued a list of instructions, then turned to me. "Come on," he said.

He led me to a small corner that served as his office. Embracing quickly and standing back to look at one another, I saw his skin was tanned and his hair was longer, but he was the same smiling Simon that I'd missed. Pouring two glasses of some dark spirit, he said, "Only a few months it's been, yet it feels like years. It's good to see you, Pat – a toast."

We toasted and tossed back the drink. It was stronger, rougher than the brandy I was used to drinking with Christie, but not unpleasant. "This isn't bad. What is it?"

"The local rotgut." He poured a second glass each. "Your tastes have deteriorated."

I sipped this one a bit slower, enjoying the raw flavour. "I could get used to this stuff," I told him and he made a face that said, *well that's typical of you.* "So," I went on, "what happens with the child now?"

He shrugged sadly. "Same as happens to all of them. If a family doesn't come forward, she'll probably end up over at the camp, working for a living."

"Working at what?" I demanded.

"What do you think?"

I stared at him, aghast. "She's a child, and after what she's been through …"

"She has to eat," Simon was coldly pragmatic. "I can see you've been seasoned in battle but not in war. In here," he gestured to indicate the makeshift hospital, "I see it from a different angle. You will too, soon enough. You won't like it – none of us do – but you'll come to accept it."

"Christ, two months and you're already a cynic."

"Excuse me, Doctor." It was Annika. "The child has eaten some broth and Ana has taken her to be bathed."

All the while Annika was speaking, she was sliding sly glances at me from the corner of her eye. It wasn't lost on Simon, who suppressed a smirk. "Good," he said. "When she comes back, put her to bed and write up the chart for Doctor Hurst. He'll examine her tomorrow and decide what's to be done."

As Annika continued to linger, smiling openly at me now, Simon added, "That will be all, nurse."

"Of course, Doctor."

Simon and I watched, admiring the outline of her arse as she sidled away. I groaned, "It's been a long time, Sime. I've been faithful to our wager, but that one …" I shifted uncomfortably and downed the remains of my drink.

"Stay away from her," Simon warned. "Nothing but trouble." He straightened and rolled his shoulders with a cracking sound. "Now, I must go and check my patients before I finish up. Will you be in your tent this evening?"

"Until I go to Christie's."

"Christie?"

"Major Thorpe – friend from Devon – we share a brandy each evening. Join us?"

"Good brandy?"

I grinned. "Normally the pick of the Bonaparte stock. But Christie has something new tonight."

"How could I refuse? See you then."

I'd left Barnabus outside the hospital tent. He was no longer there, and I assumed Niall had taken him. There was no great danger of anyone else taking him – the horse's reputation preceded him. I still owed the bugger a piece of my mind, but it could wait.

My step was light as I made my way back to my tent; the effects of strong liquor. I grinned to myself, feeling Simon's rotgut warming my stomach. More than that, though, I was happy to see my stepbrother again.

After an absence of almost three months, I saw Simon in a different way. Yes, he was still beautiful, but he seemed more mature – he'd seen and experienced things that had changed him, as I had.

But there was more. Something in the pleased way that his smile twisted when he first saw me. I'd never seen it before and it caused my stomach to tighten.

It was the first time, in all our years of acquaintance, that I'd seen Alex's face reflected in her brother's – a sibling similarity. It made my heart hurt and I hoped never to see it again.

ON A MISSION

Simon straightened with a wince. He'd been bent over a patient for so long, working so closely, intensely, that now he found his back almost frozen in a hunched position. He rolled his shoulders and moved his head from side to side with a loud cracking sound.

The fighting had been particularly fierce this last two days – more than mere skirmishes or belligerent uprisings, these had been battles, full-blown, with heavy losses to both sides.

He and the rest of the medical team had been on their feet for the greater part of forty-eight hours. There'd been no time for sleep and only briefly snatched moments where he could stuff small amounts of food into his mouth, handed out by the young girls helping in the hospital.

Simon was exhausted beyond measure, and they kept coming – the wounded, the dying, the dead. Hobbling under their own efforts or carried in by comrades, they were a steady stream – as steady as the thunder of the cannon and the distant cracking of rifle fire.

Every roar, every crash and boom, would likely result in another man arriving at the hospital, another body to add to the unmarked, mass graves. Simon tried not to think of it. Just as he tried not to think of the inadequacies of the hospital, the unanswered medical questions that frustrated him so – he could only do that which was within his capability.

The wounded filled the pallets, initially singularly. Before long they were lying head to toe, two to a bed. Then they filled the floor spaces at the back and front of the hospital, the aisles between rows of pallets, and finally they spilled out to the ground in front of the hospital.

Boys, too young to join the fighting, were put to work erecting a canvas sheet affording some small relief from the Spanish sun, over men that lay moaning in fly-blown filth, wrapped in stinking, bloodied bandages. Other, smaller children filled tin cups with water and assisted the wounded to drink. Those wounded who were unable to drink unaided, were given squares of water-soaked linen to suck.

It was the only help available until Simon, Andrew and Henry – the camp's three doctors – could attend to them.

Women were recruited from the camps to assist. They bathed wounds, cleaned up vomit, blood and other bodily substances. Those with the stomach for it, assisted with surgical procedures, while others sat, holding the hands of the dying, offering a final human contact, a soft feminine voice, a gentle touch. It was, in many cases – too many cases – all that could be done, and yet it was an invaluable occupation of compassion.

Simon sighed wearily and passed a hand over his eyes, unknowingly leaving a smear of blood across his brow. He felt the stubble on his cheeks, felt the dry grittiness of his eyes, and the dull throb in his temples.

ॐ

Lack of sleep, lack of food – they were taking their toll on him, but he couldn't rest.

He looked around at the sea of wounded men. There would be no rest for hours yet, not while these poor wretches needed him.

Across the tent, Andrew was setting a broken arm. The pained shrieks of his patient were drowned in a chorus of other such screams. It was a continuous assault on the senses.

The hospital had long since run out of laudanum and were using willow bark, brewed into a tea by one of the camp women. Albeit not ideal, it was the only pain relief available besides the half-dozen bottles of brandy Major Thorpe's aide had brought around.

This, they had reserved for amputees and patients of other major procedures.

Thoughts of Major Thorpe brought Patrick to mind. Simon knew that his stepbrother was out there, fighting somewhere. It occurred to Simon that with so many wounded arriving every minute, it was by some miracle that Patrick had not appeared among them.

Then again, there were literally hundreds of men here, lying or sitting about in bloodstained, filthy rags; it was unlikely that he would recognise his stepbrother if he were among them. Much less likely if he were numbered among the men lying insensible on the battlefield, vacant eyes wide with shock and disbelief – the final thought to cross their minds.

"Doctor Simon?" Simon turned. It was the young girl, Maja, that Patrick had brought to camp five months earlier. She was holding a tin cup, a bottle of ale in her other hand.

Simon took the mug and gulped its contents gratefully. Returning the empty cup, he smiled, "*Gracias*, Maja."

He leaned against a table, allowing himself a brief moment's respite and feeling the sweat trickle down his back, watching as the girl made her rounds of the nurses and the other doctors, pouring from her bottle for each one.

People more adept at the Spanish language than Simon, had

questioned the girl and discovered that she had been raised in a small village outside of Badajoz. A score of French soldiers had raided the village, looking for food and carrying off whatever they found. Both Maja and her mother had been raped and Maja's grandfather had been shot while trying to defend his womenfolk. Maja's mother had been killed shortly after.

It was a common enough story; all too common.

Maja couldn't say why her life had been spared, but a young girl, alone in the world, could not be expected to survive any great length of time. She had decided her only hope was to follow the British army. So, she had set out, trailing at a distance, hoping for an opportunity to mingle and become part of the human sea.

Without anyone noticing, Maja had slotted herself into the hospital's routine. She cleaned, she prepared food and was keen to make herself useful – and the nurses and doctors, overworked as they were, were only too grateful of the extra pair of hands.

Maja was possessed of a surprisingly strong stomach. Simon and Andrew were already assigning her to assist the nurses as they bathed and dressed wounds and performed some even more unsavoury cleaning tasks.

"Doctor Simon!" The shout came from a nurse by the entrance of the tent. It was Annika, crouched over a soldier stretched out on the bare earth. Even at this distance, Simon could see the man's left leg was shattered; from the knee down, it was little more than a pulpy mess with shards of white, jagged bone poking through the torn flesh.

He sighed sadly and raised his hand in response. "Coming."

Another amputation, he knew, and he hated performing them, but in cases like these, amputation offered the only hope of the patient's survival – unless of course, the stump putrefied, and gangrene set in. Then the odds of survival diminished further.

Simon pushed off the table, bent to collect his bag and made his way across the hospital to Annika.

❧

Patrick stood over the inert body. Panting in the aftermath of a fight to the death, he turned, wrenching his sword from the Frenchman's chest as he did so and grimacing at the ugly sound of steel scraping on bone.

Sweat, mixed with the blood from a gash on his temple, was running into his eyes. It stung and made it difficult to see, but as he surveyed his surroundings, it seemed to Patrick that the heat had gone out of the battle – if only momentarily.

Wounded men sat or lay where they'd fallen; those still alive or not badly hurt stood swaying on their feet or staggering around in confused, aimless circles.

The war had been raging in and around Salamanca for months, now, and as Wellington led the march towards the Douro River, the French had fallen back, although they'd maintained a strong position on the opposite bank.

Patrick was a quick learner and the realities of war no longer offended him. In fact, it was reasonable to say that over the course of the last six months he'd both witnessed and perpetrated the kinds of actions humans should simply not do to other humans.

To be above such barbarity, is what many claimed set humans apart from the rest of the animal kingdom. But such claims could well be challenged by anyone witnessing the savagery of a battlefield.

The intensity of the battle was waning. With many of the French in retreat, only sporadic shots were being fired, and Patrick, exhausted and smeared with sweat, grime and blood, simply stood, hunching over, hand on hip and sword trailing on the ground from fatigue and watching impassively as one of his own men finished off an enemy soldier.

"Captain!" a voice behind him called. Christie's aide was cantering towards him on the major's horse. As he drew near, he slowed the horse to a cautious walk, the grey mare picking fastidiously, a path through death and destruction.

"Captain," Fitchen repeated breathlessly; he was dismounting almost before the horse had stopped. "Major Thorpe requires you attend him at your earliest convenience – he's on the east flank, Sir. You're to take his horse," Fitchen added, with a barely contained snigger – Barnabus's fear of just about everything was a source of great amusement.

It was well known that Captain Washburn marched into battle on foot alongside his regiment. While it earned the captain a degree of respect among the enlisted men, it resulted in considerable taunts from the other officers – many of whom did not bother to hide their smirks.

Patrick did not care. It was far more important to him that he won the support and loyalty of his men than his fellow officers.

"Thank you Fitchen," he said, mounting and pulling the horse's head around towards the east, and with a quick kick to the flanks, went in search of his commanding officer.

∽

Patrick found Christie on a hill that afforded a good, operational view of the battlefield. He was leaning over a makeshift table made from a broken door balanced between rocks, two other men beside him, poring over a map.

The first man Patrick recognised was Emerson, one of the other young captains under Major Thorpe's command, the second was a man dressed in a rather unremarkable dark suit.

Dismounting, Patrick saw the men were in a deep, muttered conversation, so rather than announce himself, he hovered on the outskirts, holding the reins of Christie's horse, until such time as he could respectfully interrupt.

As he waited, the stranger in the sombre clothes drew his attention. He was a handsome, slender man, dark-haired with a long, straight nose, and Patrick estimated him to be in his early forties.

Softly spoken, the man seemed to naturally command attention. Even Christie, a major, who in the civilian world was the son of a duke, seemed to defer to him.

At length, Christie looked up and gestured for Patrick to join them, at the same time calling over a boy to take the horse.

Patrick approached, nodding a greeting to Emerson. His eyes then moved to the stranger and was formally introduced to General Arthur Wellesley, Viscount Wellington.

"General, this is Captain, Viscount Patrick Washburn," Major Thorpe, said, "the man I mentioned."

Patrick saluted respectfully and stood at attention as the general looked him up and down. Turning back to Christie, he said, "I have no taste for this mission, Major, and would urge the captain to avoid conflict wherever possible."

Addressing Patrick directly, he added, "Take nothing at face value, Captain."

"Yes, Sir."

"Agree, Sir," Christie said, "which is why I believe Captain Washburn is the man you need."

"Very well." Turning again to Patrick, the general continued, "Captain, the major here has recommended you for a specific task. I am assured you are cool-headed and unlikely to engage in unnecessary aggression. I expect you will operate true to the major's assessment."

"I shall do my best, Sir," Patrick said, although he had no idea what was being asked of him.

"Good. Now, I am otherwise committed, so I will leave the major to explain what is required of you. Please report to me before sunset."

"Yes, Sir!" Patrick saluted as the general turned.

The three men watched as the general strode to where his horse was tethered to a sapling. Two mounted aides stood by, and once Wellesley was similarly mounted, the three rode away.

Emerson spoke first. "Why does the general not wear his uniform?"

"Because," Major Thorpe said, turning towards the table and the map, "he stands alongside his men in the field of battle. By dressing the way he does, he presents an anonymous figure to the enemy. Imagine the fire he would draw if they knew who he was!"

"Now Captain," Christie said, turning to Patrick. "As the general mentioned, we have a task of particular importance for you."

Patrick said, "This all sounds terribly interesting, Major, and more than a little intriguing."

Emerson snorted. "Rather you than me, Washburn. Good luck!" He saluted the major, nodded to Patrick, and departed.

Patrick watched him leave, a thrill of excitement stirring deep down in his stomach.

He turned to find the major regarding him speculatively. "You're already looking forward to the adventure and you don't even know what it is," Christie observed.

"You know me too well. So, you'd better tell me."

"Very well." Christie smirked at him. "A young woman was picked up on the road last night – hear me out!" Christie said quickly as the other man opened his mouth to speak.

"Not just any young woman – and not one of those women. She is a lady … claims to be the wife of Lieutenant-Colonel Armand de la Fontaine, a member of Napoleon's trusted circle."

"And she's here? In camp?"

Christie nodded. "Although technically she is the enemy, and technically she is a prisoner, she has been treated with the respect she is due. However, she says she is here deliberately, and, apparently, unbeknownst to her husband."

"Why?"

"Ah, here's the key." Christie said with a wry smile. "It appears the lady has a ... er cousin, if you understand me, an officer of minor rank and who we captured during a battle about week ago."

"We don't generally take prisoners – not from the lower ranks."

"Correct, but this fellow was different. This fellow may only be a junior officer, but he is – we believe – an Italian prince. Don't ask me why he's fighting with the French."

"Bored, I expect."

"Perhaps, or his family's making a political alliance. Regardless, there would be a tidy ransom payable if it were proved that he is that valuable. The point is, the lady was so desperate to see him that she tried to sneak into our camp – not successfully. She was caught and taken to Wellington. This is where you come in."

Now Christie leaned over the table, rotating the map ninety degrees to the right and pointing. "This is us ... this is the Douro River as you can see, and here," he stabbed a finger at a spot across the river from where the British campsite was marked, "is where her husband is. The lady has agreed to share certain documents with us if we could assist her in furthering her liaison with our prisoner."

"*Une affair de coeur,*" Patrick murmured.

"Precisely, and one we can use to advantage." Christie sat back and regarded Patrick with mild humour. "You are to escort the lady back to her husband, smuggle both yourself and her into the enemy camp – hopefully before she is recognised – stand by as she locates the documents we need, take possession of them, then get out of there without detection."

Patrick exhaled slowly and rubbed thoughtfully at his beard stubble. "What are we offering her in return?"

"That all depends. If the documents are what she claims they are, we will allow both her and her *cousin* to go free. If they are not, she'll be promptly returned to her husband and he can deal with her."

"Must be important documents if you're prepared to forego an impressive ransom," Patrick said, eyeing his friend suspiciously.

Christie laughed. "You know I'd tell you if I could. Suffice to say that yes, they are very important documents, and although Wellington claims to have little taste for the mission, it's merely the deceit of it he dislikes. He does, very much, want those papers."

Patrick snorted and Christie said, "So, you'll do it?"

"Of course I'll do it. Sounds like an interesting diversion."

"Good – I knew you would. Just remember what the general said. Try to avoid conflict – get in quickly, get the papers and get out. And one other thing – don't trust the woman."

At Patrick's look, Christie added, "If she can betray her husband, she can betray anyone. But she is single-minded where that Italian fellow is concerned. Now," Christie began rolling up the map, "I have a meeting so I'll leave you here – sorry I can't offer you a ride back to camp."

Patrick grinned at his friend, "Won't kill me to walk."

"Ha! Word is that you do a lot of that. Seriously, Patrick, you need to get yourself a better horse. Perhaps steal one from the French while you're over there," Christie added, laughing.

He mounted his grey and Patrick scratched the horse's neck, "Wouldn't dream of it. I'm becoming quite attached to Barnabus. Poor fellow's troubled."

"Being the camp laughing stock will do that!" Christie retorted, gathering his reins. "Well, good luck Captain. Report to me when you get back."

∾

Simon leaned wearily against a table in the surgery. Maja was there instantly with a cup of ale and a wedge of bread with a slice of ham on it. He thanked her fondly.

The child was very useful, evidently deciding this was where she was going to stay, the story she'd told them all had been accepted and she was now part of the hospital.

Perhaps because Simon was the first person to show her any kindness – other than Patrick, but he was rarely around – Maja took special care of him, always sensing his needs before he spoke them, always ready with food or a cool cloth to mop his brow. He suspected she had something of a young girl's fancy for him.

One morning, after a night of surgery, Simon had staggered into his tent for an hour's rest and found her asleep in his pallet. Too exhausted to deal with it at the time, he'd merely collapsed beside her and been instantly asleep.

Later though, he explained that it was inappropriate for her to be in his tent and that she couldn't stay with him. Despite her brimming eyes, he'd led her back to the hospital and asked one of the Spanish nurses to find a bed for the girl.

Maja had been resentfully silent for a day or two afterwards, but very soon got used to the arrangement and now seemed quite settled.

Simon swallowed the last of the bread and ham, allowed her to top up his ale mug, and then with a flash of a pretty smile, she disappeared into the hubbub of a field hospital.

Just then an ensign ran in announcing another wave of wounded making their way off the field. Resignedly, Simon drained the last of the ale and pushed away from the table.

The wounded were laid out in the foreground of the hospital tent, there being no space for them inside. Simon followed a nurse outside, preparing to make his rounds, triaging the patients.

He hated this part of the job. It was always his fear that Patrick would be among those lying there, green eyes opaque and lifeless, or bright with pain, limbs blown apart – the truth of war was that such fears could become reality and Simon dreaded the thought of having to advise Lord Thorncliffe that his only son and heir had been killed or maimed.

In any event, it was a risk that the brothers had knowingly accepted, even if neither had fully appreciated the extent of it.

Simon saw immediately that Patrick was not among the dead or wounded for he was standing in the inadequate shade of a tall, thin cypress tree Wearing a clean uniform, he appeared freshly shaved and bathed, although smudges of fatigue ringed his eyes.

As Simon approached, he watched the thoughts on his stepbrother's face shift from pleasant greeting to concern. By the time Simon stood before him, Patrick was frowning, not bothering to shutter his expression as he generally did back in England.

"When was the last time you ate something?" Patrick demanded.

"About two minutes ago." Simon ran a hand through his hair causing a hank of it to stand up in a crest, stiff with sweat and dirt.

"And slept?"

"About two months ago."

Pat's smile was weak. He gestured towards the wounded being stretchered in or carried in the arms of their comrades. "Work cut out for you?"

"Never stops. How's it out there? Are we winning?"

Patrick snorted derisively. "Nobody's winning. We make ground, they take it back. They make ground, we take it back. It's all push and shove; blood and mud and death all around. The fighting stops for a half-day, maybe more, through sheer exhaustion, then it starts up again."

They stared hard at each other for a moment, assessing, words of regret that neither would admit to, hanging between them.

Finally, Simon said, "You know, Pat, it would be going on whether we were here or not. I'm glad to be here ..." he waved a hand at the men hobbling in behind him, "I'm content to be doing what I can.

Patrick nodded. "I'm happy you said that – and glad to be here too."

He paused for a moment as the nurse, Annika, rushed up to ask a question. Simon responded briefly and Annika flashed a meaningful smile at the men, then hurriedly returned to her patient.

Patrick was watching her over Simon's shoulder. He said, "What is it about Annika? Everyone warns me about her, but she seems—"

"She's not what she seems," Simon said with a vague smirk. "Best you just smile and nod and stay away."

Their discussion broke off and they watched as a horse and cart arrived bearing a further three wounded.

"Look," Patrick said, "I can see you're busy. I just came to tell you they're sending me on a mission tonight. They want me to sneak into the enemy camp ..."

His eyes gleamed at the prospect. "Some papers they need. I'm to take a woman – the wife of one of the French officers and—"

"Annabella de la Fontaine." Simon smiled at him. "Have you met her yet?"

Pat shook his head. "You've heard of her? They picked her up last night and brought her in."

"Oh, I've heard of her," Simon confirmed, "and I stitched up the arm of the sentry she slashed with a nasty little knife she keeps in her bodice. Piece of work she is – oh, you're going to love this!"

Now Patrick grinned. "Sounds like a challenge. And I thought the soldiers were the enemy."

ON A MISSION - *THE CLIMAX*

Midnight, and the Douro River looked like an oily, black ribbon. A slice of moon cast a faint, buttery shimmer over the topography of the far bank and a warm wind blew, bringing the mingled scents of camp-fires and the excuse for coffee they used here, in the absence of the genuine product. It was a welcome change, though, from the acrid smell of gunpowder and death.

A night bird, probably an owl, screeched overhead, and a dog barked in the distance. Otherwise, the night was silent.

Patrick, dressed as a local farmer, sat astride Barnabus. Niall, behind him, rested comfortably on the horse's round rump. Madame Annabella de la Fontaine perched side-saddle on a borrowed mare. She cut a mysterious figure with a rather femme-fatale air about her.

Damn but she's attractive, Patrick thought, *and she's thoroughly unpleasant – dangerous too. Is that part of her attraction, I wonder?*

They were waiting for a boatman, a local who had agreed to take them across the river in exchange for a promissory note – a debt the boatman knew would never be paid, for the British army was broke, and it was no secret.

Yet it was not in the man's interest to deny the request, coming as it had from the general himself. The boatman knew that at the very least, the general would order his men to bypass the boatman's home as they scoured the countryside for provisions.

For as the British army was broke, it was also starving. While many of the soldiers were billeted with local Salamanca families – eating them out of house and home – the majority remained in a tent village just beyond the city's boundary.

Of these, groups regularly made raiding expeditions to outlying farms and villages and into Salamanca itself to acquisition – by any means – provisions to feed the army.

Patrick adjusted his position on Barnabus's back and leaning forward with a squeak of leather, he gave the horse's neck a vigorous rub. Barnabus was relaxed; happy to stand for hours in one position, providing there were no loud noises or sudden, unexpected movements.

Sighing deeply, Patrick could *hope* the general would issue the order forbidding the men from putting together their own foraging parties, and he could *hope* that order would be obeyed. Might as well hope for Napoleon to visit for tea.

Christie regularly gathered small parties of men and accompanied them on foraging excursions, and by sanctioning their operations, attending as a senior officer, he managed to minimise the violence and aggression of the men's actions – and the resistance with which they were received.

The soldiers were, the locals tended to forget, there to assist them in driving out the French. But it seemed to Patrick that the Spanish were an ungrateful lot.

He sighed through his nose as he remembered a recent battle during which the British suffered heavy losses, while the Spanish soldiers had turned and fled. When the French chased absconding troops down to a nearby village, the Spanish death toll had been horrendous.

Patrick had led his men to the village and successfully repelled the French troops, forcing them into retreat. Counting his losses in the aftermath, he was dismayed to learn that the surviving Spanish soldiers had, again, fled, leaving their dead scattered around the village.

Returning to the village two days later, Patrick was horrified at the sight – and smell – that met him. The dead Spanish soldiers were unclaimed. Bloated, fly-blown bodies, from which rose an evil, pervading stench, were lying where they'd fallen; the villagers, evidently, content to step over the rotting corpses rather than remove them.

Moreover, the Spanish soldiers had not returned to bury their fallen comrades – it was incomprehensible.

Patrick shuddered at the memory. Two weeks later and he felt he still had the foul smell in his nostrils. He'd immediately put his men to work, digging graves and removing the bodies, all the while seething and disgusted by the apathy of the Spanish people.

"I think I heard somethin', Sir," Niall whispered behind him, drawing his attention back to the present.

Patrick sucked in a deep breath, enjoying the clean air, and squinted into the darkness.

Sure enough, limned against the black river, he could just make out a small boat. It moved smoothly over the water, its rag-wrapped oars breaking the surface so silently that only someone listening for it would have heard it.

"Alright," Patrick said, "time to go."

Slipping off Barnabus's back, he moved over to the mare and reached up to assist Madame de la Fontaine to dismount, hands about her waist, conscious of her pregnancy.

As he did so, her distended belly brushed against him. He was surprised by how soft it felt – he thought it would be firmer. His inexperience with pregnant women was telling on him.

Landing her safely on the ground, Madame gripped his forearms and squeezed. "Ever the gallant gentleman," she purred.

"Young *and* strong – what a combination!"

Patrick grunted irritably. She was wearing some heady perfume that caused his senses to swim. "Patchouli," he murmured.

"Very good, *Capitaine.* Do you like it?"

"You have bathed in it," he snapped. "You will give us away." Madame had been a thorn in his side since they'd left camp. No opportunity to sharpen her tongue on young Niall had been wasted – even going so far as to suggest that the boy's affinity with horses was due to his equine parentage. On top of that, she'd taken particular delight in baiting Patrick himself.

Niall had ridden in silent misery while Patrick had boiled in fury. The general had warned him to be cool-headed and controlled – clearly, the woman had a reputation. In any event, this mission was more important than any self-satisfied slut, so he'd gritted his teeth and murmured, "Ignore her," to the boy sitting pillion behind him.

Now, he snatched up the mare's reins and turning abruptly, led the horse to where Barnabus waited. Niall had moved up to sit in the saddle and Patrick tied the mare's reins to the pommel. "Alright, Niall, take the horses back to camp, and advise Major Thorpe that we have met the boat. Return in the morning for us."

∾

"Yes, Sir," Niall agreed dejectedly. When Captain Washburn requested Niall to assist him on the mission – albeit in a limited role – he'd been proud and excited. Now his part was over, he was sorry – although he was not sorry to see the back of that arrogant lady.

Niall wanted to warn Captain Washburn about her – for Niall was gifted with the kind of clear sight that accompanied an uncomplicated life. This woman was trouble, and she was going to make trouble. Niall hoped that the captain would not be caught up in it; Captain Washburn had been good to him.

He watched as the captain spoke quickly to the boatman before handing the woman on board. Once the two were settled in the shallow hull, Niall pulled Barnabus's head around. Hannah, the little mare, followed, and they disappeared into the night.

∾

The boat moved with barely a sound, cutting smoothly through the inky water. The young *capitaine* sat in the hull watching silently as the boatman strained at the oars, propelling them swiftly across the river.

Madame sat opposite, scrutinising the young *capitaine* with a practised eye. He could be older than he looked, but not much, she guessed. When he'd lifted her down from that bony little horse, she'd been surprised by the wiry strength of him.

Virile too – no poncing foppery about him at all. And those green eyes! She couldn't see them now in the dark, but when she'd met him earlier in the *général's* tent, she'd been taken aback by the intensity of their colour.

She gave a languid sigh and turned away to watch the water rippling in their wake.

∾

Ten minutes later the boat reached the opposite bank, driving into the mud as the river bottom rose up at the edge. The boatman indicated with a jerk of his thumb that his passengers were to disembark.

Patrick assisted Madame de la Fontaine, taking her elbow and guiding her across the mud – much to her disgust. "An officer you may be, but you are no gentleman – I have changed my mind," she grumbled, examining the sodden and filthy hem of her skirt.

"You were offered breeches," he responded absently. He was watching as the boatman pushed back out into the river and was quickly swallowed by the darkness.

Madame snorted rudely. "You may not be a gentleman, but *I* am a lady."

"Debatable."

"Titled," she added smugly.

"Irrelevant."

She glared at him in outrage, "Peasant!" she spat. "How dare —"

He cut her off with an impatient gesture, "Come on, we've no time to stand around debating culture – or lack thereof."

"Foolish little boy!" she snarled in her accented voice. "Child with a purchased *grade de capitaine* playing at being a man. I have seen your type: rich merchant papa buys his son a commission to get him out from underfoot while the heir to the family wealth is cosseted and spoiled. You are bitter with jealousy."

"Ah, you have me pegged," Patrick confessed, and sweeping the woman a mocking bow, said, "Now, if it please your ladyship – move your arse!"

Her eyes widened with indignation, nostrils flaring. *God she was beautiful*! She tossed her hair, but beautiful or not, Patrick was not in a mood to pander to her. Taking her elbow again he disregarded the quickening of his pulse and roughly tugged her up the bank to where tufts of late autumn grass were crisp beneath their boots.

She jerked her arm away from him. "Take your hand off me, Sir! Your *général* will hear of this! I am a lady, *with child*," she emphasised, curling her lip, "and you are manhandling me!" She pushed past him, snarling something over her shoulder and striding confidently towards a dirt track, only barely visible through the darkness.

Patrick snorted derisively and followed her to the track, a cloud of patchouli hanging in the air. He noted with a certain satisfaction; Madame might speak with a strong French accent, but she had just cursed him in Italian. In that moment, he instinctively knew that the general was wrong: his Italian prisoner was not Madame de la Fontaine's lover – he was something else, and Patrick could guess what.

Smiling to himself, he decided that this was going to be an interesting night indeed.

∾

Side by side, they walked briskly, following the track for two miles or so before arriving at the rim of the French encampment on the edge of a small forest.

As they came to a screen of thick, thorny shrubs, Madame halted and edged closer to Patrick, pointing towards a scattering of cypress trees and sparse undergrowth. "It is there, the camp, among those trees. See the fires?"

"And where are the documents?"

She slid him a contemptuous sideways glance. "Where do you *think* they are? Lying about on the ground? The documents, *Capitaine*, are in my husband's writing desk – in his quarters."

Patrick contained his rising irritation and watched through the trees. Between the trunks were small camp-fires, each identifiable by its curling plume of smoke and small gathering of men. The usual collection of camp followers was milling about and while he continued to observe his enemy, the familiar sounds of an encampment of men settling down for the evening, attended by women and a handful of barefoot children – the typical rag-tag tribe that followed an army – were filtering through to him.

Snatches of song, a strummed guitar, all carried on the breeze, along with cooking smells and the occasional voice raised in triumph over some competition. It all made for a relaxed atmosphere, jovial and careless.

At length, the small groups were breaking up. Women were folding children in blankets and laying them like sausages close to the fires; the men were wrapping themselves in their greatcoats, the night was falling silent.

"Where are the sentries?" Patrick whispered suddenly.

"Oh, there are no sentries here, *Capitaine*, this camp is bordered by the river, *n'est-ce pas?*"

"Bullshit!" Patrick responded smartly. She made a derogatory sound in her throat and tossed her hair, swamping him in exotic patchouli. He felt his balls tighten and contained a groan – *It's the hair thing*, he thought. *She better not keep that up all night!* "There *will* be sentries so what's the best way in?" he asked irritably.

Smiling, she leaned close to him, pressing her bosom against his arm. Her face was like new cream in the pale moonlight, her breath warm on his face. "You really must learn to ask more sweetly, *Capitaine*."

"Don't play with me, Madame!" he hissed.

"*Allors!* You are very grumpy for one so young. Is it the frustration of your virginity that causes such ill humour? Why do you not visit one of th— *ack!*"

Patrick grasped her jaw in a firm hand. Leaning into her face, he growled through gritted teeth, "I said, *don't play with me*! If you want to see your Italian prisoner again, best you stop acting the coquette and ..." he released his grip, "honour your side of the bargain. Now, lead the way!"

Rubbing her chin, she glared at him, dark eyes flashing angrily. "Follow me."

༄

She led a circuitous route around the outside of the encampment. There were sentries – as Patrick had suspected – but she knew where they were posted and how to avoid them.

Eventually, she stopped abruptly, and they crouched behind a wide cypress. A sentry stood, chatting idly with a fellow guard, some fifteen feet away from where Patrick and the woman hunkered, watching.

"The fat one there, I know him," she whispered. She was so close he could see her teeth shining like pearls in the dark. "He is lazy and stupid. He is also in love with me and will do whatever I ask."

"What about the other one?"

"Oh, if he is not in love with me now, he soon will be," she said with a sure smile. "They all fall in love with me. Even you will."

"You know what I mean—"

"Of course, I know what you mean, *Capitaine*. The other one, I do not know him. I have not seen him before so we must wait until he leaves."

Patrick exhaled and continued watching the two men through the low branches of the cypress. It didn't look like the other one was going anywhere. It might be a long wait.

"You know, *Capitaine*, I do think that you are already in love with me." She held her finger and thumb an inch apart, "Just a little, *oui*?"

Patrick snorted, without taking his eyes from the two sentries visible through the trees. "Don't wager your honour on it."

"An experienced woman could teach—"

Turning abruptly, he snarled at her. "You trying to get us caught? Shut— *ah*!"

Before he realised what was happening, she had grasped him firmly through his trousers. "Eager young virgin ..." she murmured against his mouth. "The things I could teach you ..."

His body responded immediately and intensely, blood draining south to pool in a painful tightening in his groin. Ironic, he realised, that his celibate body was certainly behaving as eagerly as a virgin's would.

She laughed scornfully and with a final squeeze, released him.

Head swimming, angry and more than slightly embarrassed, he roughly shoved himself away. "Madame!" he growled hoarsely, trying to control his breathing while keeping his voice down. "Enough of your games!"

"You cannot deny that you want me, *Capitaine*. The evidence is —"

"I shall keep my virginity, Madame, for a worthy maid – not some painted slut in a forest."

"*Connard*!" she swore, turning back to the sentries, only to find they'd gone. "Where are they?"

"Over there," he pointed to the right. The two men were accepting mugs from a boy. They drank deeply, wiped their mouths on their sleeves and promptly returned to their post.

"How well do you know the fat one?" Patrick asked.

"I told you – he is in love with me."

"Do you think he would let us pass into the camp?"

Shrugging, she said, "Perhaps yes, perhaps no."

"What about …" he paused and looked at her speculatively.

Madame raised an eyebrow in inquiry.

"What if you were to call them over? Distract them. Could you do that?"

"I could, *Capitaine*, but that would put me in the position where they would be expecting something from me. A young man, lean and strong like you – that is one thing, but …" she looked across at the pair and shuddered.

Patrick grinned. "Discerning, eh? Well, who would have thought! Still, any whore can close her eyes and spread her legs, *oui*?"

"Be very careful, *Capitaine*! One word from me and you will have nothing to grin about!"

He snorted rudely. "We're all victims of our circumstances, are we not, and right now, you're here and so am I, and we need to get into that camp so …" he waggled his eyebrows. She may not have seen the movement through the darkness, but she certainly understood the tone of his voice.

She sighed. "How will I get away from them without … without—"

"Without sacrificing your honour?" he suggested, facetiously. "Can't imagine you've been too troubled about that in the past. Just follow your instincts."

With another toss of her mane, she cleared her throat, rose to her feet, and moved in front of the tree, standing in full view. While her conversation with the young *capitaine* had been carried out in hissing whispers, she now raised her voice to the sentry. "*Bonne soirée, Etienne. C'est moi, mon cher.*"

The man's head lifted. He shot a quick glance at his companion, then squinted into the woods. "*Madame de la Fontaine? Est-ce vous?*"

"*Oui mon amour. J'ai été chercher pour vous. Venez ici …*" adding with emphasis, "*S'il vous plaît.*"

The soldier grinned at his companion and immediately began moving towards the cypress.

Patrick sighed. *Christ, man*, he thought, *do you have to be that easy? You make us all look bad!* Regardless, he leaned toward Madame and whispered, "And his friend too."

She curled her lip at him but he gestured impatiently. "Just do it! Call the other one as well."

Glowering, she nevertheless obeyed. "*Non, pas seulement vous, mon amour. Votre ami trop – je ne suis pas seul.*"

The two men exchanged eager looks, glanced around briefly, then immediately abandoned their posts.

Behind the trees, Patrick made a tutting sound. "I cannot believe how easy that was. Bloody fools – led by their pricks."

"You are no better, *Capitaine*."

"I like to think I am."

She sniggered and made to grasp his crotch again but Patrick leapt aside. She laughed seductively. "*Non,* you are but a boy … you are no better!"

At that moment the men appeared among the cypress branches and Patrick melted into the shadows.

Madame turned to face her admirers. "*Hullo, mes amis. Etienne …*" she beckoned the rotund sentry towards her, gesturing to the other man to wait by the trees. Taking Etienne's hand, she led him into the darkness.

Etienne's companion stood alone, head bobbing uncertainly as he craned his neck to see where his friend had gone. In that instant Patrick stepped up behind him.

"*Bonjour monsieur,*" he said, affecting a girlish voice. As the soldier spun about, the smile on his face died in an instant as the butt of Patrick's pistol clouted him on the head.

The man dropped to the ground and Patrick stepped over him, darting through the trees to where Madame was half-hidden within the foliage. Etienne was pawing at her bodice; his face was pressed into her neck.

Her expression was a picture of disgust as Patrick stealthily approached. Madame watched over Etienne's shoulder, eyes wide and imploring as if to say, *hurry up!*

"*Ah, mon amour, aller lentement,*" she murmured to the man slobbering over her throat.

"Huh?" fat Etienne raised his head. He did not see the blow coming.

Madame de la Fontaine glanced briefly at the unconscious body at her feet then back up at Patrick. "You took your time, *Capitaine!*"

"You seemed to be enjoying yourself." Gesturing with his eyes, he added, "Fasten your dress."

☙

Having disposed of the sentries, if only temporarily, it was relatively easy to get into the camp. It was quiet now; most people had turned in for the night. No one accosted them or enquired as to Patrick's identity; although, walking calmly beside Madame de la Fontaine, he attracted a curious glance from the one or two people still about at the late hour.

Madame guided them unerringly towards a tent almost in the centre of the camp. They stood some twenty yards away, ostensibly chatting casually, all the while watching the tent for signs of Madame's husband, the Lieutenant-Colonel de la Fontaine.

Patrick was reminded of a time at Whitehall Palace, when as a fourteen year old, he'd been dared to infiltrate an area strictly off-limits to all but the King's closest advisers. Adopting the demeanour of one who had every right to be there, he was able to move freely and unquestioned through the King's most private council rooms.

Appear nervous or uncertain and you were lost, he'd told himself. *Appear as though you belong, and you can go anywhere.*

Following his own advice, he relaxed and moved confidently. Though Patrick's heart was thumping beneath his borrowed shirt, he was neither nervous nor afraid – he was excited. The familiar thrill of adventure was spiking hot, adrenalised blood through his veins.

It was the same tingling rush of sensation he felt just prior to marching into battle; the same urgent build toward sexual climax. He contained a groan.

I don't care what anyone says, he thought, when I get back to camp I'm going to find that Annika!

"What are we waiting for?" he demanded heatedly. "He's your husband, isn't he? Just go in!"

She shot him an uncertain glance and didn't respond. "To hell with this! Come on ..." He grasped her elbow and made to move towards the tent.

"Wait!" She dug in her heels. "He cannot see me. He will ask questions."

Patrick regarded her narrowly. "Madame, if you have something to confess, I suggest you do so now, otherwise you are going into that tent. You will locate the paperwork and rejoin me here."

"And if he is there?"

"Find a way to signal to me. I will take care of it."

She looked doubtful but Patrick wasn't about to be fooled. He reached to take her arm in the same moment as she moved, and he inadvertently grasped a wad of thick padding in the front of her gown.

In an instant he realised his mistake. It wasn't that he was unfamiliar with the feel of a pregnant belly, it was that she was not pregnant!

She saw the realisation dawn on his face and, evidently deciding she would rather face her husband, she dodged his grasp and ran towards the tent.

Patrick cursed softly and watched as the tent flap fell into place. Preferring not to draw attention to himself, he sucked in a breath and casually strolled after her.

Outside the tent, he squatted in the shadows cast by a table and a crate of supplies, listening intently for any sound from within. There were no voices, only muffled bangs and thumps – the kind of sounds made during a search.

He waited, biding his time, until the sounds stopped, and silence descended. And still he continued to wait, ears straining, and the silence from inside the tent continued.

Rising, he lifted the tent flap and went inside.

∞

A lantern flickered in the corner, sending a warm yellow glow around the room that contained a bed, a writing desk, and a few trunks and personal effects. Annabella de la Fontaine sat on the edge of the bed. Clothes and papers were strewn about, tossed in her frenzied search but she sat quietly, defiantly, empty-handed.

As Patrick entered, she rose and regarded him coolly. "He is not here – as you can see." She gestured about the room. "The documents are not here either."

"Madame," he strode purposefully towards her, "if you told me the sun was shining in the morning, I would check for myself before believing you."

"So little faith," she sneered.

"Lift your skirt."

She cocked an eyebrow. "Ooh, *Capitaine*, I thought you would never ask."

When he didn't respond, she shrugged, then unexpectedly and immodestly, lifted her skirt. He caught a quick glimpse of fine white lawn bloomers as she unfastened a thick pad from her abdomen. Flinging it contemptuously to the ground, she stared defiantly at him.

"Congratulations – it's a boy." His voice was low and menacing. "Now, the documents."

"We might as well leave now *Capitaine*. I told you – there is nothing here."

Ignoring her, he suddenly asked, "Why did you pretend to be with child?"

"I wanted your *général* to believe the man he holds as his prisoner is my lover."

"And he's not." It was a statement not a question.

She shook her head. Patchouli.

"He's your brother," Patrick guessed and was gratified by the surprise on her face.

"How—?"

"Beside the fact that you curse in Italian, there is a family resemblance between you – I visited him before we left camp. What I do not understand is why you're going to such lengths to save him – they will ransom him. Is he as valuable as the general suspects?"

At that she clamped her mouth shut.

"Ah, so he is. Well," Patrick decided to call her bluff. "You are right. There is nothing here for me. I shall inform the general." He made to leave.

"I am coming with you!"

He smiled to himself before turning back to face her. "No, you're not. You don't have the documents."

"I – no, but … my brother."

"*Do you have the documents*, Madame?" Patrick's tone was dangerous. "This is the last time I ask nicely. Be honest with me or understand that I will have no hesitation in plumbing your every orifice to find where you've secreted them."

Suddenly her mouth twitched. "They are stern words from a virgin, *Capitaine*. Or did your papa purchase you a lady to go with your commission?"

"Give me the papers." He held out his hand.

She lifted her chin and drew the dagger from her bodice. "Come and get them."

He snorted and reached for his pistol.

Her large eyes widened further. "You would not dare. That would bring every man running."

"You're right." He reached into his boot and extracted his own knife. "But this won't." Within a heartbeat he'd deflected her knife with a blow that sent it skittering across the tent, then with an arm about her waist, he pulled her back against his chest and pressed his own blade to her throat.

In a stream of snarled, colourful Italian, she again delved into her bodice, pulled out a leather pouch and flung it across the room. "Take it, *bastardo*! But I am coming with you."

"Of course you are," he said, flinging her away, "because my commanding officer keeps his promises and will allow you to see his prisoner. Now, your ladyship," he bowed elegantly, "let us get the fuck out of here before those two sentries wake up."

～

But the sentries had already woken up and as Madame de la Fontaine and Captain Washburn emerged from the tent, the two guards were running about, shouting, and stirring the camp into wakefulness.

"Come on," Patrick grasped her hand and they crouched low, creeping along in the shadows. As chaos erupted around them, they slipped quickly behind a neighbouring tent, and paused briefly, hearts racing. From there, they darted from shadow to shadow until they were close enough to run into the seclusion of the cypress forest. Patrick waited, watching the camp, while Madame caught her breath.

Fortunately, fat Etienne was so enamoured of Madame, that he had chivalrously excluded her from his description of the gang of unidentifiable thugs that had attacked him and his companion.

Thus, nobody was particularly looking around the Lieutenant-Colonel's quarters and the fugitives made a clean escape.

The first pale fingers of dawn were edging above the eastern horizon as they stepped out of the forest and started down the track towards the river.

And as they walked, she confessed that her family name was Annabella Maria Giovannelli and she was the sister of Barone Victorio Fausto Giovannelli, the prisoner held in the British camp.

Hmph, Patrick thought. Only a baron. Wellesley and Christie had him for a prince.

The Barone was the last of a proud and ancient line of Italian noblemen, the valuable only son of a family too poor to afford a ransom. "I knew the only way to secure my brother's freedom was to sell French secrets to the British. They were all I had to bargain with."

"And why you did not want to hand them over."

"I must take my brother back to Italy, *Capitaine*. I can show the documents to your *général* but I must return them before they are discovered missing."

Patrick ignored her. "Or risk your husband learning of your deceit and hunting you down."

"*Capitaine*, he might have killed me for this."

Grinning, Patrick said, "Marriage to you must regularly cause him to consider killing you."

She looked sideways at him as they walked. "Were you bluffing, or would you *really* have used that knife of yours on me?"

Something about her then struck him as rather sad, and since she was being honest with him – or seemed to be – he responded in kind. "Yes," he admitted. "I would not have enjoyed it, but yes, I would have used it. I am a British soldier, Madame, and you are a traitor to France, your country by marriage. Neither my countrymen nor yours would condemn me for it."

They walked in silence for some time after that.

Eventually she spoke, "I did not actually claim Victorio was my lover, but it was easy to let you think it."

"And if we thought you were with child and that was the reason you were desperate to see him, we would not realise how valuable he is?"

"Yes, but he is valuable in name only. My family are destitute." She shrugged and brushed the hair away from her face. In the pale light of dawn, she looked exhausted, dirty and dishevelled – and he wanted her ... he ached with it. "Still," she went on pretentiously, "we have what you call a pedigree, we are titled and respected. Far better to have that, than be a—" she shrugged.

Patrick drew in his breath. "Than be a peasant like me?" he finished for her. "You are a snob, Madame. You should not judge people."

"Perhaps," she snapped. "But I cannot help it and I dislike, *intensely*, that my brother is being held by ... by *Englishmen*. No doubt you will all betray us. You English are foul creatures – not to be trusted, ever!"

"Some of us," he conceded, wearily, "although I suppose our willingness to honour our agreement will depend on the validity of those documents." Her pomposity was wearing him out. In the aftermath of the night's excitement, he was crashing rapidly to earth and couldn't think beyond returning to camp and crawling into bed.

But first he must find Annika and ... he didn't pursue the thought for they'd arrived at the riverbank.

The boatman waited for them as arranged. This time they sat in the hull side by side, in a fatigued silence. They could see Niall waiting with the horses on the opposite bank. Once again Patrick neglected to assist her over the mud. She glared at him, and he grinned at her.

Madame chose to ride pillion behind Patrick. She seemed to enjoy the feeling of his lean young body as she coiled her arms about his waist. He, in turn, enjoyed the soft, feminine weight of her resting on his back. Pity she was such a bitch!

Safely back in the British camp, Patrick rode Barnabus directly to General Wellington's quarters. Dismounting, he announced himself and Madame de la Fontaine. The sentry on duty advised that they were expected and ushered them directly into the General's presence.

∾

For a long time, Patrick sat with the general giving a complete account of the night's activities: the layout of the enemy encampment, what provisions he had seen and how many soldiers there seemed to be. He had handed over the wallet of documents and waited quietly, struggling to stay awake as the general flicked through them.

Long minutes had ticked by, and finally the general looked up, and smiling, congratulated the young captain on a job well done.

Earlier, Hywel had taken Madame away to see her brother, so Patrick was alone now as he walked towards his tent. He realised, with some surprise, that he'd been awake for roughly thirty-six hours straight. Strange to think that he'd fought an exhaustive battle yesterday at dawn, spent the night roaming a French encampment with that infuriating woman, and finally spent an hour briefing the general.

His mind was buzzing with fatigue and his body felt charged with the kind of exhausted energy that caused his hands to tremble and his heart to race. It felt like he'd had too much coffee. Huffing humourlessly, he tried to remember the last time he'd had a steaming cup of the genuine brew. Just the thought of it made his mouth water.

So distracted was he that as he entered his tent, he did not immediately see the woman standing by his desk, although the smell of patchouli was intense. She turned as he came in.

"What are you doing here?" he asked gruffly. Unselfconsciously, he peeled off the filthy, sweat-stained shirt and flung it to the floor. "Surely you have other souls to torment?" Pulling over a chair, he sat and began untying his boots – a fiddly job as the laces were caked with mud.

Annabella de la Fontaine watched, her eyes running over the lean form of the young man as he first stripped off the shirt and then his boots. Eventually he stood before her, barefoot, bare-chested, wearing only his breeches.

"Well, Madame?" he demanded tersely. "You should not be here so the least you can do is explain yourself."

"I came ..." she paused uncertainly, then, "I came to apologise ... for insulting you."

He cocked an eyebrow. "You have me at a disadvantage. Of the many insults you threw about, which one do you feel sufficiently apologetic for?"

She smiled and looked at the beaten earth floor. "I called you a peasant – you do behave as one."

"Ah," he turned away and reached for a jug of ale. Pouring two mugs, he handed one to her and remained standing at arm's length. "I would not consider that an insult. There are peasants I know with better manners than you."

She shrugged carelessly and took a sip. "Your man, Hywel ... he told me ..." She drained the mug and looked at him. "My brother is *un Barone* – a baron. He is minor nobility, where you ... you are an earl – and yet ... and yet you behave so—"

Patrick tossed down the ale. "My father is an earl. I am not."

"Your language is coarse; your behaviour is so ... *common*. Yet you are daring and ... how old are you, *Capitaine*?"

Smiling, Patrick refilled his cup, then offered the jug to her. She shook her head. "*Capitaine*?"

"Madame, I am young enough to call you Mama. Old enough to make you forget your own name."

Patrick watched with amusement as the blood rushed into her cheeks. But she dropped her empty mug to the floor and, grasping the waist of his breeches, pulled him towards her. The bulge within his trousers made unlacing them difficult but she was quick and deft, and when she touched him, her hands were cool and confident. He swayed on his feet.

"I've not touched a woman," he gasped, his hands ruching up her skirt, "for more than eight months ... *ah Madame* ..." she had removed the cotton bloomers and was naked beneath the skirt, soft skinned and ... patchouli filled his senses. He growled and they collapsed onto his narrow bed. "I must apologise ... in advance," he continued breathlessly. "This will not take—"

"Hush, *Capitaine*. My husband is an old man – *ah!*" She inhaled sharply as he neglected the preliminaries and immediately slid into her. "For me, it has been longer."

WRITTEN CONFESSION

*B*roughton Hall is lovely in the spring. Elbows resting on the cool stone, I leaned over the old, lichened porch balustrade, breathing deeply: freesia, jonquil and rose, sweet fragrances hanging in the crisp early morning air.

Close by a dog barked. It was the distinctive, incongruously high-pitched yap of a border collie and my heart lifted.

The lawn stretched before me, smooth billiard-table green, divided by the neat gravel drive that swept in a gentle half-moon curve to the left where it disappeared into a grove of birch and beech.

Jemima barked again and I straightened, peering to the right where the ancient oak rose sturdily from the lawn. Its wide trunk supported boughs thick as a man's torso, its new spring growth fluttering in the breeze.

A flash of black and white disappeared behind the tree; if I looked closely, I could just make out a dusky-pink woollen gown spread out on the grass; its wearer was propped against the base of the oak, just hidden from sight.

The ripple of pleasure started in the pit of my stomach and swelled upwards; a rare pleasure known by a fortunate few – the pleasure of a true love acknowledged, requited. It pulsed through my veins, flooding my chest, and engulfing my heart.

Smiling to myself, I made my way down the porch steps, four of them; I counted so that I took my time – enjoying the moment. I stepped onto the drive, feeling the shifting of the gravel beneath my boots, hearing the comfortable crunch of it as I strolled, casually, easily.

Then over the border onto the lawn, its moist, earthy smell, its silent carpet beneath my feet as I approached the great oak.
Jemima ran to greet me. She pushed her head up to meet my hand and my knuckles stroked absently over her brow, as I passed on my way to the giant tree.

It was said that this massive oak had been a mere sapling when the first Broughtons settled on this land. I trailed my fingertips over its craggy skin, the thick damp bark; I moved languidly, approached gently.

Slowly, I rounded the great tree trunk. The skirt of her gown was visible there, pooling on the grass. My eyes travelled by inches upwards, her knees were bent, the curve of her thigh, her sweet round bottom resting against the base.

Her head was bent, hair escaping from its clips in curling tendrils against the silk of her cheek. She looked up with surprise. Her young bosom rose and a soft blush of welcome crept into her face.

Hunkering before her, my mouth had suddenly gone dry – I licked my lips and moved close. I could smell her, the fresh green fragrance of her. I wanted to taste her.

"I love you," I whispered, leaning forwards, my eyes on her mouth.

"And who the *devil* are you?"

I awoke with a start, sitting bolt upright, heart thumping. It was a woman's voice, accented and aggressive.

"Why are you entering the *capitaine's* quarters uninvited?" The voice continued. "Remove yourself immediately."

Patchouli. Memory rushed at me. I was in a tent ... Spain ... patchouli. Bloody patchouli!

"What time is it?" I mumbled. Nobody responded. Squinting blindly, I recognised Simon's silhouette against the sunlight streaming through the opening of my tent, while Madame Annabella de la Fontaine positioned herself, hands on hips, before him, wearing only her underwear.

Simon swept her a courtly bow, mocking, and I sensed him peering into the dim recesses of my tent to where I sat, bleary-eyed and worn out from my activities over the previous forty-eight hours.

"Pat?"

"You will address the *capitaine* appropriately ..." Madame eyed his apron contemptuously, "*docteur.*"

"It's alright, Madame," I said, yawning and scratching at my chin. A sprouting beard was always a bit itchy.

Madame glanced towards me then back to Simon. Her mouth looked swollen, her hair suitably dishevelled – Simon took a step forward into a beam of sunlight and cocked an eyebrow in an expression I read easily. I shrugged helplessly in response. "The doctor is my brother," I said, swinging my legs to the side of the bed.

"If he were Napoleon himself, he should not come barrelling in like—" she stopped abruptly, then went on distractedly, "like …" The sunlight was streaming over my brother's head and shoulders and Madame had just noticed his face. Simon's face had that effect on women.

"Like nothing." I snorted humorously. Simon gave me a significant look. It held a question and a hint of incredulity.

You *slept with her*? His expression spoke clearly.

With a vague nod, I got out of bed and lurched wearily across to the trunk where Hywel leaves my laundered uniforms. "Madame," I said, pulling on a clean pair of trousers. "My brother and I have a family matter to discuss so if you wouldn't mind …" I stooped to pick up her gown from where it had earlier been discarded.

"Are you dismissing me?" she asked. Her voice was restrained, but quickly rose in outrage, "You are dismissing me!"

"Ah, yes. I am dismissing you. Arms up if you will." I gathered her gown and held it above her.

"How dare you! We have … we … I …" her eyes slid to my pallet where the rumpled sheets spoke more eloquently than she did. "*Salaud*! *Con*!" She spat and I smirked at the foulness of her language.

Nevertheless, she obediently raised her arms above her head. The movement caused her breasts to edge above her chemise. The tips peeked tantalisingly at me. I smiled, conciliating, and whispered, "Later, perhaps," then I dropped the gown over her head.

"Not if you were the last man on earth!" she screeched. "*Sei un bastardo, sei un—*"

"Alright, sweetheart, I get the message." I turned. Simon was valiantly maintaining a neutral expression.

Behind me, Madame had been buttoning her bodice, now she

shoved past me, pausing to grasp a handful of my crotch and give my cock a savage squeeze.

What is it with her and ... shit! I yelped in surprise and pain, and she laughed scornfully. "You can take this and shove it up his arse!" she indicated Simon with a jerk of her head. "*Cazzo!*"

∾

"Madame de la Fontaine?" Simon said incredulously. We were sitting opposite one another sipping hot coffee that Hywel had delivered.

"Madame de la Fontaine," I confirmed. "She has a sharp tongue in both Italian and French. Rather talented! Apologies – I have welched on our wager."

"Don't apologise – I didn't expect you'd last *this* long. But Madame de la Fontaine?"

"It was either Madame or Annika."

Simon's expression was coy. "Better Madame then."

"Why? What's the big mystery surrounding Annika? Everyone warns me about her, but nobody says why."

"Ah," he waggled his eyebrows. "You'll find out. Now," he raised his apron and reached into his trouser pocket, extracting a wad of crumpled letters. Rifling through them, he singled one out and threw it across to me. I caught it and he said, "Arrived yesterday while you were ... um ..."

"Sleeping – that's pretty much what I was doing. Escaped the general around midday ... Madame was waiting ..." I grinned sheepishly. "I must say I was embarrassingly quick ... so was she! We slept away the afternoon and all night. What time is it now, anyway?"

"It's after nine. I thought you should be woken."

Glancing down at the letter in my hand, I recognised Maeve's handwriting. "I didn't expect to hear from her so quickly."

"Nothing of concern?"

I shook my head. "No." Simon's mouth opened – he was about to probe but I cut him off by getting up to put the letter on a table. Reaching for my shirt, I was thankfully, pulling it over my head as Simon spoke – he couldn't see my face when he said, "I received a letter from Zan. She's quite upset."

Years of managing my reactions stood me in good stead as, without missing a beat, my head popped out of the neck of the shirt and I said, blandly, "What's troubling her?"

Simon sighed and looked at the letter in his hand. "She's asking me to intervene – again – to break the betrothal contract Mother has arranged."

Feigning mild disinterest, I stated, "But you won't."

"I cannot. How can I, Pat?" he sounded frustrated but that could be because we'd discussed this before. "Perhaps if I'd attained my majority but ... I can't."

"Would you intervene if you could?" I regarded him speculatively. Knowing Simon, if he'd genuinely wanted to help his sister but was unable to, his expression would have been apologetic. His expression was not apologetic.

He made a rueful face and shook his head.

I exhaled through my nose. "I know Hamish Glendenning," I told him. "I know things about him that are ... he's not a nice person, Sime. You'd be—"

"I know – I'd be condemning her to an unhappy life. You've said as much before. But honestly, do you really see us finding someone more suitable?"

"More suitable than what?" I demanded. "More suitable than a sodomite that—"

"Is it because he's a sodomite you don't like him?" Simon rose from his chair to face me. "I never picked you for a bigot."

"Jesus, Simon! Don't put words into my mouth!" I threw down the dregs of my coffee and slammed the mug on the table. It occurred to me that the only times Simon and I quarrel are when we discuss his sister.

It occurred to him, too, because he looked at me curiously. "I'm
—"

"It's not that he's a sodomite," I went on, placatingly, "God
knows I've met a few over the years and they're decent chaps. But
Glendenning—" Simon opened his mouth again and I raised my
hand. "Listen to me. Glendenning is ... he's ..."

I leaned against the edge of the table. "When I was at court ...
there were rumours. Very *unsavoury* rumours."

I was staring at my bare feet, seeing in my memory the tear-
streaked face of a small boy I'd discovered hiding in the stables
behind a bale of hay. I could still hear the child's stammered report
of a dark-haired man ... a man with a Scots accent ... a man who
had done unspeakable things to him.

The memory continued to distress me. I'd had no evidence that
it was Hamish the boy had been talking about, but in my heart I'd
known. I looked across to where Simon stood watching me.
"Look," I said. "In fairness, I don't know for sure that Hamish was
ever involved in ... some of the things I've heard, but ..." I shrugged
helplessly. "I don't know that he wasn't involved either."

Simon didn't speak for a long time. He looked away from me
and down at the letter in his hand. Finally, he said, "Zan simply
says she doesn't like him. She begs me to break the betrothal but
can't explain what it is she dislikes about him – she just doesn't
want to marry him."

"Astute girl, your sister," I said, carefully modulating my voice.

"She didn't like you at first either," he pointed out
mischievously. "She couldn't say why, she just didn't like you."

"No one's infallible," I admitted. "But she came to see her
mistake. This is different."

Simon frowned and shook his head. "What am I supposed to
do, Pat? She's little more than a child – a wilful, obstinate one at
that. Mother is doing the best she can under the circumstances."

"Bullshit." I grumbled. "Why is there such a hurry with this? Why are you so determined to marry her off to the first offer – an unsuitable one to boot?!"

"I'm not," he said. "But this opportunity has arisen. It may well be the *only* offer – Mother worries that's all. It wouldn't matter anyway – Zan would reject any offer that meant she wouldn't be able to sit beneath the Great Oak reading books for the rest of her life."

I gave an involuntary snort of laughter and conceded that Simon was right in this particular summary. "So, what's the answer?"

"Mother is no better or worse than any other mother of daughters. She wants the best match for them."

I nodded, grudgingly acknowledging that Mim Broughton's ambition to find the best husbands for her daughters was a focus consistent with every other society mama. I'd fended off enough of them myself.

"And Glendenning is a Viscount," I conceded. "A worthy catch, if you were to disregard the rumours." I checked the coffee pot and found enough in the bottom to top up both our mugs. "Though wouldn't you rather an earl?" I suggested, not meeting his eyes.

Simon inhaled, about to say something, then paused. Finally, he said, "Are you volunteering your services?"

It crossed my mind to wonder what he'd say if I offered for Alex, and I shocked myself by actually considering it.

If only for a split second, then I turned to look at my brother and chose to ignore his question. "Or you could aim higher. Christie is the son of a duke – and unwed. I could put in a good word."

Simon laughed. "This is Zan we're talking about. You know how prickly she is – it may completely destroy your friendship with the good man!"

❧

Later, after Simon had left, and I had broken my fast on a binding meal of bread and boiled eggs, I instructed Hywel to ensure I wasn't disturbed for an hour as I needed to write up my report of the mission to the French camp.

This was not exactly true as I'd already given my report, albeit verbally, to the General. The truth was that I wanted privacy in which to read, and respond, to Maeve's letter.

Maeve's letter was a reply to one I'd sent to her several weeks ago, and clearly by the promptness with which this one arrived, she'd been jolted by what I'd written.

Bracing myself for my sister's reply – which would be either a caustic harangue on the loss of my wits, or a gentle mocking as though hoping I'd written in jest – I broke the wax seal with a snap and smoothed the two pages out on my desk.

Morocco

4 August 1812

My dearest brother,

Have you taken leave of your senses?

"Ah," I said aloud, "she has taken the first option."

Alexandra is our sister and need I remind you that even though that relationship is by marriage, in the eyes of the law, any congress between you is considered incestuous!

Consequently, when you wrote to me of the intensity of your feelings for her, I was torn between joy that you have at last been struck by Cupid's arrow – serves you right! and irritation that you have chosen so unwisely – are you never wise where women are concerned?

Oh, of course, I hasten to add, that I am feeling rather smug at the moment and the urge to say, "I knew it!" is beyond my powers of resistance. Therefore, I will say it: I knew it! And I believe I have known it all along – ever since our first arrival at Broughton Hall when you were always so quick to defend her and spend time with her. I knew it also when we were last at Broughton Hall together and you were so outraged at my suggestion that you wanted to bed her!

Which thought has suddenly sent chills up my spine. You have not bedded her have you?

I trust you have not for surely even a roué such as you would not be so foolish! In any event, it certainly seems to me from your description of the summer you spent together in Devon, that Alex has grown into a lovely and witty young woman.

I assume that such emotions as those you describe have come as something of a shock to you – this brings me much mirth, despite the seriousness of the situation.

Love is an odd thing, my dear brother, and to cause you, so long after your summer in Devon, to confess your sentiments, indicates more than anything, the depth of your feelings.

I have known you to believe yourself in love several times – a Miss Whitmore comes to mind! But I have also known you to regain your senses after one or two months. Yet now, nearly two years since you last saw our stepsister ... how did you say it? To quote *from your letter ...*

The attraction I felt for her when we first met years ago has grown from platonic affection and the appreciation of a sharp mind to a love more passionate and commanding than I could ever imagine. To keep her at arm's length caused a physical pain within my heart. After all my youthful love affairs, I was quite unprepared for such a reaction and unaccustomed to the amount of restraint I was forced to employ.

You have chosen a feisty and energetic young woman upon whom to level your affections. You also could not have chosen more foolishly for she is beyond your reach ... you must know this, which is why I urge you, most emphatically, to put her from your mind.

You must, of course, wed and get children, but Alex Broughton is unattainable. A future with her is impossible!

I beg you, my dearest, upon your return to England, participate in a London season and expose yourself to the marriage mart. You need not marry for love, but with the abundance of young ladies coming out each year, you are sure to find a suitably lovely – and even intelligent – brood mare to make your Countess.

I know you for a rare man, Patrick, a man of strong values and intense passions. That you have loved Alex, without touching her, for so many years, and are now so sufficiently overwhelmed by your growing desire for her that you are confessing your feelings to me, tells me more than words how genuinely you regard her.

How you must detest such vulnerability in yourself! I pity you, my dear, for she is a young girl, innocent and naïve. No doubt her attraction for you is, as you say, a result of a pleasant summer in in your company and quickly forgotten.

Most likely she is now embarrassed when recalling her infatuation for you – only a loving sister would say that!

I will not lecture you further, and though I am secretly giggling at your situation – not the hard-hearted rake you'd like to be, eh? – I am also terribly worried for you.

Please put her from your mind, my love, as she will have put you from hers. I would prefer you focus on your military service – it is a dangerous occupation; you must keep your wits about you – I would not have you distracted by the fickle fancies of a young girl.

All my love to you Patrick. Please be safe and sensible – in all things.

Your Maeve

~

Granted, it was not as bad as I'd expected. Maeve, of course, poked fun at me and admonished me, but she was also sympathetic and surprisingly understanding.

Moreover, she believed me – and I knew, given my licentious behaviour over the years of my uninhibited youth, that not many, probably not even Simon, would believe that I could genuinely care for someone as I cared for Alex.

I had thought for a long time about whether I ought to write to Maeve about my feelings. Perhaps I had hoped that by disclosing my love, my sister would ratify my decision to make a career in the army and remain unwed for life.

A miniscule part of me had vainly hoped the dizzy romantic in her would urge me to resign my commission and fly immediately into the arms of my beloved – never to be parted again.

Foolish notion! Dizzy romantic as Maeve may be at times, she is also level-headed and brutally honest. My sister and I are two sides of the same coin. Tossed in the air, one of us will, at any given time, be the steadying influence over the other.

In the one point we agree: that Alex's attraction to me was merely the romantic fancy of a young and inexperienced girl. Maeve's wish that I attend a London season and select for myself a suitable bride was not for the likes of me – and well she knew it! I detest the frivolous artifice of it all and refuse to put myself through it.

My love for Mary, the one woman I'd truly grieved for when our time had ended, did not come close to the intensity of my feelings for Alex. This was how I came to understand the difference between fucking and making love.

I have fucked many women, but I have never made love ... to anyone. Though I desire Alex and hunger to make love to her, I accept, resolutely, that I never shall. I will never know that most sensual, spiritual joining of two people in tender harmony.

I blew out my cheeks in a heavy exhale, took up my pen, dipped it into the jar of ink, and began to write.

Spain

21 August 1812

My dear sister,

Yes, I do believe I have taken leave of my senses and yes, I do understand the futility of my desires. Our stepsister is undoubtedly off-limits to me – I know this.

Why I decided to confess to you, I cannot explain. Perhaps something in me hoped that you would urge me to go to her and declare myself? However, in exercising your characteristic pragmatism, you have bludgeoned such fantasies from me with the force of your logic. Your arguments introduce nothing new – I have bludgeoned myself repeatedly with the same logic.

Therefore, have no fear for my sanity, dearest Maeve. I am resolved to enjoy a lasting career in the military – however lasting a career in the military can be.

Given all that I have confided, and your subsequent chastisement, I have decided never to marry. You, my dear, must therefore be the one to wed and produce a son and heir to my fortune and the future of the Thorncliffe line.

My love to you

PW

∾

Later that day, Fitchen brought a request for me to attend a meeting with Major Thorpe. As I walked to Christie's tent, Captain Emerson fell into step beside me, and we arrived together to find General Wellington already there.

"Ah, Captains," Major Thorpe said as we entered. "Come in and make yourselves comfortable. The General requires your services."

We sat at Christie's large map table and Fitchen served small glasses of Douro port while we listened as the General outlined his plan.

The mission was simple in theory. In deference to my knowledge of the layout of the French encampment, I was to lead Captain Emerson across the river and into the camp, whereby we would locate and disable the French army's heavy artillery. Additionally, we were to locate and detonate their ammunition supplies.

"We know that there are women and children in that camp so you must engage the enemy only as necessary to carry out your mission," the General stipulated. "We understand they have at least six large cannon and, of course, a storage facility for powder, cannon balls, rifle and pistol shot and shot-making moulds and materials, et cetera. Your mission is straightforward: find it all and destroy it."

The General regarded the three solemn faces gathered around the table. "Any questions, gentlemen?"

"Sir," I spoke up. "How do we know they have ordnance? While I was in the camp, granted I wasn't on the lookout for heavy artillery, but I did not notice any at all."

The general nodded sagely. "Yes. You did tell me that in your report. However, in discussions with Madame de la Fontaine, she claimed that the French do indeed have such weaponry. In any event, even if they do not, they will have their armament supplies stored somewhere."

"Is it possible that Madame de la Fontaine was laying a trap?" Emerson asked. That would have been my next question.

Again, the General nodded. "It's more than possible. However, since Captain Washburn here is familiar with the encampment, and has successfully infiltrated its boundaries, we would be remiss if we did not return to investigate for ourselves."

"Captain?" Major Thorpe was looking at me. "What do you think? Do you feel confident in your knowledge of the camp to be able to sneak into it again?"

"Yes, I do." I didn't add that I considered the prospect of another midnight mission exceedingly exciting.

"Very well," the General said. He drained his glass of port and rose. The three of us rose with him. "Then it is settled. Have yourselves ready to leave at dusk tomorrow evening."

Each man in the tent acknowledged the General's command with, "Yes, Sir!"

"Major Thorpe," the General continued. "Please make the logistical arrangements with the horses and the boatman again ... er ... send him a cask of ale to sweeten his temper."

"Yes, Sir." The major saluted and the General was gone.

Major Thorpe turned to Emerson and me. "Captain Emerson, you will be under the temporary command of Captain Washburn. Follow his instructions, and work as a team when you get to the camp."

"Yes, Sir!"

"Are there any further questions?"

Emerson and I looked at each other. "No, Sir," I answered.

"Good. Then I shall make the arrangements as required. Report to me tomorrow afternoon to ensure you have everything you need."

"Thank you, Sir," Emerson and I responded.

We left Christie's tent together. "Well, Washburn," Emerson said, "do you think we'll find anything?"

I shrugged. "I honestly don't know but if they do have ordnance I know where it's likely to be."

He slapped me on the back, "Excellent! I'll be looking forward to this. Life can become rather routine around here." We parted then, he to his own tent and I to visit Simon.

Upon arriving at Simon's tent, I found my stepbrother seated at a writing desk, finishing a reply to his sister's letter. "What are you telling her?" I asked, sitting on his bed, and allowing myself to flop backwards with my legs hanging over the edge. I peered over at him.

He shrugged. "Exactly what I said to you – that mother is trying to do her best for her daughters."

"Very well. They're sending me on another mission," I told

him. "Tomorrow night, across the river again."

Simon laid down his pen and regarded me thoughtfully. "Be careful, won't you? I don't want to have to write to tell your father you've been blown apart."

I made a rueful face and sat up. "Don't worry. I've no intention of being blown apart. Shall I see you at breakfast?"

"Not tomorrow. We have a new doctor – an Arab, name of Mallah."

"An Arab?"

Simon nodded. "The Arabs are even more advanced than the Greeks when it comes to medicine. I'd have given a year's allowance to have had the opportunity to spend time with an Arab doctor when I was at Oxford."

"Better than the Greeks, eh?" I was impressed. I'd heard the Greeks were very progressive.

"Anyway," he went on, "he arrived this morning and brought some interesting ideas with him around surgery and sanitisation – even goes so far as to boil his surgical instruments after every use. I'd have scoffed but for the fact that he has a remarkable reputation – he loses very few patients to fever or putrefaction. Andrew and I have been invited to observe his work."

He looked down at his letter, ensuring the ink had dried, before folding it. "Where are you going now? We could have supper."

"Ah, yes, I am hungry but not for the kind of sustenance you're suggesting. I thought I'd go find Madame and—"

"Don't bother. She's gone," he said off-handedly.

"So suddenly?"

"Yes. Seems our prisoner was her brother. She spent a couple of hours with the General after leaving your tent this morning and managed to negotiate passage for the two of them back to Italy."

"I see."

Simon's eyes glittered mischievously and my own narrowed suspiciously. "What is it?"

"Oh nothing ... not much anyway, except that she left your bed and immediately requested an audience with the General."

I shrugged. "So?"

"So," he huffed a laugh. "I wouldn't want that getting around if I were you. Doesn't look good."

"Perhaps," I stared hard at him. There was something else in his face ... something I ... couldn't quite ... I stared harder. "What are you not telling me?"

He waved his hands in a helpless gesture. "She came to see me after visiting the General. She claimed I was prettier than you and made me a proposition."

"Did she indeed? And did you take up her proposition?"

Now my stepbrother's expression grew smug "Well ..." he prevaricated.

"Ha!" I was on my feet in an instant, grinning widely – it wasn't the first time that Simon and I had shared a woman. "You did, didn't you! And so quick to judge me for bedding her!"

He shrugged and sealed his letter, dripping gluey, red wax onto the page and pushing his signet ring into it.

"That's more likely why she left so suddenly," I said, self-righteously. "Between us we weren't enough for her."

Simon took his time sealing his letter before looking up at me, his expression devious. "Apparently, I may be the prettier one, but you ..."

"I am what?"

He waggled his eyebrows but before he could answer, an unearthly shriek rent the morning air. "Wha—?" I started.

"Shh!" Simon held up his hand, grinning. "Wait for it."

The shriek became a series of piercing cries that sounded like a kind of bird – or wounded animal. It rapidly built to a crescendo, rhythmically rising in a gasping soprano.

It seemed that the entire camp had stilled, waiting and expectant. Then suddenly the crescendo exploded into a full, climactic scream.

I stared at Simon in alarm aware that my mouth was hanging open. "What the hell was that?" I demanded.

"That," Simon said, grinning broadly, "was Annika. Seems she's received a visitor this morning."

DUTY, HONOUR AND GALLANTRY

Emerson and I crouched in the shadow of a twelve pounder – one of three deadly cannons intended for use against the British army. Guarded and well maintained, these machines were heavy enough to cause terrifying destruction, while light enough to be dragged across battlefields by contracted gun teams.

Dressed in civilian clothing, we each bore two pistols tucked into our belts and a knife. We also carried a bag containing the equipment we would need. Having quickly infiltrated the French camp, we mingled with the French soldiers learning what we could. It had been ridiculously easy – I hoped it wasn't as easy to infiltrate our own camp, although I suspected it was.

Emerson's excellent French had enabled us to ask carefully worded questions and to pass unchallenged among the regiments; they'd foolishly assumed we were from the camps of tradespeople that regularly followed armies.

Foolish because we'd moved freely about, unquestioned ... until we'd approached the guarded field, ringed by trees, where the artillery was kept under the watchful eyes of a pair of armed soldiers.

It had taken the better part of three hours to scour the camp and locate the ordnance, but once we had, our orders were clear – destroy all the artillery – or at least render it useless.

Watching from behind a small forest of fig trees, we'd formulated our plan of attack. There'd been no time for nervous contemplation. We'd identified our targets and known what we had to do.

"We need to wait," I'd said cautiously. "Once the guards have been relieved, we know we'll have at least two hours before anyone approaches. By then we should easily have finished."

Emerson had nodded, his teeth flashing in the dark. He was enjoying the excursion as much as I was.

The adrenalized blood had pumped through my body. I'd felt charged, alert and eager. The waiting had been tedious. Emerson had checked the mixture of lime and powdered volcanic ash, requisitioned from a stonemason in Salamanca. He'd taken out his flask and added just the right amount of water to make a mortar.

"The Caesars would be proud," he'd whispered to me, holding the small canvas sack containing the wet concrete.

Well into autumn now, the Spanish night was dark and crisp, the stars were bright in the sky and our breaths hung in the air before our faces. I'd kept my hands tucked under my arms for warmth and forced myself to stop fidgeting with eagerness.

We hadn't waited more than half an hour before a pair of guards approached, exchanged a few words with their fellows and had then traded places.

Emerson and I had glanced at one another and drawn our knives from our belts. I'd had little taste for the task ahead of me, but war was war. If these cannons were used against my countrymen, many more than these two guards would die or be horribly maimed.

Having planned our attack, Emerson and I had agreed on the best tactic: the only way we could achieve our objective was a silent kill.

These guards had drawn the short straw this night. Signalling to Emerson, I would take the guard on the left, he the one on the right. Crouching, moving with stealth, we'd circled and come up behind the pair who stood some five yards apart facing opposite directions to observe anyone approaching from either side.

The practices of silent killing are intended to take the enemy quickly and unawares. In a single fluid movement, the attacker gags the victim's mouth and kills with a single strike. He must then lower the lifeless body soundlessly to the ground.

Emerson and I had needed to attack simultaneously. We'd gestured to one another, one ... two ... *now*!

We'd run out as one, focused on our individual targets.

With deadly efficiency, my arm had gone around my guard, my left hand over his mouth, pulling him backwards and off balance. The only sound had been his muffled grunt against my palm as my right hand rose; my blade found its mark. I'd nursed him gently to the ground.

A silent kill, perfectly accomplished. Emerson had done likewise.

Regrouping, we'd crouched, and keeping to the shadows, run towards the huge guns hunkering in the dark like great malicious beasts, their long snouts glistening beneath the stars.

Now, squatting beside the first cannon, I ran my hands over the firing mechanism, dipping into crevices and nooks, quickly locating the vent holes. Emerson stood by, keeping watch; then, as I found the hole, he took out his bag of mortar and we set to work.

Simon had supplied us with small iron spoons, sturdy yet dexterous enough to scoop and pack mortar tightly into the vents. By the time our vandalism was discovered, the mortar would be solid concrete, virtually impossible to excavate, rendering the fuse mechanisms permanently dysfunctional.

We fumbled the first one, scooping the mortar clumsily in the dark. By the second, we'd become more efficient, finally mastering the task by the third.

Nodding at one another with satisfaction, we darted through the darkness, keeping low and quiet, past the two unfortunate guards, until we found the path through the trees back to the French camp.

It made sense that the shot, powder and other weaponry be stored somewhere close by. As we straightened and began walking normally to avoid attracting attention, I discretely pointed out a building, more sturdily built than a mere tent, and Emerson nodded.

Another pair of guards would need to be taken care of. I sighed, regretfully, but knew my duty.

Once more, we ducked into the shadows and edged closer to the building. Slinking along, keeping to the wall, we came as near to the guards as we dared.

Again, we struck mercilessly, carrying the guards' limp bodies to the ground and dragging them out of sight, before approaching the door.

It was bolted, but not locked – I considered the oversight foolish in the extreme. Nevertheless, it served us well.

Emerson slid the bolt while I kept watch. As the door swung open, we ducked inside and closed the door softly behind us.

The room was crowded with crates and trunks. Pyramids of six- and twelve-pound iron shot were piled against the walls and dozens of kegs of powder were stacked in rows two levels high, almost to the ceiling.

"This is going to be too easy," Emerson whispered.

"It's not over yet," I countered. "Have you the flint?"

Emerson pulled the flint from his bag while I set to work with hands that were sticky with blood and grainy with cement. I quickly breached a keg of powder with my knife, then holding it in my arms, I ran a trail of powder from the remaining kegs across to the door.

While I was doing this, Emerson was scraping dried leaves and sticks into a little pile. At my nod, he began striking his flint into a piece of char. It didn't take long. Shortly he was blowing on it, causing the tiny piece of cloth to glow red.

"Ready?" he asked.

"Let's go."

He dropped the smouldering char onto his kindling; we waited a moment to ensure the fire had caught. Almost immediately, it set the line of powder I'd drawn into a sparking tail, a bright flame running quickly towards the full powder kegs.

With only seconds to spare, we threw open the door and dashed from the building, sprinting into the cover of the small fig-tree forest surrounding the camp.

My heart was pounding, sweat was running into my eyes, stinging, and we waited interminable seconds while nothing happened.

"What's—?" Emerson started.

Just then a deafening explosion rent the air. It was accompanied by a red-and-gold flash, and the entire building erupted in one terrific inferno. Smaller, sporadic explosions were blasting like thunderous aftershocks as people came running from every direction.

Soldiers, officers and civilian men, women and children all charging about in confusion, shouting and screaming; orders, questions, demands, all clamouring to rise above the din of chaos.

"Holy Christ!" Emerson breathed; his face was glowing orange from the flames. He turned to me. There was a momentary flash of his teeth before his expression turned to surprised horror and he fell forward.

His fall revealed a young soldier wearing only trousers and shako. He had a look of fear on his beardless face as our eyes met. The dripping knife in his hand wavered as he faced me.

"*Ici!*" he suddenly shouted, "*Ils sont ici!*" Fortunately, we were hidden among the trees and in the pandemonium around us he would not have been heard anyway.

In the split second it took for me to realise that Emerson was still alive, I had drawn my own knife, leapt over my companion and tackled the Frenchman to the ground.

We rolled and tumbled in the matted undergrowth and while we were matched in age and size, I was the stronger – I also seemed to be the smarter because I quickly realised that if I spent my energy trying to attack him, I would never better him.

As soon as the thought entered my mind, I had the advantage. I allowed him to roll on top of me, but then forced the momentum so that we continued to roll. Suddenly I was sitting astride him. His knife flashed in an arc through the air, but I was ready for it.

Anticipating its trajectory, I leaned back as though riding down a steep slope on horseback, then I grasped his wrist in one hand and his throat in my other and leaned forwards with all my weight.

He dropped the knife, and I heard the cracking of the bones in his forearm, felt their snap echo through my chest. He let out a great bellow of pain. Immediately, I leapt off him and he curled on his side screaming and nursing the injured arm.

By now, Emerson was on his feet. I turned to him, and he grinned bravely. "Can you run?" I asked.

"Well, I'm not fucking walking if that's what you're asking!"

I grinned back. "Let's go!"

And we ran.

Emerson had been stabbed in the shoulder. He wasn't losing a lot of blood, but the pain was slowing him. I guessed that it wouldn't be long before a party of soldiers was sent to chase us down.

Yet by the time we left the forest and were jogging down the road towards the river where the boatman was waiting, there was still no sign of anyone.

Perhaps we'd be lucky.

I doubted it.

Pausing momentarily for Emerson to catch his breath, I examined his wound. It had opened further with our run, and the back of his shirt was now sodden with blood "You'll survive," I told him with false bravado. His face had taken on a waxy sheen visible in the starlight, and he was swaying on his feet.

I was worried for him, but he must not know that.

"Go," he gasped. "You run; I can hide in the forest … easier if we separate."

"No." I grabbed him, forcing him to straighten. He grimaced with the pain. The boatman would be hiding in the reeds some two hundred yards ahead. We could make it. "I'm not leaving you behind," I told him firmly. "You're under my command for this mission – you'll do as I say. Now, come on!"

So we hobbled together down the dirt track, following the riverbank towards the crossing point as quickly as we could. Yet as he weakened, Emerson's feet began to stumble and I threw an arm around his waist, virtually dragging him along.

By the time we rounded the last bend in the track, I could see the boat bobbing on the edge of the water – a black shape against a thick, inky background.

Just as well, I thought, as the sound of hoof-beats echoed through the night. They're coming.

"Thank God he's—" Emerson began, but he stopped abruptly as the horses pounded into view on the track behind us.

"Get in the boat!" I ordered.

Four mounted soldiers were galloping around the last bend, almost upon us.

"They're—"

"Just get in the fucking boat – *now!*" I shouted, shoving him roughly down the riverbank.

"Hurry!" the boatman yelled. "I ain't waitin' 'round!"

Emerson slid down the bank but had not even reached the boat. He turned to where I was crouching, readying myself to slide down the grassy slope after him. "Washburn! Behind you!"

I spun around. Two of the horsemen had dismounted and were sprinting towards me, one brandishing a pistol, the other a sword. With no time to get to the boat, I rose, resignedly, to face them – at least Emerson would have time to get away.

The only weapons I had were my two pistols and my knife. As the soldiers ran at me, I pulled out both pistols and discharged them simultaneously. The explosion tore open the night.

One soldier fell silently, the other screamed and dropped clutching his stomach. They were quickly replaced by a third man wielding a sword. Bereft now of my pistols all I had was my short knife, next to useless against the reach of the sword.

I leapt sideways, backwards, dodging the slashing blade. I could hear the boatman shouting; Emerson shouting … I had no time to respond – no time to order them out onto the river.

The fourth man now circled me, coming up from behind bearing a heavy cudgel while I dodged and danced around the swordsman.

This was one fight I was not going to win. I ducked a mere split second before the soldier with the club swung like a tennis player.

It hit me. A glancing blow, but it sounded like a hammer on an anvil. I saw a flash of light and suddenly it was as though time had slowed. As I fell backwards, I watched the other soldier's blade descend, heard it slash the air with an evil hiss.

My leg gave beneath me and a searing, white-hot pain shot through me as I hit the ground.

I didn't scream. I know I didn't, but I should have for the pain was so fierce, so instantaneous that I reeled, momentarily dazed with disbelief. But I didn't scream; I was too shocked by the rapid swell of dark blood welling through the long gash in the thigh of my trousers.

But the man with the sword was readying himself for the death blow. As I lay on the damp grass, I stared up at him, dazedly realising that I was about to die.

Suddenly Emerson was standing above me, weaving unsteadily on his feet, a pistol in each hand.

I heard the shots ring out.

I heard the men scream.

I felt the cool grass beneath my cheek.

❧

"Is he alive?" It was Simon's voice.

I thought it was Simon's voice.

I tried to open my eyes, but they were too heavy.

My leg ...

My leg hurts.

What are they doing to my leg?

It hurt like the blazes. I tried to squirm away from the pain but it followed.

Simon's voice again. "Hold him still ... I need to ..."

❧

My head hurts ... I can't see ... and why can't I move my leg?

❧

I'm hot. I can't breathe.

❧

"But he keeps throwing them off."

It was a woman's voice. *A woman... Alex... no, not Alex. God, I want to see Alex!*

"Then put them back on. He has a fever – we need it to break."

"Yes, Doctor."

That's no doctor – that's my brother!

"S – Simon?" My voice was a faint croak, but he heard me and I felt him lean close to my face.

"It's alright, Pat. Sleep … you've been wounded and you're ill. You need to sleep. You'll be alright."

"Em – Emer—"

"Emerson's alright." Simon said. "He's better than you … now sleep."

I felt a hand, cool and gentle, on my forehead.

A woman's hand. Cool and gentle …

Cool … gentle … soothing …

❧

I'm not afraid of dying. In fact, I think I would welcome it for I am ill … gravely ill … and I have never been ill in my life.

No. I am not afraid of death's creeping approach, its icy claws on my shivering body, but I have such regrets as to wish that I were not dying.

If I had the strength to snort, I would do so now at my own perversion, for I have always professed to disdain those who regret.

Yet I find, as I lie here, wracked with pain and ravaged by the poisons of a festering wound, that I have such regret that my heart aches.

For I will never kiss the one woman I have ever loved.

She will never know that I loved her.

I will never hold her in my arms as a lover.

So that's three regrets really … my body is about to combust I am so hot. And yet I shiver uncontrollably, and so violently that my teeth rattle.

If death is planning to take me, I wish it would not drag its feet so.

∾

"Bathe him in cool water. I don't care if you have to sit there all night. Get that fever down!"

"And the leg?"

"Keep draining it … keep it open, the pus … it's poisoning his system. Put the maggots to it."

"Yes, Doctor."

"Call me immediately if anything changes."

"Yes, Doctor."

Silence.

Alex, my darling … I think I'm dying.

❧

"Here now, Captain. Try to drink … just a little …"

"How is he?"
"Not good, Major …"

❧

"How …?"
"Nothing … changed, Doctor, … weakening … write to his family."
"Not yet … feverish. Hmm. If it doesn't …"
"I don't know … do. … maggots have cleaned … but the poison … even Major Thorpe … but …"
"… dire. You've done all you can."

❧

"Patrick …?"
"He needs water … I can't … Doctor. … not responsive."
"I can't do any more … I don't think … last the night."

❧

"Patrick …?"

✧

"Captain …?"

✧

"I'm right here, Pat … not leaving you …"

"Nurse! … quickly! Help me hold …"

"… bindings. We could tie … hold him do—"

"Hold him!"
"Captain! Lie still … it's alright!"
"I've got you, Pat! You're … don't fight … hold him still while
…"

✧

"Doctor?"
"Hmm …?"

"… been here all night, Doctor?"
"Oh Annika. Yes."

"He looks … not so … happened?"
"Fever broke … for now."
"Hope … Doctor?"
"We'll see …"

∿

I'm alive.
Alex, I'm still alive but … so tired.

"Al-ex …?" My throat is so dry I can't talk. My lungs are burning. I can't breathe properly.

∿

"Al-ex …?"
"Captain?" The voice was close to my ear, soft and feminine. "Captain … are you awake?"
"Alex …?" I'm confused. Where am I?
"Doctor! Come quickly! He's awake!"
Rapid footsteps … a man's voice. "Pat … Can you hear me?"
I groaned. I felt as though a carriage and six had run over me.
"How do you know he's awake?" Someone was touching me … my wrist, my neck, my forehead.
"He said a name," the woman responded. "A man's name."
"Hmm," the doctor said absently. His voice was familiar, gradually actualising through the fog in my brain. "Patrick are you awake?"
Simon! I'm at Broughton Hall!
Alex is at Broughton Hall!
But, I can't be in England … I'm in Spain.

Suddenly I wanted to weep. I drew a short breath. My chest felt tight, I couldn't take in much air, but the man's name came clear in my mind, "Sssime ..." my voice was raspy.

"Yes! I'm here."

"Sssimonn ..." I tried again but I was quickly tiring.

"Yes!" My brother laughed. "Yes ... thank God!"

I briefly wondered why he was so joyous while I was lying here so ill. And then I slept ...

જ

She was shaving me. I could feel her pulling the skin of my face this way and that, soft feminine fingers, and she was humming a sweet tune I didn't recognise; I felt the rasping scrape of a razor.

I opened my eyes, and the world swam as though I was under water. I closed them again. "Wha—"

It came out like a croak, but she paused in her work and waited. I swallowed, tried again, "What is ... that tune?"

"Welcome back, Captain," she said, cheerfully. I knew her voice but couldn't put a name to it. "It is a country tune my grandfather used to sing to me. But Captain, I cannot tell you how pleased I am that you are awake. We have been so terribly worried for you."

"I have been ill." I whispered the words without opening my eyes.

"Oh yes. For a long time, we thought we would lose you."

I nodded. I had known that I was close to death, so the news came as no surprise to me. I was more surprised to discover that I had lived – and now I felt so weak and ill, I almost wished I hadn't lived.

"Now," she continued. "Let me finish making you presentable – it's not easy, you've lost a lot of weight. Then I shall go and fetch Doctor Simon. He has been beside himself with worry over you."

I must have slept again for the next thing I knew Simon was

standing over me. I squinted up at him and his handsome face beamed down. "Christ, man! You gave me a hell of a scare. I thought I was going to have to write that letter to your father."

Something a bit like a congested snort came out of me and he helped me to sit up, holding a pan before me as I coughed and spat. Finally, my coughing subsided, and he lowered me to the pillows and pulled over a chair.

"How do you feel?"

"I don't know," I responded, fluid wheezing through my lungs. "I can't breathe properly."

"That's because your leg wound suppurated. It poisoned your body, and you took a fever. You've been lying there, unmoving, for so long your lungs have filled with fluid. Once we get you up and moving about, we'll give you a tea of liquorice root – it'll help with that."

"How …" I swallowed over the lump in my throat. "How long … have I been here?"

Simon's expression grew intense. "Nearly three weeks."

I drew in a quick breath.

After my second coughing fit ceased, my brother nodded. "You … you've been very ill, Pat. Very ill." He rose suddenly, turning his face away from me. "Alright, let's take a look at this leg of yours."

While conducting his examination, Simon continued talking, filling me in on all that I'd missed, and I recognised the tone he adopts when he's trying to keep the discussion light. He had genuinely been afraid for me, and I was touched.

"Emerson and Major Thorpe," Simon was saying, "have both sat by your bed at various times. Even the General visited briefly. You're a hero, you know."

I grunted and Simon looked up in alarm. He was examining the sword wound on my left thigh, "That hurt?" he asked.

I was sweating with the pain. "Bloody oath it hurts!" I growled.

"Hmm." Simon was satisfied. "I used maggots on you – good

old-fashioned remedy. They only eat dead flesh, you see. Remember that Arab doctor I told you about? Well, lucky for you he's still here. Practically saved your life."

I was growing sleepy again. My eyes were becoming heavy and drooping. I allowed them to close – *ah … blissful.*

"The General is recommending you for a gallantry medal," Simon said. "You and Emerson both … Emerson wrote a report, detailing everything you did – even down to facing four armed men so he could get away."

I had a sudden flash of Emerson, wounded, swaying, blood soaking the back of his shirt, standing over me, pistols cocked. "Emerson saved me too …"

"Oh yes, he did say that, but if not for you he may not have survived – he was wounded, and you might have left him behind but you didn't."

"Very detailed … report," I murmured on the edge of sleep.

"They're going to decorate you, man," Simon said. I felt him pull the sheet over me, his examination complete. "And they're going to send you home."

"Home!" My eyes shot open, and I stared at him aghast. "They can't … they wouldn't discharge …"

"They're not discharging you," he said quickly, pressing gently on my shoulders, easing me back to the pillows. "You're going home to convalesce – they're sending you to your father. They want you back – you're a war hero! You and Emerson completely destroyed the French artillery and supply store. They broke camp within a week … marched away … even abandoned the cannon you sabotaged."

I could feel my heart racing and since I could only breathe in short shallow gasps, I stared up at my brother, unable to speak. But his words were bouncing around in my head. *Home. Home to convalesce.*

"I'm proud of you, man," Simon said, quietly, a little

embarrassed. But he laid a hand on my forehead and smiled. "I'm proud to call you brother."

Lying there, I stared up at him, too stunned to respond, still reeling from his words. *Home to convalesce.*

And as he left me, I lay gazing at the sagging canvas ceiling of the field hospital until my eyelids grew heavy once more and I allowed sleep to overtake me.

Home, I thought on the brink of consciousness. But the word did not conjure images of Waterville Place.

In my mind's eye, I did not see my vast jewel of an estate, the seat of my ancestors, to which I owe my enviable fortune, my title, my lands and villages and people.

They were sending me home – to my father.

My father was at Broughton Hall.

And so was Alex.

WHERE THE HEART LIES

"How's the patient?" Christie came striding into my tent, uniform immaculate, as ever, and smiling as though he'd just been out for a relaxed stroll in the English countryside.

I was sitting up in bed, eating stew. "*Impatient.*"

"Ah yes, Simon did tell me that you've been up and hobbling about." He pulled over a chair and sat next to my bed. "Have you seen the scar on your thigh? Quite the stunner! If that were to open again—"

"It's not going to open again," I growled, scraping my spoon around the bowl. The stew was horrible, and I was trying not to think about what it may contain, but I knew that if I were to regain my strength I needed to eat. "Anyway, I need—"

"What you need is to take your time. Simon tells me that you refuse to rest. You lost considerable weight while you were ill, and —"

"Anything else Simon tell you?" I snapped.

Christie took the hint and shut up.

"Did Simon also tell you that he wrote to my father?" I demanded, angrily. I dropped the empty bowl to the floor beside my bed and the wooden spoon clattered against the tin. "Did he tell you *that*? Did he tell you he told my father that I'd been wounded and was being sent home to convalesce?"

Christie's face remained calm. He nodded. "What's wrong with that?" he asked. "It's the truth."

"There's a lot wrong with it," I grumbled, flopping back against my pillows like a petulant child.

"It would do you good to go to Waterville."

"My father's not at Waterville," I muttered.

"Eh?"

"My father's not at Waterville. He's in Yorkshire."

"Simon's estate? So, you go to Yorkshire, but you need to make sure that leg is properly healed before you get on a horse."

I exhaled grumpily through my nose while he merely stared at me. Who has purple eyes like that, for God's sake? Christie's eyes were purple – a fact for which I'd teased him incessantly when we were children.

Suddenly he smirked at me. He knew what I was thinking – seen the look cross my face often enough. "Alright, Patrick," he said. "It won't work."

"What won't work?"

"There's something you're not telling me and you're even trying to distract yourself." Christie settled back into his chair and rested an ankle across the opposite knee. "What is it?"

"What is what?"

"Captain, do I need to order you to tell me what's troubling you?"

I snorted rudely. "Go to the devil, Christie."

"Are you upset because Simon's letter would have worried your father?"

"Well, what do you think? Of course I'm upset about that! He should not have worried him."

"Your family needed to be told, Pat," he said, reasonably. "You're going home. There was a time when your life hung in the balance. Simon was worried sick – he delayed writing as long as he could. Once it became clear you were going to survive, orders were issued for you to go home to your father. The general's sending a lot of men like you home to convalesce – consider it leave."

"I know that!" I snapped. I was unusually irritable and not inclined to curb my temper. The long days of inactivity were driving me to distraction; I had already read every book that Simon, Christie and Emerson had in their possession and my attempts to teach Niall to play a decent game of chess had only served to frustrate me further.

In an effort to entertain myself, last week, I had impulsively summoned Maja to my tent and begged her to teach me the Spanish language – something constructive to think about.

The girl had come grudgingly, making it clear that she thought her time was better utilised helping Simon in the hospital. Reluctantly, I agreed, and my lessons ceased after only two.

"Pat?" Christie's voice brought me back to my present situation. I looked up at him. He was no longer smiling. "Tell me what's wrong. I know you well and this ..." his gesture indicated my attitude, "this uneasiness, this agitation ... it's not like you."

I continued to stare at him. He was right, of course – I was frustrated by my slow recovery, and I was also anxious about going to Broughton Hall. Not to mention the grief I would see in my father's face and his distress when I told him I was leaving again.

These concerns were nothing compared with my anxiety at the prospect of seeing Alex. I'd have preferred not to be going to Broughton Hall. Avoiding Alex was one of the reasons I came here. Yet at the same time I was longing to see her, but afraid of baring my soul to her, and my greatest fear: that I may burst into tears like some foolish schoolboy at the first instant I lay eyes on her.

Suddenly aware that Christie was watching me, I drew in my breath and looked at him.

"Christie," I said softly. "I want to tell you something."

∾

Major Sir Christopher Thorpe was feeling rather odd as he left his friend's bedside. Deep in thought, he hardly noticed the rain. Patrick's confession amused him insomuch as Christie had always known that Patrick had a heart, even if he were at pains to hide it.

Yet conversely, it had worried him because Christie believed that if Patrick were to follow his heart, it could result in an enormous rift between the Washburn and Broughton branches of the family, and the closeness Christie had witnessed between Patrick and his stepbrother, Simon, was too special a relationship to risk.

Additionally, it brought Christie's own family concerns to mind – issues about which he was loath to think. He didn't need reminding that the hostilities between his brothers remained unresolved. Christie would rather that his friend did not put his own familial harmony in jeopardy.

One thing was certain: Christie had never seen his friend so agitated. What was it Patrick had said?

I'm afraid to see her, Christie. Those weeks in hospital; all I could think about was seeing her again and wondering if she still felt the same. And yet I'm afraid at the same time. I would rather that my father were at Waterville and I could avoid her altogether. But with Simon writing to Broughton Hall, that is where I'm to go.

Christie paused beneath a tree with large, spreading branches. He leaned against the trunk, as the rain dripped steadily off the leaves around him.

Patrick was the sole heir to the vast Thorncliffe fortune. There was pressure on him to marry and continue the line. To find himself in love with an unattainable woman was an unenviable situation.

For a fleeting moment, he thought sympathetically towards his elder brother, Thomas, and could almost understand the man's coldness – *almost.*

Christie had continued to probe, "And you don't wish to have any physical interaction with her?" he asked. "Your intentions are purely honourable?"

Patrick's face had darkened. "What do you think? Of course I do. I love her and want to be with her every way, but it is impossible – regardless of her affections for me. She is Simon's sister. I could not touch her if a future were possible – which it's not. And she is a maid – I could not touch her if a future were *not* possible."

Patrick had sighed sadly. "The general has ordered me home to convalesce, hasn't he? And since my father's at Broughton Hall, that's where I'm to go."

Christie had nodded in agreement.

"Besides," Patrick had continued, "I came here ... I enlisted early to remove myself from her but continuing to stay away from her is torture. I now know what is really important to me. I must see my father – there are things I must say to him ... thank him for ... And," here he'd paused, raking his fingers through his hair, "and I must see Alex. Though I'm afraid as well, I must know, for my own sanity, one way or the other, if she—"

Christie had watched his friend struggling uncomfortably, reluctant to say the words. "If she truly loves you," he'd supplied. "Is that how you feel? Are you prepared for possible disappointment?"

"At least I will no longer have the question in my mind. I can return to the war and build a career. Whatever," he had shrugged, "a career in the army involves. Either way I will not be wondering. I will always know that someone had once loved me for the right reasons, not for any financial or social gain they saw in me."

Christie pushed away from the trunk of the tree. Patrick Washburn was his own man; he would do what he would do. There was nothing Christie could do to help, and he was due in a field meeting with the general and other majors.

༄

Annoyingly, it had been my left thigh that had been wounded, the leg most important when mounting a horse. I stood on the mounting block – I hadn't used a block since I was ten years old – and leaning heavily on Niall's shoulder, painstakingly lifted my left boot into the stirrup, grasped the pommel on Barnabus's saddle, and clumsily hauled myself up, swinging my right leg over his round rump.

I felt the scar pull and tighten and tried not to wince, but Niall wasn't fooled. "You'll be in fer a tongue-lashin' from the doctor if you open that wound."

"And you'll be in for an ear-boxing from me if you tell him," I retorted.

Niall didn't say anything more but his expression was eloquent enough. He stood back and watched as I walked Barnabus out of the horses' enclosure before nudging him into a loose-reined canter.

With every stride, the scar on my thigh felt like it was stretching and tearing. Barnabus seemed to sense my awkwardness and tried to adjust his movement to match my seat, only to make it worse.

It was the sitting position that was most uncomfortable. I tightened the reins and rising off the saddle into a half-standing position, clucked the horse into a gallop.

Barnabus was always delighted to run – generally away from situations that displeased him – but today, surrounded by the sounds of a camp at peace, he was relaxed and obedient. He snorted with pleasure, flared his nostrils, and bolted like the wind.

His tail and mane flew behind him and his hooves beat the sodden earth raising muddy divots behind us.

It was exhilarating and the most enjoyment I'd had in a long time. We charged through the camp and out onto a field beyond and Barnabus ran as though he'd sprouted wings from his hooves.

But I was quickly tiring and the muscles in my legs were screaming from holding a crouching position for so long after the weeks in bed.

I hauled on the reins and Barnabus reluctantly pulled back to a canter, then a walk, and I returned to a seated position, gritting my teeth as the skin on my wound tugged.

Determined not to give in, I stubbornly ignored it and returned to where Niall was still standing by the mounting block.

Barnabus compliantly moved alongside the block, and I eased myself out of the saddle, noting as I did, the blood staining my trousers. Not a lot – only a few drops, but as Niall's eyes met mine and he opened his mouth to speak.

I pointed my finger. "One word out of you and I'll—"

"You'll what?" Simon came marching over and I realised that Niall had not been idle while awaiting my return.

"Fucking little traitor!" I growled at him.

He merely smirked and led Barnabus away, leaving me to face Simon's anger.

∽

It was another month before Patrick was able to sit properly on a horse and ride without opening his wound.

Simon had issued instructions to Niall and Hywel that under no circumstances was Captain Washburn permitted to ride until Simon gave his approval. Deprived of this pleasure, Patrick was seen hobbling about the camp on foot, gradually rebuilding his strength – determined to be back in the saddle as quickly as possible.

It seemed to Simon that the thought of going home had his brother quite rattled, but the general was unlikely to change his mind. Several other wounded were to return to England and Patrick was going whether he liked it or not.

Nevertheless, it was almost Christmas by the time Simon conceded that his patient was well enough to travel.

He had been watching his brother's progress with interest. The Arab doctor had done wonders with the leg – Simon hadn't wanted to admit how close his brother had come to losing it, or even his life – and every day he'd studied Doctor Mallah at work. He was particularly intrigued by how the doctor regularly sniffed at the wound, checking for signs of gangrene.

Patrick had always enjoyed robust health, and accordingly, was a difficult patient, intolerant of his rehabilitation and impatient with his recovery. Simon had expected that, but he hadn't expected Patrick's irritability.

Usually controlled and unreadable, Patrick was moody and distracted. One moment he seemed eager to return to England, while anxious about it at the next. Something was plaguing him, but in his typically shuttered manner, he denied any suggestion that he was troubled.

Nearly two years ago, when they'd first bought their commissions, Patrick had claimed that his early enlistment in the services was due to a romantic involvement with one of his tenants. At the time, Simon had been happy to accept his brother's explanation; it allayed a nagging discomfort concerning his sister Alex.

Now, though, the suspicion returned with an intensity that caused Simon's stomach to twist. Had he been too quick to dismiss his earlier suspicions? Too ready to accept Patrick's story?

Simon huffed through his nose. If so, it was too late – there was nothing he could do about ... God, he couldn't bear to think it.

Alex?

Alex and Patrick?

Surely not, but what other explanation could there be for Patrick's uncharacteristic restlessness?

When at last the day came for Patrick to leave, Simon watched his brother's preparations with growing trepidation. What if his worst suspicions were true? No ... impossible. Patrick was merely worried about facing his father – after all, he really just up and enlisted without his father's consent.

Yes, that was it! The more Simon thought about it, the more he was convinced – Patrick was worried about facing his father.

Niall was holding Barnabus's bridle as Patrick buckled his saddlebags, and now he turned to Niall, bending his head to listen as the boy whispered urgently into his ear.

They broke off suddenly as Simon approached. Patrick's expression was guarded until he realised it was his brother standing behind him, but Niall's face reddened with guilt.

"Alright you two, what's going on?" Simon asked.

"Nothin'," Niall lied, adding, "Doctor-Sir."

Patrick, however, grinned wickedly and said, "Better say your goodbyes to Barnabus."

Simon raised his eyebrows in question.

"Don't say nothin', please, Doctor-Sir," Niall begged, eyes wide and pleading, "but Barnabus ... 'e ain't cut out for this life ... too gentle, 'e is."

Too skittish, Simon thought. He turned curiously to Patrick.

Shrugging, Pat said, "I'm riding Barnabus to Gijon. He can stay there until I get back to Spain. But he's such a nervous wreck, I expect he'll shy at something, bolt off like an idiot, step into a rabbit hole and break a leg. He probably won't make it."

"That would be unfortunate," Simon said, rubbing his chin thoughtfully. "But I believe you're right. You'll have to buy another horse before you return."

"Yes, I think I'll have to. Well," Patrick quickly embraced his brother. "This is goodbye, for now." They slapped one another's backs, then he turned and swung into the saddle.

Niall held Barnabus's halter in one hand and was stroking the horse's face with the other. The boy was murmuring softly, and Simon distinctly heard a tearful sniff, although Niall kept his face carefully turned away.

Patrick sat patiently, allowing the boy to whisper his farewell. Finally, Niall planted a self-conscious kiss on the whiskery muzzle and stepped back.

Leaning from the saddle, Patrick ruffled the boy's hair. "So," he said with a casual touch to the brim of his shako, "Adiós por ahora."

Simon stood beside Niall as Patrick and Barnabus rode away. The boy suddenly seemed frail and lost and Simon realised that without Pat's presence, Niall would have no occupation at camp – ergo, no reason to be there.

Draping a casual arm over the lad's shoulder, he said. "Don't worry about the nag. He'll end his years at Captain Washburn's estate – you should see that place ... he'll have the best life! Now, let's go. I need your help in the hospital and I don't have time to loiter here."

∾

The road to Gijon was long and muddy. It rained persistently for the entire first week of the journey – not that Barnabus complained. Most of the fighting had moved inland so we had a fairly uneventful trip.

There was one time when I guided Barnabus off the road to hide in a thicket of bay trees as a small party of French soldiers passed by. I suspected they were deserters and wouldn't have taken kindly to being identified, whether by their own kind or by me.

Due to the rain and cold of early January, I slept mostly in haylofts, while Barnabus dozed casually in a stall beneath. Local farmers were happy enough to have me stay, provided I paid, which I did

One night, I passed in a wine cellar, which was bloody cold – although the vintner offered, for a price, his wife's services as a means to warming me. Seems the vintner enjoyed a diverse income.

Needless to say, I declined his generous offer, and Barnabus and I made an early start the following morning.

At Gijon, we were required to wait four days until a ship bound for England could take us both. There was another ship that was leaving earlier but the master had no room for Barnabus.

The four-day wait was frustrating, but my leg had grown very stiff and sore on the ride to the coast, so it was probably better that I rested it.

Finally on board, we waited for the dawn high tide for our departure. We sailed across the Bay of Biscay, rounded the western tip of France, and entered the English Channel.

I visited Barnabus in his stall below decks several times a day – both to entertain myself and to ensure he was travelling well. To my surprise, Barnabus settled into ship life far more easily than I expected. Pity the navy had no need for horses.

I was aware, as we sailed up the Channel that we passed within hailing distance of my home in Devon. I considered asking the master if we could pull into Exmouth.

As we passed Torquay, I overheard a group of sailors discussing the extensive smuggling activities carried out in the region. Aware that some of my own villagers were involved in the area's various clandestine operations, I decided against suggesting a detour.

The next day, we sailed through the strait between the Isle of Wight and Hampshire and finally docked at Southampton.

❧

London, early February 1813. Grace was kneeling in her small courtyard garden, vainly trying to coax life into a bed of daffodils. A shadow fell over her and she recognised the rotund shape of her housekeeper. "What is it, Mrs Cockell?"

"A soldier here to see you, Mrs Poole. Lord Patrick. Are you at home?"

"Lord Patrick is here?" Grace was immediately on her feet.

"Yes." Mrs Cockell inclined her head.

"Of course I am home." She strode into the house, entering through the kitchen, Mrs Cockell behind her. "Where is he? In the parlour? Good. Have some refreshments sent in."

She found Patrick standing on the hearth. A fresh log had been placed on the glowing coals and the room was warm and inviting.

Grace went to him immediately and was received into his arms. He embraced her tightly, and she felt his weight loss through his clothes.

Stepping back, she regarded him critically. "You have been ill?"

"I have been wounded," he admitted, taking the seat she indicated.

"But you are well now? I am so very happy to see you, Patrick, I have worried about you and—" she broke off as the maid, Jean, came in carrying a tea service and plate of sandwiches on a tray.

Patrick was tired, but he was also hungry. He fell gratefully on the sandwiches, and between bites, told Grace about his injury and subsequent illness. He did not tell her about his mission to destroy the French artillery, nor did he tell her that he'd been decorated with a gallantry award.

Grace called for a second plate of sandwiches; as Patrick continued to eat, he asked if he could stay with her and George for a day or two to recover after his journey.

Grace happily agreed and later that afternoon, Jeremy was

brought down from the nursery to greet his Uncle Pat, and George returned home from work.

"So you'll be eager to go down to the stables to visit your mare, I expect?" George asked over port later that evening. "You'll find she's been well taken care of."

"Yes, I am looking forward to seeing her, although I suspect Barnabus will have his nose out of joint when he finds I've forsaken him for another."

George laughed. "Is Barnabus that big gentle fellow I saw when I came home?"

"*Si*," his wife said. "He will remain here until Patrick returns to the war."

"Ah, not quite," Patrick replied. "Barnabus has been retired from military service – he's simply not cut out for it. I plan to send him down to Waterville. I will arrange for a pair of my grooms to come up to London to collect him."

"Excellent," George said, "and in the meantime he can stay here. He can have Equus's stall – right next door to Sir Simon's Oliver."

And so it was settled, and later, when Patrick visited Equus, he spent a few minutes with Barnabus, scratching the sweet spot on his breastbone and explaining his new living arrangements.

He greeted Oliver who was as cheerfully relaxed as always, noted that he was a little overweight – which was Oliver's usual condition – and made a mental note to ask the stableman to have him exercised more regularly.

When next he turned to Equus, she snorted and whuffed at him in great pleasure. She butted her head against his chest while he laughed, rubbed her face, and combed his fingers through her coarse black mane, equally pleased at seeing her again.

❧

The following morning, George and Grace sat in their meals

room finishing their breakfast as Patrick rode past on Equus. As horse and rider disappeared up the street, George turned to his wife.

"Do you think he looks unwell still?"

Grace put down her morning coffee and nodded, her face grim. He is very tired, and I feel that his ... how you say... his spirit is not yet recovered."

"Hmm," George agreed. "Keep him here for a couple of weeks if you can. The roads to the north will be better if he stays for a while. He should at least wait until the spring has properly arrived."

"He will not wait." Grace spread butter on a slice of toast. The English habit of toasting bread for breakfast had grown on her. "He is eager to see his stepsister."

"He told you that?"

Grace smiled knowingly and shook her head. "He did not need to."

∾

Grace and George persuaded me to stay with them in London for a week longer than the two days I'd originally planned. In truth, I enjoyed the delay. Grace was concerned about my weight loss – and my filthy, travel-stained clothes.

She forced me into a set of George's clothes while my uniform was being cleaned and pressed, and stuffed me so full of stodgy English food that in just seven days, I'd replaced some of the weight I'd lost during my illness.

Equus and I began our journey north as the sun was rising on the last day of February. Spring had arrived in London and Grace had been celebrating the blooming of a bed of daffodils over which she'd been fussing.

Over the previous days I'd enjoyed reacquainting myself with Equus. Her smooth rocking-horse gait and the saddle I'd had made to fit both her back and my arse were as comfortable as I remembered.

Now, feeling much recovered, I set a good pace early in the trip, and we maintained it over the days of our journey. The travelling was relatively easy, although the further north we moved the more evident were the lingering signs of winter.

Parts of the road were still frozen and treacherous. The nights were bitterly cold, but the days were bright and crisp. We stayed in inns and the occasional barn, working steadily northwards, and the roads grew slushy with melted snow. By the time I arrived in Wakefield, I was exhausted, as was Equus, so I found an inn for what I hoped would be my last night on the road.

It was Saturday morning when we set out towards Leeds. I'd spent a restless night in an uncomfortable bed so was not feeling especially refreshed when I collected Equus from the inn's stables.

She at least seemed better rested than I was. We soon passed through Leeds, and I turned her north-west, moving into higher country. The moon had risen by the time we crested the Chevin and as we descended the other side, farmhouse lights twinkled between the rise and fall of the hills.

We rested in the shadow of giant rock formations on the hillside, and I think I slept for a short time. Equus grazed and relaxed, but it was the cold that forced us on, despite the dangers of darkened roads with hidden potholes and obstacles. It was cold but my pressing need to complete my journey saw me ride through the night to do so.

The sun was a thin gold line on the horizon by the time Equus's clops echoed along the empty lanes of Wolstone. It was hovering above the misty paddocks as we finally turned onto the lane to Broughton Hall.

I was all but asleep in the saddle as we entered the gates and started up the drive, but some miles back Equus had sensed home and a warm stall filled with hay. Despite her fatigue, her ears had pricked and she'd picked up her pace.

The lawns were white with frost as we crunched along the gravel of the drive. Its half-moon curve was bordered by twiggy branches, almost naked but for the bright green, spring growth trembling and glittering with dew.

Then as we emerged from the trees, Equus and I both started at the sound of a dog's single bark.

Jemima!

My heart jumped into my throat. If Jemima is here ... I couldn't finish the thought. I nudged Equus into a canter towards Broughton Hall's porch. Before I got very far, there came another bark and a black-and-white shape barrelled across the brittle lawn and arrived in a scattering of gravel to dance around Equus's feet.

I worked to steady the horse as she sidestepped and snorted in alarm. It was then that I saw her ... walking calmly along the terrace above the orchard.

My heart was pounding as I dismounted, and I crouched beside Jemima. My hands shook as I raked my fingers through the dog's thick coat.

Jemima was squirming and twisting with delight, but my eyes were on Alex as she approached. In that moment, I don't believe I'd ever seen her look as lovely.

The morning sun was pooling on her shoulders, raising bronze sparks in her chestnut hair; it hung in tousled ringlets down her back. She was slender and elegant, mature in a way she'd not been three years ago – she was a woman now, and beautiful in my eyes, old enough to know her own mind.

Alex came towards me, her eyes fixed on my face. The hem of her pink gown was almost red with dampness, but she continued obliviously across the white lawn.

With a final touch to Jemima's head, I rose to my feet. Swallowing anxiously, I didn't have time to consider my own emotions for Alex had stopped and was staring at me. She had pressed her hands to her breast as though to still the hammering of her heart. Her lips were slightly parted and trembled as she breathed.

Waiting uncertainly, she regarded me through luminous eyes, and as a single tear spilled over her lashes and trickled unheeded down her cheek, I had my answer.

She loved me.

And not as a lonely, infatuated child. She loved me with the passion of a woman who had grown in my absence into a young lady of spirit and independent mind.

But she continued to stand irresolutely before me, and I decided that I hadn't travelled these hundreds of miles to simply stare at her.

I bridged the gap between us, pulling her roughly into my arms and holding her hard against my heart. My breath hitched in my throat, my eyes burned, and I realised that I was in danger of weeping.

Her arms had gone around me with equal desperation and as she pushed her forehead into my chest, I buried my face in her neck, breathing the clean smell of her hair, the enticing scent of her. I pressed my lips to her skin ... God I wanted to kiss her ...

"*I love you ... Christ how I love you,*" I murmured against her throat, brushing my lips over her skin ... so close to kissing her it was hurting.

I could have stood there, with her like that, for the rest of my life – indeed I felt my heart could have stopped, and time with it but for Equus's impatient snort.

Finally, with a control I have never exercised before, I relaxed my arms and we moved apart. The tears were streaming down her cheeks now. I wanted to wipe them away but was afraid to touch her again.

Her eyes were scanning me, my uniform, my boots, and back to my face. Finally, she spoke. "Are you hungry?"

The taut air between us relaxed; I could have laughed with the relief those three words brought. "No," I responded softly. "I'm tired though. I need to rest."

She seemed to exhale as though she'd been holding her breath. "We didn't know you were arriving this morning – I'll have a fire made up in your room."

A fire – the thought was delicious but I'd have sooner remained in the cold so long as I was with her. Impossible though and I swallowed again, aware that I was behaving like a schoolboy and hoping she didn't notice as the emotions roiled inside me.

"I'll take Equus to the stables," I told her. Alex nodded mutely, hands hanging at her sides.

Gathering Equus's reins, I turned away. My heart was near to bursting with a kind of joy I've never known. All I could think was, *she loves me ... she loves me and I love her*!

I was walking away when the first tears I'd shed in some ten years spilled down my cheeks. Not trusting myself to face her, I said, without turning, "It's good to see you, Alex."

God help me, I thought. *What am I going to do now*?

MOMENTS OF HUMANITY

First on my list of priorities, upon my arrival at Broughton Hall after travelling from Spain, was sleep. I stripped off my filthy clothes and fell, naked, into bed and was immediately and deeply unconscious.

At some point my father came into the room. I vaguely remember making some perfunctory response to his enthusiastic greeting, then rolled over and returned to sleep.

I must have slept some seven or eight hours before I woke, called for a bath, and promptly returned to sleep. I was shortly awoken by a troop of footmen carrying a tub and kettles of steaming water.

Dismissing them – I prefer to bathe unaided, which to these footmen was outrageous given my father's exalted rank – I set about washing and shaving off the facial hair I had allowed to grow while on the road.

As a rule, I don't like facial hair on myself. I feel that a man with facial hair is hiding something – *it is a meek dog that barks from behind a hedge*, as the saying goes! If I choose to keep my thoughts to myself, I school my expression accordingly. So, my hedge was removed and I regarded my scrubbed and beardless self in the mirror.

Now what?

∽

I found my father in the library. He was seated in the window, reading a newspaper from Yorkshire, and looked up as I came in.

His face split in a wide smile as I approached and he folded the paper, rose and took me in his arms. I could feel the small tremor of emotion running through him as he held me. Yes, despite my misgivings, it was good to see him.

Bloody Simon! I thought, but immediately remembered Christie's words:

Your family needed to be told, Pat. You're going home. There was a time when your life hung in the balance. Simon was worried sick – he delayed writing as long as he could …

Of course, Simon was right to send a message to my family. Of course, I couldn't simply arrive unannounced, but I still didn't enjoy the fact that my father had been distressed.

When, finally, he released me, he resumed his chair and I pulled its opposite over and sat across from him. "So, tell me son, how bad was the injury?"

I shrugged. "Bad enough. I have a scar so spectacular I ought to go about without pants to show it off!"

He gave a brief laugh and said, "Your stepmother thinks you go about without pants enough as it is!"

I grinned. "Well, she lifts her sk—"

My father interrupted me with a raised hand, "Have a care – she's my wife."

Any number of retorts sprang instantly to my lips, but I mastered my tongue and kept them to myself, saying instead, "Do you want to see my scar?"

"Here?" He looked shocked and I grinned again.

"Why not?" I had already risen and was unfastening my

breeches. Slipping them over my hips, my shirt covered my privates, but not before my father noticed my nakedness beneath.

"You don't have a need for underdrawers?"

"Occasionally, but you can tell my stepmother that I dress like a gallant – she'll relish the vindication. Here—" I indicated the puckered red gash along my left thigh, although it couldn't be missed. "What do you think?"

"Bloody hell!" he breathed. "Looks deep. Almost to the bone?"

I nodded. "Hurt like the blazes too. Simon couldn't stitch it up until they'd cleaned it out properly. So it had to remain open for a week or so."

"Was that when you took the fever?"

"Apparently. I was unconscious much of the time. But they only managed to clean it out properly by using maggots."

"Maggots, eh? An old remedy." My father was thoughtful for a moment. He poked a fingertip gently at the flesh beside the scar. "Hurt now?"

I shook my head.

"Sews a neat seam, that brother of yours. By the look of it – patched you up well."

"I owe him my life," I said solemnly.

"As do many owe you, I heard," he said, locking his gaze with mine.

I pulled up my breeches, buttoned the flies and resumed my seat. I didn't respond.

"Two years in the army and you've already been decorated. Quite something to be proud of."

I shrugged. "I don't think about it." It was the truth.

"Hmm," he said again, and allowed his eyes to drift out of the window to the lawns and gardens beyond. I watched him for some moments, and the expressions that flickered across his gentle face. A look of indulgent exasperation was forming and I turned, following his gaze and my heart stopped.

There was Alex, lying spreadeagled on the lawn in the sun. Drawing in my breath, I realised that my mouth must be hanging open like some idiot's and quickly adjusted my expression.

Father turned away from the window. "She is Mim's despair, and certainly challenges everything a lady ought to be, but ..." he huffed a little laugh, "she has her charms. Lovely girl ... lovely, unpretentious girl. Pity about that betrothal but look at her ... I can see why Mim accepted the first offer she received."

"She could have waited."

Father shook his head sadly. "No, she couldn't. Your sister is —"

"But Hamish Glendenning?" I interrupted. "You know him – he'll not make a happy wife of her."

"That's true," he conceded. "I did try to explain the boy's ... proclivities but Mim was adamant that the sooner the girl was betrothed the better for all concerned."

"All concerned except the girl herself," I said bitterly.

He looked at me sharply. "What's your interest in all this?"

"I'm interested because Mim is trying to arrange an understanding between Anne and me. I know what it's like to have your life organised without consultation."

"Feel badly done by, do you?" he asked, eyes twinkling. "Well, you could do worse than Anne."

I snorted rudely. "I could do better too – any Wolstone slattern for starters."

"Alright," he said, with finality and rose from his chair. He spoke firmly but his mouth twitched with sly humour. "It's good to have you home in one piece – even if that piece has been patched and mended. Now, I must leave you as I've some letters to write."

He hugged me again and left the room.

Standing in the window, I continued to watch Alex lying in the grass. Jemima lay panting beside her, as always. My God, it did my heart good to see her like that! I didn't care what my father said – or society for that matter. I loved that she enjoyed the sunshine so much that she would lounge like a starfish in the grass. I loved that she didn't care what anyone said about it.

Without warning, I was struck with a thought so devastating that I was shocked I hadn't realised it before. *Alex was betrothed to marry*!

Oh, of course, I knew it as a fact – but standing there in the window, it suddenly became real. She is *contracted to marry*.

Forget for a moment that I have only contempt for Hamish Glendenning. My previous experience with what I thought was love, was Mary Whitmore. When Mary told me she was married, I received the information as a matter of inconvenience.

Yet now, it had occurred to me that Alex is betrothed, and the reality of all that implied was like a punch to the gut. She will never be mine. I will never hold her, make love to her, or know her in any way other than as a brother.

She will be sharing the life, home and bed of a man other than me. She will be protected and supported by a man other than me.

She will bear the children of a man other than me.

She will grow old with a man other than me.

Watching her now, the reality of her situation – and mine – seemed to be revealed in all its unwelcome detail. I could not bear to think of her belonging to Hamish Glendenning; could not bear to think of the things he, in his husbandly role, would be entitled to do to her.

Nor could I torture myself with these thoughts. In an instant, I decided that while I am here, I will enjoy my time with her in perfectly respectable pursuits and she must never know how I feel about her. We will pass the days left to us as innocently as any brother and sister, and then I will return to the war.

For me, this must be enough. It *must* be enough – there was no alternative.

Resolved, I turned away and left the library.

∾

Alex didn't hear my approach. Perhaps she was asleep. Certainly, Jemima saw me and thumped her tail softly in the grass.

Alex's skin was turning an unfashionable shade of golden brown and her face was smooth, turned up to meet the sun's warmth. She was a grown woman now, and so much about her had changed in the almost three years since I'd seen her last.

Three years that had not dulled the intensity of my feelings. Three years that had, if anything, honed a youthful attraction into a sharp, undeniable passion. I stood over her so as to cast a shadow across her face. She murmured something and cracked open a single eyelid.

"Mind if I join you?" I asked. She smiled lazily though her young bosom rose quickly as she drew in her breath.

Extending a languid hand, she patted the grass beside her. I sat where indicated, leaning back on my elbows – it was pleasant being able to sit with my legs out before me. Bending them still caused an uncomfortable stretching of my scar.

"How've you been?" I asked.

"Oh, you know how it is around here," she said, cheerfully ironic. "Something new and exciting every day. More to the point, how are you?"

"Simon filled you in on the leg and fever. Other than that ..." I shrugged, "I haven't had the best of times, but I've had it better than others."

We fell silent for a moment, and I contented to watch a bee do the rounds of the freesias bordering the park.

"I'm glad you're home, Pat." She spoke quickly, as though embarrassed, then looked away adding, "I've missed you so much."

She closed her eyes and I watched the flush spread rapidly up her neck and across her cheeks.

My heart swelled and throbbed at the honesty in that simple sentence. My resolve wavered and I unhinged my elbows to drop onto the grass, and lay flat on my back with my head cradled in my hands.

"I've missed you too," I said, so softly I am not even sure I said it aloud. But I had and she lay there with her eyes closed, as though hoping I would not see her discomfort, and all the while I was thinking about that kiss – the last time I'd seen her – on the porch at Waterville.

I closed my eyes. What I wouldn't give to kiss her now.

Sensing her movement beside me, I opened my eyes just as she rolled onto her stomach and turned to me. She faltered, then collected herself. "How about those whiskers you arrived home with?" She pinched my chin. "Trying to look all grown up, were you?"

Playfully, I flipped her onto her back and leapt across to straddle her, a knee either side of her middle.

She squealed and wriggled, and we wrestled as innocently as children before I locked a hand around her wrists, pinning her arms above her head.

Alex's eyes danced and her face was flushed with merriment. My other hand flicked at a chestnut curl. "I could say the same of you ... expecting royalty perhaps?" She was squirming beneath me, trying to unseat me but I wasn't going to let her get away so easily – besides, the game was too delightful. "And what about these ..." I'd spotted an earring dangling from her lobe. I deftly unhooked it and held it against my own ear, "I'm Hamish, I'm Hamish ..."

We were both laughing, the mood between us more relaxed. I released her hands and she gasped, "Get off me, you great lump, I can barely breathe."

I did as requested, helped her to a sitting position and

returned her earring. The tension between us had broken and I was glad of it. Now we relaxed into the easy banter that we'd enjoyed before I discovered my love for her, before we individually realised that she loved me.

We talked and poked fun at each other. I discovered that she was nearly nineteen and my heart twisted anew. *If things had been different* ... I thought wistfully.

Alex told me that she was holding a gathering of her friends on Sunday and asked if I would like to attend. I wouldn't ordinarily have been interested but my chum Deon Morehead was among the invited guests.

When I said that I would look forward to seeing Deon, she told me that Deon was betrothed to her friend Julia.

I smiled to myself thinking that Deon would no doubt be unhappy with any betrothal, though I kept the thought to myself. Instead, I told her I knew Deon's sister, described as the *glorious Adrienne*, and felt an uncommon sense of satisfaction at Alex's undisguised jealousy.

I should have told her then, that Adrienne had already set her cap at me and that I'd rejected her, but what good would that have achieved? It wasn't as though Alex and I had any kind of future together.

Besides that, to my discredit, I found that I enjoyed her jealousy – at least momentarily as I reminded myself that in anyone else, I'd have scorned such pettiness.

Until the next moment when I discovered that Hamish was currently in residence at Broughton Hall. The intensity of my own jealousy took me completely by surprise. It was as though a red fog had engulfed me in its folds: I was immediately and unreasonably furious.

"Is he here too?" I managed to get out, struggling to bring myself under control.

Too late, for she stared at me, eyes searching my face. "He

knows you're here. With all the carrying on ... the earring ... I thought ..."

I shook my head as though to clear it. "Where is he?"

"Gone to Leeds for the day."

"Without you?"

"I didn't want to go."

"Can't say I blame you," I grumbled, pulling myself together.

She looked confused. "It's not that ... rather ... I was worried about you. I was waiting for you to wake ... to see you were alright."

I stared at her for a long time. I didn't know what to say ... I felt like I'd said too much already. The fact that Hamish was here and she was holding a party to introduce him to her friends was like a knife in my heart – and I hadn't seen it coming.

Any lingering doubts over my earlier decision were throttled in the coils of the jealous green serpent writhing within my stomach. I knew I was right to steel myself from her.

More resolute than ever, I determined to enjoy such moments that I could; they will need to last a lifetime, for when I leave here, I shall wish her luck for her future and be done with it.

She will be married and living in Scotland with him; I should have no reason to see her again. I must take what small pleasure in her company was possible over the coming weeks.

All this crossed my mind in a fleeting second, during which I carefully shuttered my expression. Finally, I offered a gentle smile and touched her cheek. I wanted to do more, but this was all I had – a fingertip caress. "I'm alright," I told her, "believe me."

Alex lay back on the grass then, apparently satisfied with my response. "Will you be staying," she asked, "or will you go to Devon?"

So soon? This was the moment I'd dreaded. I rested casually on my elbows and spoke as though it were of no consequence. "Those of us who were wounded were sent home to recuperate. I shall be returning to Europe in time for the summer."

She sat bolt upright and gaped at me. Her face was white. "You can't, Pat, it will kill your father, and what about the rest of us ... Oh God, not again; haven't you had enough?"

I wanted to reach for her, pull her into my arms and promise to stay, but that would be foolish. The most I could do was try to avoid a quarrel with her. "Alex, I have to ... I'm a soldier – it's not over yet. Wellington sent us home for a spell, but we're still needed."

"Of course, it's over!" she cried. "The French are out of Spain, Napoleon's starving his troops in Russia – what more is there?"

I was impressed by how informed she was, but now was not the time to say so. Her response was a physical pain in my chest. I wanted to avoid conflict with her at all costs. These days will be the last I will see of her ... it would break my heart to leave her with only memories of quarrelling.

"Please," I implored her, "I didn't come here for this."

I stared up at her as she scrambled to her feet and glared down at me.

"Then why'd you bother coming at all?"

∞

Well, I should have seen that coming, I thought ruefully much later. Father and I sat in the library sharing a bottle of wine before supper. We talked about the situation in Europe and my arrangements for the continued management of Waterville in my absence.

I had hoped to enlist my cousin Aden to act as a steward but having recently married, he was reluctant just at the moment.

"I'll give him time to settle into marriage and then will ask him again," I told my father, who agreed that Aden would make an excellent steward.

"Seems everyone's getting married," Father mused, draining his glass.

"Don't remind me," I said with a grimace. He smirked at me. He thinks I'm opposed to marriage – he wouldn't like to know the truth, that I would not be opposed to marriage if—

My thoughts were interrupted when supper was announced. Father and I made our way to the dining table. Alex joined us – alone. Nobody mentioned Hamish's absence; we were all privately relieved that the poncing popinjay hadn't yet returned from Leeds.

Alex was clearly still annoyed with me, which upset me a great deal.

Why did she have to be so childish about this? I am committed to my commission – I have a job to do!

I assumed she was worried about my safety – for whatever good that might do either of us. In any case, her attitude irritated me.

Father tried to maintain a flow of polite conversation; he was evidently aware of the tension between us, but he carried on, nonetheless.

Alex, sulky and petulant, continued her foolish behaviour. Alright, so I loved the girl, but that didn't mean I should tolerate such idiocy.

Suddenly my father said, "Did Alex tell you she is having a gathering tomorrow?"

"She did," I said, casually taking a sip of wine. "Seems I know some of the guests."

"So, you'll be attending, Lad?"

"I shall – if permitted." I shot a glance across the table at her, willing her to say something welcoming, hoping she would put aside her petulance.

Instead, she glared at me and snapped, "Don't feel obliged!"

That was enough for me. "Would not miss it for the world," I snarled savagely, then nocked my verbal arrow and released with precision, "You and your Lord Whatsit, publicly displaying your happy togetherness – so quaint."

The hurt leapt immediately into her face, but still dealing with my own irritation, I wasn't finished with her yet. "Besides," I said to my father, "I understand the beautiful Adrienne will be in attendance."

"Oh ho! Yes indeed, *glorious* girl," my charmingly guileless father cheerfully raised his glass. "To the glorious Adrienne."

"Oh!" Alex spluttered. "You two are disgusting – she's my age!"

"A young filly – easy to break, easy to train," I told my father, in a deliberately lecherous tone. He and I laughed like children, and I was satisfied to see Alex growing pink with outrage.

"I can't believe you're talking about our visitor like that," she cried, adding, "my friend."

My father looked contrite. "Cheer up, Lass, we're teasing you. Your brother's home and we must enjoy his company while we can. Here – have another wine."

Alex's sulky moods were one of the things I disliked about her. No doubt my cruelty was something in me she didn't like.

Nevertheless, as the wine was drunk, we were both able to put aside our less pleasant characteristics. Eventually I stopped being cruel and she stopped pouting and rather than bait one another, we relaxed into a comfortable evening.

∾

Alex was foxed. I was foxed. Father was beyond foxed and slumped, snoring, in his chair. Alex slurred something about friends coming and needing to go to bed but when she tried to get up from her chair, she swayed and stumbled.

"Here, I'll help," I told her, extending a steadying hand.

I rose to assist her and though I'd more experience with alcohol, I'd drunk a lot more than she had and was in not much better shape.

Together, we stumbled and staggered our way up the grand staircase. She giggled, I shushed her. I bumped against the wall, she shushed me, and we snickered like children as we bumbled along the darkened hall to her door.

I had my arm about her waist and it felt good – like she was a perfect fit against my side. She was wearing a silk evening gown and it was slippery and sensual beneath my fingers.

We finally reached her door and she turned into me, her face against my collar. She was too drunk to know what she was doing, but I was sobering rapidly. My heart was racing and every nerve was jumping at the touch of her hands on my back, her breasts crushed against my chest, her breath hot on my neck.

Don't think about it, I told myself firmly. I wrapped an arm around her to steady her as I fumbled for the latch on her door.

Her maid jumped up from a chair when I entered. She summed up the situation very quickly and rushed to help me as I stumbled through the door. Alex was almost asleep in my arms – or passed out, whichever was the nearer.

"Help me get her to bed," I whispered. Janet nodded as I laid Alex down, and she crouched to remove Alex's slippers.

"I'll do from here, Master Pat," she said but I was already preparing to leave her to it.

"Shall I rouse one of the other maids to help you?"

"No," she shook her head. "Thank you. I'll be able to get her into her nightgown."

Janet turned away to rummage in Alex's wardrobe. I stood looking down at her relaxed face.

No indeed, she was not the great beauty to rival her sister, but she was beautiful to me, with her cheeks flushed with wine and her hair tumbled over her shoulders.

My heart ached for what I could never have. And in a moment of weakness, I allowed myself one last touch.

I leaned forwards, and whispered against her cheek, "My

darling girl. I love you ... I will love you forever."

Then I pressed my lips to the little space between her eyebrows, lingering, feeling the soft skin of her brow, the violet scent of her hair lingered in my nostrils.

Alcohol? Weariness?

Were these the cause of the welling of my eyes, the lump in my throat? Foolish behaviour! I straightened, turned abruptly and left the room.

∾

I was coming out of my bedroom the following morning as Janet emerged from Alex's, closing the door softly behind her.

"Morning, Master Pat," she said, bobbing a quick curtsy as I passed in the hall.

"Morning Janet." I continued past her but something in the maid's face caused me to turn back. "Is there a problem?"

Her expression told me that there was. "It's Miss Alex. She's ill ... I can't get her out of bed, and she has guests coming today."

"I see," I said. "Leave it to me." I opened Alex's door and marched determinedly into her room. The foul smell of stale alcohol told me all I needed to know about Alex's illness.

"Janet said you weren't well," I said, approaching her bed. My quarry was a moaning mound beneath the counterpane.

I stood over her, my mouth twitching with mirth. *Oh yes, I've felt like this many times!*

"Whatever did Cook do to that fish last night? I feel terrible," her voice was thick and pitiful, and I couldn't restrain myself further. I burst out laughing.

"It's a little unfair to blame poor ol' Cook," I said trying to control myself. "You were well and truly foxed last night. Now you've one hell of a hangover by the sounds of it and it serves you right."

"Why does it serve me right?" Her voice was muffled beneath

the bedclothes. How she managed to breathe the fetid air under there I'll never know.

"Restitution for all those times you raged at Simon and me," I replied smugly.

"That's mean; I feel like I'm dying."

I laughed again. "That's right, your head's throbbing and your tongue's swollen and furry."

"I have friends coming today," she wailed.

"Not going to be looking your best, are you?" I was enjoying this immensely.

She moaned and gulped loudly, then suddenly launched herself out of the bed and threw herself to the floor before her chamber pot.

That was quicker than I expected, I thought, as she heaved painfully, expelling the contents of her stomach.

She was wearing only her nightgown and I tried to avert my gaze from the outline of her naked body beneath the sheer lawn. Now was not the time.

There never will be a time. She belongs to Hamish.

The thought quelled my laughter, and then I began to feel sorry for her. I moved to her side so I could hold her hair back from her face, murmuring sympathetically as her body contracted and convulsed, so violently that she could barely breathe.

Finally, she sat back on her heels, gasping. I could tell from experience that it wasn't over for her yet. And just as the thought entered my head, she gave a small whine and collapsed over the chamber pot again.

Alex continued retching, even after her stomach was empty, and I cringed knowing how painful that could be.

At last, she curled on the floor, weeping and exhausted. I brought water and a cloth to bathe her face and hands. Then I briskly chafed her arms to ward off the shivers that were beginning to overtake her.

"How do you feel?" I asked, gently. "Are you going to be ill again?" I felt so sorry for her. She looked up at me and her eyes were great, brown-velvet pools.

"I don't know ... I ... don't think so."

"Then, you'll soon be feeling better now you're rid of all that."

She took a shaky breath. "Doubt it."

"Oh, you will. Believe me; I'm exceedingly experienced in these matters." I smiled brightly. "Now you need something nourishing to put in your stomach."

"I'll be sick again."

"No you won't – you'll be surprised."

I scooped her up and carried her back to bed. She was light and trembled slightly in my arms. Laying her gently, I tucked the bedclothes around her shoulders. Suddenly her eyes widened and she gazed up at me.

"Did you kiss me last night?" she asked softly.

"I did." I glanced down at her, slightly embarrassed that she recalled my moment of weakness. I also wondered whether she remembered my impassioned whisper. It didn't seem that she did. I spoke quickly to cover my unease. "You looked very appealing – I couldn't help myself. Do you mind?" This last to reassure myself – I knew that Alex would not mind, but I was feeling uncommonly awkward and needed consolation.

"No." Her eyes were drooping. Her cheeks were flushed and her brow was damp with perspiration, but I could have kissed her again.

"Good," I said decisively, adding for my own benefit, "but you'll not be getting another now; you're all sticky and smelly."

Turning to leave, I said, "I'll let you sleep for a while, then I'll bring you some food. You'll be ready for your friends. Don't worry."

She was already asleep before I closed the door.

Outside Alex's room, I slumped against the wall and exhaled

heavily. *God help me! How am I going to make it through the next couple of months?*

HEY JEALOUSY

"I regret that we did not get off to a good start." Adrienne's small, white hand rested on my sleeve as we strolled along the lawn. Alex's afternoon gathering was under way, and the music from the string quartet on the porch was blending with evening birdsong.

Aware that Alex was watching, it was with superhuman effort that I forced myself to focus on my companion. I bent my head towards her. "You're right," I agreed, "yet we can put that behind us and be friends."

She paused and cocked her head prettily, looking up at me through dark lashes. "Just friends?"

I smiled and nodded firmly. "Just friends."

"I am afraid that I behaved most indelicately during my stay in Oxford. While you are here, I do hope that we can spend time together and you will come to see that I am better than that. I would like to be more than *just* friends."

With a gentle tug on her arm, I urged her to continue walking. "Miss Morehead, I—"

"Adrienne, please. And you are Patrick. Let us remove the formality since you and my brother have been friends for so long –

we are practically family. Oh my, look at the colour of this rose! I declare it's as gold as the sunset."

She had effectively changed the subject and I couldn't be bothered to turn the conversation back. Instead, as she bowed her head to sample the flower's perfume, I shot a quick glance over my shoulder, just in time to see Alex turn away from the balcony to rejoin her guests.

Alex looked exquisite this afternoon. She was wearing a blue silk gown, far more fashionable than anything I'd previously seen her wear. The fabric flowed sensuously over her slim body, and the cut and shape of the bodice sent my imagination into paroxysms of fantasy.

Her maid had swept her hair into an elegant pile with a cascade of glossy curls down her back and sapphires dangled from her ears. Her eyes shimmered with a mysterious beauty that I alone knew was a result of her illness that morning.

My pulse had quickened at the sight of her.

Seeing her standing with Hamish, greeting her guests as they arrived, caused my heart to ache with a pain that shortened my breath. I couldn't bear to think of their pending marriage; his hands on her – filthy pederast!

Was this why I accepted Adrienne's invitation to walk in the gardens? Was I jealous?

Bloody oath I was jealous! And it was an unwelcome and unfamiliar sensation. Particularly as Hamish's admiring eye followed Deon about the room; for he would have the right of Alex's body, with no appreciation for her as a person of intelligence or a desirable woman.

"Patrick ...?" Adrienne was looking at me curiously. "You're miles away. I asked when you were returning to Europe."

I gave myself a mental shake. "I must be in Belgium before the end of May."

"Then, before you go, perhaps we can—"

"Let's go back to the house," I said suddenly and turned without waiting for her response.

❧

Deon and I sat on the lawn together in the darkened garden. While the last of Alex's visitors were calling for their carriages, I had managed to extricate myself from Adrienne's attentions, avail myself of a bottle of wine, and grasping my friend by his collar, had gone to sit beneath the Great Oak.

"My sister is relentless," Deon said. He put the neck of the bottle to his mouth and drank deeply. "It's because she's so beautiful – she's accustomed to getting her own way."

"She is beautiful," I conceded. He passed the bottle back and I took my turn.

"Your sister," Deon continued, "was radiant this evening. I had not noticed before – it's odd, but Alex is ... she has some quality that makes her rather ... fascinating."

I carefully modulated my voice before I spoke. "She's betrothed."

"So I understand. To that sodomite – he *is* a sodomite, isn't he?"

Taking another mouthful of wine, I wiped the back of my hand across my mouth. "Yes."

"Poor form, handing a virgin over to a fucking sodomite and expecting—"

"Here," I thrust the bottle at him. I wasn't happy with the direction of the conversation. I certainly didn't enjoy discussing Alex, particularly in the context of her future. "What about you," I countered. "Betrothed to Julia Chapman, I hear."

"Hmph!" He swallowed a mouthful of wine. "That wasn't my idea."

"You could do worse," I told him.

"I won't go through with it. I'll find some way out." He looked up to where Julia could be seen on the porch, silhouetted against the house lights. He gave a protracted sigh. "She's looking for me now. Well ..." he hauled himself to his feet and passed the wine bottle down to me. "Looks like I'm escorting her home. Come to visit soon ... don't worry, I'll keep my sister away from you!"

I watched him stroll away while draining the last of the wine, then I flopped back on the grass to watch stars drift between the fluttering leaves of the old oak tree.

Alex seemed to be developing an understanding with Hamish that, while not affectionate, seemed amicable enough. It was hard to witness.

I sighed wearily. The situation with Alex was unworkable. It was not possible to stay here, to love her as I did and bear witness to the growing accord between her and her betrothed.

And since it appeared that the marriage was going ahead, surely it was good that they were able to deal amicably with each other – wasn't it?

The trouble was, I wanted her to be happy, but I wanted her to be happy with me – not Hamish – and the tension was making me unreasonably short tempered. It had taken every ounce of my self-control not to wipe the smug smile off Hamish's face earlier when Alex asked me to put on a coat before her friends arrived.

It seemed there was only one solution: I must leave. I will go to Waterville for the spring planting and perhaps return to Europe early.

I will tell my father tomorrow, pack my things and leave the day after.

∾

I awoke the next morning feeling surprisingly refreshed after all the wine I'd drunk the night before. It was not yet light – rising early was a habit I'd acquired in the army – and only the earliest of birds were beginning their morning chorus in the garden below my window.

The sky was a lovely shade of palest blue and a few harmless clouds hung above the trees. I felt restless, fired with an odd eagerness to be up, to begin the day.

Rising and dressing quickly, I washed my face and, fastidious as ever, brushed my teeth with a bristled toothbrush and a little pot of powder I'd purchased in Spain.

My chin was raspy with a day's growth and my hair needed cutting; neither of great concern and quickly forgotten as I stepped off the porch onto the gravel drive. Crossing the low border, I wandered over the grass towards the top terrace, where I could look over the rose garden and down towards the orchard.

A stone wall beyond the fruit trees marked the border of Simon's land with his neighbour's. In residence next door was a large bull and from where I stood, I could see him standing, bored, in his paddock.

I drifted down to the wall, and leaned on the rough, morning-damp stone, to watch the poor creature gaze into the middle distance.

Separated from others of his kind and used at the will of an owner for the purposes of breeding, it was a lonely existence for a sentient being, and I felt a ridiculous sense of solidarity with this animal. For wasn't my position similar?

Perhaps I was drawing a long bow, but in that moment, I felt myself truly alone in a world that would have me disregard my own feelings and desires, to find a suitably qualified female with which to breed a future generation of my line.

Was Alex's position any different from that of a cow, presented to a bull – regardless of her own desires – for the propagation of the species, the continuation of the name?

Lost in such depressing thoughts, I was startled as Jemima bounded between the rows of trees to greet me. "Hello there," I addressed the dog. "Where's your mistress? She won't be far behind, I'll wager."

As I spoke, Alex strolled into view, between the columns of apple trees. Petals from the new blossoms floated and swirled around her feet as she came towards me, and my breath caught in my throat.

She was wearing a plain woollen gown and pelisse. Her hair was uncombed and hanging in untidy curls over her shoulders while her eyes glistened with pleasure; she was happy to see me.

That was when I knew myself to be a coward as I resolved to speak with my father immediately after breakfast; I must definitely leave tomorrow.

∾

Rising to meet her, making some inane conversation to distract myself from the hammering of my heart, Alex and I fell into step, walking leisurely through the orchard.

I don't remember much of the actual conversation we were having, except that she attempted to continue our usual teasing banter that ended with me saying something about Hamish to which she took offence.

It irritated me that she would defend him. And then, as though to deliberately taunt me, she brought Adrienne into the argument, calling us *lovesick poodles*.

Under normal circumstances, I'd have found Alex's turn of phrase amusing, but these were not normal circumstances. I knew that Alex was jealous of Adrienne, just as I knew that I was jealous of Hamish.

Yet neither of us had a right to jealousy, and it was this fact that pushed me to the edge of my limits.

"This jealousy of yours is quite tiresome," I told her, nastily. Then I turned away, intending to return to the house.

Why couldn't she have left it there? Why couldn't she have let me walk away? But it was not in Alex's nature to surrender in the face of a battle.

"Don't you walk away, Patrick Washburn," she shouted, and the sound of her voice echoed through the still of the morning.

"Shut up!" I hissed, whirling around. "Do you want to wake the whole house?"

"Then don't say something like that and walk away like a coward," she retorted. "I don't want to have that old argument with you again, but—"

"Really!" I demanded. And then it was on ... neither prepared to yield to the other. I don't remember the entire argument. We stood only yards apart, hissing unkind things at each other – the kinds of things people in love say ... the way they hurt one another for no good reason.

She called me conceited. I called her jealous and childish. She said I was hateful and a philanderer – a rake. I responded by likening her to a spider, lurking, spying on me and interfering in my business.

I can only speak for myself, but this argument tore at my heart. I wanted an end to it for it was painful to me that we would say such things to one another, and as I felt the sting of her words, I retaliated mercilessly.

And I was better at it than she.

I attacked, unleashing such a verbal storm that she had no response and stood frozen in place. Her mouth fell open and the tears streamed, unheeded, down her face. She knew I could be cruel and began pleading with me to stop.

But I went on ... relentlessly, pummelling her with unkind words.

Why did I do it? I did it because I was in such pain that it was the only salve to my wounds.

And even as I hurt her, I wanted to fold her in my arms and never let her go. I loved her so desperately that something in me snapped. I lunged towards her and clutched her wrists.

She seemed alarmed and recoiled slightly – as if I would physically hurt her! The thought horrified me and yet I continued to snarl at her, words designed to wound. She tried to pull away, but I would not release her.

Now she was begging me, and I was beyond hearing. I continued berating her: about Hamish, about herself, about me ... on and on I went, as my own grief poured from me.

And then finally I said it; I said the one thing I vowed I would never say, and I listened helplessly as the accusation flew, without restraint from my own mouth:

"Tell Hamish you can't marry him because you're in love with me!"

As the words spilled out, I stood in profound shock, struck dumb by what I'd just said.

I released her wrists and she fell back, covering her face and sobbing into her hands.

Dazed and vaguely befuddled, I think I lost track of time as I stood for a long moment, watching her weep.

I felt sick, appalled by my own behaviour.

There was no way I could rectify the situation; I had destroyed everything. My relationship with Alex was never going to be the same. I should walk away now and never see her again.

But I stood paralysed with grief and pain. *Walk away ... now!* I commanded myself.

A wise man would have walked away. A strong man certainly would. A better man than I, would walk away and never turn back.

I was not wise, strong or better.

"Sweetheart, don't cry," I whispered, on the brink of tears myself. "I never wanted it to be like this. I should have gone while I still could." I drew in a deep, shaky breath. I wasn't even sure if she'd heard me. "I can't be strong for both of us."

She had heard me. Slowly she lowered her hands. Her face was stained with tears, her lips trembling.

I felt the tears stinging the backs of my own eyes as she turned her face up to me. I knew in that moment I was utterly defeated. If I did not touch her, take her in my arms, declare myself – however futile it may be – I might collapse in an unmanly mound of grief at her feet.

So I did the only thing I could do.

∾

The moment I first kissed her will live in my heart forever. I pushed her hard against the trunk of a tree, my mouth fused to hers with an intensity of feeling I'd never known.

I felt that every moment of my life, every breath, every step had led me to this pinnacle. Every lover I have taken, every man I have killed, all fell away as though I were an innocent again, eager for experience.

I kissed her, tasted her, touched her face, her hair, my tongue in her mouth, my weight pressed against her, her breasts crushed against my heart. I was frenzied, untamed, driven by an urgent hunger that left me crazed with desire and painfully hard.

And she returned my passion with an ardour that was entirely instinctive, a lust as desperate as my own; her body responding with a primitive need that I doubted she was even aware of.

It would have been so easy to lift her skirt, to slide into her warmth, to take her with a greed borne of long-suppressed desire – but I could not.

I wanted more of her ... and more *for* her.

I could not throw her to the ground and rut with her beneath a tree. I could not do that and then turn away, return to Spain and leave her to Hamish as though it never happened.

With that thought the fog began to lift from my mind. We sank to the ground and I cradled her in my arms while she rested her head against my heart, softly weeping into my shirt.

I sat quietly holding her, shaken and bewildered, trying to make sense of what had just happened, and trying to cobble together some plan for the future.

At length, she raised her face to me. The tears were glistening on her lashes, her lips were red and swollen. She whispered, "You love me?"

It was like someone lifted a great, burdensome cloak from my shoulders. The relief was phenomenal. I nodded and said, "I do – have for a long time."

⁕

Alex and I sat beneath an apple tree for longer than we knew. We talked and confessed our love for one another. We kissed some more, and I told her I wanted to marry her.

It wasn't something premeditated, but as soon as I said it, I knew it was the truth – I did want to marry her. I wanted her children to be ours. I wanted her to be my future countess and the mother of the heirs to the earldom and Washburn estates.

How to extricate her from her current situation was the difficulty, but it was not impossible. In the meantime, I had to fulfil my military obligations, although it may be possible to resign my commission early and return to her.

I told her that I would not lay with her until we were wed – it was important to me that Alex's first sexual experience be unhurried, loving and in a proper bed rather than the drunken and hurried trysts in which I usually engaged.

I also was concerned about pregnancy. Although I knew there were ways around that, I could not imagine presenting her with a sponge and cup of wine and explaining what she was required to do with them.

While I was determined not to bed her, I also promised Alex my fidelity. I promised to abstain from whoring and all other encounters, saving myself for her alone. To my mind, I was affianced; I had made my commitment to one woman, and I could not be happier.

❧

My father asked me to ride into Wolstone to speak with a carpenter about repairs to the stable doors. Ordinarily, I would give Equus her head and we would cover the two miles in no time.

Today though, I needed to think. I set Equus to a restrained walk and let my mind drift over the morning's events.

I had not risen from my bed with the intention of declaring myself to Alex. If anything, I'd been trying to come up with a feasible reason to leave Broughton Hall.

Now, of course, everything had changed and my greatest challenge was ensuring I left Alex as intact as I have found her. For now, I have kissed her – properly – and I want more. She was eager and surprisingly passionate – she wanted more too and seemed disappointed when I told her I would not lay with her.

"Well, that's women for you," I told Equus. "Pretending a dedication to the preservation of their virtue while eager to give it away."

No, that's not fair. Alex has never played the coquette – not to me, nor, to my knowledge, to anyone else. She's far too ingenuous for that.

Alex would give herself to me without question – the knowledge made my head reel – but I wouldn't touch her that way because she was no slattern. She was no whore or taproom slut. She was the woman I wanted to grow old with and there was a vast difference.

I didn't know how or when I would be able to extricate her from her betrothal; before I could though, I would have to return to the war. If I were to be wounded again, or killed – it was a reality – I must ensure she could make a good marriage.

She must be a virgin, and this was not something I wanted to discuss with her – it was the way the world worked.

"She's too naive," I told Equus who slapped me with her tail. "Alright. I'll shut up about it now."

The horse snorted appreciatively as we crossed the bridge into Wolstone.

DELICIOUS TORMENT

When thou sigh'st, thou sigh'st not wind,
But sigh'st my soul away;
When though weep'st, unkindly kind,
My life's blood doth decay.
It cannot be
That thou lovest me as thou say'st,
If in thine my life thou waste,
That art the best of me.

I sat in the taproom at the Black Bull. The words of Donne's *Sweetest love, I do not go* were running in the back of my mind like distant music while I nursed a mug of ale, which was gradually growing warm as my mind wandered, distracted.

I loved Alex. I loved her as a man who has had experience of many women and knew the difference between love and lust. Yet I had my doubts about her.

Alex was a young girl, inexperienced and unhappily betrothed. I'd no doubt that she loved me, yet I suspected that love was as fickle and changeable as that of any young girl.

And I was driving myself to great heights of idiocy with it for Alex was a temptress. She worked on me both consciously and unconsciously, tempting me with her smiles, her laughter and the sly, slanting looks from the corners of her eyes.

Fool that I am, I want to marry her. I want to extricate her from her betrothal and take her to my home.

"Ha!" I scoffed into my mug before draining its contents. I am a fool, but worse than a common everyday fool – I am a wealthy, well-educated one, which means I am dangerous to myself and others.

It's just one of many reasons I cannot bed her because I expect that once I've returned to the war, she will grow weary of waiting for me and will accept marriage to Elginbury – or someone else. She is the sister of a baron; even if Simon is a minor baron, he is a man of means and both his sisters will be well-dowered.

If she did not wed Elginbury, someone would offer for her. I don't think I was biased in my assessment; I thought I was realistic in a way that Simon and his mother were not. They only saw Alex as a hoyden, a child with wild ways and a smart mouth.

I saw past that. I saw a spirited, energetic young woman with a quick mind; and I wouldn't be the only one to do so. Not only that, but although her dowry meant nothing to me, she was considerably valuable on the marriage mart, which was why the Elginburys would be reluctant to release her without compensation.

I sighed heavily. I was driving myself to distraction with all these thoughts. Alex had me tying myself up in knots. The easiest solution, of course, would be to say, *To hell with Simon, his mother and everyone else, I'm marrying her and that's the end of it!*

But that was not my way. I would never leave Simon – or anyone for that matter – to a legal mess on my account.

In any case, I couldn't marry her until I had returned from Europe – that way I would know her affections were not those of a young and naive girl with little knowledge of life. No, if she was prepared to wait for me, I would have certainty of her steadfastness and her commitment.

Regardless, I—

"Milord?"

Vaguely irritated by the interruption to my brooding, I looked up to find a very young girl with a very knowing smile standing before me.

"Hmm? What can I do for you, lass?"

She smirked prettily causing dimples to form in her cheeks. "It's what I can do fer you, milord."

"What's your name?"

"Kate," she replied, coiling a blond ringlet about her index finger.

"And how old are you, Kate?"

"Sixteen, milord."

My expression was sceptical. She was tiny, frail like a bird, her body had not yet fully developed those womanly curves that came with maturity. "Thirteen if you're lucky – too young for me, lass."

"Don't matter how old or young, milord, still gotta eat."

I studied her for a moment. Her face would've been pretty but for the pinched look that hunger had stamped on it. I jerked my chin towards the bench opposite. "Sit."

She made a reluctant face but obeyed. "I've got a room down the lane, milord."

"We're not going to your room." I clicked my fingers at a passing serving maid. "Bring a plate of today's stew," I told her.

"Aye, milord."

"I'm not interested in food, milord!" Kate objected. "It's money I need."

"Well, if it's money you're after you've come to the right place." Deon Morehead slid onto the bench beside the girl. "This fellow's made of it."

"He's not payin'," she grumbled.

"Not paying, eh? Not like you, Washburn."

"Wants to buy me food," Kate continued indignantly.

"*Food*!" Deon repeated in mock outrage.

"Stew."

"*Stew*? Well, I say. I wouldn't stand for that. What are you about, Washburn? Offering a lovely young thing like this a plate of stew? Should be ashamed of yourself."

I grinned and shrugged. "She was hungry."

"Ah, but money buys gin, doesn't it sweetheart," Deon said, sliding an arm about the girl's bony shoulders and pulling her towards him. "And gin fills the belly as good as any stew."

Kate beamed. "Aye, milord."

"Anyway," Deon said, releasing her. "I'm not a lord, sorry to say, but he is – pity he's so sour tonight. He's not normally ... what's got into you, Washburn?"

I shrugged, aware that I was being very sour. "What brings you here?" I changed the subject.

"Heavy balls and a heavy purse."

"Good," Kate's sly hand slid beneath the table and Deon drew in a sharp breath.

"Tempted as I am," Deon deliberately removed the girl's hand from his crotch, "you look young enough to get me locked up or ..." he looked around, "beaten up. Your father or brother's probably lurking about somewhere ready to knock me on the head and relieve me of this month's allowance. So ..." he grinned cheerfully, "stew it is!"

Kate sighed and slid off the bench. "You can jam your bloody stew!" she snapped and stalked away just as the food arrived.

"Do you mind?" Deon asked me. I gestured for him to go ahead but he'd already taken up the spoon.

"I'm impressed," I told him.

"Hmm? How so?"

"You picking that girl for a lure."

He shrugged and swallowed a spoonful of meat and gravy.

"You taught me well."

"I didn't pick it. Thought she was a genuine whore – just too young."

The spoon hovered above the plate as he regarded me narrowly. "Losing your touch. What's wrong with you? You're … distracted?"

"Just thinking. The war … I suppose."

"Got yourself a Spanish girl?"

I shook my head.

"Screw anyone over there?"

I thought of Madam and nodded.

"Missing her, are you?"

"No, not at all." I smiled, adding, "besides, Simon stole her from me, then she buggered off, out of the camp."

"Simon, eh?" Deon scraped the last of the stew from the plate. "That was surprisingly good, you know," he said indicating the empty bowl. "Never mind. None of us gets a look-in with Simon around. You need to bed someone …" he pointed the spoon at me. "You have that look about you. All … hungry-like. Been a while, has it? Had anyone since you been home?"

I shook my head. I was hungry alright – every time I looked at Alex I—

"Alright then," he rose. "Come on, let's go to Leeds for the night."

I rose with him but resisted when he reached for my elbow. "I'm going home."

"No …!" My friend was aghast. "You can't!" He gestured around the taproom. "The night is but young, the women are warm and willing … anyway, what's this I hear about you being contracted to your stepsister – Anne, is it? My sister was very upset. Tiresome business, the machinations of women! If anyone needs a damn good whore, it's you. Now, let's go."

"I'm not contracted to Anne and I'm going home. I suggest you do too. *You're* contracted, remember?"

"Phht! I'm trying *not* to remember. Well," Deon adjusted his coat and flicked at the lace on his shirt cuffs, "Looks like I'm going to Leeds without you. *Adios*, Captain!"

❧

I was drawn to Alex, as I'd always been drawn to her. It was different now, though, because I'd declared myself, so the nature of our friendship had been changed. Father and my stepmother were too concerned with their own affairs to notice any alteration in the way Alex and I acted towards one another.

As for me, I felt like a fourteen year old overburdened by rampant urges. I was unused to having my lusts unfulfilled and it was a kind of delicious torment that I had no relief in her body – or anyone's body for that matter. I'd promised Alex my fidelity and I did not regret it.

There were opportunities, of course, because Alex was eager and trusting. She delighted in teasing me, and I delighted in her attentions.

It seemed to me that Meg's nurse, Clara, often accompanied us as we wandered through Broughton Hall's gardens and neighbouring forest. Meg would skip gaily along beside us or ride on my shoulders – it made for very pleasant hours of easy companionship.

If Alex was unaware of Clara's chaperonage I was not, for the cunning woman would wink at me and turn away. She allowed us a modicum of privacy to kiss and embrace, while ensuring we were not truly alone. If she was trying to protect Alex from me, she was misguided. She should have protected me from Alex!

The acts of kissing and fondling were new to Alex; she was eager to explore and experiment and regularly teased me into dangerous territory – not that I went kicking and screaming – I was thoroughly enjoying her.

There were, however, occasions when I came perilously close to giving in to my baser nature that caused me to truly question my decision not to take her to bed. It would have been so easy – and such a blessed relief!

Alex tested my resolve, regularly asking me to tell our parents about us. She said that if I truly loved her I would prove myself; I would announce our engagement, I would take her to my bed. I wavered; I was tempted.

Christ! I wanted her and it was a sensual torture. Her eagerness frustrated me, angered me and delighted me at the same time.

One particularly trying occasion was the afternoon that we were told Simon had been horribly wounded. A letter had arrived from Simon's colleague, whom I had met, Doctor Andrew Hurst, detailing the horrific injuries Simon had sustained during a mission to a village. There'd been an explosion and while Simon had lived, a second man he'd taken to assist him had been killed.

Shaken to the core by the information, I'd sat in my room for a long time considering how quickly one's fortune could change. Growing increasingly morose, I questioned what I was doing to myself and Alex by denying us satisfaction of the love between us.

What was it all for when a life could be extinguished, or irretrievably altered, in the space of a heartbeat?

Finally pulling myself out of my brown study, I was dressing to attend a dinner when Alex tapped on my door.

Irritable, discontented and grieving Simon's misfortune, I pulled her into my room. I was wearing only breeches and aware that I was dangerously naked and she dangerously alluring in her evening gown. I nevertheless clasped her to me and kissed her with passionate brutality.

My body reacted immediately, and I quickly released her. She slumped against the wall; the rise of her bosom above the bodice of a daringly low-cut green dress did nothing to assuage the ache between my thighs.

"I presume you're not in the habit of visiting the bedchambers of men so you must have heard about Simon?" I said.

She nodded and I saw the stricken look in her eyes – I'd been too interested in her mouth until now. "I can't believe it," she cried. "It's so ... I can't believe God could be so cruel."

I sighed heavily. "God had nothing to do with it – damn frogs! All the more reason for me to get back there – the sooner the better!"

"You can't punish them all. Oh Pat ..." she began to cry, and my heart twisted in my chest.

"Shh ..." I soothed, unable to resist pulling her into my arms again. She rested her head against my naked chest, and I stroked her hair.

Finally, she pulled away and looked into my face. "I also came to tell you Mother is writing to Lord Elginbury to confirm the date of my wedding."

My stomach lurched but I steeled myself and didn't react. This was exactly why I couldn't allow myself to be carried away by her. "When's it to be?" I asked calmly.

"A day in December."

I could see the longing in her face and knew I was asking a lot of her. I said as much – I was trying to mollify her but it wasn't working. She was afraid so I tried a different tack.

"Is this what you're wearing?" I touched a glistening ruby at her throat. "You look lovely."

She smiled without humour. "Shameless flattery won't distract me." Could she not see that I was trying to distract myself as well? Those gloomy thoughts I'd had earlier were threatening to come flooding back.

"Pat, what if something happens to you?" she went on. "Oh, why do we deny ourselves? We love each other ... there's no shame in expressing it."

Christ she was tempting. Not only her body but her logic. Why should we deny ourselves? When a life can be snuffed out so easily, why shouldn't we find some happiness, some pleasure in each other's arms while we could?

Society would condemn us – her more than me – but for the first time in my disreputable life, I'd be taking a woman purely out of love.

It was too much to think about. I took up a shirt and turned away to finish dressing. I didn't get very far. Still unresolved but willing to push the boundaries, I reached for her and began kissing her again.

Did she sense the change in my embrace? As my passion rose my kisses grew demanding and urgent. I needed relief, I needed to touch her, be inside her.

With a supreme effort, I drew back and cupped her breasts, murmuring something – I knew not what as my senses swam with desire.

Helpless with need, I kissed her again, deeper. It would be so easy ... and she would welcome me; her body was instinctively sensual, wantonly pushing her hips into my groin. She was breathing hard, her arms were around me, one hand had crept up my back beneath my shirt.

Suddenly all reason fled. I could no longer recall the reasons – supposedly very good reasons – why I had decided not to lay with her.

My bed was just behind me.

We continued to kiss as my hand slid up her back to the lacing on her gown. The ends of the ribbon were between my fingers. Suddenly there was a knock at my door.

Alex and I leapt apart as though scalded. Her face registered guilt and fear but for me it was like a fog lifting. I'd come so close to throwing her on the bed. Even now my loins throbbed and my evening trousers were painfully tight.

But I pressed a silencing finger to her lips – trying not to notice how red and swollen they were – and I calmly called out, "Who is it?"

It was not the first time I'd been interrupted at such a crucial point but it was certainly one of the most welcome as I realised how close I'd come to making Alex my lover.

I had some brief discussion with Alex's maid through the closed door, before dismissing her and turning back to find Alex smoothing the skirt of her gown with trembling hands.

"A timely interruption," I said with a grin, but she was having none of it. She was sulky and unhappy. Dissatisfied too; I could have told her that sexual frustration goes both ways.

Still, I should not treat her as entirely naive, and even as I suppressed my own urges, I explained to her that I feared pregnancy. I also worried for her future if I were not to return from the war.

What I did not, could not, explain, was that I continued to doubt her. I could not shake the fear that I was merely the personified fantasy of a bored and sheltered young woman, betrothed to a man she disliked. Only time would prove one way or the other and until I knew for certain, I could not weaken and take her into my bed.

She meant too much to me for that. I would not have her *ruined* for if she were not virgin, a husband would easily know. I knew that Hamish would not take lightly such an insult to his dubious honour – most men would share his attitude.

Further, I, for the first time, had a care for my own heart. I loved her with such single-minded devotion, that if I made love to her now, I risked losing my mind entirely to the detriment of my other responsibilities.

If I married her, Simon would suffer as the Elginburys would be sure to take a breach in contract to the highest court in the land, and the army would consider me a deserter – the punishment being death. Call me materialistic, but I was not ready for death; not quite yet anyway.

∾

So, but for the occasional tests of my resolve, I allowed my relationship with Alex to flourish and grow. I promised her that once returned from the war, I would initiate proceedings to nullify her betrothal contract.

I had no doubt that the Elginburys would demand a large settlement, but it's a price I would gladly pay.

Tackling our families should be no trouble provided I discussed the matter with Simon in Europe and engendered his support. I was certain, by the way, that he would support my claim since I was sure he already suspected my regard for his sister. And even if he didn't, providing there was no financial or social loss to him or his family, there should be no practical reason to not bless our union.

Hmm, that's another reason I should not bed Alex: Simon would not tolerate my taking advantage of his innocent sister. To stay in his good graces, I must abstain from touching her in any way inappropriately.

As for Simon himself, before the news of his severe injuries, we had received a letter he'd written to tell us of a Spanish nurse he'd fallen in love with. At the time I'd left Salamanca, there'd been no such nurse, so she must have arrived shortly after my departure.

That being the case, his relationship must be very new. Given that Alex and I both pledged our support of his desire to marry this girl, he would surely support our desire to marry one another.

Well, that's how I saw it.

∾

In any event, the date of my departure loomed. Soon it was the middle of April – I was required to report to Christie in Belgium by the end of May, meaning I'd have to leave in a matter of weeks to get there in time.

The general would be in Brussels, planning, what we all hoped would be a final push to defeat the French once and for all.

Although the sea crossing was longer, it would have been simpler to sail directly from Hull to the Netherlands and travel overland to Brussels.

Father asked me to go via London and check on one of his properties. After giving it some thought, I decided it would work because I could leave Equus at Grace's home again before I sailed. Perhaps I would have time to go to Waterville and look over a few things.

That was an idea! Barnabus was still in Grace's stables. I could ride him to Waterville myself and ensure he was comfortably settled before I left. It would be better to face Niall with the truth: that I had personally settled Barnabus in his new home.

Decided, I wrote a letter to Christie advising the change in my plans but assuring him I would be in Brussels at the appointed date.

Afterwards, I sorted through my clothes, checking my uniform and discovering, to my dismay, that my pants were tight about the middle.

Alex came in. By unspoken agreement, she left my door open while she sat on my bed and teased me. She called me Butterball – some name Simon had given Anne when their sister had been a chubby child.

"Hmph!" I said, mildly amused. "I'll ride it off on the way to London – if I can sit my horse without bursting my seams."

"London?" her eyebrows rose. "I thought you were leaving from Hull?"

I explained the situation but she merely shrugged. I imagine it made little difference to her. She went on to tell me that the date of her wedding had been agreed – 14 December.

I was momentarily taken aback – I'd not realised the plans

were truly so advanced.

"What shall I do, Pat?" she asked me. Her lovely brown eyes were wide and anxious.

"Nothing." I said firmly for I'd been struck by a thought. "Simon will be home soon. He's marrying a woman for whom there'll be no approval yet he's following his heart." I looked at her steadily. "Did you ever ask his opinion of your betrothal to Hamish?"

"No," she confirmed.

But *I* had. I knew that Simon was unhappy about the betrothal but saw it as an opportunity for his sister where no other existed. Once, I had even dangerously suggested that I might offer for her.

Simon's reaction had been oblique and difficult to read; I had deflected his speculation with an obtuse comment about Christie.

Now I realised that Simon may well be the answer we've been looking for. Alex looked relieved but suggested it would mean admitting our relationship.

Well, of course it would, but I suspected it wouldn't come as too great a surprise. I didn't think he'd have a problem with it either – unless I'd taken advantage of his sister before approaching him.

I resolved to talk to him when I returned to Spain. He was not due at Broughton Hall until October – time to discuss the matter with him and gain his approval.

While thinking this over, I took my sword from the back of my wardrobe. Withdrawing it from its scabbard, I slashed the air in a practise move to test my arm.

Alex dragged in her breath. "I don't like that."

I considered the weapon in my hand. It had saved my life more times than I could number; I had used it to kill men – innocent strangers – more times than I could number.

Swords were beautifully crafted, decorative and a fashionable addition to a gentleman's outfit. They were also deadly, capable of inflicting horrendous injuries in even the clumsiest of hands.

It must be terribly worrying for those remaining at home when another was risking his life on a battlefield.

The look on Alex's face gave me pause – perhaps she did genuinely love me as much as I hoped she did.

"Sorry," I said with sincere contrition. "I wasn't thinking. We were instructed to practise four times in a sennight but I've been lazy – hence the paunch." I patted my stomach, which beneath even my own hand felt tightly muscled.

Alex rose to leave.

If anyone had been watching through my open door, they would have seen a brother offering a very proper military greeting to his sister. However, my gesture, a correct click of my heels and a formal swordsman's salute, was generally reserved for those most respected – or loved.

I doubt even Alex recognised the level of regard my gesture implied as she left my room.

∾

It was 15 April, the morning of my last day. I rose early and went to the stables. Greeting Equus with a handful of oats, I then slipped the bit into her mouth and the bridle over her ears.

By arrangement, Alex met me there shortly after. I hugged her quickly, and wordlessly, we walked out into the pre-dawn light. The sky was clear, and our breaths steamed before our faces.

I mounted Equus's bare back and walked her to the mounting block where Alex waited. Reaching down, I pulled her up behind me.

Jemima trundled alongside as we made our way into the woods. Alex's arms were around my waist, her head on my shoulder. I covered her linked hands with my own, and leaned back, tilting my head to kiss her.

It was a long, lingering kiss; more emotional than passionate.

When we parted, she rested her head on my back and I could feel the warmth of her breath on my nape.

At length, we arrived in a small clearing I'd found years ago while wandering the forest on my own. I'd always fancied this place to be a woodland temple with its high arching branches and curtains of vines. That spring morning, the green ceiling was dotted with little white flowers.

I reined Equus in and slipped from her back, then lifted Alex down. She came lightly into my arms, clasping my neck and I held her there against Equus's warm side, kissing lovingly and slowly.

There were not many mornings when I did not wake and think sadly on the evil of war and the men I have killed in its name. I think of the blood that has run over my hands; how I have scrubbed the rusty stains from the whorls of my fingerprints or picked the dried residue from beneath my nails.

Yet that morning, I felt renewed. With Alex, my heart knew only love. I felt forgiven and imbued with a sense of peace.

Alex and I dug a heart-shaped bed in the forest floor and planted iris bulbs – her favourite flower. We made a pact that we would return here next spring and make love beneath their purple witness.

I recited Donne, my favourite poet, and we kissed to seal our agreement. I was truly a romantic at heart – I had learned this about myself only recently.

We left the clearing as the first rays of sun filtered between the branches of our temple. We didn't mount Equus, simply walked beside her, and Jemima beside Alex.

I was holding Alex's hand when I felt her shiver.

"What is it?"

She was looking over her shoulder.

"I ... I'm not sure. The candle went out." She looked genuinely unsettled.

It seemed to me that a cloud suddenly shadowed the clearing, and I suppressed a shudder of my own. I spoke lightly, "Ooh – a portent of misfortune?"

"Don't." She squeezed my hand. "You mustn't scoff. I feel strange ... like something is wrong."

"And so it shall be if we will it. C'mon." I gave her hand a little tug.

∾

I spent most of my last day in Simon's study with my father. I was going through the arrangements I'd made with Simon's tenants for that summer's harvest – although it was a few months away yet. I also wanted to discuss various matters pertaining to Waterville that I needed him to be aware of – things he needed to know if I were not to return.

We didn't mention it, but the possibility was uppermost in both our minds.

I thought, for the first time, of what it would mean to my father – to our name and the peerage – if I were killed. And suddenly I wondered whether I should tell him about Alex, my feelings for her, my desire to marry her.

Was it too late? Could we ride, as she had implored, to Gretna, be married over the anvil and ...

Was it too late to leave her honourably with child and secure the earldom?

It was a mercenary way of looking at things, yet I'd made my choice as far as whom I wanted for my countess, was it not reasonable, *responsible*, to ensure I put my affairs in order before I leave for war?

My father was jotting figures into Simon's household ledger, a pair of spectacles perched on the end of his nose.

I framed the words in my mind:

Father, Alex and I would like to marry. I'll explain later but we must do it before I leave ...

Father, Alex and I are in love and wish to marry. May we have your blessing so that I can leave her with child and ...

Father, I have an urgent desire to bed my sister ...

I drew in my breath, "Father—"

"I wonder what Simon would say about this," he said, cutting me off.

Momentarily disoriented, I stared dumbly at him. "What ...?"

"This," he pointed to a figure at the bottom of a receipt. "Mim bought a new strand of pearls – the jeweller sent the account here. Look at the price! That's extortion!"

"Oh ... yes. Well, it's done – it's not for me to question her."

"Yes, yes ... let Simon worry about his mother when he gets home. Problem is, of course, that the Broughton estate can only support so much of her spending."

"She's your wife," I told him, impatiently. "Perhaps you should be footing the bill."

"Quite right too – we can afford it more easily and she *is* my responsibility."

He scratched a line through the entry in the ledger and put the account aside. "I'll take care of this."

My moment slipped away.

ॐ

And the day similarly slipped away. After a specially prepared farewell dinner, I went to bed, heavy of heart, knowing that whatever destiny awaited me, my opportunity to alter it had trickled through my fingers.

The wheels of fate were now in motion. If I were to die on the battlefield without a legitimate heir – it was out of my hands.

If Alex were to wait for me until I returned – that was also out of my hands.

In my room, I made a final check of my bags and uniform. All seemed ready. I peeled off my clothes and folded them neatly – it was the last time I would dress as a civilian for ... I knew not how long – and I climbed into bed.

∽

"Patrick ..."

The voice was soft, close to my ear. It sounded like ... what was Alex doing in my quarters in Belgium?

I murmured something and returned to sleep.

"Pat, wake up."

Something touched my cheek and my eyes snapped open, my mind fuddled. "Mmm? Alex? What are you doing?"

"What do you think, you idiot?"

I was not dreaming! I heard her sob. She was crouching at my bedside wearing a silky nightgown. Over her shoulder I saw the furnishings of my room in Broughton Hall – unlike the boxy, functional trappings of my field tent, these were classic, handcrafted items shining like polished silver in the dark.

Instantly awake, I held open the side of my bed and she slipped beneath the covers beside me.

I rolled her in my arms and she was murmuring, weeping, shivering with cold and emotion. Her hip moved against me and I hardened instantly. "Please Pat," she whispered through her tears, "I want this ..."

"And if we should create a child this night, what then?" My resolve was melting by the second.

"Then I shall go to Devon and wait for you."

"Good idea – they'll never find you there," I responded flippantly, although I felt nothing like flippancy. I was trembling with desire and love of her.

She lightly reprimanded me but I barely heard her words. All I heard was, "... make love to me."

My body responded with a leap but still I held myself in check. "I won't be here for you if—"

She kissed me and it was over.

It was her first time. I wanted it to be special for her. It was our first time together and I wanted it to be special for both of us.

So, I took my time. I needed her to be ready. I knew it would hurt her and it was important that I did not rush this.

As with most unmarried men of my time, I had never laid with a virgin. The sum of my sexual encounters was in the arms of experienced women: married, widowed, professional. I knew what to expect when I entered her, but only in theory.

I went slowly. I started by removing her nightgown, kissing her, stroking her. And she touched me, experimentally trailing her fingers over the contours of my back, my buttocks, before hesitantly drawing her hand between us and moving down.

My hips shot uncontrollably forwards, my body was on fire, and I gritted my teeth as she clasped me, curiosity in her touch.

I sensed her wonder and felt the urgency rising within her. When I parted her and caressed her most secret places, she writhed beneath my hands, she gasped and whimpered, and I knew that she was ready.

I shifted and lay above her, my weight on my elbows. Her eyes glistened in the dark, gazing trustingly up at me. She knew the question I would ask.

"Yes!" she breathed and I could not wait.

I pushed into her; felt the resistance, felt it give and heard her small cry of surprise.

Trembling with desire and the effort to control myself, I lay as still as I could. "Tell me when it stops hurting," I murmured against her mouth.

She didn't respond, but I felt the tension in her shoulders relax, her grip on my biceps loosened as she accustomed herself to sensual intrusion.

I began to move.

We made love twice that night and both times I cautiously

withdrew at the crucial moment. I doubt she was aware of my precaution and though it was not fail-safe, it was all I could do.

Alex and I slept in one another's arms after the first time. After the second time, I heard the first dawning calls of birds in the forest. I lay awake, propped on one elbow, watching her sleep, recording in my mind the erotic beauty of her sated face and tumbled hair. There were tear stains on her cheeks.

The sky had lightened at the edges when she awoke and slipped from my bed. I stood at the door and held her in my arms. We kissed, she promised to wait and I pledged my fidelity.

Then she was gone.

Before I could change my mind, before I dissolved into a snivelling heap on the floor, I dressed, grasped my saddle bags, belted my sword, and strode from the house – a changed man.

DAMN LIES

Patrick rode into Brussels on a hired horse, late in the spring of 1813. He went directly to the allied encampment and reported to his commanding officer.

Major Christopher Thorpe was eating a light lunch of cold ham, bread and cheese with a group of officers. "Good to see you returned to us, Captain," the major said. "Join us," he waved towards the spread of platters on the table, "we were discussing the latest information we've received from the general."

Patrick took a seat, nodding a greeting to Emerson across the table, while a young lieutenant laid a place for him. Patrick helped himself to food and poured a cup of what passed as coffee.

Major Thorpe took a sip of tea and continued briefing the men around the table. "Now, latest intelligence suggests that Napoleon is rebuilding after that disastrous expedition into Russia."

"He'll be licking his wounds and determined to save face," added an officer Patrick had not previously met. He was an older man, with a thick red beard, ruddy complexion and distinctive highland burr. Catching Patrick's eye, he introduced himself as Captain Ian MacGregor of the Scots Greys.

"Exactly," the major agreed. "From what we know, they're camped somewhere near Burgos. Wellington has ordered a hard march into Vitoria to block the road to France before Bonaparte can move on us."

The officers around the table nodded pensively.

"Ready your divisions, gentlemen," Major Thorpe directed. "We're moving out in two days. Apologies, Captain," he added, turning to Patrick. "You've only just arrived and we're on the march again."

As the men filed out of the room, Major Thorpe asked Captain Washburn to remain.

Alone, the two men embraced as the old friends they were. "Good to see you Patrick," Christie said. "How was ... everything at home?" He looked significantly at the other man.

Patrick couldn't prevent the silly grin creeping across his face. "I'll tell you later – have you any good brandy?"

"Of course! Only the finest. Let's meet this evening in my quarters. Meanwhile, I have an assignment for you. When we march out, I want you to take a small party of men and journey to Salamanca. There's a chest of money sitting here. I need you to take it there. Wellington has been hounding the British government for money for the troops' wages – they finally sent it. I need someone I can trust to take it to Salamanca."

Patrick nodded. "Very well."

"I don't need to explain the danger of this," Christie went on. "Take a pair of Spanish soldiers with you. You'll be riding close to the enemy camp – make sure you don't attract attention. Dress as local farmers but arm yourselves well. We can't lose that chest!"

Patrick nodded again. "Is my brother still at Salamanca or has he left for England?"

"That's the other reason I'm assigning this mission to you. You'll find Simon still at Salamanca. He's not in a good way, Pat.

It will do him good to see you. Take a week or so before you join us in Vitoria."

"I'm not looking forward to seeing him," Patrick admitted, "but I think you're right. I need to – hopefully I can be of help, somehow. Besides that," Pat added on a lighter note, "I promised Niall a full report of Barnabus's condition and how well the blasted horse settled into his new home."

At that, Christie's face changed. "You don't know?"

"Know what?"

"After you left, Simon was using Niall as something of an assistant. The boy had accompanied him on that mission – to that village. When the blast went off and Simon was wounded, Niall was with him. The boy was killed, Pat."

Patrick stared at his friend, stunned. "Niall? Niall was killed?"

Christie nodded sadly.

"I'd heard that Simon had someone with him … that the other man was killed, but I never thought. Jesus Christ!" Patrick ran a hand through his hair. "Poor bloody lad."

"War." Christie said in disgust. "The innocents always suffer the most. Now," he drew a breath, "you need to bathe and rest. We'll talk again later."

∾

Within days, the British army, led by Major Christopher Thorpe, had decamped and was on the march towards Vitoria.

Before leaving, the major had prearranged a wagon and pair of sturdy but unremarkable mules. On the day of departure, Patrick dressed in civilian clothes, loaded the chest of Sterling into a cavity beneath a false floor in the wagon.

Then, accompanied by two Spanish soldiers, also disguised as farmers, they loaded the wagon with sacks of grain and potatoes.

If accosted by French soldiers, the plan was to allow the Spanish men to do all the talking. If need be, the freight would serve as payment to secure their passage past the French camp.

It was known that the allies had – for the most part – moved out of Salamanca; a group of farmers heading to market in that direction should not attract undue attention.

The journey was expected to take no more than five days and Patrick was content to drive the wagon at a steady pace – a relaxing change from riding on horseback.

Sure enough, five days later, the trio arrived in Salamanca. Along the road they'd been unburdened of almost half their cargo of produce over two encounters with French soldiers, but other than that, they were unscathed.

○∾

Knowledge of Simon's condition didn't prepare Patrick for the reality of his brother's disfigurement.

Simon had been an incredibly handsome man. In Patrick's opinion, only the magnetic, masculine beauty of Major Christopher Thorpe could rival Simon's looks.

However, the difference between the two men had been mostly evident in their diverse temperaments: Christie was more serious, where Simon had been cheerfully irreverent.

Such cheerfulness was understandably absent, Patrick observed, as he sat by his stepbrother in the dim light of the other's tent.

Simon passed his days in the false twilight of his quarters, merely sitting, hour after hour in a chair, and pondering a spot on the wall. Although initially brightened by Pat's arrival, Simon rapidly returned to the state of abject depression in which he'd been mired since that tragic explosion.

He regularly closed his eyes and lapsed into such deep silences that Patrick thought he may have fallen asleep. It was only as Simon stirred and asked some half-interested question about his estate in Yorkshire that Patrick found him even remotely engaged in the world beyond his grief and pain.

And what pain that must be – with his torn face and broken body, and his shattered spirit. There were no words that Patrick could offer to adequately express his sorrow, his own grief. So he sat, quietly reading or doing paperwork and just keeping his brother company.

Simon was learning to dress himself one-handed. Each morning Patrick made a point of visiting so the brothers could eat breakfast together. And each morning Patrick found Simon irritable and frustrated, cursing his clumsiness and inability to manage the simplest tasks like buttoning his trousers.

Patrick quickly learned that he should ignore Simon's fumbling and pay no particular attention to the bad-tempered growls and the occasional boot thrown about.

He also discovered that asking after Maria, Simon's affianced, was one of the few means by which he could elicit the grimace that passed for a smile on Simon's ravaged face.

"She's in Burgos," Simon explained, when Patrick demanded an introduction to his soon-to-be sister-in-law. "They seconded her there after a series of skirmishes in the region. She'll be back in a couple of weeks – they're discharging her so she can accompany me home."

"Pity," Patrick remarked. "I was looking forward to meeting her."

"Looking forward to finding out what's wrong with her, you mean, since she's still going to marry me," Simon said bitterly.

Patrick regarded his brother steadily. "Something like that. You're so stubbornly content to sit in that chair – what *would* she want with you?"

∾

"It's bloody hard, Pat!" Simon cried one morning.

Patrick was reading a memo that had arrived in a dispatch from

Burgos. He looked up at his brother – half-afraid, half-relieved that Simon now seemed ready to open up about his disability.

"Look at this!" Simon demanded. He held up his right hand. "What kind of surgeon has only one hand? What kind of wife wants an ugly cripple for a husband? What kind of future can I possibly have now? How can I expect Maria …?"

Simon's voice trailed off, then he bowed his head and wept. Patrick held his brother in his arms as Simon's shoulders shook with the force of his grief. There were no words to answer those questions, but the reassuring touch of a loved one can do so much more.

And Patrick did love Simon. He loved him as though they'd sprung from the same loins and had fed at the same breast.

Simon's outpouring of emotion was perhaps the crumbling of the wall he had built around himself. Patrick hoped it would allow Simon's spiritual healing to finally begin.

The next day, the medical team tending Simon's injuries, declared him fit to plan his return to England. Later that same day, a message from Maria arrived reporting that she was on her way to Salamanca, and Patrick began preparing his journey to Vitoria to rejoin his commanding officer and resume his position in Wellington's thirty-second division.

∽

It was the morning before Patrick was to leave Salamanca. He arrived at Simon's tent with their breakfasts on covered plates, as usual, and lifting the tent flap, Patrick was pleased to find his stepbrother standing beside his trunk, finishing his packing.

"Morning," Patrick said, brightly. "Almost done? I've—"

Simon whirled around. His distorted face was twisted into an angry and gruesome mask and Patrick took an involuntary step backwards.

"Did you fuck my sister?" Simon demanded, furiously.

In all the years of their friendship, through all their adventures and misadventures, Patrick had never known Simon to use such language.

Genuinely shocked, and more than a little rattled, he stared at his stepbrother, momentarily lost for words. "Your sister?" he repeated like a fool.

"*Alex!* Alex – my sister! You *do* remember her, don't you?" Simon's voice was low and menacing. He waved a sheet of paper in the air significantly. "*Did you fuck Alex?*"

Patrick quickly regained his senses, and he was immediately insulted.

Fucking was what he did with whores, bar wenches, society sluts. He fucked when he was foxed. He fucked for sport, for larks, when he was bored or randy. In this, Patrick knew a very clear distinction.

His expression firmed and he met his brother's fury with a calm response.

"No," he said. "And don't you ever speak to me like that again."

Patrick snatched the letter from Simon's hand, turned and stalked from the tent.

∾

Alone in his own tent, Patrick spread the crumpled sheet of paper on his desk and leaned over it to read.

It was from Simon's mother, Mim. She described what she called: *an uncomfortably suspicious intimacy between Alexandra and Patrick during the latter's convalescence at Broughton Hall.*

Mim explained that the pair had enjoyed a rapport that she believed had led to Hamish Glendenning, Alex's betrothed, cutting short his visit and returning home. It was a closeness that had prompted much innuendo and sly whispering among the staff – stemming, damningly, from Alex's own maid, Janet.

Mim went on to say,

Upon your stepbrother's return to Europe, Alexandra fell into a dreamy melancholy from which the girl roused only to express a stubborn refusal to participate in her own wedding arrangements.

Reading between the lines, Patrick realised that Mim had no firm facts at hand but believed there was enough backstairs gossip to warrant writing to the head of the Broughton household.

Mim ended the letter on a tone that left Patrick in no doubt as to her thoughts.

A county determined to undo this family's position and reputation will not allow the truth to interfere with its tale of a girl's ruination at the hands of a notorious rake – regardless of whether such allegations are without foundation.

You, as head of this house, my son, must take this matter in hand upon your return. Determine the truth and ensure that steps are taken to quell the tide of scandal. I regret, however, that I remain persuaded towards the veracity of the stories – hence this letter.

ல

Patrick and Simon avoided each other for the remainder of the day. Neither brother was comfortable with their estrangement, particularly since they were soon to part ways – Patrick back to the war and Simon to England.

With Pat's reaction, Simon was filled with remorse over his attack. He knew in his heart that under normal circumstances he'd never have behaved so – but nothing about Simon's current state of mind was normal.

Patrick was equally distressed although for different reasons. He refused to feel guilty for lying to his stepbrother, though he felt he'd avoided the truth rather than actually lied.

As he prepared the mules and wagon for their journey to Vitoria, Patrick wondered whether he ought to approach Simon and admit everything.

It would mean confessing that he and Alex had spent the night together. That would no doubt send Simon into a fit of fury; although once Simon had calmed down, Patrick hoped to seek Simon's blessing for his relationship with Alex – the outlook wasn't promising!

Patrick was certain Simon would eventually accept the honesty of his intent – at least he hoped so – providing Simon allowed him to speak. But Patrick had never seen Simon so angry and given the delicate nature of Simon's physical and emotional state, Patrick was loath to inflame the situation further.

"All done, 'ere, Captain," a sergeant said, interrupting Patrick's thoughts. "Everything's loaded and ready to go."

"Good, thank you Bain."

The sergeant saluted and turned away, and Patrick decided to go and look for his brother.

❧

Patrick leaned against a stone wall. Dusk was colouring the Spanish countryside in shades of lavender and mauve as a colony of bats flew overhead. Fleet little bodies silhouetted against the sky, they moved rapidly, first one way, then the next, changing direction in the blink of an eye, and then they were gone, along some invisible skyward highway.

The locals call them *los murciélagos* and Patrick enjoyed watching them. At dawn each morning they passed overhead, streaking across the pale sky to their dark daytime lairs. Then, each evening, they emerged and took the opposite route to pursue their nocturnal activities: feeding, mating, socialising.

As the colony disappeared into the evening, Patrick pushed away from the wall. He wasn't looking forward to seeing Simon, but he had to. War was a strange thing; he didn't know when he'd see his stepbrother again – if ever. He had to clear the air between them and, he had decided, he would not tell Simon of his involvement with Alex.

Before Patrick left Yorkshire, Alex had been determined to talk to Simon herself and enlist her brother's help to extricate her from her betrothal. *Let that be*, Patrick thought. *Let Alex be the one to decide what Simon knows – she'll be the one living with the repercussions.*

Besides that, Patrick was returning to the war; he did not want bad blood between himself and his brother, in case the worst should happen.

Simon's homecoming would be difficult as it was, Patrick didn't need to add to it with any conscience-salving confessions.

Patrick paused outside Simon's tent, listening for sounds from within. There were voices, low and masculine, in private discussion. Patrick tapped on the frame of the tent and was invited to enter.

Simon sat with his medical colleague Doctor Andrew Hurst. Lord Draven, as he was known in England, was pouring some dark liquor into two glasses and as Patrick entered, he automatically poured a third.

The brothers eyed each other cautiously as Andrew toasted Simon's continued recovery and safe journey back to England. The three men raised their glasses.

༄

Shortly after, Andrew left to check on his patients, leaving Simon and Patrick alone.

"You're going tomorrow?" Simon asked.

Patrick nodded. "At dawn. We've timed it so we should be passing the French camp during the night. We'll be stopped, of course, by guards, but it's more difficult for them to identify our nationality."

"Hmm." Simon said. Then, "Pat, I'm sorry about this morning. I—" he made a rueful face, uncertain how to continue.

Patrick rescued him, relieved that Simon had spoken first as he'd been considering ways to raise the subject. "It's alright," he said. "I read the letter – your mother ..." Patrick shrugged helplessly.

Simon nodded with solidarity. "You and Zan have always rubbed along well. It's no surprise my mother's suspicious mind would eventually lead her down this path. And with servants gossiping – particularly Janet ..."

Guilt stabbed Patrick's chest. Much as he disliked Mim Broughton, she was in the right on this one. Nevertheless, he said, "Don't go on, man. I'm returning to the front tomorrow, and you're going back to England. Let's not discuss your mother."

"Agreed," Simon said, and shared the last drops from the liquor bottle between their glasses.

∾

It was dawn on the morning of 22 September 1813. Simon waited while Patrick checked his cargo of sacks of wheat and potatoes bound for Vitoria.

Two mules waited patiently in the traces. Their long ears pricked to the sounds of a camp slowly coming awake around them. Though they'd already eaten, they eagerly accepted the handful of oats Simon shared between them, whuffling into his palm until every grain was gone.

At length, Patrick was satisfied that all was ready. He turned to his brother as Simon was wiping his slobbery palm down the leg of his trousers.

"So," Patrick asked, coming over, "when's Maria due to arrive?"

"Tomorrow or the next day," Simon replied, automatically glancing towards the road. "You may even pass her on the way."

"I'll be sure to introduce myself."

Simon smiled. "Do that. She'll be pleased to meet you."

The brothers regarded each other silently for a moment, each lost in his thoughts. Though the war had brought many such partings, they felt instinctively that this was somehow different, even if neither understood why.

"Well, brother," Simon said, "I don't know when we'll see each other again, but I'm certain that we will. Best of luck to you and keep yourself safe. Even if I'm no longer your physician, I still have no desire for your father to receive a letter."

Patrick grinned. "It'll take more than some random frog to do me in."

"I'm counting on it."

They hugged then, awkwardly as Simon was not yet accustomed to having only one arm and Patrick was mindful of the continued tenderness of his brother's wounds.

They released each other and Patrick went to the wagon. He checked the traces, the mules and their harness before climbing into the driver's seat beside the two Spanish soldiers. He suddenly thought of something and leaned from his seat, "When are you getting married? Will you wait until you get home or—"

Simon shook his head. "Maria wants to get married here, in the chapel on the other side of the village. It's where her grandparents wed – it's sentimental."

"Christ! Your mother won't be pleased."

"She's never pleased."

Patrick chuckled. "Does your bride know about Mim? It's only fair to tell her in advance and allow her to decide whether you're worth it."

Simon laughed. It was the first time Patrick had heard him laugh since his return to Spain – it raised his spirits. He added, "Well, my best regards to the bride – of course, if I see her on the road, I'll provide a full brief on her future mother-in-law."

Simon was still smiling when he asked, "You're still resolved never to wed?"

In an instant Patrick's stomach twisted.

Shit! Patrick had told Simon his future was with the army. Having lost their wager on the basis that he would wed for love or not at all, Patrick had chosen not at all. *Shit-shit!*

He silently cursed Simon for reminding him. His brother's face was open and unaware of the import of his question. And he expected a response.

Guilt and irritation rippled through Patrick at the playful look on his stepbrother's face – guileless, honest Simon.

Now, Patrick felt like a complete and utter bastard as he flicked the reins over the mules' rumps. "Walk on," he ordered without answering.

Simon's smile faded as he watched his stepbrother disappear down the road. Patrick might pretend he'd not heard Simon's question, but Simon knew otherwise.

SOUL SEARCHING

*T*hursday, *1.45 am*

"Major! He's here!" The shout seemed to come from somewhere above me.

"Move aside, please ma'am." A second well-modulated voice; authoritative – a voice I vaguely recognised, but the effort of opening my eyes to address its owner was too great. I sank back beneath the waves of a sickening, undulating crapulence.

"How long's he been like this?"

"Long enough to make me rich." This last was spoken in a coarse, unfamiliar female voice. "Paid by the hour, I am!"

There was a derogatory snort from the first person, who added, "How'll we get him up, Major?"

"I don't know." The owner of the voice gave me a rough shake. "Captain!"

I groaned.

"Wake up, Captain. *Now!*"

Someone had hold of my arm. I felt my head lolling; I was incapable of supporting it myself. There was a growl of frustration, followed by a stinging slap to my face.

"Patrick!"

I forced open an eye – just a crack. Black hair, purple eyes ...

"Chr-Christie?"

"Yes, it's me," he snapped. "Hywel too. Get up! On your feet, now!"

"Lea—" I gulped. I was about to be violently ill. "Leave me al —"

My stomach convulsed and the last thing I remember was a feminine exclamation and the disgusted curses of the two men at my side.

∾

Previously ...

Tuesday, 8.20 am

Patrick strolled through the allied campsite. It was a fine winter's morning and he felt energised, eagerly anticipating a new mission with Emerson. The pair had been successfully teamed several times over the months, which had led Major Christopher Thorpe to team them again for this latest assignment; a midnight reconnoitre of a farmhouse on the outskirts of Cogollos.

Apparently, the French were using the house as a supply store. Patrick and Emerson were charged with the task of infiltrating it, mapping its floor-plan, and identifying the rooms that held weaponry, including the types and numbers of weapons.

They were not to engage the enemy – the major was adamant – he would send a division to do that once his two captains had safely returned with a sketch of the house's layout and contents.

Being January, it wanted another month before the real battles recommenced; so, for Patrick, this assignment was the perfect diversion – exactly the kind of excitement he needed.

He'd just visited the supply store where he requisitioned a

472

pouch of shot for the two pistols he carried, tucked into his belt during his missions.

A small crowd had gathered around a lad with a mail satchel. Letters from England were always a cause for great excitement. Those who didn't receive mail from loved ones, often sat close to those who did, listening avidly as news from home was shared.

Patrick rarely received mail and it didn't bother him in the least. Occasionally, a letter might arrive from his sister. Other times, he heard from his father or his cousin Aden, who was acting as steward at Waterville in his absence, but that was all. He'd welcome mail from Alex but knew she was unlikely to write until he wrote to her – and he was a woeful correspondent.

"I'll get round to it," he muttered to himself, not feeling too guilty about his lassitude – he had enough writing to do, what with reports, requisitions and other documents.

Thus, he was skirting the group when the lad called out, "Capt'n Washburn! Mail for you."

Patrick arched his eyebrows in surprise. He paused and stared at the boy to be certain he'd heard correctly. When the boy waved a letter in the air, Patrick shouldered his way through the crowd to retrieve it.

It was a letter, sent from Broughton Hall, and Patrick recognised his father's handwriting.

༄

Tuesday, 7.50 pm

Louis Hywel had just returned to Captain Washburn's quarters with the battered old hat the captain had asked him to source for the night's mission. He had not seen the captain since the morning, which wasn't that unusual for a normal day, but on the day of a mission, the captain would normally be checking his weapons and making his final preparations by now.

From what Hywel could tell, the captain hadn't been around all day and no preparations seem to have been made. Everything seemed to be in its place with nothing to indicate an excursion was about to be undertaken.

Yet the captain was due to leave in an hour or so and Hywel found his captain's absence curious.

Additionally, there were several papers scattered about the captain's desk. Hywel thought this was unusual too – the captain was normally fastidiously tidy with his paperwork.

Hywel gathered the papers and stacked them neatly. The orders for the night's mission were there – Hywel placed them to one side and gathered the remaining papers into a pile, sorted by date, the most recent on the top.

"Washburn? You there?" A head peeked through the opening flap of the tent.

"Captain Emerson," Hywel saluted the officer. "Captain Washburn's not here, Sir, can I help you?"

"You know where he is?"

Hywel shook his head. "I don't. Haven't seen him all day, Sir."

Emerson frowned. "Strange. We're due to ride out soon. He's normally ready before I am. Has he organised his things?"

"There's a new bag of shot over there." Hywel pointed to a trunk at the foot of the captain's pallet upon which rested a leather pouch. "He got it this morning – that's all as far as I can tell."

"Well," Emerson said, scratching his chin, "send a boy to fetch me as soon as he comes in."

"Yes, Sir."

❧

Tuesday, 8.30 pm

"Captain Emerson sent me," the scruffy urchin announced from the tent entrance. "Wants to know if Captain Washburn's ready."

Hywel sighed. There'd been no sign of the captain and what had begun as a small annoyance had suddenly become more serious. He stroked his moustache thoughtfully then said, "Please tell Captain Emerson that Captain Washburn hasn't returned to his quarters yet."

∾

Tuesday, 8.40 pm

Captain Jeffery Emerson burst into Captain Patrick Washburn's tent without announcement.

Hywel was sitting in a chair reading a book by the light of a lantern. He leapt to his feet in surprise.

"Where's Washburn?" Emerson demanded.

"I – I don't know, Sir. He hasn't returned."

"Shit! I don't believe this!" Emerson paced the tent in frustration, moving random items about as though the errant captain may be discovered beneath a shako, a pillow, a bottle.

"Shit!" he repeated. He turned abruptly and strode from the tent.

∾

Tuesday, 9.05 pm

"Are you Hywel?"

Hywel glanced towards the tent opening. Since Captain Emerson's agitated visit earlier, Hywel had been pacing back and forth across Captain Washburn's tent in a quandary of indecision.

The same messenger boy from before was peering at him between the tent-flaps. "Yes," he responded.

"Major Thorpe's asking to see yer," the boy said.

Hywel nodded, relieved to have something to do. He was

increasingly concerned that Captain Washburn was missing. Equally worried, as was evident by the summons, were Captain Emerson and the major.

"Coming," he told the boy, and left the tent.

∾

Tuesday, 9.10 pm

"You sent for me, Major?"

"Hywel, yes. Thank you for coming so promptly." Major Thorpe was relaxing in a chair. His uniform coat was laid across a trunk and his shirt was unbuttoned at the throat. The remains of a meal were still on a table.

Captain Emerson was standing by the major's writing desk. His face was hard, his mouth a thin-lipped, grim line.

Major Thorpe said, "Captain Emerson tells me Captain Washburn has not been sighted this afternoon or this evening."

"That's correct, Major."

"When did you last see him?"

"This morning, Sir. He went to the supply store to get pistol shot."

"And did he return?"

"I believe so. The shot is there. I was running an errand; he'd been and gone by the time I came back."

"Hmm." Major Thorpe rose from his chair and stood before his writing desk, seeing nothing, thinking. "Did he leave a note ... any indication of where he may have gone?"

Hywel shook his head. "No, Sir."

Thorpe exhaled gustily and turned to Emerson. "Obviously the mission will need to be postponed. We can reschedule it later, but we need to assume something's happened. Washburn's not the sort to just take off. We'll get to the bottom of it."

Emerson seemed dissatisfied with the major's attitude but

nodded reluctant agreement.

"Very well," the major continued, "Emerson, take half-a-dozen men and search the camp – top to bottom. Washburn's around somewhere."

"Yes, Sir!"

"Hywel," the major turned to the aide. "Go speak to Rogers in the supply store and find out what he knows. Washburn may have said something, given some hint as to … I don't know what. Just go and speak with him."

"Sir!" Hywel acknowledged. He and Emerson left the major's tent together and parted to attend to their individual tasks.

∾

Wednesday, 2.30 am

Captain Emerson exited Major Thorpe's tent. When he'd first become aware of Captain Washburn's disappearance Emerson had been irritated. Then, irritation had become frustration, followed quickly by anger. Now, however, in the early hours of the morning, after an exhaustive search of the British camp, he was worried.

As was Major Thorpe, for there was absolutely no sign of the captain. Nobody had seen or heard anything that could provide even the smallest clue as to where the captain may be.

But he must be somewhere, Emerson reasoned, a man doesn't simply vanish into thin air. For now, though, Emerson was exhausted.

He went back to his own tent and fell, fully clothed, onto his pallet and was immediately asleep.

∾

Wednesday, 11.20 am

Major Christopher Thorpe strode purposefully across the encampment. He was on his way to the yard where the horses were corralled.

Patrick had now been missing for over twenty-four hours – if nobody in the blasted place could tell him where the man might be, Christie was going to find out for himself. Time was running out for Patrick – and Christie – because very soon, Christie would be required to report his friend as absent without leave.

The longer Christie delayed the report, the worse it would look for him. But if Patrick had, in fact, deserted … Christie did not want to be the one to make such a report, yet as Patrick's commanding officer, he'd have no choice.

The crime of desertion was punishable by firing squad.

Christie shuddered to think of it as he arrived at the horse-yard. He immediately attracted the attention of one of the grooms. Recognising a senior officer, the man ran over.

"Yes, Sir, Major. Can I help ye with something?"

"Yes. Are you familiar with Captain Washburn?"

The man grinned. "We's all familiar with 'im, Major."

Christie decided not to pursue the obvious line and continued with his own. "Can you tell me if the captain's horse is here?"

"No, Sir. Cap'n collected 'is 'orse yesterday. Little roan mare, Sally."

"I see." Christie considered for a moment. "Thank you."

He went to turn away, then thought of something. "Tell me, did the captain say where he was going?"

The man's eyes narrowed as he pondered. "Nope. Not that I recall. But 'e weren't looking too good. Weren't 'is normal friendly self, neither. Didn't say much, just told me to get Sally ready and 'e rode off without another word."

"Was anyone else with him?"

The man shook his head. "Nope."

Christie sighed deeply. It wasn't much but it was something –

enough for him to know that Patrick had left the camp under unusual circumstances.

"Thank you."

The man saluted. "Major!"

Christie turned away and retraced his steps to his tent, but he went slower now, thinking as he walked. It wasn't a lot to go on: Patrick had left the camp alone, and without a word of explanation to anyone.

He was certain now, that something serious had happened – Patrick would never have simply absconded – especially not after having just received orders for a new mission. He was too conscientious, too professional – and he loved the excitement provided by the assignments he and Emerson had been undertaking.

It was a mystery, but one thing was certain, Patrick Washburn was absent without leave. Christie could cover for him for a short time but not forever – Patrick had to be found, quickly, before he would be forced to issue the order for Pat's arrest.

ᖆ

Wednesday, 4.45 pm

"Major!" Christie's head jerked up from the report he was reading. His aide, Fitchen had barged unannounced into his tent and was approaching with a folder in his hands. Christie groaned internally – more work!

"Dispatch from the general, Sir."

"Thank you." Christie took the folder and noted that Fitchen continued to stand before him.

"What is it?" he asked, somewhat abruptly. Besides the worry of all the paperwork he had piling up, Patrick was still missing. Christie didn't know how much longer he could delay filing a report.

"Sir, I think you should know that the messenger boy asked me if I knew Captain Washburn's whereabouts."

Blast! Christie frowned impatiently. "Why should he need to know that?"

"Because, Sir, he has dispatches for both Captains Emerson and Washburn."

Christie gestured with annoyance. "Seriously, Fitchen? The captains receive dispatches almost daily – why are you telling me this?"

"Because, Sir," Fitchen said slowly to emphasise a point, "the boy commented that it was unusual for Captain Washburn to receive so much mail. Along with today's dispatch, he received a letter from Morocco."

Christie blew out his cheeks in an exasperated sigh. "The captain's sister is living in Morocco – it's hardly anyone's business if—"

"The boy said," Fitchen interrupted, "the captain received a letter from England yesterday. Two letters in two days for a man who rarely receives mail."

"I'm starting to lose patience, Mr Fitchen," Christie snapped irritably, bowing his head once more over his work. "Tell the boy to keep his gossip to himself and I'll thank you, in future, to refrain from going about camp repeating it."

"Yes, Sir, Major," Fitchen said, doggedly. "But I felt you should know – under the circumstances of the captain's absence."

Now Christie hesitated. Lifting his head, he regarded his aide with new interest. Fitchen was red-cheeked from Christie's rebuke, standing at attention, and holding his ground. "The messenger boy said the captain received a letter from home early yesterday morning. By my reckoning, Sir, that would've been shortly before he left camp."

"Damn," Christie muttered under his breath. He was on his feet in an instant. "Not a word of this to anyone – you hear!"

"No, Sir!"

"Go find the captain's aide – Hywel. Tell him to meet me at the captain's tent."

"Yes, Sir!"

∾

Wednesday, 4.50 pm

Christie had just got to Patrick's tent when Hywel arrived at a run.

"You sent for me, Sir?"

"Yes. Tell me, did Captain Washburn receive a letter from home yesterday?"

"I believe so, Major. It's on his desk."

"I see. Come."

The two men went into the captain's tent and Christie immediately went to the writing desk.

"I left it top of the pile on the right, Sir," Hywel said. He waited just inside the entrance.

Christie saw the letter immediately. It was a single page, signed at the bottom by the earl, Gerald Washburn, Patrick's father.

He guessed, immediately, that it must contain bad news – he hoped Patrick hadn't deserted and returned urgently to England. Unlikely, he knew. Patrick was too professional; he'd surely have sought leave. So …

Christie picked up the letter and began to read.

My dear son,

How pleased I was to receive your confirmation regarding Anne. Of course, I had always suspected as much but in your absence, it was difficult to argue your case.

Meanwhile, I have been able to secure a match for Anne – a young man, minor noble looking for a well-dowered bride. Certainly not the prestigious match her mother would have preferred but under the circumstances – and those circumstances being that we cannot be choosy – I believe George and Anne will rub along quite well.

If your stepmother is disappointed in the match, at least she can take satisfaction in her other daughter's situation for your stepsister Alexandra was married to Hamish Glendenning last week.

The pair wed in the small parish vicarage that lies, you may recall, just beyond the Broughton boundaries. They departed only a couple of days later for Hamish's seat in Scotland.

So, all three of the Broughton children are spoken for. Now, I must turn my attention to you and your sister – though I am certainly doomed to disappointment where you both are concerned.

I do believe your sister is married to a trowel in an archaeological site in the deserts of Morocco, while you seem wed to your sword.

A father can only do so much before he throws up his hands in surrender. Ah, but I am rambling, and you, I am sure, have more pressing duties.

Stay well and stay safe, my son.

With love,

Your father

Christie came to the bottom of the letter, then skimmed up to re-read the line, ... *your stepsister Alexandra was married to Hamish*

Glendenning last week.

His hands suddenly felt cold, and he dropped the single page onto the desk. He, who rarely swore, demonstrated a vocabulary worthy of a drunken sailor.

Turning to Hywel, he said, "Mr Hywel, can I count on your loyalty and discretion?"

Hywel approached, tentatively, nodding. "Yes, Sir. Of course."

"Good." Christie passed a weary hand over his face. "Good, because I need both from you now. Captain Washburn … I fear, may have deserted. We must find him and bring him back before it's too late."

∽

Thursday, 6.25 am

I awoke to the smell of frying onions and bacon. It was still too early to be light so about all I could make out in the dimness of the room, was that I was in a bed – not a pallet in a tent, but a proper bed, with a mattress, and blankets.

Without warning, the cooking smells caused my gut to rebel. I rolled over and was violently ill.

In the midst of my convulsions, a metal bucket was thrust across the floor, directly beneath me. As my tortured body expelled the last of the rancid concoction in my stomach, I noted weakly that I was not alone.

Gasping, exhausted and debilitated, I lay back on the bed and promptly passed-out – again.

∽

Thursday, 8.50 am

I was lying flat on my back, an arm flung over my eyes. My head hurt something savage and there was the most disgusting taste in my mouth.

That alone made me groan and roll over. I heard the bucket slide under my face.

Groaning pathetically, I swallowed hard as my stomach lurched, then stabilised.

"Returned to us, are you? Going to throw up again?"

I managed to move my head negatively, then tried to open an eye – it seemed to be stuck, encrusted with Christ knew what. I prised my lid up and despite a stab of pain, tried to focus on the man seated across the bucket from me.

"Christie. *Urgh* …" I groaned again and rolled over, burying my face in the pillow. A sudden flash of memory caused such a brilliant, searing pain in my chest that I gave an involuntary sob.

I hadn't wept since I was a child, yet as I lay there, on that bed, the pillow beneath my face grew damp.

Christie didn't say anything as he left the room, gallantly providing me a moment of privacy.

It was probably half an hour later when he returned. By then I had composed myself and was sitting up in bed. I can only imagine what I must have looked like because I had the Devil's own hangover and had been sobbing like a maid.

Christie was dressed in his shirtsleeves and carrying a tray with a bowl of soup and chunk of bread on it; the smell rising from it caused my stomach to growl.

"How long since you've eaten?" he asked, placing the tray on a table.

I shrugged. "What time is it?"

"It's nearly nine o'clock, two days since you disappeared from camp." Christie resumed the seat next to my bed. He looked weary and jaded. "I read your father's letter. I know about your sis— … about Alex."

Hearing her name spoken aloud was excruciating. My heart shrivelled to a desiccated husk in my chest. Besides that, a hard lump was forming at the back of my throat; there was a real danger I'd begin weeping again. "Please," I whispered, swallowing, "Don't ever speak that name again."

Christie nodded, thoughtfully, his face carefully blank. "Very well, but that at least confirms the reason for this … unfortunate episode."

"This is not an unfortunate episode," I snarled.

"Well," Christie gestured dismissively. "Whatever you call it, if we get you back to camp before nightfall, we'll be able to cover your absence."

I turned away to stare at the ceiling. The thought had barely formed in my mind before the words came out. "I'm not going back."

Christie breathed steadily. "I see. So what you're telling me, your commanding officer, is that you're deserting."

I shrugged, carelessly.

"You understand the implications, don't you?" he went on. "You understand what this means?"

Turning on him, I said, "Of course! But I'm telling you as my friend, not my commanding officer."

"I can't be one and not the other," he said angrily. "Not here at any rate. You're behaving like a child and putting me and Hywel both in a difficult position."

Sitting up suddenly, I growled, "Then fuck off, Christie! No one asked you to come and—"

"What about Emerson?" he demanded, his eyes following me as I leapt out of bed.

My head swum but I ignored it. "You were assigned a mission," he continued. His face was growing red. "You just vanished without a word – where does that leave him?"

"You sort it out!" I shouted, pulling on my trousers. "You're the commanding officer!"

"That's—"

"And," I rounded on him, my finger aimed at his chest, "don't you fucking dare tell me I'm behaving like a child."

"Sit down!" he barked, pointing at the bed.

I did, but only to pull my boots on. "If you *are* my friend, I'm asking you to turn your back long enough for me to get out of this blasted shithole."

"And as your commanding officer, where does *that* leave me?"

"You can leave this …" I glanced around uncertainly. I had no idea where I was. "You can bugger off back to camp and act surprised when I can't be found!"

"I can't do that, Patrick," he said. His tone was gentler now, but he was still angry.

"Just say you haven't seen me."

"It's not that simp—"

"*For God's sake, Christie!*" I shouted. "Just bloody—"

"*Will you listen!*" he shouted back. "You're in my house!"

I stared at him, all fight draining away. "Your house?" I repeated like an idiot.

Christie sighed and sat on the bed beside me. "This is my house. It's the only place I could think to bring you till you'd sobered up."

He ran a hand through his dark hair. "I told you about my situation … I bought this house." His voice drifted away and I nodded.

In my self-absorption and grief, I'd forgotten Christie's own troubles, confided over a brandy several months earlier. I threw a sidelong glance at him. He looked unhappy and tired.

"You've hardly had any sleep," I said, feeling a twinge of contrition.

"I've had Hywel and Emerson scouring every inch of camp, the local villages and every bloody brothel and inn within a ten-mile radius. We finally found you passed out in some filthy hole with a whore."

I stared at him. "A whore? I don't remember—"

He grinned for the first time and quickly shook his head. "No. She even confirmed it. Apparently, you weren't interested, possibly the only time in your life."

I snorted. "Not since I returned to England. Not after that night …"

The unfinished sentence hung between us. I couldn't say her name. I couldn't bear to call her face to mind or think about her body beneath mine.

I drew in my breath and looked at him. "Christie, I'm asking you to leave – go back to camp and tell them you couldn't find me. Give me until tomorrow – please?"

"Tomorrow? To do what? If you desert now, I'll have harboured a fugitive."

I thought for a long time while he waited in silence. Finally, I said, "I'll either return to camp with some …" I shrugged, "some excuse for my absence. Or, I'll be gone."

"Gone where?"

I gave a wry grin. "As my commanding officer, I can't tell you. As my friend, well, I've often thought America seemed interesting. Alternatively, I could sign up as a mercenary for one of our allied divisions in Austria or …" I shrugged. "I have options – returning to England is not one of them."

Christie's face registered shock. "You would sacrifice your estate, your inheritance … everything for this?" He got up to pace the room. "You're mad!"

"They're not that important to me. And *this* just happens to be —"

"You selfish bastard!"

I stared at him in surprise. "What?"

"What about your father? Your tenants? All those people relying on you and you can just abandon them so petulantly!"

"Christie, I'm trying to be honest with you! You asked."

"Very well." He took his jacket off a chair and slipped into it. "Very well," he repeated and the disappointment was clear on his face. "You're leaving me no choice. I'll give you twelve hours. After that, I hope I see you in camp. If not, I wish you luck. As your commanding officer, you have twelve hours to come to your senses and return to camp with a damn good excuse. If not," he paused and drew a deep, regretful breath, "if not, you better not show your face anywhere near a British division."

"You will put a warrant out for me?" I asked dispassionately.

He nodded. "You'll be leaving me no choice. It's the law for deserters – you know that, Pat."

"Yes."

"Just … think carefully, *please*. Think about the people who need you, your future in the army. You're well regarded. If you don't want to return to England, you can build a career here … think about it."

I didn't answer.

"Listen, I know you're in pain. I know … I read the letter. I understand what this has done to you but …" Christie sucked in a long breath. "Don't do this, Pat," he implored. "Don't destroy everything over this. They will find you, you know. And they will execute you."

Still, I didn't answer, but not from any belligerence – I just didn't know what to say. I looked at him sadly.

"Alright, then," he said, going to the door. "Stay here until you've made up your mind. I hope …" he grimaced and didn't finish. Then, with a dejected sigh, he was gone.

∽

Thursday, 8.45 pm

Christie sat at his desk, a glass of brandy at his elbow. He had a pile of paperwork to read through and a report to finish. Fitchen had earlier brought a requisition form for a dozen pairs of boots and new uniforms; Christie could sign the form but he knew the supplies would not be forthcoming – the army was broke and not even the general could get requisition orders filled.

But boots were the last thing on Christie's mind as he sat there. Before him was an arrest warrant – almost completed. It only needed the reason for the arrest, the name of the person being arrested and Christie's signature.

His hand hovered above the page, then resolutely, he wrote, *for reason of desertion.*

Desertion.

Patrick Washburn, his friend since boyhood, was a deserter. Christie had given him a twelve-hour deadline, but Patrick had not appeared.

Now, if found, he would certainly be executed.

At the top of the page, Christie had written the words, … *to be arrested.* Angry that he'd been placed in this position – all the for sake of a woman – Christie glared at the words. He hadn't yet filled in Patrick's name.

Of course, he had sympathy for his friend. Hadn't he, Christie himself, his own problems in petticoats? Yet he wasn't a deserter! In fact, he'd chosen to make a life for himself in the army and thus avoid all troubles of the female variety.

In any case, as the third son of an illustrious family, there wasn't much else for him –it was either the priesthood or the military. That was just the way it was for a third son.

Patrick's life was a different story. As the eldest child, the only son, Patrick Washburn was titled and independently wealthy. In the future, he would be an earl, a peer of the realm and entitled to a seat in the House of Lords.

But Patrick was absent without leave, and as soon as Christie signed the document before him, Patrick would be a deserter – most despised of any military order.

"Damn you, Washburn," Christie ground between his teeth. "You leave me no choice."

He lifted his pen and, drawing a deep breath, signed the document.

"Major?" Fitchen came into the tent.

Christie sighed. "What is it?" Wearily, he lifted his head and laid down his pen.

Fitchen waited at attention. In the shadows behind him stood another man.

Dirty, dishevelled and looking decidedly unwell, Captain Patrick Washburn, stepped forward and stood at attention.

Christie swallowed and slowly rose from his chair.

The man before him saluted. "Captain Washburn reporting for duty, Sir!"

Relief felt like a weight lifted off Christie's shoulders. "Thank you Fitchen, that will be all."

Fitchen saluted and left the tent. Meanwhile Christie walked around the desk to stand before his friend.

"Thank God you've seen sense," he said softly. "At ease, soldier," he added with a small smile.

Patrick visibly relaxed and only then allowed his gaze to drift to his friend's face. "I've nothing else, Christie," he whispered.

Christie noted the other man's haggard features; the weary disillusioned eyes, grim mouth, and tight, unshaven jaw. He nodded. "I understand you feel this way, but it's rubbish."

"Is it?" Patrick's voice sounded tired. "She changed me, man. Turned me into a person I didn't think I was."

"Thought you were immune to love, did you?"

Patrick smiled weakly. "Something like that. But no more. It'll take time, but I've decided to throw everything I have, everything I am, into the army."

"Cauterise the wound," Christie commented flatly.

Patrick nodded. "Or die trying."

The men quickly embraced, then stepping back, Christie said, "You stink and you're filthy. Go and get yourself cleaned up. I'll put around the story that you've been unwell."

Patrick bowed his head. "Thank you."

"You ..." Christie started, then a sudden thought occurred to him. "Your sister is in Morocco? Is that right?"

"Yes."

"Go to her. It'll take you a week to get there. Spend a week, then a week back. Three weeks in total."

Christie moved to his desk to prepare the leave notice. "I'll sign the papers."

"Christie—" Patrick began but his friend rounded on him.

"This is not open for discussion – it's an order, soldier. Go to Maeve. She always was the sensible one – talk to her, get it out of your system; then come back here and give me all you've got. I need you fresh and ready for the spring campaign."

Patrick felt his throat growing tight again. He swallowed and blinked up at the canvas ceiling of Christie's tent. "Thank you," he muttered.

The two men saluted, regarding each other for several moments.

Then Patrick turned on his heel and strode away.

Christie watched his friend leave, then, moving to his desk, stared at the arrest warrant.

Snatching it up, he scrunched it into a tight ball, then grasping his lantern, went to the rear of his tent where he could take the edge of the rug and pull it back to reveal the hard, packed earth beneath.

Removing the glass casing from his lantern, he held the ball of paper to the naked flame until it burst alight, then he dropped it to the bare ground.

Christie watched the arrest warrant roil and glow, smouldering, smoking, before collapsing into a pile of dead cinders.

Then, with the rug returned to position, he strode to his desk and threw down the glass of brandy in one gulp.

A MESSAGE FROM KAREN

Let me begin by saying that I'd never planned to publish *Counterpoint*.

In 2013, I started re-writing *Torn* as a series of short stories from Patrick's point of view, purely as a writing exercise, because I've never been good at writing graphic bedroom scenes.

After *Torn*, we *all* suspected that Patrick had been getting up to some seriously juicy stuff and I was itching to reveal all the gory details – if only as writing practise.

So I embarked on a project to tell Patrick's story, but to align it with *Torn* and fill in the gaps; the parts that Alex didn't know, hence, what the reader didn't know.

Yet, as I got into it, *Counterpoint* became so much more than simply a gossip session and bed-to-bed romp. To my surprise, I discovered that Patrick was a way more complex character than I'd realised.

Additionally, in researching and writing about Patrick's years in the war against Napoleon, I had the opportunity to explore his daring and sense of adventure, and he demonstrated a maturity I hadn't expected.

Coming to the decision to publish these stories has been a

journey of nearly 10 years. Oh I did dabble with some online releases, but as a mainstream, commercially available publication, well no – after all, who'd want to read a collection of racy stories about a Regency bad boy?

Turns out a lot of people.

So, after all these years, I had my fingers prised from the manuscript, and an amazing team of professionals took over, working tirelessly to produce this publication.

Firstly, *of course!* there's my amazing editor Jane Woodhead who never fails to offer the best and most professional editing services a writer could ask for.

Next there's my wonderful husband Stuart, who took the edited manuscript and painstakingly typeset and produced the finished book. He then got creative and designed an iconic and beautiful book cover.

Special mention at this point goes to Kerry from *38th Parallel Productions*, who waved her magic wand over the cover design to truly bring Patrick and Alex to life.

A physical book can only go so far without committed support. Many thanks to my lovely media representative Tamara Jenkins from *Esencia Communications*, and to my brilliant friend and event manager Meagan Taylor.

Last but not least are you: my very important readers. Without your loyal following there would be no books at all! A big thank you to you!

I hope you enjoy my books. If you do, I'd be grateful if you could leave a review on Goodreads or Amazon so that others may discover my books and enjoy them for themselves.

Additionally, you could visit my website, www.karenturner.com.au, sign up to my newsletter or send me a message – I'd love to hear from you.

Karen

Other books by Karen Turner

ALL THAT & EVERYTHING

Ever wondered what life looks like from a cat's perspective? What about the funny side of daily train commuting? Are things really what they seem in the mirror?

From Regency London to the Australian bush, *All That & Everything* is an enchanting collection of award winning short stories.

Karen combines a selection of her late father's sketches with these carefully chosen stories to offer something for everyone.

Other books by Karen Turner

TORN

Yorkshire 1808

When 14 year old Alexandra meets Patrick, her handsome and notorious step-brother, she is confused and resentful as he shakes the foundations of everything she has ever known. Driving a wedge between Alex and her brother Simon, he tears apart the fabric of her quiet world. Yet she is intrigued by the enigmatic Patrick and finds herself increasingly drawn to him.

These are the years between childhood and womanhood, during which Alex begins to realise that her growing affection for Patrick owes nothing to sibling fondness.

But these are turbulent times for England and Patrick and Simon, answering the call of adventure, join the fight against Napoleon with devastating consequences.

In a family ravaged by war and deceit, Alex finds herself betrayed in the worst possible way.

This is the story of one woman's passionate struggle for love and hope against all the constraints of her time.

Alex's story continues in *Inviolate*.

INVIOLATE

Yorkshire 1813

Numb after the pain of an intolerable betrayal, 19 year old Alexandra Broughton turns to her only source of hope – an arranged marriage. Resolutely accepting this as her last chance to make a future for herself, she journeys to Scotland to face the unknown.

Although Alex makes every effort to settle into her new life, she struggles to suppress the memories of her lost lover's passionate yet faithless embrace, and remains haunted by a fleeting and impossible love affair.

For Alex, this is a time of growing; a coming of age where she turns to her husband in a desperate effort to carve out a life with him, and just as it seems that contentment is within her grasp, disaster strikes.

As the war against Napoleon reaches a crescendo, Alex discovers a web of deceit that slowly unravels long-held secrets to reveal the true meaning of treachery.

Trapped in a loveless, violent marriage, and with nothing left to lose, Alex embarks on a fight for survival. Battling the irresistible forces ranging against her, she remains bound to the one man she can never forgive – the one man above all others she can never forget.

Other books by Karen Turner

STORMBIRD

Yorkshire 1941

Stormbird returns readers to the once beautiful rural home, Broughton Hall, the setting of Karen's previous books, *Torn* and *Inviolate.*

It's now 1941, England is at war and Broughton Hall has fallen into disrepair. New owner, war-widowed young mother, Jessica is struggling to raise her two children and run a small dairy.

When she encounters a wounded German fighter pilot hiding in her barn, she commits to helping him.

At first, the barriers of ignorance and prejudice separate them. Yet in a world where danger lurks behind every door, an unlikely friendship becomes a story of love, loyalty and understanding.

www.ingramcontent.com/pod-product-compliance
Lightning Source LLC
Chambersburg PA
CBHW060811120726
47909CB00006B/1866